An Uprig

NAUTICAL

Throughout the centuries, sail
language to describe the high
processes that they use to live and work at sea. This still
holds true in the twenty-first century.

While counting the number of nautical terms that I've used in this series of novels, it became evident that a printed book wasn't the best place for them. I've therefore created a glossary of nautical terms on my website:

https://chris-durbin.com/glossary/

My nautical glossary is limited to those terms that I've mentioned in this series of novels as they were used in the middle of the eighteenth century. It's intended as a work of reference to accompany the Carlisle & Holbrooke series of naval adventure novels.

Some of the usages of these terms have changed over the years, so this glossary should be used with caution when referring to periods before 1740 or after 1780.

The glossary isn't exhaustive; Falconer's Universal Dictionary of the Marine, first published in 1769, contains a more comprehensive list. I haven't counted the number of terms that Falconer has defined, but he fills 328 pages with English language terms, followed by an additional eighty-three pages of French translations. It's a monumental work.

There is an online version of the 1769 edition of The Universal Dictionary that includes all the excellent diagrams that are in the print version. You can view it at this website:

https://archive.org/details/universaldiction00will/
***

PRINCIPAL CHARACTERS

Fictional

Captain George Holbrooke: Commanding officer, *Argonaut*

Lieutenant Carter Shorrock: First lieutenant, *Argonaut*

Josiah Fairview: Sailing master, *Argonaut*

David Chalmers: Chaplain, *Argonaut*

Jackson: Bosun, *Argonaut*

Ann Holbrooke: Captain Holbrooke's Wife

Capitan de Navio Don Ezequiel Mancebo: Commanding officer, *San Sebastian*

Teniente Fernando Guterres: First lieutenant, *San Sebastian*

Historical

Lord George Anson: First Lord of the Admiralty until June 1762

Charles Wyndham, Earl of Egremont: Secretary of State for the Southern Department from October 1761

Lord Alexander Colville: Commander-in-chief North American Station

Major General Sir Jeffery Amherst: Governor-general of British North America

An Upright Man

The Fourteenth Carlisle & Holbrooke Naval Adventure

Chris Durbin

Chris Durbin

To Olivia

Who proves that Unicorns walk among us!

An Upright Man

Copyright © 2023 by Chris Durbin.

All Rights Reserved.

Chris Durbin has asserted his rights under the Copyright, Design and Patents Act, 1988, to be identified as the author of this work.

No part of this book may be reproduced in any form or by any electronic or mechanical means including information storage and retrieval systems, without permission in writing from the author. The only exception is by a reviewer, who may quote short excerpts in a review.

Editor: Lucia Durbin

Cover Artwork: Bob Payne

Cover Design: Book Beaver

This book is a work of historical fiction. Characters, places, and incidents either are products of the author's imagination or are used fictitiously. For further information on actual historical events, see the bibliography at the end of the book.

First Edition: November 2023

Chris Durbin

CONTENTS

	Nautical Terms	vii
	Principal Characters	viii
	Charts	x
	Introduction	1
Prologue	Opportunity	4
Chapter 1	Creative Entry	9
Chapter 2	Suspicion	18
Chapter 3	Don Mancebo	27
Chapter 4	Do Something!	35
Chapter 5	Just One Man	44
Chapter 6	The Human Condition	52
Chapter 7	The Passing Bell	61
Chapter 8	A Man Set Apart	71
Chapter 9	A Particular Service	81
Chapter 10	The Iroise	91
Chapter 11	Decision	102
Chapter 12	Painful Memory	114
Chapter 13	Where in the World?	122
Chapter 14	Fog on the Bank	132
Chapter 15	A Banks Schooner	141
Chapter 16	First Blow	151

Chapter 17	Lord Colville	159
Chapter 18	Avoidable	169
Chapter 19	Bacalao	178
Chapter 20	Collision of Interests	185
Chapter 21	A Fine Cutter	194
Chapter 22	Fall From Grace	203
Chapter 23	The Intendant	211
Chapter 24	The Laurentian Channel	222
Chapter 25	Attrition	232
Chapter 26	A Lonely Vigil	242
Chapter 27	Other People's Letters	247
Chapter 28	Unlimited Liability	258
Chapter 29	A Master Stroke	268
Chapter 30	de Ternay's Fog	278
Chapter 31	No Refuge	290
	Historical Epilogue	300
	Fact Meets Fiction	304
	Other Books	308
	Bibliography	310
	The Author	312
	Feedback	314

LIST OF CHARTS

1	The North Atlantic	x
2	The Iroise	xi
3	The Gulf of Saint Lawrence	xii
4	St. John's, Newfoundland	xiii

An Upright Man

Lieutenant Colonel William Amherst: Land forces commander of the Newfoundland relief force

Étienne François, Duc de Choiseul: Foreign minister of France

Chef d'escadre Charles-Henri-Louis d'Arsac, Chevalier de Ternay: Commander of the French expedition to Newfoundland

Joseph-Louis-Bernard de Cléron, comte d'Haussonville: Commander of the land forces of the French expedition to Newfoundland

***

Chris Durbin

The North Atlantic

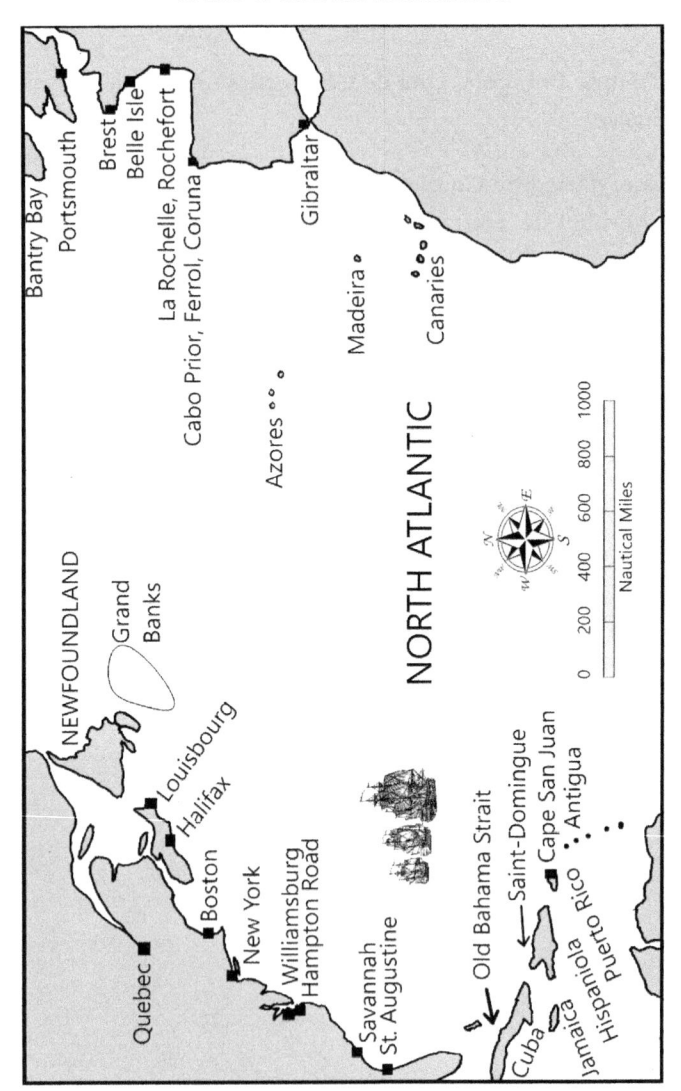

An Upright Man

The Iroise

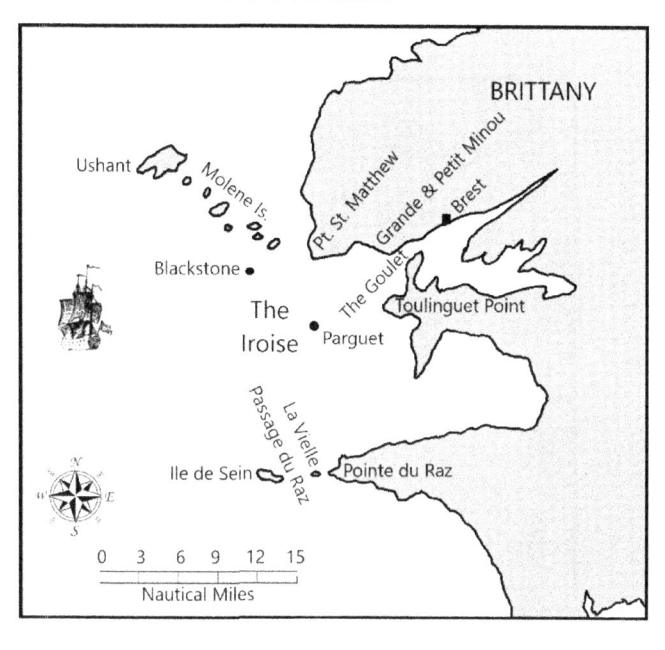

Map showing the Iroise sea area off Brittany, with labeled locations: Ushant, Molene Is., Blackstone, The Iroise, Parquet, La Vieille, Passage du Raz, Ile de Sein, Pointe du Raz, Pt. St. Matthew, Grande & Petit Minou, Brest, The Goulet, Toulinguet Point, and BRITTANY. Scale: 0–15 Nautical Miles.

Approaches to the Gulf of Saint Lawrence

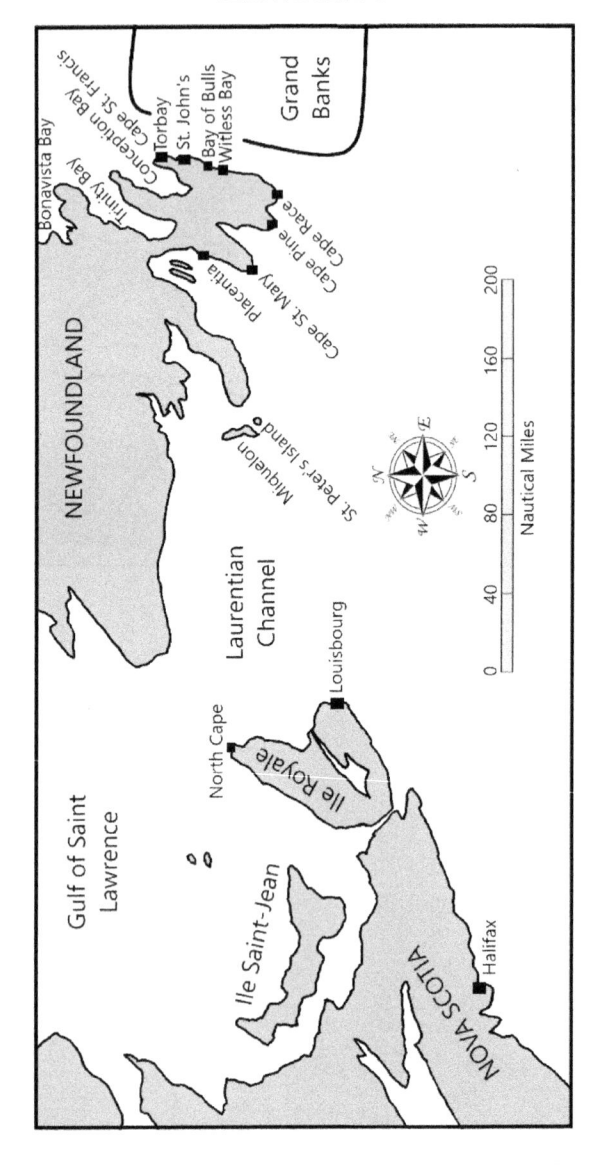

St. John's, Newfoundland

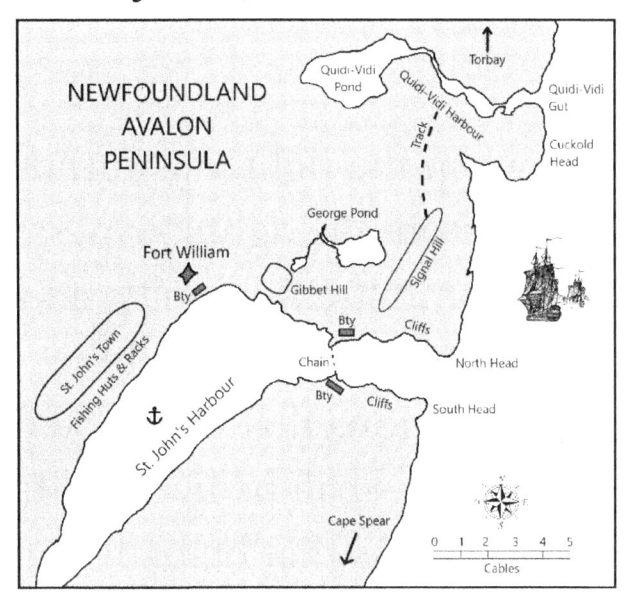

But when the righteous turneth away from his righteousness, and committeth iniquity, and doeth according to all the abominations that the wicked man doeth, shall he live? All his righteousness that he hath done shall not be mentioned: in his trespass that he hath trespassed, and in his sin that he hath sinned, in them shall he die.

Ezekiel 18:24

A new, compleat, and more accurate Translation of the Bible, 1611.

INTRODUCTION

The Seven Years War in 1762

In January 1762, at the urging of King Louis of France, King Charles (Carlos) of Spain agreed to join the war against Britain. Louis and Charles were first cousins and this alliance was known as the third Bourbon family pact. As well as an underlying belief that Spain and France, both devoutly Catholic countries, should be natural allies against the heretic British, King Charles had three principal war aims. First he wanted to invade his neighbour Portugal, then Britain's ally, and bring its territory into the Spanish Crown. Second, he had a number of grievances against Britain that he hoped would be addressed in an eventual peace treaty, including access to the rich fishing grounds off Newfoundland. Third, he wanted to reclaim Minorca, the island that had been held by Britain since 1713 and captured by France at the beginning of the war.

France staked everything on Spain's entry into the war and another hugely expensive push to take Hanover, but the strategy was crumbling. The third King George considered himself more British than Hanoverian and it became evident that even if Prince Ferdinand – the commander of the allied armies in Germany – could be defeated, Hanover wouldn't be a particularly valuable asset at the peace negotiations.

Canada had fallen, and the French possessions in America were reduced to a toehold in the Gulf of Mexico and nominal ownership of the vast but unexploited hinterland that they called Louisiana. The Caribbean sugar islands that provided much of the state's wealth were being picked off one-by-one and all their plans for an invasion of England had come to nothing. The King's ships were either destroyed, blockaded or sailing under British colours and it would take years to rebuild the French fleet.

In Britain, William Pitt resigned after a disagreement over the war with Spain, and the government entered a period of turmoil. Anson remained as First Lord of the Admiralty, but his successor, Lord Halifax, a politician and no seaman, was waiting in the wings. Although he was in ill health Anson still drove the planning for the expeditions against Havana and Manilla.

Even before Spain joined the war, it was obvious that it wouldn't have the strategic effect that the cousins, King Louis and King Charles, had hoped for. France needed a success to bring Britain to the negotiating table. Nothing grand – Louis didn't have the force for that – but something that would hurt the City of London in its pocket. It was against this background that the Duc de Choiseul scraped together a naval squadron to strike at British interests.

Carlisle and Holbrooke

In 1761, Edward Carlisle's ship-of-the-line *Dartmouth* was sent from Jamaica on what looked like a trivial mission intended to demonstrate friendship to Spain, carrying a cargo of lost furniture to the Spanish governor-general of Havana. However, in Havana he found evidence of growing co-operation between the French and Spanish navies and was requested to carry the new governor-general of Guatemala to his domain. There he uncovered further plots, and his wife, Lady Chiara, used her talents for languages and diplomacy to earn a seat at the ship's councils of war.

Carlisle's search for evidence of preparations for war took him further west into the Gulf of Mexico, and to a final battle with a more familiar enemy.

In December 1760 Holbrooke's frigate *Argonaut* joined Admiral Hawke's blockading squadron off the French Atlantic coast. He narrowly missed capturing a French frigate that had escaped from the Vilaine estuary in company with two ships-of-the-line. That was his first encounter with the Chevalier de Ternay, who would appear again in the story. Holbrooke was called to the Admiralty where he was given a new task, to insert and then extract agents from Brittany. He hazarded his ship and himself on moonlit beaches and estuaries, and didn't recognise the signs of his own mental fatigue. He had a respite when he joined the force to invade the French island of Belle Isle, but then it was back to the blockade of the Vilaine, a duty that ultimately took its toll. In the summer of 1761 he returned to his home in Wickham suffering from what we'd now call post-traumatic stress disorder or PTSD. After a period of recovery he returned to sea in his frigate *Argonaut* and was sent to the Caribbean, to his old theatre of action, the Jamaica Station.

***

PROLOGUE

Opportunity

Friday, Eighth of January 1762.
Spanish Ship San Sebastian, at Sea. Cabo Prior east-southeast 3 leagues.

Capitan de Navio Don Ezequiel Mancebo stood with his feet wide apart, lightly touching the poop deck rail to keep his balance while he allowed his body to become accustomed to the long Atlantic swell. He was always happiest when he was at sea with the cares and woes of the shore slipping away behind him. Things were so complicated on land, but here he was master of all he surveyed. He need ask permission from nobody and if a task could be accomplished within his ship's resources, it was done. If it couldn't, well, there was nothing more to be said on the matter. Don Mancebo was careful to keep his face severe, but inwardly his heart was singing. He had a good sailing master, an excellent first lieutenant and a competent set of lesser officers; as he cast his eyes around the deck, he could see that the ship was being secured for sea efficiently. He took a last glance at the fast receding shoreline and said a silent farewell to Ferrol and all its anxieties. He recalled his last conversation with the admiral, who spoke of the probability of war with Britain as though it was something to be feared, but from his own perspective it couldn't come soon enough. He longed to be let loose against the English trade in the Caribbean, to take prizes and to gain renown, and it looked like he'd be in a prime position to reap the first rewards. He was determined to drive his men and keep his ship in good order so that when he reached Havana he'd need only stores and water before he was ready to be sent out. God grant that the glorious King Carlos had declared war by then.

Don Mancebo's reverie was disrupted by the sailing

master who clumped up the ladder and saluted when he reached the poop deck.

'We've made a good offing now sir, and we're clear of the coasting traffic except for that sloop to windward of us, but it looks like he's running for Coruña. We should bear away for the sou'west and take advantage of this nor'easter while we have it. All hands are already on deck and we can be settled and on our way in time for their dinner.'

Don Mancebo nodded in agreement. It was as well that the sailing master was concerned with the crew's welfare; it was all too easy to forget that men must have food and rest when so much needed to be done merely to keep *San Sebastian* at sea.

'Is the ship properly secured?'

'Aye sir, it is. From the main truck to the hold, from the jib boom to the taffrail.'

The sailing master was a loquacious man and he still hadn't learned that Don Mancebo valued brevity.

'Very well…'

'Captain, sir.'

Don Mancebo's order was interrupted by a call from the officer of the watch who had run half way up the poop deck ladder to deliver his report.

'The sloop close on our starboard beam is letting fly its sheets, sir. I believe it wants to speak with us.'

A quick glance showed that his officer was correct. A young man dressed in a presentable suit – clearly no common sloop's master – was waving urgently at him as his little vessel's sails flogged and chattered to the gentle breeze. It was probably nothing, but a prudent captain didn't ignore the chance of news, even when he was only a few hours into a voyage.

'I think we can afford to hear what he has to say. Heave to, if you please. I'll be in my cabin.'

***

'I regret, Captain, that I have only a few minutes to spare and then I must be away…'

Don Mancebo's face flushed with anger. He wasn't used to being spoken to in this manner in his own cabin, and by such a stripling as this who hadn't even properly introduced himself. He opened his mouth to deliver a stinging rebuke.

'...excuse my urgency, Captain, but my errand is to King Carlos himself and I must make all speed to Madrid.'

'Very well, and what is it that excuses your delaying a King's ship?'

The young man drew a breath.

'It's war, sir, war with the English. I left London in the greatest haste four days ago at the bidding of our ambassador, and sailed from Southampton to bring the news that King George has declared war upon us. I'm told that he cited a secret treaty that King Carlos made with King Louis, but I know nothing of that. It'll be made clear in the dispatches that I'm carrying, I'm sure.'

'Good God, man, then why are you delaying to tell me? You should waste not a moment.'

A courier with such important information shouldn't stop for anything, and now that Don Mancebo knew his mission he was as impatient that the courier should be on his way as the young man himself was. He couldn't delay this messenger more than a few more minutes.

'Excuse me again, sir, but his Excellency told me that I must stop any King's ship that I meet along the way and tell of the news. He said that it could affect your plans.'

Don Mancebo considered for a moment. This was momentous news, if it was to be believed. He looked appraisingly at the courier. He certainly looked the part, and his story had a ring of truth about it.

'You're sure of this?'

'Oh yes, sir. His Excellency sent me on ahead but he'll be following by now. All of London was abuzz with the news and my carriage was stoned and abused whenever I passed through a town that had heard of the declaration. I was fortunate indeed that I was given an English army escort.'

'My congratulations on your deliverance,' he replied with heavy sarcasm, 'and in what way does his Excellency believe my plans should change?'

The courier looked nervous at the idea of giving advice to this hard-looking naval captain, even if he was only a bearer of his master's words.

'He was most specific on that subject, sir. He expects that you'll return to port and await new orders. His Majesty will certainly want to consider this matter before committing his navy.'

***

Don Mancebo watched from the poop deck as the sloop squared away and ran down towards Coruña. The courier would be there by the end of the afternoon watch and the commandant of the garrison would surely give him a coach and escort once he knew his errand. The road to Madrid was generally bad in the winter, but the weather had been fair for a few weeks and it wouldn't be impassable. The ambassador's dispatches would be at the Escorial Palace in three days, or four at the most.

Then should he turn back to Ferrol? Every fibre in his being protested at the idea. It would incur interminable delays as requests for orders were sent to Madrid, questions were asked, and clarifications required. He doubted whether he'd sail again before February. Nevertheless, it was probably the right thing to do and at least by doing so he couldn't be called to account for exceeding his authority. He looked over the rail and saw his officers talking among themselves. His first lieutenant looked up and their eyes met, but he wisely left his captain to his own counsel. They knew nothing of the courier's news and there would be wild speculation in the wardroom and the gunroom, and even among the men.

Yes, he could be severely criticised if he didn't turn back. However, if the courier spoke the truth about the sloop's fast passage from Southampton, then, if he squared away before the wind now, *San Sebastian* would be the first

Spanish ship to reach the Americas with the news. The governor-general of Havana would hear about the declaration of war at least a week faster than he would otherwise. That was certainly a consideration. First with the news! And not only the first Spanish ship but likely the first ship of any nation to carry word of the declaration of war across the Atlantic. The English merchant trade wouldn't have been warned and even their men-of-war would be unconcerned at the sight of a Spanish fourth rate. He felt almost dizzy at the opportunities that came with knowing he was at war when his opponents didn't.

He looked over to leeward. In an hour the sloop would be so far away that nobody on its deck would see *San Sebastian's* movements. Good; that courier had a sneak's look about him and Don Mancebo didn't want the news of war to be closely followed by a report of him ignoring the ambassador's advice. For his mind was made up. He'd cram on all sail and make for Havana as quickly as possible. Months would pass before any criticism could reach him and by then his country would have other things to worry about.

***

An Upright Man

CHAPTER ONE

Creative Entry

Monday, Fifteenth of February 1762.
Argonaut, at Sea. Off St. Johns, Antigua.

Lady Chiara held Joshua's hand tightly. He was inclined to make a break for anything that looked interesting if given the chance, and she'd already hauled him back from a determined effort to reach the mizzen shrouds. His plan was simple, if somewhat terrifying for his mother. When he broke free from her grip he'd climb over the gunwale, down to the mizzen chains and thence up the lanyards until he found the convenient-looking ratlines. At three-and-a-half years old he was becoming loudly articulate, fully mobile and distressingly adventurous. It had taken Chiara's constant supervision to save him from self-destruction on the two-week passage from Port Royal to St. John's.

Enrico watched all this in amusement. He'd already offered to take charge of Joshua but his cousin had still not salved her conscience after more than two months of voluntary separation from her son, and she wasn't going to relinquish his charge to anyone. Two months during which time she'd sailed in her husband's ship *Dartmouth* to Jamaica, Havana, the Gulf of Mexico and the Yucatan coast. She'd enjoyed it, certainly, and especially she'd delighted in using her skills in the Spanish language and her deep knowledge of diplomacy to assist in her husband's mission. However, that was all over, and she was determined now to settle down in her new home in Virginia and bring up her son to be a credit to her family.

Joshua made a sudden lunge and was hauled back from the brink of disaster by the quartermaster, an unusually nimble man for his age, who scooped him up, straightened his breeches and shirt, and returned him to his mother.

Enrico had missed the incident because he was busy

watching the convoy coming out of St. John's. Each ship that glided towards the rendezvous had its own ideas of the appropriate sails for the occasion with some setting their t'gallants while others had nothing but their courses and stays'ls. Viewed as a whole, it gave them an untidy, disorganised appearance.

'Well, Mister Angelini, what do you think of all this?'

Captain George Holbrooke didn't need a telescope to see the apparent chaos of a convoy gathering for departure. The six ships and brigs that he'd brought up from Jamaica were in a reasonable order, lying hove to two miles to the north of Sandy Island where, if they had any difficulty, the northeasterly trade wind would blow them clear of danger. It was the Antigua ships that were causing the problem, all nine of them. They hadn't profited from Holbrooke's eagle eye for the past fourteen days of beating to windward across the Caribbean and they were inclined to take their escort's signals as nothing more than suggestions.

Enrico Angelini picked up the telescope from its becket on the binnacle as though he had a right to it. Indeed, only two weeks before he would have had that privilege, as he'd been a lieutenant in the Sardinian navy seconded to the fourth rate man-of-war *Dartmouth*. All that had changed with the arrival of a letter from his minister of marine, informing him that his naval commission was terminated and he was to report to his old cavalry regiment in Turin. Enrico had no intention of taking the demotion that was entailed in that order and he was determined to make a new life in Virginia, where the convoy was bound. He was dressed in an unfamiliar plain grey suit that had travelled with him since *Dartmouth* last visited Nice. It was the first time he'd worn anything other than a blue uniform coat for over half a year, and he didn't like it.

'I expect they'll come to some sort of order before sunset, sir. These merchantmen really have no idea of convoy discipline. Just look at that brig, haring off before the wind as though he's determined to put himself ashore

An Upright Man

on Sandy Island.'

Holbrooke was an old hand at convoys. Despite being only twenty-three years old, barely older than Enrico, he'd fought right the way through the present war and this was his second command. Convoy escort was one of the principal roles of frigates and he'd had his share of the pain and the tedium. There was nothing that could surprise him when it came to the behaviour of convoys.

'Oh, they'll do well once they settle down. It's their small crews that are the root of the problem. They've enough men to keep two watches with the bare minimum for sail trimming, but anything else needs all hands, and if they reef their tops'ls every time they start to draw ahead, they'll exhaust their men in a day or two. Slow and steady is the way with convoys, and always give them plenty of time.'

Enrico was mentally tallying the ships as they arrived. Eight were due to come out of St. John's and another, a large ship-rigged West Indiaman, was coming around from Old North Sound, and had sailed the previous day in order to work her way around the island.

'Ah, there she is, just rounding the Salt Fish Tail and bearing away to join us. She'll be here in no time.'

Enrico couldn't help a note of regret. He knew that Holbrooke had promised to put him and his cousin's party into the big West Indiaman as soon as it arrived. He looked at the sea and felt the wind. There was no help there, it was a perfect day with the mildest of trade wind breezes, and he mentally resigned himself to a passage in a merchantman when what he really wanted was to stay in *Argonaut*. It would probably be his last chance to tread the quarterdeck of a man-of-war, and already he felt its loss most keenly.

His cousin too wanted nothing more than to take the passage in *Argonaut,* but Sir James Douglas, the commander-in-chief Leeward Islands was most insistent that women weren't to take passage in his ships. He'd been inveigled into allowing Chiara to sail with her husband in

Dartmouth, because of her ability to speak Spanish and his lack of any suitable alternative, but he was determined that it wouldn't happen again. His final words on the subject rang in Holbrooke's ears, like the echoes of distant gunfire.

***

Slowly, slowly, the convoy gathered until Holbrooke had fourteen merchantmen all hove to, with only the ship from Old North Sound to join, and she was coming down fast with the trade wind.

'Should I bring the longboat alongside now for her Ladyship, sir?'

Carter Shorrock, *Argonaut's* first lieutenant, was keen to get the transfer over and done with. He'd told off the men to carry Lady Chiara's baggage onto the deck and the captain's coxswain was ready with a picked boat's crew. It would be a simple affair to take Chiara, her manservant Rodrigo and her maid, her cousin Enrico and her son Joshua over to the merchant ship, but the convoy couldn't get underway until it was completed.

'One moment Mister Shorrock. Would you ask Mister Fairview to join us at the taffrail?'

Shorrock was bemused. The taffrail was the place for private conversations when the captain didn't wish to go below, but what was the need for secrecy now?

'Ah, Mister Fairview, thank you for joining us. Now, Sir James made me promise to transfer Lady Chiara and her suite as soon as this ship joins the convoy. I agreed, of course, but I did point out to Sir James that the weather would have to be suitable. I couldn't possibly endanger her in a longboat in bad weather; in a heavy swell for example. Now, gentlemen, what do you think of this,' he asked looking pointedly at the benign and regular waves approaching from the northwest in stately procession, with never a breaking crest nor steep entry, 'a little too much for safe boatwork, perhaps?'

Shorrock and Fairview exchanged glances. The weather was as perfect as they had ever seen it and the swell, in particular, was nothing out of the ordinary. However, they both knew that the height of the swell wasn't one of the items that were usually recorded in the log, unlike the wind strength and the visibility, for example. It was quite clear what their captain wanted of them. Shorrock, loyal as ever, spoke first.

'It would be imprudent, in my opinion, sir.'

Holbrooke turned to Fairview and gave him a questioning look.

'I agree, sir, it's not to be attempted, not with Lady Chiara's safety to be considered, nor that of Master Joshua. I'll make a supplementary note in the ship's log and in my own regarding this unusual swell. I expect it's caused by the wind piling up against Sandy Island over there.'

'Thank you for your professional judgments, gentlemen. I'll endorse your log entries once you've made them.'

Holbrooke sounded stiff and formal, not wanting any hint of this collusion to be seen in his face or detected in his words.

'Now, make the signal for the convoy to get underway if you please. Close that ship and let her master know that Lady Chiara won't be taking passage with him. You don't need to give a reason. When that's done take station to windward. Perhaps you'd both join me for dinner; I believe Mister Petersen can take the watch.'

***

Holbrooke strode the weather side of the quarterdeck as the convoy gathered up its skirts and bustled away to the northwest to weather St. Kitts and pass to leeward of Anguilla. There was a little too much northerly in the trade wind to risk trying to pass to windward of the shallows off the northeast coast of Anguilla. In any case he wanted to show his friend's wife as much of the islands as he could before they left the Caribbean for the broad Atlantic. They'd sight the peaks of Nevis, St. Kitts and Saba before sunset and might even catch a glimpse of St. Martin and St.

Bartholomew. Anegada would be visible in the morning and he'd pass close enough to get a departure fix, then it would be a long ocean passage before they sighted Tybee Island at the mouth of the Savannah River. The ship that was to have carried lady Chiara from Antigua was due to leave the convoy at Savannah – that was a detail that Sir James had missed – and he could hardly be expected to move her into another ship that had not been prepared to receive her, and doing this for the short four-day passage from Savannah to Hampton Road was preposterous. His officers' modest efforts at creative log entries would be sufficient to cover him, he was sure. It was quite possible that word would get to Sir James that Lady Chiara had taken passage in *Argonaut* against his express orders, but he'd be unlikely to pursue the point. If he did, the combination of the fictitious swell, the existence of which couldn't possibly be challenged against the log entries of three sea officers, and the convenient fact of the intended ship leaving the convoy at Savannah would so far obfuscate the issue that it would make a fool out of anyone who questioned it. In any case, Sir James wasn't a vindictive man and he'd certainly hear from his wife, Lady Helen, if he dragged her close friend Lady Chiara into a disciplinary matter. Yes, he was safe.

***

Holbrooke paused his walk to look again at the convoy. It was sailing in two irregular columns to leeward of *Argonaut* with the lead ship only a mile or so on the frigate's larboard bow. The trade wind had increased and they made a fine, brave sight as they reached away to the northwest. All the power and majesty of Great Britain was embodied in that view. It was Britain's trade that made her great and it was the navy that protected that trade and strangled her enemy's commerce. Of course it was a two-way street, and the wealth that the trade generated paid for the navy and it was from the crews of the merchantmen that the experienced sailors were taken – willingly or by force – for the King's ships.

'A fine sight indeed, George.'

Holbrooke turned to see that his friend David Chalmers, who was also the ship's chaplain, had joined him on the leeward side of the quarterdeck. Chalmers made a point of only using the captain's Christian name when nobody else could hear them. After all, he was under George's orders and subject to the discipline of the articles of war, as much as the lowliest landsman who hauled at sheets and halyards.

'Ah yes, I was just reflecting on the wealth that convoys such as this bring to Britain.'

Chalmers smiled slightly, just a momentary upturn at the corners of his mouth. Being a naturally reserved person he wasn't one for gross facial expressions. He'd spent a good part of his life as an unbeneficed parson and it was only his sheer good luck in falling in with first Edward Carlisle and then George Holbrooke that had turned his fortunes around. Without any particular effort he'd become moderately wealthy through prize money and head money, but he still retained the introversion that went with poverty.

'Oh, I was referring to the almost supernatural speed with which the swell reduced; I understand it was quite fearsome off St. John's. I came to congratulate you upon our survival.'

Holbrooke was a much more natural smiler and the grin spread over his face.

'You've been speaking to Shorrock or Fairview, I presume. Well, you know that I have a deep regard for Lady Chiara and I owe much to Edward. The last thing he said before we left Port Royal was that I should try to persuade Sir James to let Chiara take passage in *Argonaut*. I didn't succeed, so I've found my own way to honour Edward's wish. But you know, I'm not so sure that I'm going against Sir James' will. I had the distinct impression that he hoped that I'd find some way around his orders.'

'I expect you're right. He has a particular problem, of

course. If he once condones the taking of wives to sea he'll open the floodgates and all of his officers will want to do the same. His command would become nothing more than a yacht squadron. He left you a loophole, I assume.'

'Yes, the weather, and I think I've wriggled and wormed through it carefully enough.'

That smile again. Chalmers knew his younger friend better than Holbrooke knew himself. Perhaps it was the fault of his youth, but George never could credit how well he was thought of in the service. By dint of his own position Chalmers heard conversations that were closed to others, and he knew very well that Holbrooke's reputation would allow him to ride out any number of minor investigations, even if his superiors should feel it worth initiating one. Holbrooke, he knew, still thought of himself as an imposter in the position of post-captain, although just recently he'd shown flashes of a tendency to grow into the rank.

'You'll be spending more time on deck in this voyage, I expect.'

Holbrooke smiled again. He'd given over his cabin to Lady Chiara and her suite and he'd taken the sailing master's harbour cabin, leaving him with the tiny space that served as a sea cabin. It didn't matter to Josiah Fairview because he rarely strayed far from the deck at sea. Holbrooke still had the use of the dining cabin, however, and it was getting towards that time of the day. The watch had changed over an hour ago and he could see the marine sentry making his way along the gangway to the fo'c'sle and the ship's belfry, preparing to strike three bells in the afternoon watch.

'Yes, it's a slight inconvenience, but I know what this passage means to Chiara. She feels that this will be her last chance to sail in a man-o'-war, and you'll have heard how much she enjoys it. She's determined to settle on dry land once she reaches Williamsburg. That's why I'm shaping my course to see as many of the islands as we can. Oh, the inconvenience is nothing. But you know I won't be able to linger at Hampton Road, and it's out of the question for me to escort Chiara to Williamsburg.'

'Oh, really? Then it appears that we won't see the grand edifice that Edward has bought, just a few steps from the governor's palace. I must say that I'm surprised, convoy duty usually allows a few days at each rendezvous, for the gathering of the waifs and strays, if not for recreation.'

'Well, yes, and I had hoped for just that, until I read the letter from the navy board that for reasons known only to themselves, they'd addressed personally to Chips. The cover was so emphatic on the point that Lister quite naturally whisked the letter away before I even saw it. That man – Chips that is – may know how to set a scarf in a keelson but he just doesn't attend to his correspondence. He only read the letter yesterday and then he sat on it while he fretted over what I'd say about its delay. Apparently the navy board's world will end if our coppering is not inspected in April to inform their decision on a wider fit throughout the fleet. This is the only coppered vessel to have crossed the Atlantic and the tropic line and they must know how it's fared. Has it kept out the worm? Has it inhibited the worst of the fouling? Are the copper sheets still there, or has the ocean stripped them clean away? They insist on a full docking in Portsmouth over the neaps, two whole weeks! We must make the spring tide on the eighth of April, without fail, and hope to be released on the twenty-fourth and it appears that I'll answer for the contrary at my peril. The tone of the letter is so apocalyptic that I fear we can't linger at Hampton, not even for a day. In fact, if the conditions are right I won't come to an anchor, but back and fill in the road while we conduct our business. I sent a note to Chiara and I'm sure she'll mention it at dinner. You'll join us, won't you? I'd welcome your support.'

***

CHAPTER TWO

Suspicion

Wednesday, Seventeenth of February 1762.
Argonaut, at Sea, Cape San Juan south-by-west 30 leagues.

Holbrooke could feel the big Atlantic rollers passing under his ship. *Argonaut* was still firmly in the region of the northeast trade winds and since Tuesday afternoon had been clear of the shelter of the islands. Now there was nothing to interrupt the waves and they had built up into formidable masses of water marching down upon the convoy as it reached towards the northwest. There was no need now for Fairview to falsify his log, for the swell had risen to match his earlier fabrications and there was no question of transferring Lady Chiara from one ship to another.

He heard eight bells struck for the change of the watch and was aware of the bustle at the taffrail as the midshipman of the watch and a boy streamed the log. However, his thoughts were far away in his home in Hampshire. Being in such close proximity to Lady Chiara and Joshua had inevitably turned his mind to his own wife, Ann and his son Edward. It felt like years since he'd seen them when in fact it wasn't even six months. Edward would be seventeen months old by now. When Holbrooke had last had a spell of leave the little fellow had started to walk, and was busily destroying anything within his reach in Mulberry House. Well, *Argonaut* was bound for home but he had to touch at Savannah, Hampton Road and Sandy Hook before he could cross the Atlantic again. The best piece of news that he had in Antigua was that the original plan for taking the trade to Boston and Halifax had been dropped. At Savannah he'd just lie-to off Tybee Island to see his charges up the river, and the same in Hampton Road. He'd sent a letter ahead by the regular packet, urging

An Upright Man

any ships that wanted convoy to be ready to sail on the fourth of March, with a strongly worded warning that *Argonaut* wouldn't wait for stragglers. That should suffice to gather the trade that was bound for England. From Hampton Road he could send word ahead to New York and with a bit of luck his charges would be waiting at the anchorage off Sandy Hook. In that case he'd have to anchor for just a few hours while he sent his convoy orders to the ships' masters, then he'd be away for Portsmouth. He could be home in six weeks; his heart beat faster at the thought.

It was all due to *Argonaut's* coppering. It was still very much experimental and his ship was only the second to have this new treatment and the first to venture far from home waters. The navy board wanted to see how it had lasted over a six month voyage in the Caribbean, where the teredo worm was most active, and along the eastern coast of the American colonies. Without that he'd have been on the Leeward Islands station for years, or until the war ended.

Here was Petersen, waiting to be noticed. Holbrooke stopped and smiled at his master's mate.

'The watch is relieved, sir. The wind's east-nor'easterly and it's a good tops'l breeze as you see it, and we're having to spill wind to keep our station on the convoy. Our course is nor'west-a-half-west for Tybee Island which Mister Fairview informs me is three-hundred-and-sixty-seven leagues distant. The log shows five knots and two fathoms. There's just the one straggler, sir, that big ship-rigged West Indiaman, the *Earl of Bute,* that joined us from Old North Sound. He had to sort out his main t'gallant but he's catching up now. There's three inches of water in the bilge, the same as when I came on watch. Sunset in two hours at two minutes past six. Mister Steel has the watch.'

Holbrooke glanced over the larboard quarter. He was well aware of the straggler and he'd ordered *Argonaut* to drop back to cover her until she caught up. It would be dark in three hours and it didn't look like she'd be up with the main body by then. He considered signalling the convoy to reduce sail, but they'd probably do that anyway with night falling. No, he'd just hang back a bit so that he could see the *Earl of Bute's* taffrail light and shepherd her through the night.

'Very well, Mister Petersen. Enjoy your watch below.'

He took the telescope from the binnacle and trained it on the West Indiaman. The main t'gallant appeared to be drawing well enough now and it looked like she was closing the gap with the rest of the convoy at about half a mile in each hour. Two miles astern of station? About that, then he'd be nearly in station an hour after sunset, when it could be assumed that the tropical night would have produced complete blackness. He'd be close enough to follow by the convoy's lights.

'Mister Steel.'

The gunner lumbered over in his normal bow-legged gait.

'Aye sir?'

'Just drop back so that you can see *Earl of Bute's* taffrail light when it gets dark, would you?'

The gunner scratched his balding head and looked up at the sails towering above them, then he gave a volley of orders that were intended to spill their wind and reduce *Argonaut*'s speed. Holbrooke watched for a moment and was about to return to his temporary cabin off the wardroom when he heard a hail from the main topmast head.

'Sail ho! Sail on the starboard quarter.'

'Who do you have on deck? Young Stitch? Send him up with a telescope if you please Mister Steel, let's see if he can tell us anything more.'

Joseph Stitch was the third son of the tailor in Wickham. His family's station in life gave him no right to tread the quarterdeck of a King's ship, but Ann had pleaded his case after she'd become friendly with the tailor's wife, when she was being fitted for her wedding outfit. Holbrooke hadn't wanted to disappoint his new wife, so Stitch was entered on the books using the usual fictitious formula, as captain's servant taking the place as an ordinary seaman. He'd imagined that young Stitch would last a few months and then decide that the sea wasn't for him, but on the contrary, the lad had blossomed. He must be nearly fifteen by now, Holbrooke thought, trying rapidly to work forward from the time of his entry as a thirteen-year-old. No, he must be fifteen already and he should soon be made a midshipman. He could hardly imagine the rejoicing in the Stitch household in Wickham, for a provincial tailor's workshop was hardly the normal sort of place that produced midshipmen. From there it was but a matter of sea time, an examination and a modest amount of interest to the full glory of a King's commission and a gold-braided coat.

Stitch sped up the ratlines to join the lookout at the crosstrees. It only took a few moments for his hail to reach the deck.

'Captain, sir. It's a ship's t'gallants, she's running before the wind and overhauling us. Could be a man-o'-war sir.'

Holbrooke looked up to see Stitch handing the telescope to the lookout who he saw nodding in agreement. That was sensible, the lookout was an older hand and he'd have seen more men-of-war's t'gallants than Stitch had seen hot dinners. Not for the first time Holbrooke wondered whether it would be worth giving the masthead lookout a telescope, firmly fixed around his neck by a lanyard. So much more could be seen through the lenses than by the naked eye. It was unheard of, of course, and for two good reasons; telescopes were expensive and it was generally better that the lookout used his full naked eye field of vision rather than the five degrees or so that a telescope offered.

A man-of-war then, almost certainly. Shorrock and Fairview had both heard the hail and had immediately come on deck. Shorrock was still adjusting his stock, he must have been taking a dogwatch nap. He could feel their eyes upon him, wondering what he would do.

A man-of-war, and it sounded like it was steering to pass north of Puerto Rico, perhaps for the channel to the north of Hispaniola. It was hardly likely to be British although it was possible, just, and it was too far west for the Dutch or Danish islands. French perhaps, steering for Cape François, or Spanish for Santo Domingo or Cuba.

'Mister Steel,' he said without turning around.

'I have the deck, sir.'

That was Fairview's voice. Then the gunner must have gone to see to his guns and the powder magazine.

'Very well. Take us alongside the *Earl of Bute,* within hailing range, and make the signal to the convoy, *enemy in sight to windward.* Mister Shorrock, clear away a leeward six pounder and give the convoy a gun to wake them up.'

'Shall I beat to quarters and clear for action, sir?'

The first lieutenant was always eager to be at the enemy and now he was positively at tip-toe in his impatience.

'I think not, Mister Shorrock, not at least until we know this gentleman's allegiance. If he has evil intent then you know the old saying, *a stern chase is a long chase.* We'll have plenty of time to prepare for him and it'll do no good having the men stand by their guns unnecessarily. However, this may be a good time to have the quarter gunners go over their equipment.'

Holbrooke left Shorrock to it. He needed something to keep him active, and harassing the quarter gunners would do no great harm.

***

The reports from the masthead were coming thick and fast now. It was a man-of-war, for certain, and it looked very much like a small ship-of-the-line, perhaps a fourth rate of fifty or sixty guns. Not British; foreign by the look of her, and she was flying along with stuns'ls set to her tops'ls and courses and must be making eight or nine knots to the convoys meagre five.

Holbrooke shouted across the tossing waters at the *Earl*

of Bute's master, telling him to set every sail that he had to come up with the convoy before the strange sail caught him. That was all the encouragement the master needed and as *Argonaut* pulled away the West Indiaman could be seen hanging nameless sails from every available point of the masts and yards. Her speed increased by a good knot.

Two bells sounded from forward and the six pounder signal gun made Holbrooke jump.

'Masthead,' he called, 'can you see any other sails?'

'None, sir,' Stitch called back, 'the horizon's clear except for this one sail.'

Holbrooke walked aft and climbed onto the taffrail, holding on to the ensign staff with one hand. There was one thing in his favour; the pursuer, if that was what this ship was intent upon, had to squint into the setting sun to see his prey, while Holbrooke had a perfect view to the east. The case would be reversed in an hour when the sun set and the darkness gathered. Ah, he could just see it now, a flash of white as the stranger's t'gallants rose briefly above the horizon. Eight miles or thereabouts, he estimated. He felt a presence behind him and looked over his shoulder to see Chalmers looking up at him.

'Ah, David. Would you pass my respects to Lady Chiara and tell her the general situation? We're being chased, I believe, and I suspect he's a Frenchman of fifty or sixty guns. He'll be up with us in two hours, just as we lose the light. I hope that she and Joshua will prepare themselves to take shelter in the hold before an engagement, if there is to be one. It may be that he decides to shadow us through the night and engage in the morning, but I can't be certain of his intentions.'

Chalmers looked solemn as he replied.

'Is there no chance of escaping in the darkness? I understand there will be no moon until well into the middle watch.'

'Yes, a little sliver of a crescent moon at five bells. But it'll do us little good with this ponderous great convoy. It would be a poor seaman that couldn't keep in contact during the blackest of nights, and the way he's cracking on, I wouldn't accuse him of a lack of seamanship, not without evidence.'

'A vessel of some force then. Can we fight him?'

Holbrooke shook his head.

'Not broadside-to-broadside, he has too great an advantage. If we had no convoy I don't doubt we could outrun him, but as things stand…'

Holbrooke swept his arm across an arc to leeward, where the convoy was lumbering along, with t'gallants and stuns'ls starting to be hastily set.

'Very well. I'll deliver your message, George, but mark my words, you'll come up with something.'

***

Come up with something. Easy to say but harder to do. If that ship was French then *Argonaut* and the convoy were in mortal danger. Even if it was only a fifty-gun ship it would make short work of a twenty-eight gun frigate and then it would be hard to see how even half of the convoy could escape capture or destruction. Even if the Frenchman had an important mission to fulfil, it was hardly credible that he'd pass up an opportunity such as this. Spanish? The case could be just the same. Holbrooke recalled his conversation with Carlisle about Spain's intention to join France in the war against Britain. If this ship was coming directly from Europe then it could know about a declaration already. He'd have to treat any Spanish ship with suspicion until the facts were clear. What would he do if the situation was reversed? That was easy, he'd get close enough to the convoy to be able to watch its movements during the night and then at daybreak he'd fall upon the frigate, if it hadn't fled in the night. He'd use his superior numbers to take her by boarding, and then set about seizing or sinking the merchantmen. He played it through in his mind. The one advantage that *Argonaut* had was speed, but how could that help when he had to protect the convoy?

***

The sun was just dipping below the horizon when Shorrock and Fairview compared notes after a careful study of the stranger who was now only three miles astern.

'She's not French, sir, she's a Spanish fifty,' Shorrock announced, 'I've seen the like of her before. Twenty-four pounders on the lower deck and twelves on the upper with some sixes on the fo'c'sle and quarterdeck, just like our own fifties; same as Mister Carlisle's *Dartmouth* in fact. The question is, sir…'

Holbrooke knew the question, was Spain at war? It appeared likely, otherwise why would this ship be pursuing them so urgently? It was possible that it was a coincidental meeting, that the Spaniard was making for Florida, and if so St. Augustine, the capital city, was her likely destination. Holbrooke looked again at the ship. It was certainly in a hurry and had closed the distance so that its whole hull and its two rows of gunports were now visible.

'Mister Fairview, have you been taking bearings?'

'Aye sir. Her bearing's steady, it has been since I first saw her t'gallants on the horizon.'

'And if she was steering for St. Augustine?'

'From where we first sighted her, she'd be on much the same track as the convoy, sir. Perhaps her bearing would have drawn right a little but it would be hardly noticeable. It looks like they've come from Spain, so they could be unsure of their westing. Perhaps he intends to hail us, sir. It would make sense because he must see that we'd have had a good departure fix this morning.'

Yes, indeed. It could be an innocent encounter and the Spaniard may well be a prudent mariner seeking to know his longitude from a ship that must surely know its own. Yet it still looked suspicious. He was too far north for Hispaniola or Cuba and a little too far south for St. Augustine, and with this fine weather he should know his latitude with some certainty. Holbrooke felt baffled by all the alternative explanations; he must fix upon one. Which was the most likely? The Spanish ship had come from Europe heading to pass north of San Juan and on to Cuba. When his lookout had sighted the convoy he'd immediately altered his course to intercept. There was no good cause for a neutral Spaniard to be chasing down a British convoy, and that meant that the stranger knew something that he didn't. Holbrooke grimaced, if that was the case he had a fight on his hands.

'Thank you Mister Fairview. Mister Shorrock you may beat to quarters now, and clear for action.'

***

Should he order the convoy to scatter? He'd anticipated the possibility and the written orders that he'd sent to each of the masters included a signal to that effect, a red flag at the mizzen masthead. If they saw that red flag they'd know that it was every man for himself. They'd douse their top lights and their stern lights and steer whatever course their masters thought would best preserve their freedom. Some would cram on sail and make for Savannah directly, some would bear away and hope to lose themselves in the tangle of reefs and shoals and islands to the north of Hispaniola, and some would haul their wind and stand to the north. Each one would hope to make himself the least attractive target for the pursuer. It was almost the normal thing to do when the escort was so far outgunned by the attacker, and yet it left a bad taste in Holbrooke's mouth. He'd been given command of this convoy and it seemed like an abrogation of his duty to abandon it. Surely he could do better than that.

***

CHAPTER THREE

Don Mancebo

Wednesday, Seventeenth of February 1762.
San Sebastian, at Sea. Cape San Juan south-by-west 30 leagues.

The sailing master removed his hat and bowed briefly as his captain strode onto the quarterdeck.

'The lookout is certain, sir. There's a convoy steering to the nor'west with a ship-rigged merchantman straggling astern and a man-o'-war to windward. It looks like a frigate but he can't be sure, he can only see her t'gallants.'

Don Mancebo looked up at the main topmast head. He could see his junior lieutenant making his laborious way up the ratlines with the ship's biggest telescope slung across his shoulder. If the lookout was right then this was just the opportunity that he'd been hoping for; a rich West Indies convoy bound for the American colonies and loaded with sugar and indigo and coffee and logwood. The strongest escort would naturally be stationed to windward. If it was a frigate then anything to leeward would be another frigate or a sloop. No ship-of-the-line then, no battle-hardened English third or fourth rate to deal with; it would be easy pickings.

And yet, nothing was simple for a man-of-war's captain, and Don Mancebo frowned as he thought of the problems. The question that most engaged him was the bare fact of whether his country was at war. Could the ambassador's courier be believed? He hadn't seen written confirmation of his nation's belligerent state. In fact, since he saw the courier climb over the side and back into his boat, he hadn't spoken to a single ship, Spanish or otherwise. He'd be personally liable for the cost of damage and the deaths and delay if he engaged the convoy only to find that his King had discovered a way to avoid a conflict, and then his career would surely be over. However, he knew very well that all the talk in Madrid was of the impending war – he'd heard it himself when he visited the capital – and on balance he was prepared to accept the small risk.

The second problem was that he'd have to alter course away from his direct track to the north of San Juan and Hispaniola and through the Old Bahama Straits. That would incur a delay in bringing the news of war to the governor-general at Havana. Again, he could accept that, and if he arrived off the Morro Castle with half a dozen prizes in line astern, his forgiveness was pre-determined. The third problem was making itself obvious as his lieutenant sought to confirm the lookout's report while staring into the setting sun. It would be dark in three hours and even if he spread his stuns'ls he wouldn't be up with the convoy in time to engage the frigate – if that was what it was – and take possession of the merchantmen in the daylight. He'd have to follow through the night and attack at first light tomorrow, and perhaps by then they'd have scattered and half of them would be beyond his reach. He looked up again to the masthead where he could see that his lieutenant had taken the lookout's seat athwart the crosstrees and was peering through a telescope, right into the setting sun. He picked up the speaking trumpet.

'What do you make of the man-o'-war?'

'A frigate, sir. She's spilling the wind from her t'gallants. I'm almost certain of her, but it's the sun…'

Don Mancebo resisted the urge to berate his lieutenant, it would only lead him into reporting whatever his captain wanted to hear, and that wouldn't do, not in this case when his career rested on making the right decision. He paced restlessly. Oh how he yearned to walk the poop deck; to be able to stride out without so many people hemming him in, but for the next few hours he needed to be here, at the centre of his command, where all the levers of power were to hand. However, he surprised himself with the clarity of his thoughts after just a step or two. He turned to the sailing master and first lieutenant who were watching him expectantly.

'Steer a course to intercept that man-o'-war, Sailing Master, and set the stuns'ls to the tops'l and lower yards. First Lieutenant, beat to quarters and clear for action. Have the boats made ready for hoisting out.'

***

Don Mancebo watched the stuns'ls blossom like vast pallid flowers and felt *San Sebastian's* speed increase. It was like the acceleration of a powerful horse when the spurs were applied. He heard the beat of the drum and the trumpet's strident notes calling the men to their quarters. He felt the decks vibrate as his big twenty-four pounders were released from their sea lashings and heaved into place at the gunports. The convoy would have seen him by now and he could imagine the concern that they'd feel at this two-decker surging down upon them. It would take them some time to identify his ship as Spanish, and then the convoy commander – who would almost certainly be unaware that he was at war with Spain – would be left wondering why he was closing on them. Could he exploit that? If only he could have come up with the convoy with daylight left. He could have run up alongside the frigate close enough to hail its captain and in one sentence he'd have given him the news of war and followed it by a shattering broadside that would probably end the contest there and then. But the Englishman would surely be suspicious of a foreign man-of-war that followed through the night before hailing. No, he'd already be suspicious. The rumour of war must be as strong in Antigua and Port Royal as it was in Madrid and Ferrol. Any English captain would be wary of a Spanish man-of-war, whatever its actions. Then he must assume that the convoy already feared the worst, and in that case his task was straightforward. He'd follow the convoy through the night, leaving his opponent to be consumed by doubt. Then, as soon as it was light enough for gunnery, he'd smash that frigate, then run through the convoy giving each ship a gun to demand their surrender. He could hoist out his boats during the night without any fear of losing touch with the convoy. At the first gun, no doubt, half the convoy would take fright and scatter to escape capture, but he'd be satisfied with half a dozen prizes and in any case he could only spare enough of his crew to man that many ships. If by some chance he seized more than that, he'd have to burn the least valuable.

***

Don Mancebo paced the poop deck all through the first watch. It was still warm here despite the trade wind's cooling effect and he needed no cloak against the night chills. He'd placed *San Sebastian* to windward of the convoy's escort and doused all his lights. He'd hoist out his boats as soon as it became dark and when he was certain that they wouldn't be observed. He thought it likely that his ship was already invisible to the captain of the English escort, at least until the moon rose in the middle watch when even the dim light from that pale crescent would be enough to show his ship. As far as he could tell the convoy hadn't scattered. That indicated that his opponent was still in doubt, he must still be wondering whether Spain was an enemy. Well, let the English captain wonder; he intended to exploit that uncertainty.

'The watch has been relieved, sir.'

Don Mancebo was aware that his first lieutenant Fernando Guterres had come onto the poop deck. It was unnecessary for him to report the change of the watch but like his captain, he probably had no desire for sleep, not with an enemy convoy under the ship's lee. Don Mancebo liked his second-in-command and he had to check a tendency to become too friendly with him. Their families both came from León, just fifty leagues east of Ferrol, where the Cantabrian Cordillera and the León Mountains descended to the plain. They shared a love of the cuisine of the area, the spicy *Butiellu,* the salty smoked *Cecina* and the sweet *Mantecadas* pastries, made with the same sugar that was presumably part of the convoy's cargo. They'd both grown up speaking Leonese, a language that was much closer to its Latin roots than the upstart Castilian, and when they were alone, when the other officers couldn't hear them, that's what they spoke.

'Very well, and you've dismissed the watch below?'

'Yes, sir, after they had all been mustered, and I've left a man at each gun keeping the slow match alight.'

The first lieutenant stared hard to leeward but he couldn't penetrate the darkness. The thought occurred to him that the convoy could have used the night to turn away and run to leeward, but he dismissed the idea. There was no sanctuary for English merchantmen to leeward.

'What do you think of that convoy, sir, is it a fair prize? I'd dearly like to serve those pirates in the way they deserve.'

That was the question, of course, and when Don Mancebo hadn't been plotting its capture he'd been tormenting himself with considerations of the legality of his planned actions. In Spain it was normal to refer to the *English,* never the *British,* because that gave legitimacy to England's occupation of Catholic Ireland and its hegemony over Scotland and Wales. It was also normal to dismiss them as *pirates* and to condemn their every action at sea as being against the common laws of mankind. Ever since the first English seamen had come to the Indies to disturb the world order that Spain and Portugal had agreed between themselves at the Treaty of Tordesillas, they'd been nothing but trouble. The Spanish people had long memories and even after the passage of nearly two centuries since Francis Drake's raid, mothers in Cadiz still warned their children that if they didn't behave *El Draque* would carry them away in the night. It was too easy to assume that the English were the natural enemies of Spain, and his first lieutenant was eloquently expressing that sentiment. He knew nothing of the courier's message, Don Mancebo had been careful to keep that information to himself, and yet Fernando found it easy to believe that an English convoy could be a legitimate prize. Well, if they were to go into action tomorrow with all the personal risk that was inherent in a sea battle, it was only fair that his first lieutenant should know why they were attacking the convoy.

'It appears that we're at war with the English, Señor Guterres. That courier who boarded us off Ferrol brought the news from our Ambassador in London…'

Fernando looked attentive and nodded in the right places, but it rapidly became clear to Don Mancebo that his first lieutenant had either guessed the courier's message or – most likely – their conversation in the cabin had been overheard. He remembered that he'd taken no precautions to ensure secrecy and he was aware that his clerk could hear most of what was said in the cabin from his tiny office that adjoined it. Either way, his second-in-command already knew the essentials, and probably so did most of the officers.

'Well, none of this is news to you, I see. In that case you'll understand what an opportunity this gives us.'

'Indeed, sir. We can deliver the declaration of war to those damned English pirates through the mouths of our guns. It will be a great day tomorrow, when the sun rises.'

Don Mancebo gazed again to leeward, where the darkness was intensifying by the moment, then he lifted his head as though to study the sky above.

'O Lord, open thou my lips.'

His first lieutenant grinned and completed the phrase.

'And my mouth shall show forth thy praise.'

It was a mild irreverence, a commonplace among Spanish artillerymen, and it entirely missed the point that King David had presumably intended when he penned those lines a millennia before the birth of Christ. But then, he reflected, when it concerned the destruction of the heretics, perhaps it was no blasphemy at all.

Guterres rubbed his hands in anticipation, not at all troubled at the use of a psalm to justify a violent attack. He was too young to remember the last war but he was weaned on stories of the great Spanish navy and heroes such as Don Blas de Lezo who held off Admiral Vernon and a vastly superior English force during their attempted assault on Cartagena de Indias. He longed to do battle against the English and the matter of prize money was just an added incentive. He'd give a feast in his home town to celebrate and all the church bells would ring! There was no uncertainty in his mind; he'd followed the course of France's war against England and there was no doubt that the mighty Spanish navy would tip the balance.

Don Mancebo nodded and glanced again to leeward. He could see nothing at all, it was as though his ship was alone on the wide ocean. That there was a fabulously wealthy English convoy to leeward was an objective fact – he'd seen it with his own eyes – but like a sighting of a sea monster or a mermaid, he found it hard to believe.

'Yet it puzzles me, sir. How did we come to this situation where an English convoy can brazenly sail from the Indies with nothing more than a frigate to guard it? The Indies are Spanish by right and not a single island should be English or Dutch or Danish; not even French. The Holy Father himself gave that part of the new world to our people to hold forever. Yet here we are, with the English lording it over the most profitable islands and defending it with their navy.'

Perhaps Guterres intended it as a rhetorical question, but it was one that Don Mancebo had spent a fair part of his life pondering. Poor leadership, complacency, greed, imperial overstretch; he'd heard all the theories. Probably it was a mix of all of those deficiencies, but the real question was how to remedy the situation.

'Well, however we arrived here, I hope that King Carlos can start to regain our territories. We may not like it, but an alliance with France may be our best hope. They're cousins you know, Carlos and Louis, and they hold to the true religion. If sharing with our cousins is the price of ejecting the English, then perhaps we can swallow it, for now. But those are decisions far above our heads, Fernando, and all we have to do is make the best use that we can of this instrument of war that's been trusted to us.'

Don Mancebo was aware that he was starting to sound pompous; the conversation was degenerating into a speech delivered from on high, from the captain of a man-of-war to its second-in command. He hadn't intended that, but he could see that Guterres was hanging on his every word. Probably this would be repeated in the wardroom and filtered down to the men in their messes. Well, in that case it would have more force and would be better remembered than if he'd mustered all hands and made a formal oration from the quarterdeck rail. Nevertheless, he'd said enough.

'Call all hands, First Lieutenant, I want the boats in the water before the moon is up, every one of them. If we have to waste time getting them over the side when we're among the convoy tomorrow, we'll lose half of our prizes. Keep a man at each gun, and have them all loaded and run out. Otherwise you can take all the seamen and gunners, and the idlers. Let me know when you're ready and I'll heave to.'

***

CHAPTER FOUR

Do Something!

Thursday, Eighteenth of February 1762.
Argonaut, at Sea. Cape San Juan south-by-west 40 leagues.

Holbrooke stared to windward. Nothing. Not the slightest indication that a Spanish ship-of-the-line was out there in the darkness. Well, he must do something and it went against the grain to wait upon the Spanish captain's pleasure. That was a lesson that he'd learned from Carlisle all those years ago in the Mediterranean and the Caribbean. Take the initiative, do anything you can to disrupt the enemy's plan and to keep him on the back foot, as you would in a fencing lesson.

'Mister Fairview, where's the Spaniard likely to be now?'

The sailing master scratched his head and gazed speculatively out over the starboard quarter.

'He was doing a good speed when we last saw him, sir, overhauling us by about three knots. If he kept that up he'd be abreast of us now and drawing steadily ahead. About three miles right on the beam, I'd say.'

Holbrooke nodded. He saw Shorrock's dark shape looming up as he came aft from the guns.

'Thank you, Mister Fairview. Let's assume he's on our beam then. Now, if I were the Spanish captain I wouldn't want to draw much further ahead, that would put me to leeward of the convoy at dawn and if we had hauled our wind in the night, it could be a long chase to windward. No, I'd hold my position on the beam and bide my time.'

'He'll be concerned that the convoy might scatter in the night, sir.'

'That he will Mister Shorrock, but realistically he can't take or sink every merchantman. He has the superior weight of broadside and he'll know that a night attack will just induce risks. No, he'll wait for the dawn, I'm sure. Well,

I don't intend to let him have a quiet night. The guns are loaded and run out?'

'Aye sir, cleared for action and the hands are at their quarters.'

Shorrock's smile was clearly visible, his bared teeth reflecting in the binnacle light's meagre gleam.

'Then haul your wind, Mister Fairview, and let's see if we can find him. Now, we must not fire unless we're first fired upon, so make that clear to your division commanders and quarter gunners, Mister Shorrock. A single blast on my whistle will be your signal to engage.'

'They'll wait for the order, sir, or I'll know the reason why.'

Argonaut heeled as she came to starboard, bringing the stiff southeasterly trade wind onto her beam. An errant wave, surprised by the turn, burst over the gunwale and sent a spray of salt water aft as far as the wheel, catching Chalmers unaware as he opened the cabin door.

'Ah, Mister Chalmers, are Lady Chiara and Joshua properly stowed away?'

'They are, sir, in the hold with cushions and refreshments. I had expected some resistance, in fact Captain Carlisle assured me that I would never, ever persuade his wife to sit out an engagement in the hold, but it appears that her son's presence has focussed her mind.'

Holbrooke laughed. He'd also been warned by Carlisle that Chiara would refuse to be bundled into a place of safety. It was out of cowardice that he'd sent Chalmers to enforce his request, but he'd clearly reckoned without the maternal instinct, or without a clergyman's powers of persuasion.

'Good. I hope there will be no engagement, of course, but I fear otherwise. All the indications suggest that we're at war with Spain, and that gentleman,' he nodded towards the starboard bow, 'knows the truth while we do not.'

Chalmers looked thoughtful, staring into the blackness where it seemed that the Spaniard might appear at any moment.

'Is this not a little dangerous, then? Coming upon a much larger ship – a potential enemy – in the dead of night without giving warning of our intentions.'

'Well, that's the whole point. If he's innocently going about his business or even if he's waiting for daylight to speak to us, then he'll be surprised, but he won't fire. However, if he has evil intent, I hope to catch him unawares and force him to show his hand. I can still scurry away to leeward and I think we can survive one broadside, delivered hurriedly on this dark night. At least we'll know where we stand and I can make the appropriate dispositions for tomorrow. What I cannot – must not – do, is await his pleasure. If we're at war, then in the morning he'll run down and I'll either have to flee or commit the ship to a hopeless fight. In either case he'll take his pick of the convoy and might have a prize frigate into the bargain. If I know that we're at war then I can at least order the convoy to disperse and save half of them. And, you know, a night engagement is a chancy affair. He'll be aware of that as well as we are. In daylight he'll merely overwhelm us with his weight of broadside and he has perhaps twice our numbers for boarding. At night, anything can happen. In any case, it's hardly likely to worsen our case.'

Chalmers studied his friends face in the light from the binnacle. Holbrooke didn't look particularly worried, he noticed. Perhaps that was his growing maturity. He was still only twenty-three years old but he'd served through six years of a bloody war and he'd been in command for four of those years. He was fortunate in retaining much of the optimism of youth and its blithe assumption of invincibility. Time and increasing age would change that, but for now he had the bearing of a man for whom nothing was impossible. What would he do if the Spaniard fired upon them? Fight or flee? Perhaps Holbrooke himself didn't yet know.

'We'll be up with them in a few minutes, Mister

Chalmers, and your place is with the surgeon, but perhaps you'd like to stay until we know whether we must fight or exchange pleasantries.'

***

'The courses are furled, sir. We're under tops'ls, jib, fore stays'l and mizzen.'

'Very well, Mister Fairview. When we sight her I want to match her course and speed at long cannon-shot. Now, let there be complete silence on the deck. Mister Shorrock, keep the gun crews quiet, if you please.'

Argonaut plunged on into the black night with only the phosphorescence of a breaking wave at her bow to alleviate the deep and profound darkness. Holbrooke resisted the urge to stare out over the starboard bow, where the Spaniard was expected. There were lookouts aplenty and he could more profitably think through the likely consequences of this encounter. If the Spaniard was alert and fired upon him, then the prudent course of action would be to put up his helm and reach back to the convoy. Then he'd make the night signal for the merchantmen to disperse. He could shadow the Spaniard – *Argonaut* was almost certainly the faster ship – and make it as difficult as he could for the two-decker to take prizes. In fact, he could re-take prizes that strayed from the protection of the ship-of-the-line. Now that was a thought, a means to salvage something from this otherwise hopeless situation. The Spaniard would have to keep each prize close under his lee and that would make a real difference. But still, he, George Holbrooke, would lose a number of his charges. Perhaps he could limit it to three or four, but that would still be a defeat. He could fight to protect the convoy of course, but that made no sense, not against a fourth rate with twice his number of men. He wouldn't do it – he told himself – and he'd just have to face down any criticism their Lordships may express. Yet, a night encounter always threw up surprises, and his options may not be quite as bleak as he feared.

The minutes passed and there was no sighting of the Spaniard, no hail from the masthead, no quiet word from the sailing master. Holbrooke was starting to wonder whether he'd guessed wrong. Perhaps at this very moment the Spanish ship was creeping up astern of the convoy, ready to start engaging before dawn. In a sudden fear for the worst he walked aft as steadily as his racing mind would allow. A quick look astern showed nothing, he couldn't even see the convoy. Well, if his adversary was out there he was keeping very quiet. Holbrooke turned to scan the starboard bow and in doing so, out of the corner of his eye, he caught a grey patch on the starboard quarter. Was that a sail? He stared straight towards it but could see nothing at all but the unrelieved darkness. He tilted his head to the left and then to the right. There it was again, just the slightest patch of dark grey, only a shade or two lighter than the coal-black background.

'Mister Fairview, we've head-reached on him. Look on your starboard quarter. Haul your wind another three points.'

Fairview leaned out to look past the hammock nets. He stared for a long two seconds then turned and nodded to Holbrooke at the very moment that the lookout sang out.

'Sail ho! Sail on the starboard quarter. It's a ship, sir, with its tops'ls backed, on the starboard tack.'

The masthead lookout had the best view of the presumed Spanish ship. Holbrooke thought for a moment as Fairview went through the orders to bring *Argonaut* closer to the wind. Backed tops'ls? That was odd, unless the Spanish captain was making preparations for dawn. What preparations would require a ship to heave to? Could he be putting his boats in the water? Of course, that would take time, an hour or so probably, and in the morning he could lose half the convoy in an hour. But what an opportunity to catch the Spaniard off his guard.

'You see him, Mister Fairview? Come up onto his leeward side, I fancy he'll have a gaggle of boats in the water. Pass at half a cable if you please. Mister Shorrock, stand by the starboard battery but not a gun is to fire until I blow my whistle, not even if he fires first. Mister Murray, swivels and muskets stand by.'

'At your whistle, aye sir.'

The marine lieutenant had his men in order and Holbrooke could see their heads and muskets silhouetted above the gunwales, punctuated by the swivel guns that the aimers would insist on training and elevating in that annoying fashion. No power on earth could persuade them to keep still as they closed the enemy and Murray had long ago stopped trying.

Holbrooke's heart was beating faster now. This was an opportunity sent from heaven. With all the bustle of lifting heavy boats off their cradles and into the water, with the main yard used as a crane and with most of the gun crews heaving on braces and lifts, there would never be a better moment to even the odds. And it was a near certainty that the Spaniard intended to engage in the morning, there were few other explanations for his actions. One gun from the Spaniard, that was all he needed to be certain, and it would be odd indeed if at least one gun captain didn't panic and fire in the confusion of seeing a frigate bearing up to them out of this blackest night.

'Starboard battery ready, sir.'

'Thank you, Mister Shorrock. Do you see what I intend? We must make him fire first.'

Shorrock stared again at the Spanish ship. The outline of its stern was clearly visible now and he could just see the deeper blackness on her larboard side that could only be her boats being launched. Ah, there was something large on her side, between waterline and gunwale. It looked like her longboat was being hoisted out. He rubbed his hands, it was odds-on that *Argonaut* hadn't even been seen yet, coming up fast from astern while the whole ship was concentrating on the difficult evolution of hoisting out the longboat at night in a stiff trade wind breeze.

'Fire at his boats, sir?'

Holbrooke started guiltily. He hadn't thought of that. *Argonaut's* nine pounders would have little effect on the massive scantlings of a fourth rate, but with all the boats clustered alongside and one hanging betwixt wind and water, he had a real chance of destroying the Spaniard's ability to send away prize crews.

'Yes, Mister Shorrock. Destroy those boats for me, but we must still wait for him to open the engagement.'

The nearer gun captains had heard the conversation and were already busily tapping in their quoins to depress their guns' elevation. Shorrock turned and started calling orders to the remainder.

'Luff a little closer, Mister Fairview. Will she take it?'

The sailing master looked appraisingly at the leading edges of his mainsail and main tops'l. He caught the affirmative nod from the quartermaster who'd been watching nothing else for the past ten minutes.

'Aye she will, sir. Quartermaster…'

But the quartermaster had already give his order to the steersman and *Argonaut's* bows moved tentatively to starboard. This was no time to overdo it and end up with the ship in irons, and it took a lifetime of experience to judge it exactly so that *Argonaut* was sailing as close to the wind as possible without going too far and losing speed. He watched for the first hint of a shivering on the main tops'l luff and nodded his approval as the steersman eased the wheel a spoke or two.

'Full and by with a touch of luff, sir.'

'Very well, quartermaster. As she is, no higher.'

Fairview's smile was hidden in the darkness. He loved, with all his heart, a perfectly stretched luff.

'I don't believe he's seen us yet, sir.'

The sailing master couldn't resist commenting on the situation and Holbrooke ignored him. Yet it did appear that all the Spaniard's attention was on the boats. That was only natural and it was hard to imagine *Argonaut* acting much differently.

***

Closer and closer. *Argonaut* was racing up on the Spaniard's larboard quarter, and there was still no sign that they'd been discovered. Holbrooke had a moment to look forward. The darkness had hardly diminished but the shaded battle lanterns below the gunwales and the dim glow of the slow-match showed where each gun's crew awaited its moment of glory. The Spanish ship was plainly visible, a vast, dark presence fine on the starboard bow. There were lanterns visible on her larboard side and by their illumination he could see the boats. It was as he thought, some four or five boats were clustered near her quarter and further forward the vast and ponderous bulk of her longboat was being eased over the side. Those lanterns would prevent anyone on deck seeing *Argonaut* as she sped up alongside. Only the masthead lookout would see anything beyond the little pools of light. And yet, and yet, how would he know if he'd been discovered? He could hear no orders from the Spaniard and he could see no details on the deck. Perhaps the first indication that they were at war would be a devastating broadside at half pistol shot range. Holbrooke could imagine the damage that it would do to his frigate, perhaps he'd lose his ship in that one moment. Still, he thought it unlikely. Half of the Spaniard's broadside was masked by his longboat and the remainder of his guns must be short-manned with every seaman engaged in this most difficult task.

Holbrooke fingered his whistle, resisting the temptation to give any more orders. He could see that Fairview was handling the frigate superbly and that he'd pass so close to the Spaniard's boats that his broadside must shatter at least some of them. Shorrock had tight control of his guns and Holbrooke was confident that none would fire until he blew his whistle. The sergeant was walking behind his marines, speaking quietly to them, ensuring that no weapon was at full cock. There was nothing for him to do but wait for a gun from the Spaniard, and failing that to hail him and try to determine the situation.

'Mister Fairview,' Holbrooke was speaking softly now, so that nobody else should hear, 'if he doesn't fire on us, I'll probably ask you to heave to and put a boat in the water.'

Fairview gave him a strange look.

'Aye-aye sir. But he'll fire, you mark my words.'

***

CHAPTER FIVE

Just One Man

Thursday, Eighteenth of February 1762.
San Sebastian, at Sea. Cape San Juan south-by-west 40 leagues.

Don Mancebo looked down onto his ship's waist from the poop deck. His first lieutenant was doing well. The smallest boat, the cutter, had been towing astern since they left Ferrol, but that still left three boats to hoist over the side. The longboat had been secured to the skid beams to starboard and the pinnace and yawl had been nested to larboard. As his ship was hove to on the starboard tack it was natural that the smaller and lighter boats should be hoisted out first. He was troubled by the lanterns that restricted his vision beyond the tiny pools of light that they produced, but he wasn't unduly concerned. He could see the three boats right below the poop deck and the longboat was well on its way to being floated, it was past the gunwale now and he'd just heard the orders for the hands to ease the falls. He watched as the great boat – slung between the fore and main yards – paused as though itself waiting for the order that would set it upon its natural environment. The brisk trade wind was heeling the ship a trifle to larboard and the longboat had no great distance left to travel. Ah, the bosun had given the order and he could distinctly hear the sheaves squealing in their blocks as the boat inched downwards, then the sound stopped. He heard a sharp imperative order to halt the process.

'What's the problem, Mister Guterres?'

'The top block on the main yard tackle is jammed, sir. The bosun will have to rig a relieving tackle before it can be freed.'

'Very well. Tell the bosun that I wish to inspect the top block in my cabin, when this affair is over.'

The news of the block didn't worry him. These things

happened, particularly after a long sea passage where the boats hadn't been touched for weeks. Don Mancebo was a reasonable man and he didn't jump to conclusions. It would have been easy to blame the bosun for not properly maintaining the block, but it could be any of a number of things that had caused it to jam. He remembered finding a seagull's foot between the sheave and the cheek of a block once, and it was hard to blame a man for that.

His bosun was old but competent and this should take no more than ten minutes. The British convoy would still be under his lee in the morning and it was better that the job was done properly rather than risk damage to the boat or to any of the ship's masts and yards. Two men were already running out on the main yard. He saw one sit astride it and haul on a line that he'd been carrying. The line was but a messenger for a vast wooden block with two sheaves and its attendant cordage. He couldn't see what was happening in detail but he could imagine the seaman passing half a dozen turns of the lighter line right around the yard to offer a secure fixing for the block. Well, it was in good hands and Don Mancebo walked aft to get a better view of the sea beyond the light from the lanterns. He gazed over the larboard quarter not expecting to see anything and his first sweep of the profound darkness offered nothing new. He made a second sweep now that his eyes were adjusting after they'd been blinded by the lanterns on the deck, and he stopped dead. There was a ship coming up on their quarter. Why had nobody noticed it? But he knew the answer immediately, the only lookout who could reasonably be expected to see beyond the light from the ship's lanterns was at the masthead, and he was probably watching the interesting activity on deck and looking ahead where most sightings were made.

In a flash he realised that it must be the English frigate, come to investigate his ship, to determine whether he came in peace or in war. My God, but his guns were masked by the longboat! There was an edge of urgency in his voice as he hailed his first lieutenant.

'Mister Guterres, stand by the larboard battery, forward and aft divisions. Get the men back to the guns. Leave the longboat. Sailing Master, get us underway. Don't worry about the foresail and mainsail.'

He looked again at the sleek shape approaching their quarter. It was completely darkened with not a lantern visible but now it was closer he could see that it *was* the English frigate. Men were rushing all over his ship now, dropping the ropes that they were handling and leaping towards the guns. He heard a crash and saw the stern of the longboat drop into the sea, with the bows still held by the fore stay tackle and the fore yard tackle. The men must have just dropped the ropes that they were holding and the sheave at the end of the yard had chosen that moment to free itself. The seaman who was securing the strop for the relieving tackle was catapulted off the yard and fell with a long wail into the sea alongside.

Don Mancebo could feel a rising panic. He was in no state to engage even a frigate, and his ship was all but immobile with most of his larboard battery – from where the danger was approaching – masked by the longboat.

'Cut it free, Bosun, cut the tackles and let the longboat go. I need all the men back at the guns.'

He realised that his voice had risen to a scream. That would never do, the men must be held in check. His best chance now was to fool the Englishman into believing that Spain and Britain were still at peace. The news of war can't have reached the frigate before it sailed from the Leeward Islands, and this English captain wouldn't dare do anything to start a conflict.

'Hold your fire, engage on my word only!'

Guterres raised his hand in acknowledgement.

***

It was Miguel Crespi who started the disaster at the falls of the main yard tackle. He'd heard the order to stand by the larboard battery and he was the captain of the larboard aftermost twelve pounder on the upper deck. He was naturally in a hurry to make his way to his gun, and he could feel that there was no tension on the fall. He'd reasoned that if the sheave was jammed, it would stay that way so he just dropped the rope and ran. Behind him, the remainder of the hands did likewise and when he heard the crash of the falling longboat he just kept running. He heard none of the first lieutenant's orders before he arrived at his gun. His number two had performed his main duty and had kept the slow match alight, and he was visibly relieved to see Crespi arrive and take the responsibility.

'What's happening?' the number two gunner asked as his gun captain pulled the lighted slow match out of his hand.

'There's an English pirate ranging up on our larboard side,' he replied as he craned his neck through the open gunport.

He'd never have put himself in such a dangerous position if he didn't have firm hold of the slow match himself. Many a gun captain had ended his days when his head had been parted from his body by a prematurely fired gun. Behind him he could hear the rest of his crew skidding and jostling into place, all demanding to know who? what? where? why?

Crespi knew that he'd be in trouble over the longboat. The bosun and probably the first lieutenant had witnessed him drop the fall, they'd seen the rest of the men follow him, and would draw their conclusions as to where the blame should lie. Well, he'd make up for it with his gun. He was a good gunner – an excellent one in his own opinion – and now the English frigate was coming into his arcs of fire.

'First Lieutenant said fire on his word.'

That was the midshipman who commanded this division of guns. Crespi despised him and paid him little attention. He afforded the youngster barely a glance.

'And has he given that word?'

The midshipman looked worried. He knew that he should have more control over his gun crews but it was men like Crespi who worked insidiously to undermine his authority. He knew that he should take control and wait for the first lieutenant's orders, but Crespi's manner was insistent, and he did so want to appear decisive. The senior midshipman had a motto, it's easier to ask forgiveness than permission. If this wasn't a time act and hope for pardon if he acted in error, then there never would be one.

'I heard the captain say fire, I think…'

'Then fire it is. Stand back.'

How much of Crespi's impatience was motivated by his family history he would never afterwards admit. His forbears had lived in and around Ferrol since time immemorial and had served in the King's ships in war and fished the wild Atlantic Ocean, as far away as the desolate cod grounds off *Terranova,* during the periods of peace. His father had fought the English in the last war and he could trace a Crespi to every altercation with the English pirates since before the time of the Great Armada. To his mind there was nothing unusual in his actions, the surprising thing would have been if he *didn't* fire at an English pirate on sight. He knew nothing of his King's ultimately doomed attempts to stay out of the war and in any case it wouldn't have altered his decision. His blood was up and the midshipman's hesitation was enough for him. He nudged his hand-spike man who shifted the aim slightly. By squinting along the length of the gun barrel he could see that his shot would hit the English frigate squarely in the middle of its upper deck. He couldn't miss, and he guessed that he'd never have such a good opportunity again.

He waved his arms to keep his men clear of the recoil and pressed his slow match onto the priming. There was an instant of spluttering and a bright blue-and-red flame shot vertically from the touch hole. In the next instant the main charge exploded, sending the twelve pound ball hurtling across the fifty yards of sea. Crespi never saw what effect it had but he did notice with pride that his was the first gun to fire, and that it was soon followed by others in a ragged cacophony of explosions, as though they were all merely waiting for him to start. Good, the battle had begun and his gun must be sponged, loaded, run out and fired as fast as ever it could. His trained mind took over and he had no time for further thought as he gave his orders and lent his weight on the train tackles. He'd skin any man of his crew who failed him this night.

***

Bang!

Don Mancebo jumped involuntarily as Crespi's gun fired its fateful shot just below his feet. He should have expected it; in the confusion of this nighttime encounter with all guns loaded some fool was certain to fire his piece. Well, the die was cast and there would be no turning back, at least he now knew what to do.

'First Lieutenant! Engage the enemy to larboard!'

It was a pitiful broadside, an insult to the name of *San Sebastion*. More than half of the guns were masked by the wreckage of the longboat that the bosun was still trying to cut away. One of his own twenty-four pounders – fired without any apparent thought for its aim – smashed through the longboat's transom and rudder but not even that shock could dislodge the boat. Then the enemy frigate opened fire. He had tensed himself for the impact of the shots, but even though the frigate fired a creditable broadside his ship was hardly affected, he felt no concussions of solid shot smashing into the good Spanish oak. He looked over the side to confirm his suspicion, just in time to see the complete destruction of his boats. Each of them had been hit by at least one of the frigate's nine pound balls and at that close range even such a small shot must utterly destroy a fragile wooden boat. He felt the wind of a musket ball pass close to his face and saw the quartermaster fall to the deck with blood gushing from his neck. The howl of cannister shot from the frigate's swivel guns made a frightful noise and now he could see men falling to his left and his right. His ship was struggling to get underway, hampered by the wrecked boats that clung to its sides by their painters at bow and stern. A quick glance told him that his first lieutenant was exhorting the gun crews to greater efforts to reload for another broadside, but still his ship wasn't paying off from the wind. Another crash from forward and he was just in time to see the longboat's bows drop heavily into the swell, but still the shattered stern refused to release its embrace while it swung against the lesser boats, completing their destruction.

Crash!

That was a second broadside from the frigate, aimed at his ship this time. The damned Englishman was handling his ship superbly and moving fast away to windward, where *San Sebastian* couldn't follow, not until the chaos on the larboard side was sorted out. And then it was all over. After that second broadside the frigate disappeared into the darkness and *San Sebastian* – without her foresail and without her mainsail and with nothing left resembling a serviceable boat – was alone on the pitch-dark ocean, leaving Don Mancebo to consider his next move. It didn't take him long. With no boats to send prize crews across it would be foolhardy to follow the convoy further and further away to the north, even though he could be sure of sinking a fair number of them. He'd gambled that bringing half a dozen prizes into Havana would ensure the governor-general's forgiveness for not bringing the news of war to the Indies by the fastest means. It would be a different story entirely if he brought no prizes and a vague – and disputable – story of the destruction of a few merchantmen. The one certainty was the tangible truth of the loss of his boats and the damage to his ship. There were dead and wounded too, although the governor-general was unlikely to concern himself with them. No, he would chase no further.

'Sailing Master, heave to again. Mister Guterres, leave

half of the gun crews at their stations in case that Englishman comes back. I need at least one serviceable boat from that mess alongside and you can use every man who isn't at the guns. Officers, warrant officers, petty officers, cooks and sweepers, use everyone. I want to be reaching away for the Old Bahama Strait by the forenoon watch.'

'Yes, sir…'

'And I want the names of two men. The one who was first to let go the longboat's main yard tackle and the gun captain who fired that first shot. I'll see them suffer for this night's work.'

Guterres paused, unsure of whether this was the right moment. Well, better to get it over with.

'Sir, I fear that it may be just one man who did both of those things.'

'One man? Then may the Lord have mercy on his soul, for I shall have none for his corporeal existence.'

***

CHAPTER SIX

The Human Condition

Thursday, Eighteenth of February 1762.
Argonaut, at Sea. Cape San Juan south-by-east 50 leagues.

Holbrooke took a cursory glance to windward and astern, watching the horizon change colour and form as the upper limb of the sun started to become visible. There was nothing to be seen, as he had expected. It would have taken unusual persistence for that Spaniard to have followed the convoy with hardly a boat to his name. For he'd seen their destruction with his own eyes and it would be amazing if a single yawl or cutter could be pieced together from that carnage. A jollyboat perhaps, but even that would be a struggle.

It hadn't been entirely without loss on his side. That first shot had been the only one that was properly aimed. It had smashed through a frame beside a gunport and destroyed a nine pounder, killing one of its crew outright and putting another three into the surgeon's care. All of the other balls had either been fired into space or had added to the damage to the Spaniard's own boats. Would that unknown gun captain receive the credit for that single useful shot? From Holbrooke's perspective it appeared that it had been fired under the captain's orders and that the rest of the ragged part-broadside had just been slower in responding. He'd never know what a debt he owed to the impatience of Miguel Crespi of the Spanish navy. He'd never hear of the savage punishment that left the man barely able to stand, nor of his messmates' care in assisting him below where a half-dozen hammocks had been tenderly arranged upon the hard oak deck.

'Ah, David, how good to see you on this fine morning. I'm just about to send below for some breakfast, will you join me?'

An Upright Man

Chalmers paused for a moment to take in the sheer beauty of the scene. The extraordinary speed with which the ship could move from what had looked like a desperate battle to this attitude of peaceful cruising never failed to amaze him. The slight damage had been temporarily repaired before dawn and now the ship's normal routines had been restored. Half of the watch on deck was busy re-coiling the dozens of halyards onto their pins while the other half were pumping water over the deck and sweeping it and any muck into the lee scuppers. The dirty water was caught by the fresh breeze and instantly transformed into a substance of beauty as it was blown away to leeward in scintillating streams to rejoin the great ocean. Only the single bulging hammock that sat upon a temporary grating beside the mainmast offered a jarring note to the otherwise idyllic scene. Chalmers knew that form well, he'd known the man whose earthly remains rested inside and he'd already prepared his vestments and book of common prayer for the short ceremony that must be performed during the forenoon watch. For the majority of the ship's people, that would be the end of it, he knew. The simple act of reciting the words of a burial at sea, and the barely-heard splash as the hammock-shrouded body entered the water, would mark the end of that strange night-time encounter. Holbrooke and his clerk would still have to draft a report of the action, and the carpenter would have to make permanent repairs where Crespi's shot had damaged *Argonaut's* frame in way of the gunport and ricocheted off to carry away the rear trucks of the nine pounder gun carriage. The three men in the sickbay would have another week in which the race between healing and the onset of a fatal infection would determine their futures. Otherwise, the frigate would quickly forget the hapless Spanish two-decker.

'Breakfast? Certainly I'll join you. Lady Chiara had invited you to the great cabin this morning, perhaps you'd forgotten. Yet she's sensitive to the mood of the ship and asked me to say that she hopes you'll join her for dinner instead, after this poor soul has been sent on his way.'

Holbrooke *had* forgotten and he nodded his appreciation of Chiara's sensible change of plan. A lavish breakfast with a brave man's body still awaiting interment would have been in poor taste.

They stood together at the aft end of the quarterdeck as the last few ships of the convoy came into sight. Holbrooke clasped his hands behind his back to prevent his fidgeting fingers betraying his state of mind. It was always a nervous time, waiting to see whether he'd lost any of his charges in the night and it wasn't until Fairview reported them all present and sailing in roughly the right direction that he could really breathe easily and enjoy his breakfast. Coffee and soft bread with jam and potted anchovies. It wasn't a lavish meal but it would hold them until dinner in the afternoon watch.

'That was a curious encounter in the night, George. Do you think we're at war?'

'Oh, I've no doubt. I was almost certain of it from the moment that Spaniard altered course to follow us. She's the *San Sebastian,* by the way; Petersen read the name on the stern when all others were intent on destroying her.'

Holbrooke took another piece of bread and spread it with the anchovy paste. The intense savoury flavour complemented the strong black coffee, he'd save the jam for later.

'Saint Sebastian; shot through with arrows while tied to a tree, and yet he survived and eventually had to be clubbed to death. If that's an omen, then I fear we haven't seen the last of that fellow. Be sure to carry a strong club, my friend.'

'You believe in such omens and portents, David? I'm surprised.'

'Oh you rationalist, you man of reason! You shouldn't be surprised, the bible is full of them and there are more things in heaven and earth, Horatio, than are dreamt of in your philosophy.'

An Upright Man

'Ha! Well, quote from your Shakespeare as much as you like, but I'd cut a lonely figure among seafarers if I didn't have at least a little superstition in my makeup. I touch the binnacle for luck you know, when Fairview isn't watching. And I've no quarrel with saints, quite the contrary. However, the fact of being at war is at this present time more interesting, don't you think? Commodore Douglas didn't have any notion of it when we left Antigua.'

'Then it's quite possible that you – or rather the Spaniard to be pedantic – struck the first blow in this new phase of the war. Despite my warning – and I stand by it – I assume we've seen the last of him for the present.'

'Indeed. I expect he was steering for Havana, perhaps carrying news of Spain's entry into the war. We were just an opportune target that he couldn't resist. We were lucky to catch him with his breeches down, so to say, because we'd certainly have lost half a dozen merchantmen to him today if we hadn't.'

'Do you not feel obliged to send the news to the commander-in-chief?'

Holbrooke smiled at that. Of course he'd thought about it.

'And how do you propose that I accomplish that, Mister Chalmers? Antigua is dead to windward and it would take a week for *Argonaut*, tack-upon-tack, to beat back. The convoy would take at least two weeks and most of them would refuse to follow me. I can't abandon them now.'

'The longboat, perhaps…?'

Holbrooke looked meaningfully astern at the long, deep trade wind swell and shook his head.

'No, it's too much for an open boat. It exposes the crew to unreasonable danger and they could barely carry enough provisions for the voyage. And in the end, for what reward? The commodore is well aware that Spain is likely to join the war at any moment and a sterile account of last night's action hardly constitutes an official declaration of hostilities. It could be a rogue Spanish captain warming the bell, or just a misunderstanding. He'd find it interesting, certainly, but it wouldn't change his plans. The best that I can do is to make a fast passage to Savannah and send a report to Mister Douglas by the next packet.'

Chalmers looked sideways at his friend. In a crowded frigate there were few enough opportunities for the privacy of a conversation between captain and chaplain as equals, even less when the great cabin was occupied by a passenger and her suite.

'Tell me, George, would you have fought today? Would it have done any good if you had?'

Holbrooke didn't immediately answer and Chalmers saw his gaze pass across the pathetic bundle beside the mainmast.

'The truth is David, that I've thought about little else since we sighted the two-decker. I originally thought not but on reflection, yes, I'd have fought. I could have bought enough time for a few more of the merchantmen to escape but it's hard to imagine any favourable outcome for *Argonaut*. *San Sebastian* has twenty-four pounders and twelves, you know. Her secondary armament alone gives him a far greater weight of broadside than ours.'

Chalmers nodded. It was the answer he'd expected but he wanted to probe a little deeper.

'Then, if I may, how much of that decision was related to the harsh arithmetic of war? Would King George really profit by saving a handful of merchantmen at the loss of a not-very-old frigate? Or were there other factors at play?'

Holbrooke was used to his friend's style of interrogation and had a shrewd idea where the questioning was going, and they had a few minutes before the watch would change and then David would have to shift into his vestments. He slowly shook his head, unsure where to start.

'Well, the harsh arithmetic, as you call it, is finely balanced and it's hard to make a sensible trade of a frigate and its crew against merchant hulls and their cargoes. However, I think it would be fair to say that six of those,' he swept his hand across the array of masts and sails to leeward, 'would buy a fully equipped frigate and its people. Probably, if I could have detained the Spaniard for an hour, that number would have escaped who otherwise would have been taken. But as you no doubt guess there's more to it than the arithmetic. To start this phase of the war with a British frigate watching idly as a Spaniard ravages a West Indies convoy could have disastrous consequences for the City's confidence and for Spanish expectations. The country's prosperity absolutely relies upon trade, and that trade depends upon the navy, and the navy in its own turn can only be funded by the fruits of that trade. It's a delicate balance that Lord Anson has to consider every day. He'd face some harmless criticism for the loss of a frigate, for sure, but the devastation of a convoy – if combined with other bad news – could bring down the government and instigate a rush for peace.'

'Yes, certainly, and I hope the country understands. Yet are there not additional, more personal factors? Your own reputation, Ann's discomfort if you're killed or injured, little Edward? And then of course you have a brother officer's wife and child as passengers. I mean no criticism, but to what extent did you consider those?'

Chalmers, the keen student of the human condition, was now openly studying his friend's face. He knew very well that mere words couldn't fully answer the question. He could see that Holbrooke had lost interest in his breakfast and was staring blankly to windward, to the open, featureless sea, with a gaze that was focussed on infinity. He saw the mouth open to answer, then it closed and Holbrookes lips pinched tightly so that what was normally an open expression became hard and closed. A moment passed and Holbrooke turned towards him, valiantly trying to smile.

'Well, David, as always you've grasped upon the unanswerable, but I can at least try…'

But Holbrooke's reply would have to wait because at

that moment the bell struck eight times in four groups of two and the watch below started pouring onto the deck to relieve their mates who had stood the morning watch. And here was Fairview to report the change of the watch. The opportunity was lost, probably irrevocably. Chalmers never, ever swore and he didn't now, at least not so that anyone could hear.

***

Chiara paused in helping Chalmers to a piece of buttered toast.

'Mister Fairview told me that we should be at Hampton Road by the second of March, George, is he likely to be proved correct?'

'Oh, I wouldn't presume to question Fairview in the matter of navigation. Of course there are factors beyond his control but in general that would be a good date to work on.'

'Twelve days then. Oh I do so long to be home now that spring is coming to Virginia. Do you think my letters will be there before me? I've asked the servants to air out all the rooms; they only keep the ground floor habitable, you know, for Edward's father, but we shall need the upper floor too, and the attic rooms.'

'I expect so. The packet left Antigua two days before us and it was going directly to Hampton Road. They should have plenty of notice of your arrival.'

The dinner party was a great success. Lady Chiara, Holbrooke, Enrico, Chalmers, and Jackson looking self-conscious in his best coat and shaved to within an inch of his life. The guests were well-chosen from among the people who had been at Nice back in 'fifty-six. Edward Carlisle had been there too, of course, in command of the little frigate *Fury,* but he was far away on the Jamaica Station.

'Then it will be a parting of our ways, and who knows when we may meet again. At least I'll see you, Enrico.'

She looked fondly at her cousin who bowed in reply.

An Upright Man

Chalmers took the opportunity to ask a question that he'd wanted to ask for some time.

'Have you considered your future, Mister Angelini? Forgive me if I presume too much, but surely you'll have to find a way of keeping body and soul together.'

Enrico looked uncomfortable for a moment then composed himself.

'Well, Mister Chalmers, it's interesting that you should ask because It's been on my mind since I decided to throw up my Sardinian commission. I'm sure you understand that I wasn't brought up to consider a profession, unless one can speak of the army as one; it's completely outside the family's experience, wouldn't you say, Cousin?'

'Oh yes, can you imagine what the Viscountess would say if she knew?'

Enrico's uncomfortable moment returned. He'd burned his bridges in Nice and he was certain that he wouldn't be greeted as the prodigal nephew if he returned. He'd be lucky if the Viscountess even received him.

'However, I've given it some thought. I believe that wherever possible one should follow one's natural talents. I have few, it's true, but I can set down a coastline on paper and I can sketch a view so that others could recognise it. America is a huge country and little explored and there must be a need for surveyors and map makers. I've written to Captain Carlisle's cousin, Mister Dexter, he that owns the printer's shop, in the hope that he can give me some guidance when we arrive at Williamsburg…'

'You know, Edward has a slight acquaintance with Colonel Washington, who started out as a surveyor. Perhaps you could apply to him also; he has a plantation some way north of Williamsburg, but he's often at the capital.'

Holbrooke suddenly remembered something that Carlisle had told him.

'Yes, I've never met Washington of course, but I do know that he married a lady who's related to Edward's first captain in the sloop *Wolf*, William Dandridge. I believe she's his niece. That should be sufficient connection to excuse a letter.'

Jackson coughed discreetly.

'For what it's worth, sir, I believe that setting up as a surveyor and map maker is a very wise choice. I met a man in Jamaica who showed me a chart of the colonies on a wider map of the whole continent. Would you believe that for every square mile that's been explored and laid down on paper, there's another hundred or more to the west waiting for a man such as you? A fine choice, sir. If I didn't have my bosun's warrant I'd be tempted to set up in Virginia myself. I still might, when this war's over.'

The table lapsed into silence as each thought about a future without war. Chalmers broke the spell.

'There's a wind of change blowing, and we around this table are a perfect example of the new order. Lady Chiara has voluntarily given up her rank in Sardinian society to embrace a new life bringing up a family in the colonies. Enrico is making a similar journey but in his case he must find a way of making a living. George, the son of a warrant officer, is one of the youngest and most caressed post-captains in the navy and Jackson here, I know, was brought up by a widowed mother and now holds a navy board warrant and has a job for life should he want it. I'm but an unbeneficed parson with no hope of a country living, but since I volunteered for a place on a King's ship, I've made enough in prize money to keep me modestly until the Good Lord takes me. There's not a one of us that hasn't made choices, and sound ones as far as I can tell. Now, a toast. If I may.'

There was a scraping of chairs as the five friends rose, bending their heads to avoid the deck beams, according to how gifted they were in height.

'To old friends and new challenges.'

***

CHAPTER SEVEN

The Passing Bell

Wednesday, Seventh of April 1762.
Mulberry House, Wickham, Hampshire.

There are few sights so dismal as a house in mourning. The shuttered windows, the sternly closed doors, the smokeless chimneys, the black crepe ribbons on the lintels and the dreary garb of the remaining inhabitants; each doleful token serves to emphasise mankind's dread of its own mortality. Even when the deceased soul is unknown to the stranger, it's impossible to walk past such a place without being affected by the atmosphere. The chattering couples bow their heads and cast anxious glances at each other, the hawkers and labourers fall silent, and even the town's feral dogs abandon their usual swagger and slink past on tiptoes with their tails between their legs. And when the house occupies a central location in a town square, and the deceased is a prominent person in a small, rural community, the effect spreads to every house in the neighbourhood, like the remorseless advance of the woodland fungus' creeping tendrils.

The minute bells from St. Nicholas' church tugged at Holbrooke's conscience even as they warned him that the cortege would soon arrive. They insistently asked the question, *why this one and not you? What act of providence has preserved your earthly frame while this other's lies cold within its casket, already subject to the insidious corruption that one day must take us all?* His face was grim as he adjusted his stock and settled his cloak about his shoulders. At least he was free of the need for mourning clothes; with the country at war a sea officer's uniform was appropriate on all occasions. He turned swiftly away from his image in the looking-glass and knocked tentatively at the door to Ann's dressing room. It was opened soundlessly by Ann's maid, Polly, who bobbed low as the master of the house entered this most feminine of apartments.

'Are you nearly ready, my dear? Do you not hear the bells?'

It was the ancient custom in Wickham that mourners followed the casket to the church on foot, a carriage being thought impious except for the very old and infirm, and if they didn't leave now they wouldn't be in place in front of Bere House before the sexton's men arrived.

Ann was dressed in black from her head to her toe and where she lacked a particular sable garment, yards and yards of black fabric had been fastened in place to cover the deficiency. A veil had been stitched to her hat, covering a face that he knew was ravaged with grief. She turned to her husband and made a heroic attempt to maintain her composure.

Holbrooke had only arrived in Wickham the day before. Luckily, in the first mail to reach the ship, he'd received a letter from Ann warning him of her father's passing. Martin Featherstone's health had been fragile for some time and a chill that he'd caught while walking beside the river in the early morning had settled onto his chest. Gradually, insidiously, an infection had invaded his lungs and after a day of agonising breathlessness, he'd slipped into a merciful insensibility that, two days later, parted his immortal soul from his earthly existence. He wasn't what could be called a popular figure in Wickham, he was too stiff, too aware of his own consequence, and he was by the standards of the town a newcomer. Nonetheless, his corn brokerage business was important to the town's prosperity and its invisible and largely beneficial influence penetrated fully half of all the families in the area. A silent crowd was gathering in the square, keeping a respectful distance from Bere House, and the sexton's itinerate assistants were keeping the way clear so that the bearers could descend the steep road from the square, and across the river to the church.

An Upright Man

'I imagine Sophie will meet us outside the house.'

'Yes, she was determined to stay with father until… until he's carried away.'

'I haven't seen her at all since I came home. How is she taking it?'

Ann looked quickly out of the window. There was no sign of the Vicar's procession yet and it was only a few steps across the square from Mulberry House to Bere House.

'I don't really know what to make of her, George. A month ago, before father became ill, I would have said that they agreed fairly well, but nothing more. I never saw them arguing, but there were no real signs of affection either. They were such different people, as you know. Sophie is lively and gay while father was always too serious, he could never see the fun in anything. Oh, he was a wonderful man but I think he met Sophie too late in life, he'd been too long a widower. But when his illness became dangerous, Sophie was the very model of a doting wife and I've hardly seen her outside the house. Father couldn't have asked for a better sick-nurse, that's for certain. I do believe she's more loved in the town now than she's ever been.'

Holbrooke nodded silently. It was an awkward subject where a second wife and a child were left as the relicts of the deceased. If it were any other woman, Holbrooke would have suspected that she was establishing her position in advance of the will being produced, but not Sophie and not with a man as meticulous as Martin Featherstone was known to be. Holbrooke knew very well that a cast-iron will had been deposited at the solicitor's office in Fareham some years ago, and that it very clearly set out the beneficiaries of his estate. He knew this because Martin Featherstone had appointed him as the sole executor of his will the day after he had married the corn merchant's only daughter. He knew the contents of the will and a confidential and unasked for note from the solicitor's office had assured him that there'd been no alterations since he'd last seen it. No, Sophie's changed attitude was founded in pity and a real affection that had not been much on show to the outside world. He wondered that Ann had not detected it earlier, but then perhaps she was too close to them, too involved in their daily lives to see the ties that bound them to each other. Holbrooke hoped that he wasn't seeing the start of a rift between his wife and her stepmother. He wished most fervently that their intimacy could continue the way it had since he'd first met them, and he had good practical reason, for he and he alone among the family had seen the contents of Martin Featherstone's will.

***

The service in the church had been mercifully short and the internment in the churchyard, with only the family gathered around the grave, had been shorter still. They'd left the sexton and his men to cover the coffin and hurried back to Bere House where a table had been laid with cold meats and wine and small beer. Even that meal hadn't taken long and there were only a handful of guests; Featherstone's immediate family, Ferrers the solicitor and Hans Albach, late of the Austrian Imperial Artillery and for the past six months, since Featherstone's health had started to decline, the manager of the corn merchant's business.

Those few hadn't stayed long after Sophie retired to her rooms upstairs and Ann followed, to comfort her. Holbrooke saw the last guests out of the doors and then left for his study at Mulberry House, across the square. He called for a pot of coffee and settled himself at his desk. With a key that he kept on his fob, he opened the centre drawer of the desk and withdrew a plain, unmarked envelope. Inside was a document of thick, cream paper folded three times from its original size, sealed with a stylised anchor in red wax. The anchor was fouled of course, with the cable wrapped twice around the stock. It was rather pretentious for a Fareham solicitor but at least it couldn't be mistaken for the Admiralty seal or the variant that the navy board was increasingly using. It seemed strange to be opening the will so soon after the burial, but Samuel Ferrers, the partner in the firm of Carter & Ferrers, of the High Street, Fareham had persuaded him that in this case, and in light of Holbrooke's naval commitments, it would be forgiven.

'Two weeks, sir? Two weeks and then you'll be away to God-knows-where? Two months would hardly do justice to your responsibilities as sole executor of the will! You must open it at once and start taking action, otherwise Mister Featherstone's fine business will rapidly decay. I do assure you that there's not a moment to lose.'

The will had the usual preamble with greetings and best wishes to all and there were a number of small bequests, watches and books and candlesticks and suchlike that had particular significance to family or acquaintances. It wasn't until the second page that the important clauses were revealed.

When he'd first read the will, before Featherstone's health started to decline and while the prospect of Holbrooke assuming responsibility as the executor seemed far off, he'd paid it little attention. However he'd remembered the main points and now he re-read them to remind himself. Simple, yes, but the future of the corn broker's business relied entirely upon the good will of two people.

***

Not a moment to lose, indeed, and it seemed cold and heartless to be reading a will when the deceased wasn't yet four-and-twenty hours in his grave. However, Holbrooke had learned a thing or two about asserting his authority and he knew that if he was to carry out his duties as executor, then he must stamp his mark upon the process and he must start without delay.

There were only four people in the room at Mulberry House; Sophie, Ann, Samuel Ferres and Holbrooke himself. His insistence that it should be read at Mulberry House and not at Bere House or the solicitor's office in

Fareham was part of his plan to imprint his authority. Ferres opened the proceedings.

'*...and I do appoint as the sole executor of my last will and testament, Captain George Holbrooke of His Majesty's Navy.* Captain Holbrooke, would you like to take over from here?'

'Thank you, Mister Ferres.'

Holbrooke accepted the document and smoothed it out on the desk in front of him. Sophie and Ann sat opposite as though neither of them had any relationship to him, and indeed, he thought it better that no connection should be acknowledged during the reading. He was, after all, in a position where he might have to adjudicate between competing claims. He hoped that wouldn't be the case, but the nature of Featherstone's will certainly opened up that possibility.

'Now, the document is available for each of you to read at your leisure. However, I believe it will take some hours to extract the meaning from amongst the legal terms.'

He glanced sideways at Ferrers. It was he who had introduced all of those terms to reduce the possibilities for wrangling over the will, and perhaps to justify his own fee.

'There are some small individual bequests that I'll read after the main headings. However, in its essence it's quite simple. Mister Featherstone has left his house and all its goods and chattels to his beloved wife Sophie Featherstone to enjoy for the rest of her life. At Sophie's death, that same house and its goods and chattels will revert to his daughter Ann Holbrooke, and if the said Sophie Featherstone should remarry the same will hold true from the day of the marriage. If Ann should not survive Sophie, then at Sophie's death the whole will pass to Edward Holbrooke, being the eldest son of George and Ann Holbrooke.'

Holbrooke paused and studied Sophie and Ann's faces. It was too soon for them, he knew that, but it was important to be sure that they understood. He noticed that Ann reached across and squeezed her stepmother's hand and received a smile in return.

'Then can I assume that you understand the situation, Sophie? Bere House and everything in it now belongs to you, until you should re-marry or die.'

'Thank you, George, that's quite clear.'

Holbrooke noticed that Sophie sounded subdued, submissive even, not at all her usual self.

'And do you understand, Ann? You have no claim on Bere House unless Sophie re-marries or passes away.'

Ann just nodded. Perhaps the emotion of the occasion was too much for her.

'Now, as for the corn merchant's business, a thriving concern as you well know. Martin Featherstone has assigned the business jointly to Ann and Sophie, in the proportions of nine sixteenths to Ann and seven sixteenths to Sophie. If Sophie re-marries or passes away her share will revert to Ann. If Ann should pre-decease Sophie then her share will be passed to Edward Holbrooke, our son. The effect of the uneven split is that Ann has the management of the business while Sophie shares at seven sixteenths in the profits. Now, on the understanding that I, as Ann's husband, am necessarily away from home for extended periods, he hopes that I, as his executor, will consult with Mister Ferrers to find a good and honest manager for the business. This, of course, was written before Mister Albach was appointed as manager and we must ascertain whether he wishes to continue in that position without the benefit of Martin Featherstone's continued guidance. I must ask again, do you Ann and you Sophie understand this?'

Sophie and Ann looked openly at each other and nodded in unison. In fact it wasn't a very unusual will, it was just that Martin Featherstone, as a meticulous man, had sought a remedy in advance for all eventualities. The risk of conflict came in the uneven split of shares in the business, but it did seem as though Sophie accepted it.

Holbrooke read the list of individual bequests. It wasn't very long for Martin had enjoyed few friends outside his small family circle. When it was over Ferres offered notarised copies to Sophie and Ann.

***

After the will had been read Holbrooke interviewed Hans Albach and discovered that the Austrian certainly did wish to continue as manager of Featherstone's business. They'd negotiated a greater salary to recognise that Albach would have to control the business alone, and in Holbrooke's absence he would have to take any problems to Ann and Sophie, and if necessary to Ferrers. In effect he'd be a trusted steward of the family. Then Holbrooke's secretary arrived with the day's naval correspondence. A note from Shorrock assured him that *Argonaut* was settled into the dry dock and that the shipwrights were already inspecting the coppering and making an inventory of missing or damaged plates, so that a decision could be made on their repair. That had taken until late into the afternoon and only now could he relax. He and Chalmers had been invited to supper at his father's cottage on the Alton road. A pie of beefsteak, cheese and bread and a decent wine was exactly what he craved after a tiring day. His father sported a gold watch and chain with a jewelled fob that he'd been left in Featherstone's will and he appeared very well pleased with it.

'You fear that Sophie and Ann may not agree on the running of the business?'

Chalmers always came right to the heart of the matter and on this occasion it took Holbrooke by surprise.

'Oh, that's not quite it. As you know they're great friends, perhaps more so than a mother and daughter. No, I fear outside influences, and there will be plenty of those. Clients – farmers and customers – who try to play one off against the other and manage to create conflict where there should be none. That's why I'm so pleased that Albach has agreed to stay on. I must have a long talk with him before I leave, but as the controlling share is mine, as Ann's husband, I shall expect him to use his own judgement and defer any contentious decisions until I'm home. It does rather change our relationship, though, and I hope we can remain friends.'

Chalmers nodded but kept his thoughts to himself. Privately he wondered how far Ann would stand back from the business while Holbrooke was at sea. Legally she had every right to interfere, even though in law it was Holbrooke, as Ann's husband, who controlled nine sixteenths of the business. If it came to a point of conflict – with Holbrooke at the far side of the ocean – then any magistrate would find in Ann's favour.

'Of course, Ferrers will be a great help. He understands the situation perfectly. In fact it's not the financial risk of the business being mismanaged that I most fear, it's a breakdown of the relationship between Sophie and Ann. The business has little intrinsic value. There are no fields, the premises are all rented and it carries little stock. My father-in-law was a master of the art of buying and selling without at any point actually holding the physical goods. No, I'm not concerned for the business, but for the effect that the business could have upon my family.'

William Holbrooke would normally keep his peace in this sort of conversation, but he had a great regard for both Sophie and Ann.

'Do you really believe there's a danger, George? They seem so attached to each other, from what I've seen.'

Holbrooke took a sip of wine and thought for a moment.

'Not a danger, father, not one that I can positively identify. However, I've spent some time with Ferrers, you know, and he has extensive experience in these matters. He advises me to take care that neither Sophie nor Ann feel that they're being pushed to one side. The problem is certainly made worse by my being away at sea.'

'Well, if the news reports are correct you may be employed for some time. Spain has a vast fleet, as I'm sure you know, and they could make it much harder to bring

King Louis to see reason. You may be at sea for many more years to come.'

'I don't know whether to hope that you're right or wrong, Father, but however it turns out I must make certain that everyone understand the part that they have to play when I'm absent.'

***

CHAPTER EIGHT

A Man Set Apart

Thursday, Eighth of April 1762.
Rookesbury House, Wickham, Hampshire.

George Garnier had aged since Holbrooke had last seen him. His hollow cheeks, his stooped shoulders and his parchment-dry skin were the same, but now he walked with a limp and had an old man's way of stopping short before turning to address a companion. He couldn't be above sixty but Holbrooke could see that his time was drawing to an end. Probably his travels in Europe hadn't helped and it was said that he took his duties as apothecary to the army too seriously. Most previous incumbents had treated it as a sinecure and if they took any action at all, sent an assistant to inspect the field hospitals and the regimental medicine chests. Nevertheless, he was a good host and the dinner had been a success. They were settled now in the library to the right of the main doors to the house surrounded by Garnier's large collection of books. It wasn't only books, Garnier was a discerning collector of contemporary works of art, and the bright colours of Canaletto's paintings provided a counterpoint to the regimented shelves of poetry, philosophy and travel. It was clear that Garnier loved his paintings and he frequently gazed at them, perhaps recalling happy days in Venice.

It had been a small gathering, just Garnier, Holbrooke and Chalmers, and a man named Jean Marignac who was evidently also from a Huguenot family. He was an apothecary himself, but had said little during the dinner, as Garnier quizzed his two naval guests on the current state of the war at sea. It wasn't at all clear what winds had blown Jean Marignac to the obscure market town of Wickham, but now they were settled in Garnier's good, leather easy chairs the talk of ships and battles and trade dried up and he started to speak openly about his own affairs, a subject that seemed to fascinate him above all others.

'I travel extensively in my work and I have the honour of attending persons in most of the countries in Europe. My latest journey took me to Vienna, Padua and Paris, but I've been as far as Prussia and Russia in previous years. You see, a great man whose health is declining wants only what he perceives to be the best advice, he wants the reassurance that his physician is raking the whole of Europe for the latest cures. I flatter myself that I provide that service.'

Marignac was a boastful person but it was clear that he really was a man of some consequence. Chalmers raised an eyebrow at the thought of the astronomical fees that must be charged to cover the expense of moving so freely from country to country while the continent was embroiled in a war.

'Do you find any constraints on your movement between belligerent nations, Monsieur Marignac? Is there no suspicion of your motives?'

Marignac smiled through pursed lips, as much as to say that he was tolerating – just – this questioning from ill-informed rustics.

'The apothecary's art is universal, my dear Mister Chalmers. Oh, I take the precaution of carrying a letter requesting my attendance from each patient before I travel, but it really isn't necessary. Mister Garnier was back and forth to Padua in the last war and travelled with ease through the countries between, is that not so?'

'Indeed it was, and that's where we met, if you remember, at the university. I fear my traveling days are over now and I'll see Venice again only through my paintings.'

Garnier looked lovingly at his Canalettos. Four of them were displayed in the library but Holbrooke knew that he moved his collection around the rooms so that he had a different selection on view every month or so.

'Then I gather that even France is open to you. I beg your pardon for raising the question, but do you not find yourself uneasy with the lingering memory of the wars of religion?'

Marignac bowed slightly to Chalmers, as though he were just recognising that he might be of more consequence than a simple naval chaplain.

'Well, as a descendent of Huguenots, King Louis would have the backing of his own laws if he chose to apprehend me, but in practice the country has a rather more tolerant view of religion. I wouldn't care to live in France, but as long as I can show good reason I can travel quite safely. The King himself takes occasional advice from an émigré colleague who is based in London, although I've never had that honour…'

He managed to imply by his confidential smirk that the honour was only a matter of time in coming.

'…however, I've consulted with a family that you know something of, Captain Holbrooke. I believe you've crossed swords – albeit in a naval sense – with the chevalier de Ternay, Charles-Henri-Louis d'Arsac.'

Marignac's expression betrayed his intense pleasure at catching Garnier's other guests unawares, and Holbrooke's surprise, followed by his keen interest, showed on his face.

'De Ternay? Yes, I've never met him, of course, but as you say, we crossed swords twice…'

Marignac was a born gossip and he'd drop a name into a conversation with all the subtlety of a thirty-six pound shot. He didn't let Holbrooke finish before he launched into his explanation that was designed to illustrate his own importance.

'I was called to consult a physician in Tours who was treating a certain gentleman – a nobleman of some consequence, you'll forgive me if I don't elaborate – with a truly debilitating case of the gout. Naturally, word of my presence spread and I stayed a few days to attend a variety of people. One of them was Louise, the Marquise de Ternay. The chateau is only some forty miles from Tours, and the road along the Loire is good, although not quite so well made when it strikes south for Ternay. She sent her carriage, of course. Charles-Henri happened to be at home, while his ship was refitting in Brest, and he was most concerned about his mother. Did you know, Mister Garnier, that you may have a family connection to the d'Arsacs? I saw it in a genealogical chart that the Marquise insisted upon showing me. One Étienne Garnier married a d'Arsac some two hundred and fifty years ago. I regret that I know nothing more of the connection.'

Garnier merely bowed. He still found it difficult to speak dispassionately about his ancestors who had fled France after the Edict of Nantes was revoked and open season was declared upon all religious dissent. Holbrooke couldn't tell whether or not he knew of this possible distant relation.

Chalmers could see that Holbrooke was bursting to ask for more details of his recent adversary, but was inhibited by his position as a King's officer from quizzing this pompous man. He caught a slight nod from Garnier and a half smile that showed that their host was well aware of the nature of his fellow apothecary. Chalmers took the hint.

'Would you be so kind as to describe the chevalier?'

Marignac, in his turn, wanted nothing more than to hold the floor with his stories of great and titled men who had consulted him.

'Certainly, Mister Chalmers…'

There was no pause for thought, but an immediate flow of information delivered with a particular confidential air, as though he was imparting a great secret, or the details of a sordid affair.

'…Charles-Henri is the second son, as perhaps you know. His great peculiarity is that he spent some years of his youth with the Order of St. John – the Knights of Malta as you may know them – and there he took the oath of celibacy. Celibacy, forsooth, and he not in any way ordained! Perhaps it was a fit of true religious zeal or perhaps it was a recognition that as the second son he had no duties to perform to maintain the family name. However it was, it's a rare enough thing to be notorious, and by all accounts he maintains the oath with the greatest fidelity. Now, that gives him a certain *presence of person,* if I may call it that. He carries himself with an authority that one would expect in a man of much higher birth. His mother is clearly in awe of him and his brother tends to stay in Paris when he knows that Charles-Henri will be at home. I found him charming, but I'd certainly be more comfortable as his friend than as his enemy.'

Marignac paused for breath, long enough for Chalmers to inject a question.

'This membership of the Order of St. John, I assume he was a page to the Grand Master, or something along those lines. It implies a certain religious fervour, even if our friend chose it as an alternative to dynastic obscurity. Again, pardon my intrusion, but did you find that he was comfortable speaking to a man of your religion, a protestant, indeed?'

Marignac had recovered his breath and spoke on as though he hadn't been interrupted.

'I was always aware of a restraint when speaking to him, but I suspect he's rarely open with anyone, not even his own family. Naturally we didn't discuss religion but I didn't feel that it was a great barrier. Certainly he observes his obligations, and in fact both of our conversations were terminated by a bell calling him to the family chapel. I had the impression that he follows what we'd call *the hours.* But to continue. He's a tall man and his carriage is upright and his manner commanding. I do not imagine that his naval subordinates err more than once in his presence, and I imagine that he, in his turn, is particular in obeying his superior's orders. I didn't hear it from his own lips, rather from the physician who was attending the Marquise, but apparently his commission came at the insistence of King Louis, who had commanded that certain ships should be brought out of the Vilaine river and through our own blockade, but you'll know more about that, I'm sure.'

Marignac looked slyly at Holbrooke. It was quite clear that he knew that Holbrooke had been present on both occasions that de Ternay had brought the ships out, and that in some way Holbrooke was culpable for it.

'He commands *Robuste* of seventy-four guns, which was the last ship that he brought out. *Robuste* is refitting in Brest now, preparing for sea. I found him a paragon of virtue, a gentlemen, an upright man if ever there was one. A man who, if his birth were but a little more elevated, would prove an ornament to his King. However, as he is, he is likely doomed to the obscurity that he has fought so hard to avoid.'

***

It was only in the privacy of his own carriage that Holbrooke could really let vent to his feelings.

'What an insufferable prig! I wouldn't trust that man, nor would I favour him with any information that I wouldn't want broadcast throughout Europe. I'm surprised Garnier tolerates him.'

Chalmers smiled covertly, in the darkness of his corner of the carriage.

'They're fellow travellers of course. Both from refugee families that thrived in their new country and Garnier probably feels that he must suffer him. It's interesting that Marignac should wish to be called *Monsieur* though, and not *Mister*. I wonder just who his friends in Paris are.'

'If he's as free with his gossip in France as he is here, then I very much regret our earlier conversation over dinner. Oh, there was nothing damaging there, nothing that the broadsheets aren't saying, but then I could be cited as an authority, whether I wish it or not. Do you suppose he's a spy, I mean one in regular contact with the French navy or King Louie's people?'

At that Chalmers turned and grinned broadly.

'Never fear, my dear George, no self-respecting government office would ever employ such a person. He's completely ungovernable, and can you imagine what games could be played if our shadowy friends from the Belle Isle expedition once learned of his allegiance? It would be child's play to send misinformation across the channel merely by releasing it to him! No, he's just an everyday buffoon, but at least his picture of de Ternay was illuminating, assuming it's true.'

'True? I expect it is. It certainly fits with the man as we know him by his deeds. I tend to agree with you, Marignac is so much of a windbag that he can't help telling all that he knows and he doesn't have the wit to tell untruths. He's no liar, I believe. De Ternay is a man to be reckoned with, for sure.'

'I wonder, will we meet him again? Stranger things have happened.'

'Well,' Holbrooke considered for a moment, 'the French navy is a spent force and hardly in a position to send any sensible squadrons to sea. They're more likely to send ships in twos and threes, and given de Ternay's seniority and if he really has been given a seventy-four – remember, that's what we heard last year, so it's probably true – then he's likely to be tied firmly to an admiral's apron-strings. That's the fate of new post-captains who don't get a frigate in our navy.'

Chalmers nodded slowly in time with the rattle of the carriage. They were almost at the elder Holbrooke's cottage where Chalmers was still lodging, but he had one more point to make and leaned out of the window to shout to the coachman.

'Billy Stiles. Ease back for a while, would you?'

The sound of the hooves slowed and the rhythm of the coach changed. They were going at no more than a slow walking pace but still it would only be three or four minutes to the cottage.

'Despite it all, I find myself liking this de Ternay, George. Our own navy could do with a few more like him, men who are driven by a higher purpose than mere personal aggrandisement and the lust for wealth through prize money. I hope we do meet him again; it will be most instructive.'

Holbrooke laughed out loud and in the stillness of the early evening the nearer horse missed his step in surprise.

'Well I for one hope that we don't. He seems undefeatable, and so he's proven twice already. How does one fight a man of such high principles? He'll not spare himself in carrying out his orders, and he certainly won't spare his men. No, give me a normal French captain with the same motivations as us mortals, a venal man who can be relied upon to look to his own profit while doing his King's bidding. I can at least understand that kind of man.'

'I rather liked a term that Le Pomposo used this evening. He called de Ternay an *upright man*. I hesitate to teach you anything about the bible, dear George, for I know it's your constant companion and solace…'

Holbrooke glanced sharply at Chalmers and would have objected to the facetious comment if the chaplain hadn't continued talking right through the near-interruption.

'…but I would draw your attention to our good friend the prophet Ezekial. You should read his chapter eighteen, the twenty-fourth verse, if my memory serves me correctly. You see, he points out that an upright man – most texts use the term *righteous man,* but I prefer *upright man,* it has a more commanding ring about it – who once sins is treated the same as a man who has made a habit of sinning. No man is without that latent fall from grace, and your de Ternay is no exception. One day he'll prove fallible, and then his fall will be as great as the most dilettante, the most venal, of post-captains. The art, George, your art, is to be on hand when he commits his error, and ensure that he and his King suffer for it.'

***

Holbrooke spent an hour with his father and Chalmers at the cottage, but they didn't again discuss either Marignac or de Ternay. He'd never really seen his father as ageing, perhaps it was yesterday's funeral that had made him more alert to the signs, but there was no doubt that William was slowing down. Holbrooke made a resolution to spend more time with him when he was home from sea. There was a slight reservation in that thought because since he'd been commissioned, the father and son had lost some of their former intimacy. Perhaps it was because George no longer needed the help that his father had given him in the earlier part of his career. Holbrooke knew with a fearful certainty that without his father's intervention he'd never have passed beyond a master's mate. In fact, he'd probably have been cast adrift in Minorca to find his own passage home, or to volunteer as a deck hand on the first merchantman heading through the Straits. Yes, he'd make more time for his father, but he was by no means certain that their old terms of engagement could ever be renewed.

***

It was growing dark when Billy Styles deposited Holbrooke at Mulberry House, and the day was so far advanced that supper was already on the table. Polly fussed around until even she realised that her services weren't needed, and that Holbrooke wasn't going to let slip some juicy piece of gossip that she could re-tell in the marketplace. Holbrooke was drinking chocolate, a beverage that he found set him up well for bed.

'Something's troubling you dear…'

Ann could always see through her husband's moods.

'…was it something that Mister Garnier said? I heard he has another apothecary staying with him, come freshly from France. Is it to do with him?'

Holbrooke told the whole story. Ann knew very well how badly affected he'd been after the Belle Isle campaign and had already worked out that this de Ternay was largely to blame for his collapse. She listened in silence to the whole story, even a recounting of Chalmers' assessment of de Ternay's inherent weakness. Even so, she was surprised when her husband asked if they had a bible in the house.

'Certainly, dear. David gave us one for a wedding gift, a very beautiful copy that has rested untouched in its box. It's in the bottom drawer on your side of the bed, but be careful with it because it's still wrapped in the tissue that it came in. I'll ask Polly to fetch it.'

'Oh, no need, I'll just have a look at it before I turn in. It won't take a moment, I just want to check that David knows his scriptures.'

And indeed it took only a couple of minutes to read what Ezekial had to say about an upright man, but Holbrooke's candle was guttering before he'd finished thinking through the implications. Not that he'd ever meet de Ternay again, of course, the idea was risible. He went to sleep with the uncomfortable thought that before this evening neither Ann nor he had once opened the magnificent bible that Chalmers had given them at their wedding. Did Chalmers guess that truth? Probably.

***

CHAPTER NINE

A Particular Service

Thursday, Eighth of April 1762.
Château de Ternay, Poitou, France.

The weather had turned in the Loire valley and the trees were already in full leaf, partially obscuring the view from the chateau down to the gate house where the road to the village veered off into the main estate. Charles-Henri-Louis d'Arsac de Ternay twisted his head from side to side trying to get a clear view, but it was no good. He'd sent one of the family grooms to the village on horseback to look out for the carriage, but he knew that even if the man galloped back he'd barely get a few minutes warning of the arrival. However, there could be no mistaking the carriage. It would surely have an escort of dragoons – unheard of in this rural backwater – and in any case, as soon as it left the main highway at the village it could only be heading for the Chateau de Ternay.

Charles-Henri realised that he could be seen by any servants that happened to be passing the front of the house and that brought him to his senses. He was a captain in the King's navy and he certainly couldn't be seen to be agitated at the arrival of a guest, however great he may be in the councils of the mighty. For this was indeed an important visitor. The Duc de Choiseul was in one person the ministers of war, of marine and of foreign affairs and after the King – and not very far after – he was the most powerful man in the country. The message had come down two days ago by a mounted officer – a captain of hussars – who bore no letter, no written orders of any kind, just a verbal greeting and the hope that de Ternay would be at home on this day to receive Choiseul. The Duke must have already ascertained that de Ternay had left his ship refitting in Brest and travelled down to his family home to attend to personal business. There'd been no hint as to the purpose of the meeting, but of one thing de Ternay was certain; it was no mere social visit. He knew that negotiations were underway with the British to end this war and there must be some powerful reason to bring the minister away from his seat of power at Versailles.

The rest of the household knew no such restraint on their agitation. His aged mother Louise, the dowager Marquise, had sent all the servants into a feverish rush to prepare for any eventuality. Would the great man stay for dinner, or for supper? Would he lodge at the chateau for the night? How many would be in his party, him alone or a whole cabinet of junior ministers, clerks and advisers? Well, Charles-Henri did his best to distance himself from these speculative preparations and, as far as he was able, he continued with the personal affairs that had brought him all this way from his ship. He had no wife to add to the confusion, and he found that his vow of celibacy suited him very well. His older brother René – who had inherited the family title and was thankfully away from home and knew nothing of the visit – could worry about the continuation of the family name while he concerned himself with the great matters of the power and prestige of the French navy. He took one more look down towards the gatehouse. The gravel of the drive had been dredged from the Loire only the previous year and it still lay thick enough to offer an uninterrupted ribbon of variegated gold; it never failed to please him. He did wonder for just a moment how heavy the Duke's carriage would be. If it was one of those grand affairs that he'd seen in Versailles then it would certainly stick where the gravel lay deepest. However, if that was the case, then the carriage would hardly have made it this far into the provinces in the first place. No, there was nothing he could do and he'd learned at an early age to concern himself only with those matters that he could influence, the rest was in the hands of God. In any case it was so early, barely past the hour for breakfast, that the Duke would probably still not have left wherever he had spent the previous night. He returned to the writing desk in the corner of the library and continued studying the papers that his clerk had left in a neat, orderly pile, ready for his attention.

***

The morning passed with no sign of the Duke, and the household had settled down into a watchful silence. Every possible preparation had been made and all they could do was wait. At two o'clock Charles-Henri's mother came cautiously into the library to inquire what her son thought they should do for dinner. Only the dowager Marquise could presume to interrupt the younger son when he was working and only then in the most extreme need. Charles-Henri stood and bowed formally.

'I really have no better information than you do, maman. However, it's now well past noon and it's likely that the Duke will need some sort of refreshment when he arrives. As he's come all this way, I expect he'll want to conduct the business he has with me, but then he'll probably be grateful for dinner before he departs. My advice is to delay dinner until we know more.'

The dowager Marquise wasn't exactly in awe of her younger son, but she treated him with a deference that she didn't show to his elder brother. It was partly because of his naval rank and partly because of his strange way of life. She couldn't understand a young man voluntarily choosing celibacy, and when she'd sent Charles-Henri to the Knights of Malta it had been with the intention that he learned a military trade without committing to the ideals of the order. This grave, serious man before him was hardly recognisable as a de Ternay. He wasn't at all like his lusty father and brother, and his focussed manner made his mother uneasy. A slight bob, almost a curtsey, betrayed the relationship between Louise and her younger son, and it was evident that this was a settled state of affairs.

At that moment Charles-Henri heard the unmistakable

sound of a horse's hooves flinging up the good Loire gravel as it cantered up the drive. He rose and looked out of the library window to see one of the family grooms dismounting and hastening through the great doors of the chateau. That alone showed the urgency of the matter for a groom would invariably use one of the side entrances.

'Well, I expect this will answer our questions, maman. The Duke can't be far behind.'

Louise de Ternay hurried away to ensure that everything was prepared while Charles-Henri took a more leisurely stroll to take his place at the main doors to the Chateau.

***

The Duke's secretary officiously checked every window to ensure that it was closed. It was immediately stuffy in the library and the sounds of the chateau were muted. All that could be heard from outside was the crunch of booted feet on the gravel as a pair of dragoons paced in front of the windows, presumably to ensure that nobody came close enough to observe the great man at his business or to press their ear to the glass in the hope of hearing. Charles-Henri offered the Duke a comfortable chair, but he chose a simple hard-backed writing stool while his secretary retreated to a corner from where he could observe and record the proceedings.

'Well, it's a pleasure to meet you at last Captain. Your exploits at the Vilaine river have given you a certain fame, of course.'

Charles-Henri bowed but said nothing. Not for the world would he give the impression that bringing the trapped ships out to rejoin the fleet was anything other than the normal duties of an officer in the King's navy. He was acutely aware of his own professional position as the most junior captain on the list and without the backing of any powerful men. If he'd been called to Versailles for this meeting he'd have assumed that its purpose was to relieve him of his command, to give his third rate ship-of-the-line to a more experienced captain even though King Louis had personally promised it as a reward for liberating the trapped ships. Even the Duke's presence here at his family chateau hadn't completely reassured him; Choiseul could be on his way to Rochefort for example and merely stopping here on his way to deliver the bad news. After all, the matter would require sensitive handling if the King wasn't to be offended. De Ternay only really relaxed when he saw the unusual measures taken to ensure the meeting's secrecy; it could only mean that he was to be ordered on some particular service.

Choiseul wasn't a man to vacillate and he plunged straight in.

'I'm sure I don't need to point out that whatever is said here, in this room, is for our ears only. My secretary will record our conversation, but it won't be seen by anyone, it's solely meant as a reminder to me. You'll receive orders in due course, but you will never see the transcript.'

The Duke looked meaningfully at Charles-Henri, who nodded cautiously.

'You'll be aware that this war is drawing to its natural end, and it's unlikely that France will prosper from the peace agreement. We've been disappointed at Spain's response and, not to put it too finely, their entry into the war is having less effect than we'd hoped. Their fleet, that part of it that is ready for sea, is making for Havana in anticipation of a British attempt against that place. You may not have heard that Martinique has fallen.'

That shook Charles-Henri. The news hadn't penetrated to the Loire valley, but he immediately grasped its significance. It left Saint-Domingue as the last significant French possession in the Caribbean, and it freed up the British squadrons for other duties.

'Yes, I see that you understand. There seems to be little now to keep the British at the negotiating table and with the exception of Minorca, I have nothing to offer to induce them to return our sugar islands, not to mention Belle Isle. I need something to demonstrate to King George that he must sue for peace this year. The army can't help, it's bogged down in Westphalia and the Low Countries and this new King George has shown no affection for Hanover, so I must turn to the navy, and that's why I'm here today. I need a man with the ability to bring the war to the enemy's doorstep, and that's you, Monsieur de Ternay.'

Charles-Henri's face gave nothing away and he said little.

'I'm honoured your Grace.'

'Honoured indeed, and I hope so, but you don't yet know the extent of your fortune. You'll sail in *Robuste* as soon as possible but no later than the first week in May. You'll take under your command another third rate,' he turned to his secretary, 'remind me of its name, if you please.'

The secretary answered without hesitation.

'*Eveillé,* your Grace, of sixty-four guns, the frigate *Garonne* of thirty, and *Licorne* armed *en flute* as a storeship but with some guns remaining.'

Charles-Henri couldn't keep the surprise from his face. A small squadron, admittedly, but it comprised almost all the ships in Brest that were in any condition to put to sea.

'The King will, of course, give you a commission as *chef d'escadre* for the duration of this mission, not least because each of the other captains is senior to you.'

That widened Charles-Henri's eyes. Then he'd have his own *Cornette* at the main masthead. He'd be a temporary junior admiral with less than a year's seniority as a captain!

'Now, you'll no doubt want to know your mission and the reason for the secrecy.'

Choiseul stopped and drew a breath while watching the reaction of this strange person before him. In any other man it would have been a pause for effect, but Choiseul didn't waste his time on such theatrical devices.

'It's the Newfoundland fisheries, at least that will be your immediate objective. You'll have a small brigade, five hundred men or so, under the command of the comte d'Haussonville, but you will be the commander-in-chief of the expedition. Now, before I continue, do you have any comments?'

Choiseul wanted to be sure of his man before he went any further, and he regarded Charles-Henri with interest as the younger man sat thoughtfully for the span of some twenty seconds.

'I'm honoured, of course, your Grace, but may I observe that a brigade of five hundred men will hardly be sufficient to hold even the principal town of Newfoundland when the British are alerted. May I ask when you expect the peace negotiations to conclude?'

'Ah, you mistake me Captain, but I take your point and a force of this size is certainly insufficient to hold the territory. However, this is to be a raid, not an occupation. If I had sufficient ships I'd send out an army of five thousand to take and hold the place then exchange it for some of the islands we've already lost to the British. That's unrealistic in the navy's present situation. No, this is to demonstrate to Lord Egremont that we have the ability to hurt British commercial and naval interests. The fishery alone is worth millions and the British have commitments to supply stockfish across their possessions and to the Dutch and the Portuguese and the Italian states to name but a few. Moreover, they regard the Newfoundland fishery as a nursery – a training ground – for the seamen who will eventually man their fleet. Make no doubt that the destruction of the facilities ashore and the fishing fleet itself will be a shrewd blow. I intend that the merchants of London will set up such a cry as will force their government to take the peace negotiations seriously. You're to destroy the facilities for the fishery, burn the boats, burn all the public buildings, and if it seems necessary you're to cruise the Grand Banks and destroy any British vessels that you find there. It appears that the British have sent almost every ship and regiment that they had in the North America to the Caribbean, for the invasion of Cuba, so it should take them some time to gather a force to eject you. Nevertheless, this is a raid, not an invasion, and you're to spend no more than a month in Newfoundland; that should be long enough to complete the business. After that you'll be given wide-ranging powers to annoy the enemy in that part of the world. Île Royale also has a substantial fishery and you may feel it offers a useful opportunity. Louisbourg will no doubt be lightly garrisoned and in consultation with the Comte d'Haussonville you may see it best for the King's service to attempt that place. These orders may sound vague, and they are deliberately so because I can't say what situation you may find.'

Choiseul stopped again, inviting a response.

'May I ask, your Grace, what importance you attach to the safe return of the squadron and the landing force? It seems to me that I must hazard both to comply with these orders.'

'That's an interesting question Captain, perhaps more interesting than the answer that you'll hear only from my lips. It won't be committed to paper.'

The Duke glanced at his secretary who dutifully laid his pen aside. He continued in a lower tone.

'The loss of five hundred soldiers would be regrettable indeed, but the Prince of Soubise loses that many every week in Germany, often every day, and in an engagement, every hour. France has men and they can be trained to be soldiers without any great expense or difficulty. Ships and trained seamen are another matter entirely. You'll be aware that this squadron constitutes every ship in Brest that's ready for sea, and just as important, every trained seaman that's fit to lay aloft. In the grand reckoning of things, the destruction of the Newfoundland fishery is fair exchange for d'Haussonville's men, but not for your ships and seamen. You did not bring them out of the Vilaine merely for them to augment the British fleet. I hope that is quite clear.'

Charles-Henri nodded briefly. The Duke had made a

brutal but vital point. He hadn't realised what importance this great man gave to the rapid ending of the war. Yet it was crucial to know Choiseul's mind, because once his squadron with its cargo of soldiers had cleared from Brest he'd be on his own and would have to make decisions that directly influenced France's future. It sounded seductively easy, and perhaps the first part was. He knew little of Newfoundland but surely even the vast British navy must be stretched to protect all of its possessions. It had swallowed half the world and must need a time of reflection to digest this enormous meal. But what then? Perhaps the counter-attack would be slow in coming, but it was nevertheless inevitable. At some point a squadron of British ships and half a dozen battalions of infantry would appear at Newfoundland and then the commander-in-chief of this expedition would have some hard decisions to make.

'Now, you'll have gathered that this expedition is to be conducted in the utmost secrecy. Your orders will be delivered by courier to your ship, and within the week. They are to be shown to nobody. I'll be dropping hints in places where I know they'll get back to the British government. Those hints will suggest Ireland, Scotland and Saint-Domingue as the likely objectives for your squadron. You'll have a small number of Irishmen on board as well as two officers thinking they're rejoining their regiments in Saint-Domingue, and mail for the garrison. None of these will know the truth. When you're clear of Brest you're to do all in your power to avoid being followed by British ships. If you are, then make your destination as difficult to predict as you possibly can.'

Clear of Brest! Charles-Henri knew well how difficult that could be, and then to shake off any followers, a fine thought, for sure.

As if he was reading the other man's mind, Choiseul answered the unspoken question.

'Your first challenge is to get away from Brest without having to fight and without being pursued. I can offer no advice, and to the man who brought the ships out of the Vilaine, perhaps no advice is needed. I will however offer this assistance; a free hand to make your decisions. I'll set the date when you're to have your squadron ready for sea, and then I'll leave the departure date to you. Whether you choose an easterly wind to make a rapid descent of the Iroise, or a westerly gale when the British frigates will be standing offshore for their safety, or a fog, is your decision, but you must leave within fourteen days of the first day of May.'

Charles-Henri glanced at his writing desk where a card showing the day's date was always displayed on a small walnut stand. The eighth of April. Three weeks then, and at least two days of that would be occupied in traveling to Brest to rejoin his ship. There was evidently no time to lose.

***

CHAPTER TEN

The Iroise

Saturday, Eighth of May 1762.
Argonaut, at Sea. The Iroise.

'By the mark, fourteen.'

The leadsman's vowels were distorted by the thick, wet fog that lay like a shroud over the outer Goulet and probably the whole of the Iroise. Holbrooke knew that the man must be uncomfortable, lashed into position on the starboard fore chains, but he could rely upon his bosun to see that he was provided with a thick sailcloth apron to keep his chest and legs dry and that he was relieved at every turn of the half-hour glass. He could leave those details to his officers while he concerned himself with the overriding need to keep his ship safe while it lay in this dangerous position, so close to the principal base of the French Atlantic Fleet.

'We're right in the centre of the fairway, sir, and I reckon the ebb's running at about a knot. If we come up now, we'll just about stem the tide.'

Holbrooke glanced at the binnacle. His ship was steering southeast across the Goulet with the lazy northerly wind on the larboard quarter. Fairview was right; if he hauled his wind now so that *Argonaut* was heading right into the Goulet, towards Brest, his speed through the water would just about cancel the tide's efforts to sweep them out to sea.

'Very well, Mister Fairview, bring her to.'

He watched for a moment as the sail trimmers ran to their places at the sheets and tacks and braces. It wasn't a difficult manoeuvre and there was no need for shouting and cajoling, and in any case he'd ordered silence on the deck so that he could use his ears where his eyes were of no use. The men knew well enough what was required of them and when the ship started turning to larboard they were ready to brace the yards up sharply.

'Mister Jackson!'

Holbrooke barely had to raise his voice to be heard by the bosun and it took just a few moments for the familiar figure to reach the quarterdeck.

'You see the situation, Mister Jackson? We're stemming the tide now and I want to hold us as nearly in this position as I can. Have the leadsman feel for the bottom and let me know whether we're drifting.'

Jackson knew just what was required. The master could calculate to a nicety the effect of the tidal stream and the ship's leeway, but it would always be an estimate. With the sea bed only fourteen fathoms below the ship's keel there was a much more direct way of measuring their movement with respect to the land. The lead line could be dangled vertically so that it just rested on the seabed and then the angle that it made with the surface of the sea, and the feel of it dragging across the bottom, would give them a better idea of their movement.

'I'll double up on the leadsmen then, sir, starboard and larboard, to make it more certain.'

'Very well, Mister Jackson.'

Holbrooke paced to the ensign staff and back. There was no point in staring into the fog, he could hardly see his own ship's foremast and beyond that it was just a grey impenetrable blanket. It was hard to hide his anxiety. He'd only been on station for a few days and until now the persistent westerlies had prevented his penetrating this far into the Goulet. Somewhere to the north, about a mile away, lay the headlands of the Grande and Petit Minous. There were batteries on both of those points, as there was on the Capucins, a little further away to the east. To the south, across the mouth of Camaret Bay, lay the Toulinguet Point with its own heavy guns. There were rocks and shoals all around and grounding on any one of them in this ebbing tide would ensure his ship's destruction. If she didn't break her back as the tide fell, one of the batteries would surely find the range when the fog lifted. Yet his orders from Admiral Hawke were unequivocal. If the wind was westerly – and therefore foul for the French to escape from Brest – his station was a patrol line between the Blackstone and the Parquet. This was dangerous enough in all conscience, but if the wind was in the east – anywhere between northwest and southeast – he was to bring his ship into the far more hazardous waters of the Goulet, for that was the wind to bring a French Squadron out of Brest.

Fairview glanced again at the compass.

'Ship's full and by sir, nor'east by east. That should allow for the leeway.'

Holbrooke nodded in agreement. It was an interesting multi-factor equation that he'd have enjoyed drawing out on a chart. If the master was correct they should be holding a position right in the deepest part of the Goulet. If any Frenchman larger than a sloop was intent on escaping in this fortuitous weather, he'd have to pass within a biscuit-toss of the British frigate. He remembered a day like this in Quiberon Bay off the mouth of the Vilaine river. A Frenchman had made a fool of him that day and escaped over the bar with two ships of the line and a pair of frigates. He'd been told the man's name when he'd last visited the Admiralty in London; Charles-Henri-Louis d'Arsac, Chevalier de Ternay, a very aristocratic-sounding title. He'd been promoted from *lieutenant de vaisseau* to *capitaine de vaisseau* for that fine piece of work. De Ternay had made a fool of Holbrooke a second time when he again brought some ships out from the Vilaine, and again Holbrooke failed to prevent their escape. Their Lordships had pronounced themselves well pleased with Holbrooke's conduct on both occasions, but it still rankled with him and that ridiculous Huguenot émigré at Rookesbury House at merely rubbed salt into the wound. Well, it was fruitless to personalise this war, and even if he was pitted against de Ternay again, he probably wouldn't know it. The enemy commander was usually an anonymous figure seen at long range, and unrecognisable from any other man. His train of thought was interrupted by the bosun coming aft.

'How's she drifting, Mister Jackson?'

'Just a touch astern, sir,' he glanced at the binnacle, 'sou'west, maybe half a knot. I had that big old line heaved as well, sir, the one with the oversize tallow-hole, it brought up some crushed coral and sand.'

He looked questioningly at the sailing master. Fairview had been a channel pilot before Holbrooke had ever left his native town and he had an uncanny knack of knowing the seabed characteristics.

'No sand, Mister Jackson? Then we're west of the Pollux rocks. The sand ends there and the centre of the channel is all coral and gravel until past the Parquet. I reckon the ebb's still building, sir. If you want to hold up tight under the Pollux you could set the main t'gallant, that should be just enough.'

Holbrooke looked up to where the mainmast disappeared into the fog. It would be a miserable job climbing up there and letting fall the sail, and all for no real benefit. He knew that most captains wouldn't even consider the trouble for their men, after all it was May, and hardly very cold at all. Yet, it was an inconvenience and the next report could just as easily show *Argonaut* holding her position.

'No, I'm content to drop back on the tide. Keep the two leadlines working Mister Jackson, and let me know if the drift changes.'

Jackson replaced his hat and turned away.

'Oh, and let the leadsmen know that their work is appreciated, will you?'

***

There was nothing more for Holbrooke to do. The first lieutenant had reported the ship cleared for action with the men at their stations. That was a reasonable precaution when at any minute a French squadron could announce its presence with a shattering broadside. In fact, if the French were planning to come out, it would be in the next hour. They'd have weighed anchor at the top of the tide – three hours ago – and would have ridden the ebb through the narrowest part of the Goulet. On that schedule they'd be passing the Pollux rocks about now. But it all seemed so unlikely, and what possible purpose could a French squadron have in escaping from Brest? They'd already lost the East Indies and the west coast of Africa, New France had fallen and the Caribbean had become a British lake. They could attempt to join forces with a Spanish squadron, certainly, but every report agreed that the Spanish navy wasn't yet ready to commit forces to the war, except in defence of their own colonies. Still, that wasn't Holbrooke's concern; his only task at the moment was to plug this, the only exit from Brest. He could leave the higher strategy to their Lordships. What he was sure of was that he'd have to get used to this life. The Western Squadron had spent years on blockade duty already. Admiral Hawke had successfully made the case for a looser blockade, so the ships-of-the-line spent much of their time at anchor in Torbay or Plymouth Sound, or even as far east as Spithead, but not the frigates. They and the motley collection of sloops, cutters, bomb vessels and fireships kept the sea in all weathers and wore through canvas and cordage at an alarming rate. *Argonaut* hadn't yet spent a week off Brest but already Holbrooke could feel the tedium descending. And *Argonaut* was alone. Orders had come in a cutter yesterday that suggested a sortie by a French squadron that was known to be in Brest, and that would surely bring reinforcements, but for now only his small frigate lay between the French and the open sea. Did they know that? Was the French admiral aware that there was no inshore squadron lying off Point St. Matthew, that there was no battle squadron further offshore waiting to pounce on any enemy that dared to put to sea?

Well, there was no point in succumbing to ennui. With

a nod to Fairview he threaded his way forward, stepping over the outstretched legs of the gun crews who were dozing at their stations with nothing to do but wait, past the bosun and his leadsmen and onto the fo'c'sle.

'What, Mister Shorrock and Mister Murray? This is an unexpected pleasure.'

Holbrooke spoke in a hushed voice. He knew that his conduct set the tone for everyone on deck, and if he started speaking loudly he'd soon be copied, and then there would be no listening for the enemy. He shouldn't have been surprised; the first lieutenant and the marine lieutenant had roving commissions at quarters and each had a responsibility to visit their men wherever they were stationed. However, it was clear to Holbrooke that they were loitering at this most forward part of the ship's deck so that they could be first to spot an enemy coming down the Goulet. He smiled at that and wondered how long their enthusiasm would last as the months and perhaps years of waiting rolled by. He could see the bowsprit and the jib boom stretching ahead apparently into eternity, and as the wisps of fog came and went he could just make out the hunched figure of a man at the very extremity of the long spars. It was an uncomfortable position, for sure, but an excellent place for a lookout with keen eyes and ears.

'Who's out on the jib boom, Mister Shorrock?'

'That's Lewis, sir, the Welshman. He claims he can hear the rats yarning through the bread-room bulkhead so I've sent him out there to let us know if he hears anything ahead of us. It won't give us much extra warning and if they're bringing the wind and the tide down from Brest they'll be upon us before he can draw breath. I'll bring him in if it seems a waste of time.'

Holbrooke thought for a moment. Any advantage was worth something and he should harness the crew's enthusiasm while it lasted.

'That's true, Mister Shorrock, the French will cover that distance in a few seconds. But consider that Lewis is not only some sixty feet nearer the potential enemy, but more importantly he's sixty feet away from the noises of this ship. Leave him there and relieve him when he's had enough. I hope he'll have the sense to shout when he does hear anything. Now, if they're coming out today it will be soon. Get the men up and ready, if you please, and Mister Murray see to your marines. I'd hate to be slower than the French with my first broadside and my first volley of musketry.'

***

All along the deck the indistinct outlines of the gun crews could be seen levering themselves up and grasping the tools of their trade, the rammers and worms and handspikes and sponges. The guns were already loaded and run out and the slow match that had been kept burning in its tubs was blown into bright glowing life by the gun captains. There was something unearthly about that scene, like willo'-the-wisps over a marsh before sunrise. A superstitious man would have seen ill portents in those pallid glimmers, but Holbrooke merely saw his ship coming back to its full readiness as a fighting machine. There were so many variables, mostly known only to their Lordships, but this did seem a likely day for the French to come out. He could imagine that the wind indicator in the Admiralty boardroom would be showing this nor'easter and everyone from the clerks to Anson himself would be on tiptoe. There was nothing they could do, of course, and any message from London to the guardship at the Goulet would take three days at the least, even with this favourable wind.

A whisper from Shorrock.

'Both batteries ready, sir.'

Holbrooke merely nodded in reply. How the men were keeping quiet he couldn't tell. Perhaps one in ten were fresh from the plough having joined in Portsmouth but a week or so before and they must be finding it all very strange. At least they were all volunteers. He had no need for pressed men in his home port, not when his own followers told tales of prize money and warm, foreign shores to entice their friends to take the bounty.

Holbrooke stared ahead. There was no improvement in the visibility. He noticed with amusement that every man on deck was copying his motions, straining into the fog, hoping for a first sight or sound of a French squadron.

'The lead shows that we're drifting to leeward a mite, sir.'

'Very well Mister Jackson. Mister Fairview, will she come up a point?'

'She will, sir.'

Holbrooke gestured towards the wheel to save words and the quartermaster nudged the steersman who inched the wheel a few spokes to windward. Now *Argonaut* was hard on the wind, full and by, and the noises of the breeze against the sails increased a notch. Little chance of hearing the enemy now, not unless they were sounding trumpets and beating drums. Still, it was unlikely that they could slip by in this narrow passage.

The sound of running feet, leather-shod feet – caught Holbrooke's attention. Out of the gloom he saw midshipman Carew vaulting the train tackles in his haste to come aft.

'Beg your pardon, sir, but Lewis out on the jib boom says he can hear something. It's right to windward sir, a good five or six points off the bow, but it sounds like ships coming down the channel.'

Holbrooke turned and looked over the larboard bow. Nothing, just a vast opaque shroud. If they were truly four or five points off the bow then they were almost past and presumably were unaware of *Argonaut's* presence. Where would the reinforcing frigates be now? *Brilliant*, *Aeolus* and *Arethusa* had been mentioned and with that force they could bring the expected French squadron to action and so mangle them that they'd be forced to return to Brest. Probably they were hurrying west from Plymouth and still a day away from sighting Ushant. There was no point in firing a warning shot, it would only alert the French to

An Upright Man

Argonaut's presence.

'Did you hear them, Mister Carew?'

Holbrooke stared keenly at the youngster.

'I…I think so, sir. I ran out on the jib boom as soon as he reported. It was faint but there was something.'

There was nothing close to windward to make a noise, no tide-washed rocks, no sandbars, and Lewis was a reliable man. Holbrooke made a snap decision.

'Mister Fairview. Wear ship and bring us onto the starboard tack. Course…' he looked quickly at the binnacle, '…course west-by-south. We'll close in on whatever Lewis heard until we're certain of them. As quietly as you can.'

Manoeuvering in silence, as Holbrooke well knew, was easier said than done in a frigate, but at least wearing ship made less noise than tacking, and they were after all downwind of whatever was over there to the northwest. They must have drifted further to the south of the channel than he had thought, or else the enemy was too far north. Either way, it appeared that he had a perfect position in this fog; to leeward of the enemy where he'd hear them before they could hear him and where, when the fog thinned, he'd a have precious seconds or even minutes when they were visible to him but *Argonaut* was still hidden.

'Will you engage, sir?'

Shorrock was an instinctive fighting man, an officer with a raw courage that Holbrooke could never hope to emulate. He knew what Shorrock wanted; he wished with all his heart for *Argonaut* to work up towards the enemy, to burst from the invisibility of the fog with its broadsides blazing and to fight at whatever odds. But that wasn't why he was in the Goulet in this dangerous weather. He was there to perform a classic frigate's role, to make it possible for his own ships-of-the-line to find the enemy. No, he wouldn't throw himself into a one-sided fight. He'd cling onto the French squadron – if that's what it was – until he knew where they were bound. By the time they passed the Blackstone it would be evident whether they were for the north or the south and by then the fog would probably have burned off. Hawke had been cautious in his orders. He expected that these ships were bound for Ireland, probably to make a diversionary attack to draw off ships and men in advance of a combined French and Spanish fleet contesting mastery of the Channel. If the French were heading north, to Ireland or up the Channel, then they'd be lucky to get far without having to fight. But if they made an offing to the southwest, perhaps heading for the Americas or the Mediterranean, then they'd have a good chance of escaping, unless he could alert the Western Squadron.

***

Argonaut was on the starboard tack now and as far as Holbrooke could tell he was converging on the presumed enemy. Still, he could hear nothing and see nothing. The noises of his own ship were just too overpowering.

'I'm going forward, Mister Fairview. Keep this course but if you see the enemy, bear away.'

There was a very different feeling among the guns crews, compared with their lassitude when he last went forward. They'd heard what was up, they knew that a dangerous enemy was somewhere in the fog to windward, and like the first lieutenant, for the most part, they longed for action. Holbrooke had to step carefully over each train tackle to avoid an embarrassing fall, and yet all the time his senses were alert for a sight or sound of the French. Onto the fo'c'sle, then a scramble over the gammoning and the long walk along the two spars that stretched ahead into the fog. Lewis held out his arm for the last few yards and then he was safe with the fore topmast and the t'gallant stays for support. A moment to catch his breath and to quieten his racing heart.

'Out there, sir, fine on the starboard bow now.'

Lewis' Welsh lilt was reassuring; he at least was taking it calmly. It took a few seconds but now that Holbrooke had recovered he understood what had kept the Welshman out here. The noises of the ship were dulled and suppressed and a whole new range of sounds became evident. He could just hear the burbling of the water on the frigate's forefoot, a sound that was never heard from the quarterdeck, and he could hear the soft voice of the sea as it heaved under the unaccustomed weight of the heavy damp air. And there was something else. He cocked his ear to the direction that Lewis pointed and the unmistakeable sounds of a group of ships drifted over the water. The creak of leathered yards against masts, the rustling of hempen ropes against canvas and the groaning and squealing of rudders in their pintles. Perhaps not a large squadron but three or four ships at least. A bell! Two strokes, nine o'clock in the forenoon watch, the same as would have been struck in *Argonaut* if he hadn't had the clapper removed. He knew how hard it was to break the habits of a seagoing life in a single ship, to do it in a squadron was impossible!

***

CHAPTER ELEVEN

Decision

Saturday, Eighth of May 1762.
Argonaut, at Sea. The Iroise.

Holbrooke shifted his position on the end of the jib boom. He could sit on the cold, hard iron band that held the tack of the jib, where at least he had a good hand hold, or the barely softer pine spar from where he had to reach forward to grasp the fore t'gallant stay. He shifted from one to the other trying to ignore the discomfort and thanking providence that he'd discarded his breeches in favour of plain blue trousers that morning. It didn't look elegant and Ann certainly wouldn't approve; she was becoming more sensitive to her position in society, he'd noticed. However, at this moment it was saving a costly pair of breeches and white stockings from certain ruin. It was worth the discomfort to have this wonderful ability to hear the French squadron to windward. He was certain that they were unaware of *Argonaut's* presence while he was gathering information every moment. He could tell from the quality and spacing of the sounds that there were at least four ships, but there might be more that he couldn't hear. The voices – so many harsh commands and exasperated reproofs – betrayed ships with large crews that hadn't been to sea for some time. His ears told him that the two in the centre were ships-of-the-line, and by their relative silence those that led and followed were more likely frigates or smaller, perhaps even storeships or transports. The muffled sound of booted feet stamping and scuffing on wooden decks proclaimed that one or all of them were carrying a substantial body of soldiery.

'The fog's thinning, sir. I thought I saw a shape there for just a moment.'

Lewis had brushed away the seaman that had been sent

to relieve him. He'd assumed a particular relationship with his captain after Holbrooke had asked his advice about Lundy Island in the Bristol Channel. But that was nearly two years ago and his messmates, many of whom had joined the ship since then, frankly doubted his account. This was his opportunity to re-assert his position and he wouldn't easily be shifted from his seat of honour.

Holbrooke swivelled his head from left to right, testing the thickness of the fog through the corners of his eyes. Yes, Lewis was right. The grey shroud that hid the French squadron was less impenetrable than it had been twenty minutes ago. It had a structure to it now, a pattern of shifting, swirling veils that still hid the French squadron but hinted that it wouldn't do so for much longer. *Argonaut* could be discovered at any moment; it was time to return to the quarterdeck.

'Pass the word if you see anything new, Lewis, but keep it quiet until you're certain that we've been seen.'

Somehow the return along the jib boom and bowsprit seemed longer than the outbound journey. The space between handholds had increased, or so it appeared, and the pine spar was slippery with fog-dew. By the time Holbrooke reached the fo'c'sle his knees were protesting at the unnatural tension.

'Mister Carew, station yourself where you can hear a soft hail from Lewis and pass on his reports. Whispers only until I give the word. Don't assume that the French can see us just because they're visible from our deck.'

He saw the midshipman climb onto the gammoning and stretch his ears towards where the end of the jib boom disappeared into the still-thick fog. It was all happening quickly now and Carew's next report of a sighting came as Holbrooke made his way to the quarterdeck, again stepping over the train tackles and brushing past the gun crews. He could feel the wind changing, it was backing towards the northwest and that surely would sweep the fog away, and he could already feel the warmth of the still-hidden sun.

Any moment now…

'Ah, there they are, sir, or at least one of them. It's gone now, but it was right on our beam.'

Fairview wasn't the only one to have seen it. There was a buzz of whispered conversation from the main deck, clearly the gun crews had also caught sight of a ship.

Shorrock too had seen that ghostly shape appear for a few seconds then disappear.

'A frigate, I believe, sir.'

Another shape, a little astern of the first. It came and went in an instant, but a hundred pairs of eyes had seen it. A great two-decker that could be a seventy-four. Then another, a second two decker, perhaps a little smaller than the first. Holbrooke gulped as he realised how close he was to a formidable force. There, perhaps half a mile to windward of him, was enough firepower to blow his little frigate out of the water in a single broadside.

'Bear away three points, Mister Fairview. I think we can assume that we've been seen so let's put some distance between us and those gentlemen.'

The visibility was improving quickly and the dank fog was giving way to a clear sky overhead that promised a glorious spring morning.

'A frigate and two third rates. It's hard to see but perhaps another frigate bringing up the rear.'

Shorrock had a good eye and a lifetime's experience at sea gave him the confidence to make a snap identification from the most fleeting and partial sighting.

Holbrooke watched them intently as his own ship turned towards the southwest. The distance was already too great for an engagement, and it was unlikely that any French squadron with the open sea so close would delay to engage a lone British frigate. The lead ship was also bearing away, but slantwise, without any real conviction. Holbrooke guessed that it was positioning itself between the squadron and *Argonaut*.

'Mister Shorrock. We'll fire a full broadside just in case

any British ship is near, then single guns every five minutes. The broadside may as well be aimed at that fellow, you could just be lucky, even at this distance.'

Shorrock rubbed his hands and turned to his guns. It was easy in a frigate, all of the guns were under the first lieutenant's eye, and the orders to engage were transmitted directly, rather than through a young gentlemen shouting down a hatch to the lower decks.

The broadside tore up the sea two or three cables in front of the frigate and Holbrooke saw a flurry of activity on her quarterdeck, as though the French officers had never before been under fire, but no answering guns. He saw a uniformed man who must surely be the captain hold up his hand as though to restrain his officers.

Fairview gave a snort of derision.

'They know what we're about, sir, although it hardly does them any honour. They don't choose to add their own gunfire to ours in case it brings down the Western Squadron. They don't know where Admiral Hawke is any more than we do.'

'I think you're right, Master. But they do know where they're heading and that's more than we can say.'

'Well, they're not making for the Toulinguet Channel, sir, and I can't say I blame them, on this falling tide. They could still round the Parquet and make their offing for Finisterre, or pass through the Raz for the Basque Roads or anywhere in the Bay.'

'That's if they're making for the south, Master.'

'Aye sir, but what's to the north that's of interest to a few men-o'-war and transports? They surely won't try that same caper in Scotland or Ireland like they did two years ago.'

Holbrooke didn't answer. He remembered that chase around the very north of the British Isles and as far as the Faroes, and the final fight off the Isle of Man where they brought the infamous François Thurot to his final reckoning. Fairview might think it unlikely, but Lord Anson did not; he was still concerned about a landing in Ireland. He knew how volatile that country was, how ripe for revolt from its English overlords. Well, they'd know soon enough where this expedition was heading, at least in a general cardinal-point-of-the-compass way. The French were to the north of *Argonaut* and soon, when they were abreast Point St. Matthew, they'd have to shoulder the frigate aside if they wanted to steer to the south, or shape their course to round Ushant if they were bound for the north. They wouldn't want a British frigate hanging on their tail, whichever way they went.

***

The transformation from dense fog to crystal clear visibility was always a magical moment. Ten minutes was all that it took, from being unable to see *Argonaut's* jib boom, to having the whole of the Iroise visible in all its blue, grey and green splendour. From the Point du Raz in the south to the Molene Islands in the northwest, every detail was revealed in this clean, clear air, and far to the west the horizon presented an unbroken line where the sky met the broad Atlantic Ocean. Holbrooke even fancied he could see a bulge on the northwestern horizon close to the left of the islands, where Ushant itself stood guard over the approaches to this vital French stronghold. The masthead lookout would surely be able to see that far, and he saw Fairview sending a midshipman aloft with a telescope.

'D'you see that cutter, sir? Just coming clear of the third rate, it looks like it's heading to the frigate.'

Shorrock pointed to where the little vessel had just appeared from under seventy-four's stern. Its gaff mainsail looked far too big for such a small craft and its long jib boom thrust far out ahead. The impression of awkwardness was reinforced when the mainsail was boomed out far to larboard as the strengthening north-westerly wind hurried it on its way.

'Orders, I expect sir.'

Holbrooke made no reply. Orders for sure and he could

imagine what they were. If the squadron was bound for the south then that frigate need do nothing, and *Argonaut* would be forced to move out of range of those menacing broadsides. However, if they were bound to the north – to windward – it would be a wise precaution to have that frigate deter its British opponent from following. That would complicate things. Would the French fight to keep him away? The squadron only had two frigates and the loss of one – they could expect it to at least need repair after a fight with a British frigate, if it wasn't lost entirely – would be an important dilution of their force right at the beginning of the expedition. He could cripple that ship at least; he was confident of that. But he ran the risk of *Argonaut* also being damaged and unable to follow the French squadron, unable even to find the British frigates that were supposed to be on their way to the Iroise.

'Soldiers, sir! You can see their white coats plain as anything. There must be nigh on a hundred of them. It looks like they're forming up on the starboard waist.'

'Line infantry, Mister Shorrock, a full company at least. That'll test their hammock plan.'

Holbrooke remembered other times that he'd seen French infantry. On the coast of Brittany and again at Fort Niagara. He shuddered slightly when he remembered those wicked bayonets probing for his defenceless body as he struggled in the surf at Saint-Cast.

'Ah! Do you see, sir, the cutter's planning to round-to on her windward side, but the frigate's come off the wind a point, it looks like he was expecting the cutter to come under his lee. He won't be able to come up again, not with the cutter in his way.'

Fairview looked meaningfully at his captain, but Holbrooke had already seen the possibility. That cutter commander – probably a young lieutenant or a master's mate – hadn't thought this through. By ranging up on the frigate's windward side he was blocking her ability to manoeuvre. A moment's thought then he spat out his orders rapidly, the words of command coming easily from long usage.

'Mister Fairview, come up hard on the wind, as quietly as you can. Mister Shorrock, stand by with a full broadside to starboard. This might be our opportunity. He can't escape to windward and he may not even notice us coming upon him. At all costs, Master, don't let him come close enough to board us.'

Argonaut's bows swung gently to starboard; one, two, three points. There was no great change in the set of the sails, just the tacks of the courses brought inboard, and that was done under Jackson's eye, without any shouting. It was almost imperceptible to a casual observer, and Holbrooke could see that the French frigate's entire officer complement had moved over to the starboard side of the quarterdeck to listen to what the cutter had to say. The two frigates were converging by some four or five points with the unsuspecting Frenchman to windward.

Holbrooke held his breath. Just another minute or two and it would be too late, the Frenchman would find himself trapped between his advancing, well-prepared enemy and his own cutter.

Shorrock was eagerly judging the distance. Every gun captain had his hand raised and at each gun the handspikes were in use, levering the carriages around to keep the guns pointing squarely at their target.

'We're in range now sir, I reckon. Ah, they've spotted our manoeuvre!'

Holbrooke could see as much for himself. The French captain was perhaps more experienced than his officers, or it could have been the heightened awareness that came with command of a man-of-war. Whatever the reason, he turned to glance to leeward before the cutter had finished shouting across the squadron commander's orders. His expression couldn't be seen at this distance, but his actions told of his horror at seeing his predicament. Gun crews that had been idly watching the approaching cutter ran back to their stations as their officers shouted orders that *Argonaut's* people could hear but not understand, not this far away.

Holbrooke glanced across the stretch of water that separated the two ships. He thought of holding up his hand to keep the first lieutenant in check, but there really was no need. Shorrock would wait with the patience of a Grecian stoic until Holbrooke gave the order. There was still turmoil on the Frenchman's quarterdeck, and he could see that the guns weren't being pointed.

'Stand by to bear away as soon as we've fired the broadside, Mister Fairview, Mister Jackson,' he said in a calm, clear voice, despite his racing heart.

The sailing master and the bosun were side-by-side at the binnacle, and their *aye-aye sirs,* came as one voice.

Every yard closer would make *Argonaut's* broadside that much more destructive. Just a few moments…

Holbrooke raised his whistle and blew once. A second of time passed, and then *Argonaut's* starboard battery delivered its broadside. It was a long range, of course, but the gun crews were well-practiced and most had been in action before. Fully half of the guns found their mark and of those perhaps five or six smashed into the area of the frigate's gun ports. He could see the splinters flying and at least one gun was pointing at an unnatural angle, suggesting that the trunnions or the carriage had been wrecked. Ah, the mizzen yard had been hit in the slings, now it was suspended only by its topping lifts, and it was drooping uncontrollably to leeward. Deprived of that leverage aft, the Frenchman's head started swinging to leeward.

'Up helm, sir?'

'I think not, Mister Fairview. Hard on the wind, if you please, as hard as she'll go.'

This was one of those moments of outrageous good fortune that occurred occasionally in battle. Holbrooke's plan to offer a single broadside then withdraw to leeward could certainly be improved. That French captain would need hours of labour to make his ship fit for a hard beat to windward, and in that time the squadron commander would surely have to show his hand. Now that the enemy frigate was deprived of its ability to hold its wind, *Argonaut* could slip past and follow the two ships-of-the-line and the other frigate.

'Mister Shorrock! You see the situation.'

'Aye-aye sir. Starboard battery is almost ready again.'

'Then I'll attempt to rake her bows. Mister Fairview, as close as you dare, but don't you let him grapple us!'

The Frenchman was in a horrible state of confusion. There was a party aft attempting to lower the mizzen on its topping lifts alone, with the broken yard hanging free beside the mast. Another group of seamen were swarming out on the fore tops'l yard to furl it. The guns were an afterthought and only three shots came *Argonaut's* way, and none of those were pointed with any care. Meanwhile her bows were still paying off to leeward.

'Full and by. We'll pass at barely pistol-shot sir.'

Fairview didn't take his eyes from the Frenchman's bows; he was judging this complex problem to a nicety, assessing the differing speeds of the two frigates against the time that had elapsed and distance to run. One look told Holbrooke that they'd pass too close. The Frenchmen thought so too, and he could see grapnels being sent out on the jib boom, and a crowd of soldiers shuffling forward.

'Too close, Mister Fairview. Bear away two points if you please.'

Fairview made no acknowledgement of his error, nor did he show any sign of dissent. It was one of his best characteristics, that he never let a rebuke affect his duty.

Shorrock had the light of battle in his eyes but even he could see that they needed to keep their distance from a ship full of soldiers. Still, he must have hoped that his captain would fight this enemy until he struck his colours, was burned, or sank. Those hopes were dashed by that single order to Fairview.

'Starboard battery's ready, sir. All loaded with ball. I'd

have preferred to have some chain shot but there's no time for that, I see. The marines are ready, and all the swivels are manned.'

Holbrooke stood like a statue, watching the relative movement of the French ship.

'Fire as your guns bear, Mister Shorrock. Mister Murray, your marines may fire their swivels and muskets by volleys when they have the range.'

Argonaut was sailing two points free of the wind and moving fast towards her prey. Without really noticing, the ships had moved out of the shelter of the islands and now the Atlantic swell started to send showers of spray over the starboard bow. Holbrooke felt the sharp sting on his cheek and tasted the salt water. Any moment now!

Bang! Bang!

The great guns fired as their captains fancied they could hit the target. Now the swivels started hurling their half pound balls towards the enemy, adding their low wail to the discordant orchestra. As *Argonaut* drew across the Frenchman's bows the sharper crack of the marines' muskets joined in. It was a cacophony of sound and again Holbrooke saw the wood splinters flying from the Frenchman. The shot was taking its toll on the crowded fo'c'sle and heads. One of the brawny men who'd run out on the bowsprit fell noiselessly into the rushing water alongside, still clutching his grapnel. Holbrooke felt a moment's regret, he was a brave seaman, let down by his captain's unimaginative handling of his ship.

By rights, the Frenchman should have been hit hard by that raking fire. He should have lost his bowsprit or jib boom, if not his foremast, but by one of those chances that occurred in a battle, there was no appreciable damage. There were bright gashes in his bows and head-rail; sheets and halyards streamed away to leeward where they had been parted by *Argonaut's* shot; a few men were down, and at least one had been lost overboard, but that was all. And now *Argonaut* was past the Frenchman's bows, moving rapidly out of range, leaving his opponent to patch up his mizzen yard and make his way to windward to rejoin his squadron.

***

'St. Matthews is on the beam now, sir, maybe two-and-a-half miles, we must be right in the centre of the channel. I'd expect them to be bearing away now, if they're heading for the south.'

Holbrooke was well aware of their position, and he didn't need Fairview to tell him the implications of the French squadron's dogged persistence in their west-southwesterly course. The sun was well up and he could easily see the Brittany coast and the treacherous tangle of rocks that lay to the southeast of the island of Ushant. In an hour the French would be able to shape a course to the northwest for Ireland, if that was their destination. The bright sunshine and the exceptional visibility had shown a sea as innocent of shipping as at the day of creation. Not a coaster nor a fishing boat was abroad, and of the frigates that had been sent to prevent this French squadron sailing, there was not a sign. Holbrooke wasn't surprised. This evening, perhaps, he'd expect to see them creeping inshore past Point St. Matthews or rounding Ushant under full sail, but it was hardly reasonable to hope for them this forenoon.

That gave him a difficult choice. He could watch the French until the change of the watch, noting carefully what course they took once they had Ushant abeam, and then turn back to find the three reinforcing frigates and thus take the news back to Hawke. That was the safe choice, the classic role of a frigate to bring the battle squadrons into action. On the other hand, whatever course the French commander took from Ushant would open up a myriad of possible destinations. Everywhere from New England in the far west through a great arc past the Baltic and the low countries into the English Channel itself. Probably Ireland was the safest bet, but a squadron of that size could cause untold mischief and have an effect on the inevitable peace negotiations out of all proportion to its size.

***

CHAPTER TWELVE

Painful Memory

Saturday, Eighth of May 1762.
Argonaut, at Sea. The Iroise.

'Keep her hard on the wind, Mister Fairview. I'd like to pass ahead of that third rate if we can do so without suffering a broadside. What do you think?'

Fairview cocked his head and studied the wind on the dog-vane. *Argonaut* was undoubtedly head-reaching on the French squadron. Holbrooke's frigate was moving faster through the water and would pass ahead, but would the distance be great enough to avoid those huge thirty-six pounders?

'Touch-and-go, sir, I reckon.'

'Well, we can always tack and pass astern of them if it looks too tight. Just keep an eye on that fellow to leeward in case he has any ideas of blocking us.'

'Oh, he has a deal of work to do, sir. He'll be lucky to catch up with his friends before sunset. See how they're cracking on without any regard for him?'

Holbrooke had already noticed that. The threat of a British squadron coming down from windward must be tormenting that third rate's captain. Any French squadron that had the good fortune to pass through the Iroise unscathed would be doubly keen to avoid a blockading squadron.

'He's flying one of those *cornettes* at his main masthead, sir. What do they call their commodores? *Chef d'escadre,* isn't it?'

Holbrooke looked more closely. Shorrock was right, The seventy-four was flying the triangular flag that looked for all the world like a British commodore's pennant. That was to be expected with a force of two of the line and two frigates. Did that say anything about the experience of the

French commander? They'd put few enough squadrons to sea in this seventh year of the war, but this one would be derided as being too small for a very senior captain. So, perhaps – just possibly – this was a relatively junior man. And what did that say about their mission? Well, he could puzzle that out another time. For now, he must watch the bearing of the French third rate as though his life depended upon it, and given that he planned to cross its bows just beyond the range of its great guns, his life was certainly at hazard.

'The lead ship is faster than the second two-decker, sir. He was spilling his wind before to maintain his formation, but he's trimmed his sheets and he's pulling ahead now.'

A capful of spray caught Holbrooke square in the face and *Argonaut* lurched to larboard as a greater wave broke against the bow. They were well out of the lee of the islands now and the sea had an uninterrupted run from the northwest. The Frenchman had an extra deck and a deeper keel, and it was obvious that the waves were affecting the third rate less than they did *Argonaut*. She looked rock-steady, massive and dangerous as she shouldered the grey water aside.

'What do you think now, Mister Fairview?'

The sailing master grimaced as he studied the closing gap.

'If it's a full broadside that concerns you, well, it'll be a close-run thing, but if you want to avoid random shot then he could open fire in about ten minutes and have a fair chance of reaching us. We could tack now, sir, but in ten minutes we'll only have room to wear.'

Holbrooke took another appraising look. The sea took that opportunity to send a larger sheet of spray across the quarterdeck, soaking the quartermaster and the steersmen.

'You're right, Mister Fairview, this will never do. Bring the ship about, if you please, and clear the squadron's stern by five cables at least. We can work our way to windward before sunset, what with that sixty-four slowing them down.'

The bosun was expecting the order and the hands were at the tacks and sheets and braces before the words of command had left the sailing master's mouth. Holbrooke twisted around to check on the position of the frigate to leeward.

'He won't be bothering us, sir,'

Shorrock had left his guns to watch the unfolding race and now he took up a telescope to study the French squadron.

'I think we know one of those gentlemen over there, sir. If I'm not mistaken the seventy-four is *Robuste,* the very same that we chased out of the Vilaine estuary last summer, and the sixty-four is *Eveillé,* I'm certain.'

Holbrooke raised his own telescope. How could he have missed it? The image of that seventy-four emerging from the fog was seared into his brain, both waking and sleeping. He'd wanted to bring it to action with all his heart, and still did. He knew now that he'd almost destroyed himself in the attempt, and the extreme fatigue that resulted in a complete physical collapse had been brought on by his own determination, his refusal to take his rest while he was still able to stand. He knew all that, but still he wanted that ship with every fibre of his being.

Shorrock had his own telescope firmly focussed on the enemy ship's quarterdeck.

'That's him all right, sir, the same who had that ship last year; I'd recognise him anywhere. Nobody else on God's earth stands that straight, like he has a rammer for a backbone. See the way he turns his head and raises it in two separate motions? It's like a swivel gun with the training and elevation pins locked turn-and-turn about.'

Holbrooke steadied his telescope. He couldn't have said why this was so important to him, but Shorrock's identification had thrust everything else from his mind. For a moment nothing else existed, and the fact of his own ship manoeuvering in close proximity to a French squadron might have been a mere academic exercise, or a problem for someone else, a waking dream.

Yes, that was de Ternay, there was no possible doubt. The ink on his commission as a *capitaine de vaisseau* was hardly dry, and he must be the most junior post-captain in the French navy. The captain of the smaller third rate was likely many years his senior. How did they arrange such things in France? He didn't know as much as he should about his enemy's organisation for command at sea.

He lowered his telescope, feeling suddenly small and unsure of himself, and realised that his officers were watching him. Some stared open-mouthed and some observed from the corners of their eyes, but they all looked hastily away when he turned towards them. In a flash he understood what was happening. All of his officers had witnessed his collapse as this very same enemy ship escaped inside the Four Shoal at the east of Quiberon Bay and thence to the open sea. They must have wondered that day whether they'd ever see their captain again, or whether he was doomed to the life of an unemployed sea officer, languishing on half pay for want of the Admiralty Board's trust in his capacity for command. For their Lordships needed robust captains for their ships – how strange that his choice of adjective should mirror the name of his nemesis – and those found wanting must be discarded as one would cull the runt of the litter. His officers were morbidly fascinated in physical ailments, as everyone was when so many of their friends and family were carried off prematurely by disease and injury. They wanted to see his reaction. Nothing could have pulled him up like the thought of being an object of curiosity, even of pity, on his own quarterdeck, and his weakness was over so quickly that none noticed it, he thought.

'Well, gentlemen,' he demanded in a firm, dangerous voice, 'have you nothing better to do than to stare at your captain when you're under the guns of the enemy? I'll have every one of you attend to your duty and if I see another example of this behaviour then I'll be wanting to know the meaning of it. Mister Shorrock, what's the state of your guns? Mister Fairview, are we full and by? I haven't heard so. Mister Jackson, stir up those men at the sheets.'

The quarterdeck was suddenly abuzz with officers and petty officers finding that their duties occupied every fibre of their being. Not a man looked at his captain, and only the seamen smiled at the family drama that was played out before their eyes, for all but the newest and the most stupid knew about their captain's illness, although it was nearly a year old.

And yet, it would be wrong to say that all of his officers so studiously ignored their captain until his evil humour had worn off. David Chalmers had never seen himself as subject to the same constraints as the commissioned and warrant officers, and he watched Holbrooke carefully, albeit without meeting his eye. Yes, his young friend was still affected by that dreadful incident. It had been exhaustion and the stress of constant operations against a dangerous enemy that had caused his downfall. Fortunately, Lord Anson had been persuaded of that, rather than his collapse having been caused by some deep-seated malady. That was probably Admiral Forbes' work; he had a liking for Holbrooke and had been receptive when Chalmers had called on him as his friend was recovering. Yet he'd bear watching, Chalmers thought, as he quietly observed his subject.

'Full and by, sir, and we'll pass some six or seven cables astern of the frigate in the rear of the squadron.'

Fairview showed by the natural tone of his voice that he bore no grudge after having been so spoken to on the quarterdeck, and the other officers profited by his natural manner. The incident was all but over. Holbrooke looked around at each of his officers and was satisfied that they'd received his rebuke and returned to their duties. All but his chaplain, who met his eye and bowed fractionally. Holbrooke in his turn received the message: his friend knew what had caused the outburst and he was uneasy enough to make his concern known. Well, he could stand his chaplain's scrutiny and they could discuss it another time, in the privacy of the great cabin.

***

The ship had settled down to its task of following the French squadron and Chalmers, feeling for the letter that he'd kept in his pocket since they sailed from Portsmouth, saw his opportunity, and yet he sighed at the necessity.

'Mister Stitch, Mister Stitch, a moment of your time, if you please. Beside the taffrail, I think would be best, where we can't be overheard.'

Chalmers had no right to command, and he could expect no deference other than that owed to a man of the cloth, and most chaplains were dismayed to find that deference decayed at a frightful rate with each mile a ship sailed on a voyage. Chalmers had an advantage in that everyone knew he was a friend of the captain, but even so he had to ration the use of what little authority he had.

Joseph Stitch, however, had even less status. He was a volunteer, serving on board *Argonaut* at the captain's pleasure and he knew enough about the navy to be aware of how tenuous a hold he had on his position. Furthermore, he was fifteen and hoping to be made a midshipman. He was therefore very, very careful of his behaviour when confronted with anyone with a shred of influence over the captain. He didn't normally have a stutter, but Chalmers just made him nervous.

'Mister Chalmers, s-s-sir, h-h-how can I help you?'

'You can help me, Mister Stitch, by mending your ways.'

Chalmers fixed the young man with the sort of stare that was calculated to bring terror to anyone, certainly to an unrated volunteer in one of His Majesty's frigates, and particularly to one who laboured under a permanently guilty conscience. He let the accusation hang for a moment while Stitch's face grew paler.

'I received a letter from the captain's father on the day

that we sailed from Portsmouth. What might that have to do with you? You may well ask. Mister Holbrooke senior was approached in Wickham by your parents, now do you begin to understand?'

Stitch looked horrified. He couldn't tell exactly what he was being accused of, there were so many possibilities, but it certainly couldn't be good. He goggled at Chalmers and failed to make a sensible word come out of his mouth.

'*Argonaut* was in dock for a whole month while nameless operations were carried out on her bottom. A whole month, and you condescended to visit your parents for just one day, and not even the night. Furthermore, I understand that you wrote not a single letter home the whole time that we were in the Caribbean. Your mother complained that she learns more about you from Mrs Holbrooke than she does from your correspondence. I won't ask what kept you in Portsmouth, for I know very well that you couldn't have been berthed on board while the ship was in dock. That's between you and your conscience. So, if you're still wondering in what manner you can amend your ways, allow me to help you. First,' Chalmers counted the main headings on his fingers, 'you are to honour your father and your mother. I would have hoped that observing the fifth commandment would suffice to guide all of your conduct with respect to your parents, but in your case evidently not. Therefore, second, you are to write a letter to your mother every week – every single week, sir – and present it to me before you seal it. Third, you are to lodge at your family home whenever the ship is in Portsmouth, and you're favoured with leave; the pot houses of Portsmouth Point will flourish without your custom. Fourth… well I can't think of a fourth, but I'm sure something will occur to you when you review your own behaviour. Now, you may consider yourself fortunate that Mister Holbrooke the senior chose to inform me of your disgraceful conduct rather than addressing himself to his own son, for in that case I can assure you that the consequences to you would be truly dreadful. Now, go and sin no more.'

Stitch was utterly destroyed. He hung his head and shuffled off to his berth. It was fortunate indeed that he had the watch below for he was in no fit state to perform his duties on deck.

Chalmers watched him go and smiled wryly to himself. A good beating might have done the young man a world of good, but by the look on his face this public humiliation had an even more powerful effect; for many pairs of eyes had seen, even if they hadn't heard. He stood at the taffrail for a moment watching the coast of France slip away behind them.

'Mister Stitch is in trouble, I gather.'

'Oh, hello, Shorrock. No, not exactly in trouble, more in need of a little corrective conversation, if I may call it that.'

Shorrock laughed.

'A dozen of the best would have saved you a deal of wind, Chalmers. A dozen of the best for each offence and judging by the length of your *corrective conversation* there was more than one. Oh well, each to his own ways, I suppose.'

***

CHAPTER THIRTEEN

Where in the World?

Tuesday, Eleventh of May 1762.
Argonaut, at Sea. Ushant east-by-south 36 leagues.

'Another day, sir, and I could wish that those old hulks could make a little more speed to wherever they're going.'

Holbrooke ignored his first lieutenant. This speculation was doing no good at all, but every one of his officers was at it, and probably the whole of the lower deck too. On this heading the French could be destined for anywhere on the west coast of the British Isles and further north, or across the Atlantic to the Saint Lawrence and the American colonies. He mentally listed the possibilities; Scotland, Ireland, The Baltic, Newfoundland, Quebec, Nova Scotia, New England, New York. All of them offered opportunities for a surprise attack on British interests. And on reflection, they could even be heading for the Caribbean or the British colonies to the south of New York, or to rendezvous with a Spanish squadron in Florida or Cuba. It wasn't the fastest route, for that they'd have steered south for Madeira to pick up the trade winds, but with British squadrons holding Belle Isle and blockading every substantial Atlantic port from Brest to Cadiz, any French commodore would be well advised to make a bold offing before steering towards the sun. It would be two more days at least before the French showed their hand, and until then any attempt at guessing was probably futile.

'My guinea says Ireland, somewhere north of Bantry Bay.'

Fairview slapped his empty palm on the binnacle and stared hard at Shorrock, challenging him to take up the wager. Gambling was forbidden in King's ships, but if no money was actually shown, it was accepted with a nod and a grin. Certainly the quartermaster smiled; he was a keen illegal gambler himself, and the steersmen nodded in appreciation of this diverting entertainment. Probably there would be bets made over dinner after their watch on deck was over, their eavesdropping acquiring for them useful information to guide their betting, and from the best of authorities.

'Not Ireland, there are too few of them. They're reinforcements for Saint-Domingue, you mark my words. That's their last foothold in the Indies, and they won't want to lose it. They'll turn south as soon as they can clear Finisterre by fifty leagues. I'll take your bet.'

With that both men took up their telescopes and studied the French squadron to leeward, as though they expected a resolution of their wager there and then.

***

Holbrooke continued his pacing of the quarterdeck. It was all too easy for the captain of a man-of-war to grow idle and there were always good reasons to stay in his cabin, looking over the ship's books or attending to the myriad of administrative matters that their Lordships placed such emphasis upon. In principle, his first lieutenant and sailing master could handle everything that happened outside the great cabin, until the point where the ship beat to quarters, and he knew of many post-captains who took advantage of that to pursue their own interests. He had no great looking glass on board *Argonaut,* but when he'd last seen his reflection in his bedroom at Mulberry House, he was disgusted to see the start of an expanding belly. He knew that he was unusual in worrying about his waistline, in fact most people of his station in life thought it added gravitas to a person. Well, it certainly added *gravity,* and whatever Mister Newton said about its fundamental role in the universe, Holbrooke didn't like it. A couple of hours of stiff walking each day would, he hoped, keep himself in trim.

A day after they sunk Ushant, and with the French frigate back into its rightful position in the squadron, the friendly northerly wind had faltered and not even Fairview was prepared to guess where it would settle. Then as night fell the gathering clouds in the west settled the affair, and by dawn the French squadron was on the larboard tack, butting its way northwest into the growing westerly breeze. On their present course they were steering for the wild Atlantic coast of Ireland, but that did nothing to suggest their final destination, they'd be on this course even if they were bound for the south, to reduce the chance of running into a British squadron in the Bay of Biscay. *Argonaut* was faster than the heavy third rates and Holbrooke had worked his way up to windward and was now also on the larboard tack, heading for God-knew-where.

What concerned Holbrooke most was not, as might have been assumed, the eventual destination of the French squadron, but his own duty as a scout for Hawke's battle squadron. As far as he knew his was the only King's ship to witness the French escape from Brest. If the promised frigates had arrived in the Iroise, they'd be puzzled at *Argonaut's* absence, but with this westerly wind it would be too dangerous for them to penetrate far enough up the Goulet to see into the anchorage and deduce that their prey had fled. Probably they were keeping their offing to the west and expecting to see *Argonaut* at any moment.

It was the perennial contradiction in the duties of a frigate captain when he was operating alone. At what point did he abandon his pursuit of the enemy to carry the news back to the admiral? He could have done that two days ago, but all he'd have been able to report was the size of the French squadron and the bare fact of its escape into the wide Atlantic Ocean. He could imagine Hawke's frustration, not knowing where in the world the enemy was heading, and it would be an almost impossible task to find them again. He knew he was sticking his neck out in following the French so far to the west, and at some point he'd have to break away and report. He'd been gambling that he'd see another British man-of-war to carry his report back England, but the sea had remained stubbornly empty.

He was in a professionally dangerous position too. If he broke away now he'd have nothing more to tell Hawke than if he had steered for Torbay as soon as he'd seen the French out of the Iroise, and his report would be three days later than it might have been. On the other hand, he could follow the enemy for another month and still not be certain of their objective. And there was another problem: the French commander, probably by design, was heading for those unfrequented tracts of ocean that lay to the west of Ireland. Even with thousands of merchant ships and hundreds of men-of-war making a departure or a landfall at Ushant or Cape Clear the chances of an encounter were reducing by the hour.

Well, whatever he did, he'd be open to criticism. He'd follow for the rest of the day and when night fell and he could no longer be observed, he'd tack around the rear of the enemy and fly for Torbay with all the sail the frigate would carry. A few more turns on the quarterdeck and he'd call Shorrock and Fairview into the cabin and tell them his plan. He paused at the taffrail and studied the French for a moment. They were in good order now that the frigate that he'd mauled had patched up its rigging and sails, and he had to admit that it had been done in a seamanlike manner. He'd half expected the frigate to turn back for Brest, but a flurry of signal flags from the commodore had presumably made de Ternay's opinion quite clear. It looked as though *Argonaut* was not only faster and more weatherly than the third rates, but also had the legs of the two frigates. In fact, it looked as though the second frigate, the one that had not joined in the attempt to see *Argonaut* off, was armed *en flute*. Her tardiness in tacking had been easy to see, and she'd struggled to take in a reef when the wind came on to blow. It looked very much as though she was stuffed with soldiers at the expense of competent seamen. And there was something familiar about her even in her present reduced state, and Holbrooke couldn't quite decide whether they'd met before. Well, he had the rest of the day to puzzle it out and then this squadron would be of no more concern to him. He started to walk back to the binnacle to call his officers to his cabin.

'Sail ho! Sail to windward, eight points on the larboard bow. Right in the eye of the wind!'

Fairview didn't wait to consult his captain; he knew the urgency of identifying a sail to windward.

'Up you go, Mister Petersen. Quick as you can; whatever it is will be hull up in a few moments if it's sailing large.'

The master's mate barely paused to sling the deck telescope over his shoulder. Holbrooke watched as he swung easily over the lower futtock shrouds then lost sight of him behind the main tops'l. Fairview was right. If that vessel was running before the wind it would only be a matter of minutes before it was visible to the French. He had an advantage being to windward, but it would be short-lived.

'Deck there! It's a frigate, British I think and probably a fifth rate. All plain sail set to the t'gallants and running down to us. I can see sails beyond her, they look like merchantmen, but I can't be certain.'

'A convoy, sir, for sure. By God those French seventy-fours will give them a mauling.'

'Make the signal, enemy in sight to leeward, Mister Fairview.'

Holbrooke could see that the midshipman of the watch had already uncovered the signal locker and it looked like he was anticipating his captain's orders. It was a matter of seconds before the two flags were soaring up to the main masthead. That would alert the French of course. They wouldn't know the meaning of the flags; they could only guess, and for now, for perhaps another five more minutes, they wouldn't know whether that was a helpless convoy or a British battle squadron; would they be the hunters or the hunted?

A quick look over his shoulder told Holbrooke that the French squadron hadn't tacked, as they surely would if they were confident of the identity of those ships to windward. He'd have done the same. If it was a British battle squadron, then their present course was the best way to escape without running back to Brest. If it turned out to be a convoy, then de Ternay could tack later and still come up with them before the end of the day.

'Deck ho! A British fifth rate and at least six ships and brigs under convoy. I think I can see a sloop to windward of the merchantmen.'

'He'll come about as soon as his lookout reports those merchantmen,' Fairview looked at the dog-vane streaming away to leeward, 'and the wind's freshening.'

Holbrooke glanced at the frigate's tops'ls and t'gallants that could just be seen from the quarterdeck, then looked again at the French squadron. De Ternay would be hearing the first reports that the group of ships to windward was a lightly protected British convoy. Most likely they'd come from the West Indies or Virginia, loaded with sugar and indigo, or tobacco. In any case it would be a valuable cargo and easy pickings for two ships-of-the-line and two frigates. They could brush aside the convoy escort and only exceptionally poor seamanship would prevent them taking every one of those merchantmen. Even at this point in the war – no, particularly at this point in the war – it would be a shrewd blow against Britain if an entire West Indies or Virginia convoy was lost. It was the sort of event that could force Lord Egremont back to the negotiating table with a whole new attitude. And yet… and yet, Holbrooke didn't expect anything of the sort. He had a feeling about this de Ternay and his squadron. It can't have been sent out to prey upon enemy commerce; it was too big and soldiers weren't needed for that task. The flute that Holbrooke still hadn't had a good look at was completely the wrong vessel and all those soldiers that he'd seen on the deck would be wasted. And it wasn't like the French to make up a mission directive on the fly. That squadron had been sent out to make a raid on some British possession, or perhaps even to take and hold territory. In either case it was unlikely to be diverted from its task, however lucrative a target crossed its path.

'Beat to quarters, sir? We're already cleared for action.'

'I think not, Mister Shorrock. However, you can call all hands to bring the ship about.'

It was tempting to leave it at that, but he could see that all of his officers expected to be in action within the half hour. None had properly thought it through, and every one of them, if given the opportunity, would have had no hesitation in ravaging an enemy convoy, regardless of their orders.

'Unless I'm very much mistaken, our friends over there will ignore that convoy and press on to wherever they're bound. King Louis can't put many squadrons together – he doesn't have either the ships or the men – and this one's abroad on some particular errand. Put the ship about Mister Fairview and bring her under the lee of that frigate.'

***

She was *Lowestoffe,* a thirty-two-gun fifth rate armed with long twelve pounders, an altogether more substantial ship than the little *Argonaut*. Walter Stirling, her captain, had been posted eight months before Holbrooke, in the immediate aftermath of Howe's descents on the Normandy and Brittany coasts. They knew each other quite well as Stirling had commanded the fourteen gun sloop *Saltash* at Saint-Malo in 'fifty-eight and despite the disparity in ages – Stirling was well into his forties – they'd always got along. Stirling had eased his sheets to let his ship drop back onto the flank of the convoy, to keep between them and the French squadron, even though he knew that any resistance would be futile.

Fairview brought *Argonaut* alongside *Lowestoffe* within hailing range with the minimum of lost time, for time was of the essence, as they all knew. An hour running to leeward would require half a day's beating to windward to catch up with the French, and in that time the light would have started to fade, and a squall or thick weather could mean

An Upright Man

that the enemy would escape from their watcher entirely. *Lowestoffe* had her guns run out, boarding nets rigged and her yards chained, and Stirling clearly expected to fight.

'Who are those fellows, Holbrooke, and why have they ignored the convoy?'

A cross-wave rebounded from the larger frigate and slapped against *Argonaut's* fore-chains, sending a sheet of spray aft to sweep across the quarterdeck. Holbrooke wiped the salt water from his face.

'French squadron out of Brest, sir, only they know their destination. The seventy-four is *Robuste* but I don't know the others. I'd be obliged if you'd report our meeting to Admiral Hawke. With your permission, I plan to follow them until I know where they're bound.'

A shouted conversation was just possible, but it was difficult for Holbrooke from his position to leeward. He saw Stirling pause for a moment, apparently in thought. Stirling was the senior officer, and it was quite within his rights to order Holbrooke to take over the convoy while he followed the French. Holbrooke knew that would be the wrong decision. The convoy was important to British commerce, and it had been given a fifth rate with its greater weight of broadside just so that it could be properly defended from roving French frigates and privateers. *Lowestoffe* was no better suited than *Argonaut* to the task of shadowing the French, and each ship had already settled into its existing role. Probably all of those thoughts went through Stirling's mind, as did the certain knowledge that following the French was more likely to offer opportunities for recognition and prize money than shepherding a convoy into the Channel. Even at that range Holbrooke could see the momentary indecision but, to Stirling's credit, it was a passing thought.

'Very well, Holbrooke. I'll send Bourke ahead to seek out the Western Squadron.' He waved his arm to windward where the sloop had closed in on the convoy in the expectation of being needed. 'He's to take *Merlin* directly to

Deptford for coppering, so it'll suit us all. You have no idea of their destination?'

'No, sir. They've embarked soldiers and one of those frigates is a flute. It could be Ireland or America or Saint-Domingue, even the Baltic.'

'Well then, you'd better be off before you lose sight of them. I'll send a note to Ann when I reach Portsmouth, to say that I spoke with you.'

Holbrooke waved as Fairview brought *Argonaut* in a great sweeping curve away from the larger frigate and hard on the wind in pursuit of the French. It was a neat piece of work all around, and as Holbrooke took a last look at *Lowestoffe*, he saw a hoist of flags soar aloft, and almost before it had reached the masthead he saw the little *Merlin* bear away and start threading through the merchantmen to close on the frigate.

***

'You didn't mention the French commodore's name, George. You must have had a reason.'

Holbrooke and Chalmers were enjoying coffee and a platter of small cakes in the great cabin. They were the last of the fresh delicacies that Ann had sent away with him from Portsmouth. They weren't quite in their prime, but nor were they entirely stale, not by seagoing standards in any case. The wind had risen since they'd spoken to *Lowestoffe*, and they sat braced in chairs that were lashed to eyebolts in the deck. Fairview had been told to crack on to catch the French before nightfall and he'd taken his captain literally, spreading whole tops'ls and t'gallants to be certain of not losing sight of their enemy in the gathering gloom.

'I suppose I didn't want them to take this expedition lightly. De Ternay has been a captain for less than a year and it stretches credulity that he'd have been given a pennant already. Yet I'm sure that it's him. You get a feeling for your opponent, you know. This man is audacious and inventive, just like the man who outwitted us so thoroughly last year. If I were sat in the Admiralty boardroom and being told this story of a man who was a lieutenant only last year commanding an important expedition, I'd be tempted to discount the whole story; the flute, the soldiers, even the two third rates.'

'You don't give their Lordships much credit for imagination then.'

'Oh, I'm sure they're the very models of visionary thought. But Anson's about to go, or has already gone for all I know, and Lord Halifax is a politician and no seaman. It's better all round if I let them make their own suppositions without burdening them with mine. In any case, there's little that they can do without knowing where de Ternay is bound, and by the time they hear about it, the mischief will be done. It matters not a jot nor a tittle who commands them, my job now is at least clear; I have to follow them until I'm certain of their intentions. And there's another thing. Until a few hours ago de Ternay could have assumed that his escape from Brest could remain a secret for days or even weeks. Not now, not after he saw us alongside *Lowestoffe*. He must assume that pursuit is not far behind.

***

CHAPTER FOURTEEN

Fog on the Banks

Monday, Twenty-First of June 1762.
Argonaut, at Sea. Cape Race, Newfoundland, west-southwest 50 leagues.

'Lookout reports they're still right ahead at two miles, sir. All over the place, they are, some on the larboard tack, some on the starboard. I've sent Petersen up for a look.'

Fairview offered the speaking trumpet in anticipation of another hail from aloft. He knew that his captain liked to speak directly to the young officers when they had something to say from the masthead.

Holbrooke briefly thought about climbing to the masthead himself, but he knew he could do no better than his master's mate, and all he'd achieve would be to humiliate himself in front of the watch on deck. He did go aloft occasionally, when the bosun had something to show him – a worn stay or a patch of rot in the hounds, perhaps – but as a rule he left it to his younger officers. It wasn't a lack of ability – he told himself – but a captain's place was on the quarterdeck. Well, he knew of few post-captains who would risk their dignity by climbing to the very topmast head when there was a perfectly capable young gentleman to hand, and the last thing he wanted was to be pointed out as an eccentric.

'Captain, sir.'

Holbrooke looked up but nothing could be seen past the maintop. The fog was as thick as pea soup and there was hardly a breath of air to disperse it. The only redeeming feature was that the thick weather was confined to a thin band close to the surface. At the main topmast head the weak midsummer sun showed through the thinning layers and apparently the enemy squadron's t'gallants were perfectly visible.

'Oh, go on, Mister Petersen.'

It was his own fault. He'd schooled his officers to ensure that he had their attention before making their report, if it wasn't urgent. But really, the man must know that his captain was waiting on his word. He'd have to curb this irritability. He knew its cause well enough; it was the stress of following a powerful enemy squadron across the Atlantic for – what was it? – more than six weeks now. He'd ensured that his officers and men had enough rest but there was only one captain and with the enemy so close, he had to be constantly alert. He'd endured a lecture from Chalmers only that morning, warning him that he was heading for a collapse like he'd suffered in Quiberon Bay the year before. But really, he felt quite well, just a little on edge, perhaps.

'The nearest one is two miles right ahead, sir. It looks like the fifth rate with her head to the south. If that's so then the flute is ahead of her, and the two ships-o'-the-line are abreast of each other perhaps five cables beyond the flute. It looks like the big frigate has dropped astern to cover the flute, sir, but now she's lost the wind entirely and the other three are still making way.'

'What's their heading, Mister Petersen?'

There was a short pause presumably while the master's mate consulted the lookout who'd been up there for nearly half a glass and would at least have seen a trend.

'West-nor'west, sir, as best as I can judge. Ah, the three in the lead have the wind but the last one's still becalmed.'

Holbrooke looked up at the sails to determine what wind his own ship had, but there was nothing useful to be gained from that limp and sagging canvas. The dog vane was moving, however. There was just enough breeze to lift it from the vertical and give an indication of where the wind lay.

'Northerly, sir, what there is of it. It's bringing that cold air down from the Labrador Sea and when it meets this warmer water from the Atlantic Drift, it all gets pushed up over the Banks. Well, this is what you get.'

Fairview swept his hand around the fog-enshrouded deck. If anything, it was getting thicker and a quick look aloft confirmed that even the maintop was now lost from sight.

'Mister Petersen,' Holbrooke used the speaking trumpet to direct his voice into the heavens, 'you'll oblige me by staying up there for the time being.'

'Aye-aye sir.'

If Petersen resented having to stay at the masthead, he successfully kept it out of his voice. In fact, he sounded positively cheerful. But then, it wasn't cold up there even with the frigid northerly airs and the clammy fog. It was difficult to remember that this was the longest day of the year and today the sun would be at its highest. Midsummer on the Grand Banks, and he was cold and wet and irritable. Perhaps where the fog was thin at that height, Petersen could feel its warming rays. Down on deck it felt that the world would never really become tolerably warm. Today, was a day for waistcoats and frock coats, for comforters and mittens, in defiance of the calendar.

'Captain, sir. There's quite a gap opening between the lead three ships and the fifth rate, and the fog's getting deeper. They'll lose sight of each other soon, I reckon.'

'Can you still see them all, Petersen?'

'Yes, sir, but only the t'gallants of the leading three now. The fog between us and the fifth rate is thinner than it is further to the west. Oh, I've lost sight of the ships-o'-the-line and the flute now.'

'Can you still see the fifth rate?'

'Yes, sir, his head's still to the south and he seems entirely becalmed.'

'Let me know if you lose sight of him.'

***

Holbrooke wanted time to think, to stride the length of the quarterdeck without any interruption. He saw Shorrock brush away the purser who was approaching him with a handful of dockets. Really the man should understand the danger of this situation, the perils and the opportunities.

On one hand, he could take *Argonaut* down upon that fifth rate. He could burst out of the fog and give the Frenchman a raking broadside that would knock half the fight out of him before he'd even begun. He could… but that wasn't his task, that wasn't why he'd followed this squadron clear across the Atlantic to this God-forsaken part of the world. If he engaged the frigate, his ship would inevitably be damaged and just as inevitably he'd be unable to follow the remainder of the squadron. At the worst he could be defeated. One look at Shorrock told him that his first lieutenant wanted with all his heart to dash wildly at the enemy, and in a curious way that cleared his mind. There would be no mad heroics today; that wasn't where his duty lay. He'd embrace the fog. He'd use it to slip past the fifth rate and resume his dogged shadowing of the main part of the enemy force.

'Mister Fairview, your best approximation now, where are they heading? You thought Louisbourg or the Gulf of Saint Lawrence yesterday, but they seem to have trended to the nor'west even though the wind's in the north.'

'One moment, sir, if you please, and I'll bring up a chart.'

Now that was a momentous event. The sailing master usually kept his precious charts firmly below decks, away from the salt water and the wind. To bring one of them on deck was unusual, and in this damp, clinging fog, completely unheard of.

'Here, sir, if you please.'

The quartermaster swept the dew from the binnacle with the palm of his hand, then covered it with a clean, dry piece of sailcloth that he kept handy for just such a need; he had a healthy respect for the master's charts.

'Now, that's my reckoned position, just fifty leagues from Cape Race, as you can see, and on the nor'east point of the Grand Banks. If we had leisure we could take a cast of the deep-sea lead, but I'm confident that we'd find twenty-five or thirty fathoms. Just look at this fog and that short sloppy sea. It's exactly what you'd expect here in June. Now, given that, it looks like those gentlemen are steering for the Avalon peninsula, for St. John's or for one of the other harbours to the south.'

Fairview looked again at the chart and drew a line with his finger along the course that Petersen had suggested the squadron was steering. He scratched his head and looked again.

'The strange thing is, sir, that the obvious destination is St. John's. It's not exactly the capital of the territory, there's no such formal structure on Newfoundland, but it's the largest place, the first among equals you could say. However, they're steering too far south by about a whole point. You haven't seen the fisheries at these places I gather, sir?'

'I've never been north of New York on this side of the ocean, Mister Fairview, not even as far as Boston.'

'Well, not wishing to sound like Methuselah,' Fairview launched straight into his explanation, 'but I spent a season bringing supplies to the fishery, between the wars. There's no organization of civil society here, no colonial capital, no concept of the smaller places taking orders from the greater. Each of the principal havens, St. John's and Placentia, send their catch and receive their sustenance from England directly. It's only the governor that holds it all together and then strictly in a defensive sense, and only while the fishery's active. There are half a dozen smaller places that come and go as the season starts and ends. I say all this because the common opinion in England is that St. John's acts as some sort of capital, rather like Boston or Williamsburg; but it doesn't, far from it, and a landing in any place that serves the fisheries will be almost as dangerous as a landing at St. John's.'

Fairview realised that he was close to committing the sin of lecturing his captain and his monologue ended as abruptly as it had begun. He regrouped and fell back on the more familiar subject of navigation.

'What I'm saying, sir, is that they've been steering too far south when they've had every opportunity to make directly for St. John's. The sun was clear at noon yesterday and they'd have had a good latitude from the meridian passage, so they must know their northing. It appears to me that they're making more for the centre of the east coast of the Avalon Peninsula, not for St. John's, nor south enough to round Cape Race for Placentia.'

Holbrooke studied the chart. The coast that Fairview was considering was studded with deep bays and inlets and, although he hadn't been here before, Holbrooke knew that many of them, perhaps all, had their own thriving small-scale fishery. The destruction of any one of them would be a useful gain for France, but hardly a suitable objective for a squadron such as this. The line that Fairview had drawn with his finger ended close to one of those inlets, Bay of Bulls it was called.

'What do you know about this place, Mister Fairview?'

'Oh, I was never there, but I heard it was a small affair, just like many others. Nothing but a shingle beach with a score of drying racks and a few huts. Even so, it was home to a fair flotilla of Banks fishers.'

Could de Ternay be intending to pick these places off one-by-one? A squadron of the size that he commanded would hold the keys to the coast. Even if the governor of the Newfoundland fishery had arrived for the season – Holbrooke had heard that it was Graves in the fourth rate *Antelope,* last heard of awaiting a convoy at the Downs –he could do nothing against two third rates. In fact, with so many ships sent south to the invasion of Cuba, there weren't enough ships-of-the-line in the whole of Colville's North American command to oppose the French squadron. De Ternay could pick off the Newfoundland harbours at his leisure. Even Louisbourg, taken by assault from its French creators less than four years ago, wasn't beyond the bounds of possibility, for surely all the regular British regiments would also have been sent south. Was this the time to break off from the French squadron? To take advantage of this northerly wind to run down to Halifax and alert Colville.

'Mister Petersen,' Holbrooke turned his head to call up into the covering fog, 'can you see the third rates now?'

'No sir, the fog's thick down that way. The frigate's still in sight, sir, struggling to bring her head to the west.'

'Very well then. Mister Fairview, I'm satisfied that they're heading to St. John's or somewhere else to the north of Cape Race. In any event it's not the Saint Lawrence nor New England. That being the case, we've done our duty. Call all hands and we'll bear away for Halifax, secure the guns and revert to two watches. Keep a close lookout for fishermen, if you please; I'll be in my cabin.'

Just a few steps and he could relax. His ship would be drawing a dozen miles away from the enemy with each watch that passed and all he had to do was make the best speed to alert the commander-in-chief. He had plenty of time to draft his report as *Argonaut* couldn't possibly make Halifax in less than four days, not against the Atlantic Drift, not even if this northerly wind held. He'd forego his dinner and have his servant make up his cot, then he'd fall into a deep sleep until supper.

'Deck ho! There's another sail close in by the French frigate. It looks like one of those big Banks schooners, sir. The frigate's caught some wind and he's bearing away, looks like he's reaching across towards the schooner.'

Damn! Holbrooke turned on his heel and strode back to the binnacle, all thoughts of sleep shattered in an instant. No King's officer could ignore a clear and present threat to a Grand Banks fishing schooner. A more general, hypothetical threat such as the French squadron posed to the fishing bases could be set aside for the greater good of carrying the news to the commander-in-chief, but not this.

'We've a little wind now, sir, and it's from the north. Just a light air but we have steerage way.'

'Very well, Mister Fairview. Put her on the starboard tack and reach down to that Frenchman. Mister Shorrock, I believe the ship's still cleared for action. Then beat to quarters, if you please.'

***

Now, wasn't this a microcosm of life in a King's ship? One moment you're settling down to a four-day passage with little chance of contact with the enemy, and the next you're buckling your sword belt ready for imminent, violent action. Holbrooke looked around at the hurrying figures. In principle the men needed only to go to their quarters where all was already cleared for action. In practice there were a thousand and one things to check, from the priming in the great guns to the water in the fire buckets.

'Cleared for action, sir, and the quarters are manned.'

'Thank you, Mister Shorrock. A very creditable performance after six weeks waiting. Do you see the situation? We must prevent that Frenchman taking a prize. It's perhaps too much to expect that he'll become our prize, but at least we can let the fisherman escape, and where there's one there are likely to be others. But I can't help wondering what this captain thinks he's doing. Surely to God de Ternay will have told him that he's to stay with the squadron at all costs. Whatever that squadron has been sent from Brest to achieve, it's not furthered by this kind of squabble over a few barrels of fish.'

'A fair prize is a hard thing to pass up though, and his commodore's out of sight. Do you think there's some tension there, sir? If that is de Ternay's pennant then this frigate commander is very likely to have been posted a good few years before him. I heard that apart from de Ternay and the other fellow who helped bring those ships out of the Vilaine, there've been no promotions in the French navy for a couple of years. Perhaps this captain's exercising what he sees as his rights of seniority.'

Holbrooke said nothing although his thoughts had been

following along similar lines. There *must* be an undercurrent of dissent in that squadron. If so, then this is what de Ternay must expect and dread, his subordinate captains acting as they wish whenever they were out of sight.

'Deck ho! The fog's lifting. I can see the Frenchman clearly now; he's still moving towards the schooner.'

Holbrooke heard the flat sound of a gun, its usual sharp crack deadened by the fog.

'The schooner's boats are stretching out to reach her, sir, and she's already setting sail and casting her head to the west.'

The fog was indeed lifting. All of a sudden Holbrooke could see the foremast, then the bowsprit and then a clear sea half a mile ahead. *Argonaut* was turning fast towards the west and then, in the interval between two heartbeats, the two vessels leapt suddenly into sight. The frigate was moving slowly towards the schooner and the Frenchman's longboat was alongside and being manned. The schooner had clearly been about its business of fishing, even in this foul weather, and its boats were scattered across the face of the sea. Holbrooke counted six but there could be more lost in the fog. They were little shell-like craft that nested inside one another to save space on the deck, and now they were rowing as though their lives depended upon it while their schooner was gaining speed in a desperate race to avoid capture.

***

CHAPTER FIFTEEN

A Banks Schooner

Monday, Twenty-First of June 1762.
Argonaut, at Sea. Cape Race, Newfoundland, west-southwest 50 leagues.

Holbrooke stared at the French frigate's stern then brought his telescope up to his eye. He could see a name against a brown background, but the white paint had been eroded and dulled by the Atlantic weather and he couldn't make it out.

'*Garonne*, sir, two Ns and an E. Not a name that I'm familiar with.'

Shorrock sounded positive. Holbrooke wiped the lens and looked again. Yes, he could see it now that the telescope wasn't misted by the dew. That was a relief; he was starting to believe that everyone in his ship had better eyes than him. He could accept that in his midshipmen and master's mates and his young topmen, but his first lieutenant was considerably older.

'I heard of her before we left Portsmouth,' Holbrooke replied, for want of being the first to read the name, 'she was reported as fitting out for sea. Thirty-four guns, twelves on the lower deck and eights on the upper. A tough nut to crack, Mister Shorrock. We did well to keep her at arm's length.'

'Aye sir, but she's encumbered with soldiers.'

Shorrock had a poor opinion of armies and in any case he thought nothing of pitting a sixth rate against a fifth. He couldn't imagine that an energetic captain might have trained up at least some of his embarked soldiers to be useful in an engagement, and a six-week passage had given him plenty of time. Holbrooke shrugged it off. He had no intention of closing to a range where the issue would be decided by musketry, nor would he board a ship so overborne with fighting men. He still had to carry the word of this expedition back to Halifax, and that duty trumped every other consideration. He'd protect the schooner, if he could, but he wouldn't risk disabling his ship in the process. There was one thing; he now knew the identity of three of de Ternay's squadron, it was just the flute that still eluded him. Yet there was something about that smaller frigate; he felt that they'd met before, somewhere.

'He's seen us, sir. What will he do now? He won't want to be caught with his longboat in the water.'

Shorrock's commentary was starting to wear on Holbrooke. He could send the first lieutenant forward to see to his guns, but that would be an obvious snub. Anyone could see that the batteries were all cleared away and the gun crews looked relaxed and eager and were in no need of further instruction.

'Ah, he's calling in his boat's crew. He didn't expect us to come out of the fog like that. He probably thought he'd lost us in the night.'

'He's come to his senses, Mister Shorrock. He'd have been quite happy to take a prize and then catch up with his commodore, but he'll know that he won't be thanked for risking his ship in another fight with us. He'll tack again, or wear, and follow the squadron.'

'He doesn't have enough way on, he'll miss stays if he tries to tack. Ah, there he goes, he's put his helm up, he's wearing. That longboat is dragging though.'

It certainly was. Holbrooke could see that the Frenchman was caught in a dreadful position. His clear duty was to catch up with his squadron that was last seen heading up to the northwest. The French captain's problem was that he'd lost all of his way when he tacked to close the schooner and then backed his tops'ls to bring his longboat alongside. Now, in this weak, fitful wind, he could only take a leisurely turn to starboard to complete the circle and hope that the longboat wouldn't create so much resistance that it would prevent him wearing ship.

'Where's the schooner, Mister Fairview?'

'Almost abeam, sir, no more than six cables. He's tacked and heading nor'east. Two of his boats are alongside. It looks like he's seen the situation. Ah, he's heaving to for the remainder.'

Then he could forget the schooner. As soon as he collected in his boats he'd be off to whatever port in Newfoundland he called home. That was good, and he'd no doubt bring the word that there was a French frigate approaching the coast. But would he be believed? The fishery was an important business, and it would take some very persuasive intelligence to interrupt the steady stream of vessels heading out to the Banks.

'Mister Shorrock. Stand by the larboard battery. We may be able to rake her at long range as she wears. Load with chain shot after the first broadside. Mister Fairview, you see the situation? I want to keep the weather gage. Don't come too close, five cables will be well enough.'

***

Holbrooke felt his ship come up a point. *Argonaut* was hard on the wind now, what little there was of it. If *Garonne* continued her turn to starboard then her stern would be exposed to a raking broadside. It would be long range for Shorrock's guns, but at least it would reduce the risk of damage to *Argonaut*. It was a strange situation. Unless he'd misunderstood the French squadron's objective, *Garonne's* captain should do anything to avoid a fight with a British frigate, even one so much smaller than himself. His attempt at an easy prize had been thwarted and now he should make best speed to rejoin his commodore. And yet, there was something unusual about this expedition and particularly this frigate. Its captain didn't seem to conform to the usual behaviours that Holbrooke would have expected. Would he continue the turn and wear ship? Was there the hint of a hesitation there?

'He's bracing his yards, sir. I do believe he intends to run down on us, and the wind's backed a few points, sir, do you feel it?'

Holbrooke saw the danger immediately. The larger frigate with the wind on its quarter could dictate the terms of an engagement. If he'd ever intended to bring his ship all the way around, this French captain had clearly changed his mind. In these light airs the situation was developing at an agonising pace. He could see the white-clad soldiers mustering on the frigate's deck, and he could see the guns run out ready to deliver their broadside. No, this would never do. It would be a miracle if he avoided being boarded, and then he knew that it would all be over. His men couldn't resist an assault by what looked like a whole company of trained infantrymen.

'Will she stay, Mister Fairview?'

'Aye sir, she'll come through the wind alright, but it'll be slow.'

'Bring her about then. Mister Shorrock, the larboard battery. You should get at least one chance at her bows.'

He could see the disappointment in Shorrock's face, but he had no time for his first lieutenant's fighting madness. The situation had changed in an instant. For six weeks they'd become accustomed to the idea that they could follow the enemy squadron with impunity, relying on its commodore's sense of his duty to avoid a fight with an obviously capable British frigate. But the paradigm had changed, and this French captain had other ideas. Probably he was smarting from the way *Argonaut* had dealt with him in the Iroise, and now that he wasn't under his commodore's eye, he was determined to get his revenge. Holbrooke knew that he should have anticipated this move. The signs were all there after all, and the next few minutes would determine his fate. If he could keep enough distance from the Frenchman then he had a good chance of escaping. If he should be boarded, or even if he should fall within easy range of those twelve pounder guns, it would all be over.

***

It was all happening so slowly. *Argonaut* had just enough speed for her bows to come through the wind, but it was with painful deliberation. She was slow, but the Frenchman was no faster.

'Full and by, sir.'

Fairview was rooted to the spot, watching for any sign of the frigate starting to luff. *Argonaut* had naturally lost speed in tacking but now, with the wind on her larboard bow, she was gathering speed.

Garonne looked huge. The French frigate was under tops'ls and t'gallants with her courses furled. Her captain clearly knew his business and he was steering a course to intercept *Argonaut*.

Fairview looked over his shoulder at the approaching menace.

'She's a slug, sir. We'd have a knot over her before the wind.'

Holbrooke recognised his sailing master's less-than-subtle suggestion that he should bring *Argonaut* off the wind. And he was right, in a way. *Argonaut* was certainly the faster ship, sailing both by and large, and if he turned to the southeast now, it would be a stern chase. If the Frenchman couldn't bring down an important spar in his first salvo, *Argonaut's* escape was all but assured. But a southeast course would carry *Argonaut* away from Newfoundland and away from Halifax. If the weather didn't change, every hour with the wind at their stern would take at least four to make up when they'd shaken off the Frenchman.

'Larboard battery ready, sir.'

'On my whistle, Mister Shorrock. I want every shot aimed and then you may reload with chain.'

The sun had at last broken through. To the south the horizon was clear but the French squadron was still hidden by the fog. How far away would they be? They seemed to have a breeze when they were last seen, so they could easily be five or six miles to the northwest. Holbrooke looked all around the horizon. There were no more fishermen and the schooner was just taking in the last of her boats. *Garonne's* bow was creeping to larboard as she sought to close with the British frigate.

Six cables. It was too far, really, but Holbrooke wanted at least one broadside of chain shot. There was no question of winning this fight, he just needed to survive so that he could carry the news to Halifax. Round shot could smash through oak planks, it could unseat cannon and it could maim and kill the gun crews, but it was chain shot or bar shot that caused havoc in an enemy's rigging. Holbrooke raised his whistle and blew a single, short note.

Crash!

Argonaut's guns fired almost as one and even before the smoke had dispersed in the idle breeze, the crews were running in the guns, worming, sponging and reloading with the cumbersome chain shot.

Holbrooke watched the bows of the French frigate. It was long range but he was certain of at least one hit, low down below the ship's head. It had no noticeable effect and *Garonne* stood on as boldly as ever.

'Fire as each gun is on target, Mister Shorrock.'

The first lieutenant grinned through the powder smoke that was already blackening his face, then he turned back to his guns.

Bang!

The first load of chain shot went howling across the stretch of water and a hole opened in *Garonne's* fore tops'l. Her topmen were aloft now, letting fall the t'gallants to close the range faster. Would the courses stay furled? They'd be a huge inconvenience for the Frenchman's gunnery, and they'd be a desperate hindrance in the fine work of bringing the frigates to close quarters for boarding. But if *Argonaut* bore away and it turned into a stern chase, *Garonne* would need every sail drawing, for *Argonaut* had not furled a yard of canvas, but was under all plain sail.

Bang! Bang!

Argonaut's guns spoke at irregular intervals as Shorrock

and the quarter gunners ran from gun to gun, ensuring that they were trained and elevated to give the best chance of a debilitating hit on the enemy. It had a feeling of unreality. The ships were barely moving in this lightest of airs and *Garonne,* intent, it appeared, on closing to board *Argonaut,* had not a gun that could bear, but came on in a stoical silence.

Bang! Bang!

The range was closing slowly and Shorrock's men had found their true elevation. Every chain shot seemed to reach its mark and *Garonne's* rigging was festooned with parted halyards and sheets and braces while her sails were peppered with holes. But it hardly mattered with this wind at her stern. The minutes passed and still *Argonaut* had not been subject to a single shot in reply to the bombardment that had been directed at *Garonne.*

'He's luffing a little, sir, more than he needs to.'

Fairview was right and Holbrooke could see what was happening. In following a pursuit course to close with *Argonaut,* the French ship had come further and further off the wind and the angle between the two ships' heads had become more and more acute. Just a slight luff would allow the Frenchman to fire with at least her forward division of guns.

'Any moment now…'

Garonne's opening shots went almost unnoticed against the near constant bellowing of *Argonaut's* guns and the howling of the chain shot. Holbrooke had just a moment to notice that the Frenchman had opened fire a minute too soon and the guns, even trained as far forward as they'd go, ploughed up the water half a cable astern of *Argonaut.*

'They won't make that mistake again, sir. Look, he's coming right around now.'

Holbrooke took a quick look. Sure enough, *Garonne* was hauling her wind and coming around onto a course that would be nearly parallel to *Argonaut.* Too soon, too soon, he thought. A full broadside from the Frenchman would surely achieve a few hits if directed at *Argonaut's* beam, but it would be bad luck if they did any real damage.

'Up helm, Mister Fairview, bring us two points off the wind.'

That would open the range slowly and give the French captain a choice after this broadside. He could hold his course for another broadside but then the range would open steadily, or he could bear away and hold his fire until the distance between the two ships had decreased enough to ensure more hits. Well, having the faster ship, Holbrooke could play this game all day, so long as his luck held.

Boom!

He heard the Frenchman's full broadside this time and he felt the shock as at least two twelve pound balls slammed into his hull.

'He's bearing away again, sir.'

Now the enemy's problem was even greater for he'd need to come three points further off the wind to start closing the range again, and even that would be slow.

'He's lost at least half a cable there, sir. He'll drop some of his broadside short next time.'

Holbrooke hardly noticed his own ship's guns as they fired away in ones and twos. And they were certainly having an effect. *Garonne's* fore tops'l was so mangled that he'd felt the need to set the fore course to keep the ship's head off the wind. He could only see the enemy's quarterdeck for short intervals when he yawed, so the captain must have only an imperfect view of the British frigate.

'The schooner's out of sight now, sir.'

'Did he collect all his boats, Mister Fairview?'

'He did, sir, every last one and then he wasted no time in tacking to the north.'

'And our friend over there, will he be able to wear ship with his heads'ls and fores'ls all shot up?'

Fairview smiled through the enshrouding smoke.

'He can try, sir, but he can whistle for it. Look at the state of that fore tops'l and the jib and stays'l.'

Fairview looked up at the commissioning pennant hanging limp from the main masthead.

'He'll be thankful for having his longboat in the water just to get his head around, whether he tacks or wears. Either way, we'll be long gone, sir.'

'Very well, Master, wear ship, if you please. Mister Shorrock, you'll get a few shots in from the larboard battery then a broadside of ball with the starboard after we've worn.'

'West-sou'west to weather Cape Race, sir, then half a point west for Halifax.'

'Then make it so, Mister Fairview, make it so.'

***

'I'm intrigued to know, Carter, was that a stroke of true genius or mere good fortune? We were under the guns of a frigate with twice our weight of shot, I understand, for over an hour and yet we suffered only a few trivial holes in our upperworks, and that splinter wound for the quarter gunner, who I suspect will count it as a blessing when he gets his smart ticket.'

Chalmers and Shorrock were alone in an unusually empty wardroom as *Argonaut* sped towards Cape Race on a close reach. After one failed attempt at wearing ship that had caused huge mirth on *Argonaut's* quarterdeck, *Garonne* hadn't even tried to pursue them, but had hauled her wind to the nor'east to start the long beat to catch up with her squadron.

Shorrock took a sip of his brandy. He normally drank rum, but it was a brandy day today.

'It's hard to tell because he won't say what's on his mind until he's ready to do it. Did he plan all of that? I think not, but that's not to belittle his skill. He's a master of improvisation. He has a scheme that he works out but won't tell and then as he sees the situation change, he alters the plan. The likes of me have no chance of following his reasoning.'

'That Frenchman then was thoroughly duped, I gather.'

'Oh yes. He was confident that he had us. He thought it would take the whole day but unless the fog set in again he'd be alongside before the last dog. Then we wouldn't have stood a chance, not with all those soldiers pouring over the gunwale.'

'But was there no risk to us? Any one of those shot could have carried away an important yard and then we'd have been in trouble.'

Shorrock grinned in his wicked way.

'We certainly would, David, we certainly would. But that's what makes it all so interesting, don't you see? If we could make a foolproof plan and then settle back to execute it in the certainty that it would lead to riches and honours, where would that leave us? No, it's that element of fortune, of luck that makes life worth living. You men of the cloth may have your own views, but for me, life's a gamble and I wouldn't have it any other way.'

Shorrock smiled and looked thoughtful.

'But I'll tell you this, David. It's a very good thing to roll your dice when a man like Captain Holbrooke has already loaded them for you!'

***

CHAPTER SIXTEEN

The First Blow

Wednesday, Twenty-Third of June 1762.
Robuste, at Sea. off Bay of Bulls, Newfoundland.

De Ternay scanned the horizon and the unhospitable shore. It was a pitiless place, all forbidding cliffs and grey seas with never a splash of colour to please the eye. No, that wasn't quite true. At the very summit of the cliffs he could see the dull green that suggested a scrubby sort of vegetation. There was nothing else, no fringe of yellow gorse and even at this peak of the growing season, no sign of flowering plants. In fairness, he was two miles off the land, as close as he dared go without good charts, even in this offshore breeze, and he couldn't have seen a flowering meadow if there had been one. He'd made all the allowances that he could for a place situated so unfavourably, but still, it was a dismal land.

'The cutter's returning, sir.'

De Ternay liked his flag captain. He was the only one of his senior officers who managed to hide his resentment at de Ternay's meteoric rise from lieutenant to commodore, but even with him, his conversation was short to the point of rudeness. Each of the captains of the other ships were more-or-less openly hostile and he knew that he couldn't let them out of his sight. That buffoon who commanded *Garonne* was a prime example. He'd managed to lose himself in the fog on the Grand Banks then took it upon himself to attempt taking a prize only to be chased off by that damned British frigate. The fishing schooner would be in St. John's by now telling his tale of an enemy squadron, of a battle on the Banks and an imminent invasion. He should call for a court martial upon the man, but he wasn't at all confident that the other captains wouldn't close ranks and find him not guilty; it just wasn't worth the risk.

'Very well, Captain, I'll see the cutter's lieutenant in my cabin. If the Comte should ask after me, you can say that I'll see him a half hour after the boat's alongside.'

De Ternay desperately wanted to hear about this Bay of Bulls before the brigade commander. He'd deliberately sent the boat in without any soldiers so that he could control the information that would be gained. D'Haussonville still held to the idea that his brigade should be put ashore at St. John's. It was always a dangerous plan but now that the British had been alerted, it was positive madness. He turned away and strode back into the great cabin to await the lieutenant.

***

The cutter's lieutenant lived in fear of de Ternay and still hadn't recovered from the interview after the action in the Iroise. His report was short and to the point and he almost ran out of the great cabin when he was dismissed.

D'Haussonville was a different matter entirely. He was older than de Ternay, he held a loftier position in French society and until this expedition his military rank far exceeded de Ternay's. They hadn't openly clashed on the passage but now that the time had come to make some definite decisions about the use of the landing force, the tensions had come to the surface.

'Then there are no defences whatsoever in this Bay of Bulls, Monsieur de Ternay? Does that not strike you as a little too convenient?'

'It suggests to me, Monsieur d'Haussonville, that the British have concentrated their defences in St. John's and Placentia, the principal towns of this region…'

'Exactly. And that is where we should strike, not in some remote fishing harbour where our blow won't be noticed.'

The two men glared at each other. They had been barely on speaking terms for the past six weeks but until this moment their mutual animosity could be hidden under a studied politeness. Now, however, at the point where the main thrust of the expedition must be decided, their differences of opinion could no longer be hidden.

'I've explained the situation, Monsieur. We've approached this coast with no recent intelligence as to its defences. There should be two companies of infantry and some artillery here somewhere and if the British squadron carrying the governor hasn't yet arrived, it will surely only be a matter of days. We have no flatboats to make an opposed landing and in any case there's no suitable site nearer to St. John's. You tell me that your men can quickly reduce the fort at St. John's once they can approach it, and I tell you that the only way is by land. It's just eighteen English miles to St. John's, surely your men can march that far.'

'And the guns, Monsieur? Fort William can defy us for weeks if we have no guns to make a breach. *Mon Dieu*, eighteen miles is nothing for infantry, but for artillery…'

De Ternay cut the soldier short. He wouldn't normally do so, but he couldn't abide to hear his God's name taken in vain. He'd sworn an oath of celibacy in order to better serve his ultimate master, and he was angered to hear his name invoked so lightly. It wouldn't do to make a point of it, but he knew that a show of authority now would be understood for what it was. He turned a cold, hard eye upon the Count, who was already starting to regret his words.

'I would remind you, Monsieur, that I command this expedition and that you owe me your obedience. I must listen to your council, certainly, but where I find your arguments unhelpful it is my duty to set them aside….' He held up his hand to forestall an interruption, '…and to decide the course of this expedition alone, if necessary. I'll provide the boats to land your force – foot, artillery and engineers – in the bay of Bulls tomorrow. The boats will land sufficient supplies for a week and two hundred of my stoutest sailors and marines will assist with moving your guns across country. After destroying all public buildings and anything concerned with the fishery at Bay of Bulls, along with any vessels that you find, you're to march on Fort William and the town of St. John's. I expect you to open the siege of the fort on the twenty-sixth of this month, in three days' time. The squadron will appear off St. John's on the third of next month. I expect that will be sufficient show of force to persuade the British of the futility of resistance, if they haven't already capitulated. You'll receive your written orders this evening. Now, unless you have anything useful to say, I wish you a good evening.'

De Ternay stood stock-still, daring d'Haussonville to object. Apart from the clash of personalities and the jockeying for prime position in this expedition, he knew that he was right. He'd heard of the devastating effectiveness of the new British creed of combined arms attack from the sea, and he also knew that his own country had far to go before it could match that success. A lack of flatboats was only the most visible deficiency; it was the absence of an established command structure and an agreed doctrine that made the thing so impossible. If those two British companies were at St. John's, then they could defend against any attempts that de Ternay may make from the sea. He may despise d'Haussonville, but he knew the mettle of his soldiers, and he was confident that they could deal with whatever force the British had in this territory, once they were on dry land.

The confrontation lasted just a few seconds, until d'Haussonville' gaze dropped.

'Bah!'

The Comte waved an arm ineffectually and turned on his heel. He swept out of the cabin, leaving his staff officers to hammer out the details of the landing.

***

The wind had turned southeasterly during the night and de Ternay had been forced to move his squadron further offshore. There was an anchorage behind Gull Island in Witless Bay, just a couple of miles to the south of Bay of Bulls, but he didn't trust it, not without the leisure to properly survey the holding ground. He'd heard of it from an Irish fisherman who'd been taken from his boat. The man should have been trustworthy, he certainly swore – frequently and vehemently – that he owed no allegiance to King George, but de Ternay wasn't prepared to put his squadron's safety in the hands of such a man. The incident served to highlight just how little he knew of this shore. Witless Bay wasn't marked on any of his charts, nor was any other feature on this whole stretch of coast, all twenty-five leagues of it, beside St. John's and Bay of Bulls. And that despite his countrymen having fished the Grand Banks and – in time of peace – landed their catch here, for two hundred years. Also, he was acutely aware that he didn't know of the whereabouts of the squadron that was supposed to patrol these waters during the fishing season. His own squadron should be more than a match for the British who typically only sent a fourth rate and a few frigates or sloops to Newfoundland, if it weren't for that mad gesture of sending two hundred of his sailors ashore with the soldiers. His ships were poorly manned when they left Brest, and it was assumed that the soldiers could be used for some of the duties on deck, but now he had barely enough for a safe passage and pitifully few if it came to fighting.

Still, it was a brave sight that met his eyes. The same southeasterly wind that kept him four miles offshore was filling the sails of every boat that the squadron possessed, and each of them was heading for that bold inlet that could barely be discerned against the otherwise featureless wall of rock. d'Haussonville had left in *Robuste's* longboat with the first wave of soldiers. They were the pick of the companies, the grenadiers who would establish the French position ashore and set an armed perimeter to guard against any resistance. For it was at least possible that some British force could have been alerted early enough to march to the bay overnight. It wouldn't take a strong enemy defence to make the landing difficult and to inflict enough casualties to dishearten the rest. D'Haussonville had gone and now there was little that de Ternay could do to influence the campaign. He'd given his orders and now it was up to the landing force commander to obey or disobey as he saw fit. There was one thing though, he was certain that the Comte was fully convinced that he would face a court martial on his return to France if he deviated from his instructions. D'Haussonville was really no fool, and he knew that his impunity lasted only as long as the expedition. The Duc de Choiseul had made the command arrangements very clear, and he was known as a man who could be vicious when his schemes were frustrated by his own countrymen.

De Ternay strode a few steps along the poop deck. Yes, d'Haussonville would do as he was told, and although the man irritated him, he knew him for a competent soldier. It was his own orders that concerned him most, the orders that had been given to him by Choiseul, both orally and in writing. He was to spend no more than a month in St. John's and then he was to strike at other centres of British power and commerce in the area of the Gulf of Saint Lawrence. That sounded very easy when one was sat at leisure in Versailles in the early French spring; it was a different matter when one was backing and filling six-hundred-and-fifty leagues from home with not the slightest chance of any support. He was aware that he was poking the British lion in his own den, and that for a thousand miles in any direction the only forces of any substance belonged to King George. That frigate now, where had it gone? He was so used to seeing it that he almost missed its presence. Away to the southwest the captain of *Garonne* had said. Louisbourg lay to the southwest, so did Halifax and Boston and New York. Any one of those places could be harbouring an unsuspected squadron that could sweep his own two ships-of-the-line before them. And of course, he knew that frigate. It was the same that had followed him out of the Vilaine river, not once, but twice, and he knew its name, *Argonaut*. Its captain was a man to be reckoned with, a young man as de Ternay had seen for himself through his telescope in the faraway Quiberon Bay, a man who commanded respect and decided and acted quickly. What would he be doing now? He must be certain of his enemy's objective; it could only be St. John's, and having discovered that much, if his sense of duty matched his power of command, he'd be away to bring a British squadron to end this mad campaign.

***

It took all day to land the brigade and by the end even d'Haussonville must have been persuaded of the impossibility of doing so under enemy fire. In the early afternoon three thin columns of smoke started to rise from the head of the bay, and in an hour they had merged into one wide plume that climbed high in the sky, bending towards the northwest. De Ternay smiled thinly. Then his orders had been obeyed at least this far. There had been two score of fishing boats in the bay as well as racks full of drying cod and bales of salt fish ready to be shipped out. They were all legitimate targets and by now only the private dwellings should be remaining. Then the first blow had been struck, but that column of smoke must be clearly visible in St. John's.

'The brigade is landed, sir and all two hundred seamen are ashore. You can see that the boats are returning.'

The flag captain looked admiringly at de Ternay. He had felt insulted when he first heard that he'd be under this very junior captain's command, but he'd come to appreciate his commodore's talents. He was sure that no other King's sea officer could have so destroyed the land forces commander and sent him away like an errant schoolboy. It was a beautiful thing to witness, and he was sure that d'Haussonville's humbling was to the benefit of the expedition. He'd seen the fatal results of divided command in half a dozen campaigns and fervently hoped that he'd see no more.

'When sufficient boats have returned, be so kind as to sound the bay before I decide whether to anchor the squadron there. Tell me captain, do you have enough seamen to man a whole broadside?'

The flag captain hesitated for a moment. It was the sort of question that he'd have been reluctant to answer in front of any other commodore or admiral, and would have given an evasive answer, but he knew that wouldn't do for de Ternay.

'No, sir, and it'll be the same for the rest of the squadron. I can sail the ship with the seamen that I have, but I can't man the guns at the same time. Half of the gun crews were made up of soldiers as you know, and the other half – the seamen gunners – have gone away with the landing force. My first lieutenant is putting together as many crews as he can from the junior officers and petty officers, and any seamen that can be spared, but I'll be lucky if I can fire six guns in a broadside.'

De Ternay made no response. It was much as he had expected, and the fault lay in two quarters: in the commissioner at Brest who was unwilling to entirely denude the principal Atlantic naval base of trained seaman for this mysterious adventure, and his own for giving so many trained men to d'Haussonville. Yet he knew that he'd made the right decision. Without those seamen to drag the guns over the eighteen miles of rough tracks between Bay of Bulls and St. John's, d'Haussonville may have plucked up the courage to defy him. The Good Lord keep the British away, just for a few more days! As he thought those words de Ternay grimaced at the penance that he'd have to perform for so lightly invoking his God.

***

CHAPTER SEVENTEEN

Lord Colville

Saturday, Twenty-Sixth of June 1762.
Northumberland, at Anchor. Halifax, Nova Scotia.

'Ye're Carlisle's friend, I gather, Captain Holbrooke. He was in and out of here in 'fifty-eight and 'fifty-nine when we were dealing with the French. He brought you up from a master's mate, if I heard the story correctly.'

'Yes, sir. I served under him in *Fury* and then I was his lieutenant in *Medina* before Admiral Cotes gave me a sloop in Jamaica. I was lucky with the rash of promotions at the start of the war.'

Holbrooke understood that Colville wanted to establish some human connection before the business of reporting his news. He didn't usually attempt to justify himself; he saw it as a sign of weakness, but under Colville's gaze he felt that he needed to make some sort of explanation for his extraordinary rise through the ranks. It wasn't unprecedented, but there were only a handful of post-captains who had made such rapid progress. In any case, he liked Colville already. He was a straightforward man, a Scottish lord with an impoverished estate and only his naval pay and prize money between him and penury. It was said that he held onto this unattractive post to avoid setting foot in his home country, with its ever-present threat of the debtor's gaol. He must be close to the top of the post-captain's list, so his flag was imminent. That would mean a return to Britain, and Holbrooke wondered how Colville would manage that transition, how he'd square his creditors at the same time as suffering an inevitable drop in income.

'Well, he was the lucky one, in my opinion. You can't imagine how many disappointments I've had with my protégés. Drunken wastrels, weak-kneed ninnies and outright poltroons, most of them. Oh, a few have turned out reasonably well, but none do me the credit that you've done for Carlisle.'

Colville looked wistfully at Holbrooke. It was an important point, and in many ways senior commanders' reputations rested upon the performance of the men that they'd brought up, seen commissioned and in due course posted to a rated ship. Holbrooke could understand how it had come about. The North American command enjoyed none of the glamour of the other foreign stations, and for half of the year the squadron merely survived, battened down against the cold and damp in Halifax Harbour. Then, for the short campaign season, a senior admiral brought his own squadron across. But since Quebec fell in 'fifty-nine, there had been barely a sight of the enemy and Colville's squadron was seen as a reserve of ships to be sent elsewhere as the need arose. Colville could no doubt attract young men from his home in Scotland, but otherwise he was left with the scrapings from the bottom of the barrel.

'Well, enough of that. You've no mail for us, I understand, but you do have news of the French, and that might be a more cheerful thought.'

'No mail, I regret, my Lord. When I sailed from Portsmouth I had no notion of sailing further west than the chops of the channel. I've followed a French squadron from Brest for the past seven weeks, and I left them on the Grand Banks steering for somewhere to the south of St. John's. A seventy-four, a sixty-four and two frigates, one of them a flute. They're carrying soldiers, and I saw artillery uniforms as well as infantry. It looked like a small brigade with guns and engineers, but I can't be certain of the numbers.'

Colville stared thoughtfully out of the great stern windows of his flagship. It had been quiet on his station for the past two years, ever since the French had surrendered their possessions along the Saint Lawrence. His main occupation had been preserving his squadron through the winter and keeping a check on the colonies' growing tendency for smuggling. An enemy squadron of that size could be a problem. A month ago he had sufficient force at hand but on the news of war with Spain, most of his ships had been sent south to join the great enterprise of Cuba. Now he had only his flagship *Northumberland* and *Gosport,* a forty-four gun fourth rate that was badly in need of careening. With *Argonaut* he could achieve something in the way of disrupting the enemy's plans, but if it came to a general engagement, he'd be lucky to come out on top.

'An attempt on the Newfoundland fishery then?'

'I believe so, sir. St. John's, Bay of Bulls and those other places on the Avalon Peninsula.'

'Not Placentia?'

Holbrooke shook his head.

'They were steering too far north. We had a good noon sun only the day before so they must have had a perfect idea of their latitude. They could hardly have been intending to round Cape Race on that course, sir.'

'Well, they'll find little resistance anywhere in the whole of Newfoundland. The only places with any pretensions of defence are St. John's and Placentia, and they can only muster a company each of the Fortieth of Foot and some artillerymen for the batteries.'

Colville didn't look encouraged as he enumerated the defences of the important Newfoundland fishery. To Holbrooke it seemed an adequate force and he wondered at Colville's pessimism.

'A company with artillery should hold them for a while at Fort William, my Lord.'

'Eh? Oh, they're no better than colonial militia. They've been there for over fifty years, and they spend more time farming and fishing than soldiering. Amherst sent a mission there last year and they reported that both companies were *very defective.* Coming from a soldier, you can take that to mean whatever you like, but I wouldn't put any faith in them holding Fort William for long against French foot and artillery. Did you see the names of the ships, Holbrooke?'

'The seventy-four is *Robuste,* flying a pennant. I saw her last year when she escaped from Quiberon Bay. I believe the sixty-four is *Eveillé* and the frigate is *Garonne,* a thirty-four. The flute might be a thirty-two when she has all her guns but I couldn't see her name; she appears to be fitted as a storeship.'

'I heard that they gave *Robuste* to that strange de Ternay man; I wonder who the commodore is.'

'I beg your pardon, my Lord, but I believe de Ternay is the commodore. I'm almost certain I recognised him when we passed astern of the squadron off Brest.'

Colville again stared out of the windows in thought. As his face caught the light, Holbrooke noticed that he had a slight nervous tick in the corner of his left eye, perhaps a result of keeping a squadron intact through too many Nova Scotia winters.

'You've tangled with de Ternay before, Captain Holbrooke.'

It was a statement not a question and Holbrooke didn't feel the need to comment. It must be common knowledge that he'd spent some time ashore recovering from the fatigue of constant campaigning, and an intelligent sea officer could easily make the connection with his well-known attempts to prevent de Ternay bringing King Louis' ships out of the Vilaine estuary. He didn't want his rivalry with de Ternay to be seen as some sort of personal quest.

'Well, I suspect he'll find no great difficulty in taking St. John's, and holding it, at least for a while. The question is, what will he do next? The war's coming to an end you know, and King Louis must be looking at what he can bring to the negotiating table. Does he believe he can take the whole Newfoundland fishery from us and offer it in exchange for Martinique, or Belle Isle? Or is this a mere raid to remind us that he can still hurt us in the pocket? The Lord knows what the city will say if we lose the fishery. They send stockfish to every part of the world where King George holds sway, and a good number of other places beside. It's a shrewd move by Choiseul, a shrewd move indeed. Even if he sacks St. John's and moves on, there's a whole world of other objectives for him. Louisbourg has a scratch garrison now that we hold the whole of the Saint Lawrence and even that's been depleted for the Havana expedition. There are fishing harbours the length of Île Royale and Nova Scotia, as well as all of Newfoundland. Losing St. John's and Placentia might look unfortunate but letting the French destroy the fisheries further south would seem careless indeed.'

Colville thought for a moment; Holbrooke could see that he had some difficult decisions to make.

'Now, I must let Amherst know because it will take a land force to dislodge these fellows. He's in much the same position as me, with all his best regiments sent away to join the expedition to Havana, but I'm sure he'll be able to scrape something together from the militia and the garrisons. He's in New York, but I won't send you, I still have a couple of sloops and schooners for that kind of errand. How are your stores?'

'I need wood and water, sir, and I'll take whatever beef and bread and fresh stuff is available.'

'D'ye need no repairs?'

'No, my Lord. We suffered a little damage when we twice tangled with *Garonne,* but my carpenter and bosun have already made good.'

'Very well. In that case I'll be obliged if ye'll retrace your steps and discover what de Ternay is up to. Captain Graves will be here any week now in *Antelope* – he's the governor this year, last year too – in fact his frigate and his sloop probably came on ahead. *Siren* and *Gramont.* Look out for them and tell Graves from me that he's to make all speed for Halifax to join my squadron. I'll put that in writing. Ye'll join me for dinner, I hope, it'll be good to see a fresh face at my table, and I understand your chaplain is here consulting with mine. Carlisle told me that I mustn't miss the opportunity to meet Mister Chalmers; a quite extraordinary gentlemen by all accounts.'

***

It was a long dinner and Holbrooke had to use all his wiles to avoid overeating and worse still drinking too much. Colville was hungry for news from Britain and Holbrooke was the first King's officer to come to Halifax in months. There were five of them at the table. Colville was a first-class commodore so he had a captain under him to command his flagship. Nathaniel Bateman looked to be around forty and by his conversation he was a very experienced officer, having served through the last war. However, he'd been posted after Holbrooke, so was and always would be his junior in the naval service. The fifth diner was John Jervis of the fourth rate *Gosport*. Holbrooke knew him by reputation. His career had followed a similar trajectory to Holbrooke's, passing through the ranks of lieutenant and commander in the early years of the war. He'd distinguished himself at Quebec in the 14-gun sloop *Scorpion* and was posted just a year after Holbrooke. He was bursting with energy and left the dour, ponderous Bateman trailing in his wake as he speculated on the French expedition and how it could be frustrated.

'You were at Fort Niagara, I believe, sir. In fact, you both were,' he said with a nod to Chalmers, 'if I'm not mistaken.'

Jervis regarded Holbrooke with a frank admiration that really wasn't warranted by the few months of seniority that separated them. And Jervis had friends in high places that Holbrooke lacked. Of the two, Jervis had the better future prospects, but he was gentleman enough to refrain from emphasising the fact.

'Yes, we were both there, while you were at Quebec, I gather.'

'You were plagued by the savages, I suppose.'

Bateman's abrupt interruption was impolite at best and Colville shot him an annoyed glance. There was silence for a moment as Holbrooke considered how to reply, but it was

Chalmers who spoke first. He'd already established his role as a listener not a talker, so his intervention now carried more weight than it would have from any of the others around the table.

'Yes, we met the inhabitants of the country; Mohawks of the Iroquois people mainly but also some of the more western tribes as we came nearer the fort.'

He paused as though carefully crafting his words.

'I think I can say this with honesty, and hope that Captain Holbrooke won't contradict me. If one can isolate the virtues of a gentleman from the places that we normally associate with the term – and I take that to be the countries of Europe and the established towns of its colonies – then among the Mohawk people we met the most perfect gentleman that can be imagined. Certainly they are *savage*, but then so are we as we hurl our great iron balls at the enemy and rush upon his deck with bare steel, but I think we risk failing to understand them if we dismiss them as *savages*, as though they have no other qualities worth mentioning.'

Bateman looked uncomfortable at being reproved, and Holbrooke stepped in to avoid an embarrassing silence.

'Yes, our guide was what I suppose you'd call a leading warrior among the Mohawks, an aspiring tribal chief. He was – I presume still is – a man of the highest moral principles, utterly fearless and loyal, and perfectly schooled to survive in the wilderness. I shudder to imagine how we'd have fared without his help. Kanatase is his name, and I honour him.'

Holbrooke glanced sideways to see that Bateman was looking a little more comfortable although it was doubtful whether he'd risk another unguarded comment.

'Would you favour us with an account of the siege, sir? I've heard the most garbled accounts of your part in it. Is it true that you were at the battle that sealed the fort's fate, that you stood in the front rank of the infantry? Mister Chalmers too, by all accounts.'

Holbrooke glanced warily at Jervis, then at Colville and Bateman. Were they making game of him? He had to admit that they appeared genuinely interested, except Bateman who looked as though the affairs of a French fortress far away in the American wilderness were of no concern to him.

'Well gentlemen, if you insist. The first thing to know is that Brigadier General Prideaux' army had to traverse the lake – Lake Ontario that is – and that the French had two schooners that for lack of any opposition dominated those waters entirely…'

Holbrooke was drawn into the explanation. He had little help from Chalmers who sat silent witness to the conversation. It was only when Holbrooke looked as though he'd pass over the part where he ordered the volley that shattered the advancing French lines, that Chalmers interposed to set the record straight.

'Never before has such a thing been seen. The major who commanded fell – the wound, as it happens, wasn't serious – at the very moment when the soldiers must be made to stand and give fire. They'd been sheltering behind barriers made from felled trees. All would have been lost if Captain Holbrooke hadn't given the order and by his own example caused them to rise. You can imagine how reluctant men are to expose themselves in such a situation…'

'You stood too, my dear Chalmers.' Holbrooke was smiling now, relaxed in friendly company. 'It was the example of a peace-loving chaplain standing to receive the enemy's fire that brought the men up. And I should mention that the Mohawk Kanatase saved me from an inglorious scalping before the day was out. Gentlemen, I propose a toast, to the fighting chaplains of His Majesty's navy and to the King's allies, the Mohawks!'

That brought the conversation to a merry end. In Holbrooke's view it was becoming far too serious. He didn't relish being at the centre of so much well-meaning attention and was glad when the door opened softly to reveal a lieutenant who bowed low with his hat under his arm.

'I beg your pardon, my Lord. There's a message from Mister Shorrock, *Argonaut's* first lieutenant, to say that the stores, wood and water have been embarked and all officers and men are aboard. He's taking the liberty of bringing the anchor to a short stay. A separate message from the pilot, my Lord, and if *Argonaut* can be underway two hours before sunset, that's in an hour, he'll undertake to bring her out on the first of the land breeze. Captain Holbrooke's yawl is alongside, my Lord.'

That effectively broke up the dinner party, the best that Holbrooke could remember for a long time. There was no doubt that word of his physical collapse in Quiberon Bay had penetrated even to this far outpost of the empire, but it appeared to have done his reputation no harm. Perhaps the thinking sea officer understood that when a captain gives everything for the service, there must eventually be a reckoning.

***

The lamps of Halifax had long since been lost and now the only illumination in an otherwise pitch-dark night was the new lighthouse on Sambro Island. Fairview, with an expression of the purest satisfaction, was watching it with a fixed gaze, waiting for the moment when it would dip below the horizon as *Argonaut* dropped into a trough in the waves. When it reappeared as *Argonaut* soared up again, he'd take a careful bearing, and knowing the surveyed height of the light above sea level, he'd consult his tables and on his chart describe an arc to intersect the bearing line.

'Now, Mister Petersen. What do you make it?'

There was a pause while the master's mate studied the compass card.

'West-sou'west, a half west, sir.'

'Very good, now we may get one more chance. Stand by… now!'

'The same, sir. West-sou'west and a half west, by the mark, sir.'

'Well, the wonders of this modern age,' Fairview exclaimed rubbing his hands in pleasure, 'who would have thought that we could confidently determine a departure on a night such as this? Now, if there was just another light to the east of Halifax I could compare the bearing line and the arc with the second bearing. But beggars can't be choosers, and we must count our blessings, Mister Petersen. Record the bearing and distance in the log, if you please.'

***

CHAPTER EIGHTEEN

Avoidable

Tuesday, Twenty-Ninth of June 1762.
Sloop-of-War Gramont, at Anchor. St. John's, Newfoundland.

The sun showed its face late in the harbour of St. John's. Even this close to midsummer it had to rise above the encircling high ground before it could dispel the shadows in the tight, cramped anchorage. *Gramont* snubbed gently to its two anchors, flanked by two score of fishing boats and half a dozen of the small supply brigs that both brought the food from England and Ireland to feed the fishing communities and carried a share of the salted catch back to the mother country. Patrick Mouat stamped angrily about the quarterdeck of his sloop, casting anxious glances at the decrepit bulk of Fort William, then across to the narrow mouth of the harbour, and further right to the low ground to the west. There he could see the French infantry already throwing up earth in the first parallel of the anticipated siege. Mouat was a Shetland Islander and at fifty years he was old – very old – to be commander of an eighteen-gun sloop. He'd attained his present rank four years ago and he was as certain as he could be that he'd proceed no further in the King's navy. He knew that his service at Saint-Malo and Quebec merited promotion, but his age was against him, and this damned talk of peace had blocked all except a few promotions, and those had gone to men with powerful friends. He'd been delighted to be sent to this country; not only did it remind him of his native Shetland, but he had it in mind to look for some way of investing his growing purse of prize money in the fishery. Perhaps he could even settle here, bring his family over and set up as something along the lines of a local laird. But all of those thoughts were far from his mind today.

'If we stay much longer, we won't get out at all, sir.'

'I can see that thank ye, Master.'

Mouat's accent hadn't been modified in all his years of service.

'And what will we do for hands? That's what I'd like to know. With Mister McCloud and all of our best men away at the fort we've barely enough to win the anchors, let alone man the longboat and pull us out through the Narrows. If those French once get some artillery on that little hill, we'll be lost.'

Mouat turned his back. The sailing master was a confirmed pessimist and saw troubles everywhere he looked. But even pessimists are right sometimes and on this occasion he could hardly have exaggerated *Gramont's* predicament. What he didn't know and what Mouat had deliberately kept from the remainder of his crew, was that a French artillery train was only a day or so behind the white-coated infantry. If the garrison didn't make a sortie and clear them out within the day, before the guns arrived, it would all be lost. He should recall his first lieutenant and the hundred men that he'd sent to Fort William, and put to sea before it was too late, but that he couldn't do. His orders from Captain Douglas in *Siren* were quite clear and allowed little room for manoeuvre. He was to stay in the harbour and reinforce the pitiful company of the Fortieth of Foot until either the French withdrew or Captain Ross in the fort decided to capitulate. Well, Ross had promised to keep him informed, but he'd heard nothing this morning, not any word at all since he'd rowed ashore to the fort the previous evening. He picked up the telescope and studied the French positions. They were as busy as beavers, and he could see the earth being tossed up as the parallel lengthened. He'd never seen a siege before, but he knew the theory of it well enough. There was something sinister and inevitable about the way that the broken ground extended minute by minute, and it was clear that Fort William's doom was written in every spade of earth and rock that spewed upwards from the trenches. Mouat

An Upright Man

snapped the telescope closed.

'I'm going ashore to the fort, Master. I won't take the longboat; we may need that for other duties. Call away the yawl's crew, if ye please.'

***

It was only a walk of some two hundred yards or so from the wooden jetty, past the lower battery to the gates of Fort William, yet it told Mouat all that he needed to know. He'd seen the general air of decay in the couple of days since his arrival, and he'd witnessed the woeful state of the infantry company that garrisoned the fort, but at least, when the French expedition was first reported, there'd been a feeling that the defenders were determined to repel the invader. That resolve had gone – it had evaporated with the morning mist – and the prevailing attitude was one of deep despair. Oh, the batteries, the curtain walls and the gate were still manned, but nobody was interested in his arrival, and he could see that there were fewer soldiers than before. Were they mustered for a sortie? He thought not; in fact he was sure that they were seeing to their families and personal possessions. The company had been here for decades and most of the soldiers had settled in St. John's; they were obeying the first instinct of family men.

'Captain Ross, what's afoot?'

Mouat had spotted the garrison commander hurrying towards the gate with a subaltern who was carrying a dispatch case, and his hail was loud and clear. Ross started guiltily and hurried on with a wave, as much as to say that he didn't have time to talk to the navy today. Mouat was at a loss for a moment. He thought of chasing down the garrison commander but Ross was already through the gates and striding urgently towards the town. He cast around for inspiration.

'Captain, sir. I saw the yawl coming in and came as fast as I could. The men are gathering by the barracks ready to march down to the boat. I've left Mister Jones to see to it and Mister Fowle has a party trying to rescue what stores we can from those we brought ashore.'

Mouat stared at his first lieutenant. He was another Scot but from the lowlands south of the Forth, almost an Englishman. His meaning was clear but Mouat still wanted to have the situation confirmed.

'And why, Mister McCloud, are ye bringing the men back to the ship?'

McCloud looked as though he'd been struck by lightning, and gradually the awful truth dawned.

'You haven't heard, sir? The fort has capitulated. The French sent in terms at first light and Captain Ross called a council of war. I applied to be a member but he told me that it was an army affair and that he'd keep you informed. I don't know the details, but the garrison is to march out in one hour after the agreement has reached the French commander. Look, you can see some of them are already deserting. The sergeants won't muster more than half the strength when the time comes.'

Sure enough, there were soldiers, singly and in small groups, creeping through the gates and heading towards the town.

Mouat felt that he needed to sit down, but he hadn't served the King through two wars to find anything too outrageous to be true. He instinctively looked over his shoulder to the high ground at the south side of the Narrows. He could see white-clad figures marching purposefully in that direction, presumably in violation of the articles that were barely dry on the paper. This Comte d'Haussonville must have guessed that the garrison commander had no authority to direct the navy, and as there was no sea officer's signature on the document, *Gramont* wouldn't be bound by it. Those soldiers were moving into position to prevent his sloop's escape.

'Then hurry the men along, Mister McCloud. I can see there's no point in talking to Ross. I'm going back to the sloop, and I'll send all the boats for ye. Leave the stores.

Those men who won't fit in our boats are to be left in the charge of a petty officer with orders to commandeer any suitable vessel to rejoin the sloop.'

McCloud understood the situation; he could see that column of soldiers moving up the hill and knew just what it meant. The Narrows were less than a cable wide at their tightest point and with this light wind from the east the sloop would have to be towed out. The whole of *Gramont's* deck and the oarsmen in the longboat would have to brave the French musketry for at least half an hour; it would be a wonder if a single man survived. Nevertheless, the thing must at least be attempted. He'd seen no sign of the French squadron that the fishing schooner had reported, so they were presumably still at Bay of Bulls or on passage for St. John's. If they could win their way to the sea, there was still hope, but at the very least they must stop the sloop falling into French hands.

***

'Bring home the best bower, Master, ye can cut away the second bower.'

With so many men needed to tow the sloop out of the harbour, there were barely enough left to weigh one anchor let alone two.

'Would you like it buoyed, sir?'

A good question. Normally there would be no doubt; if an anchor was to be left behind it was always buoyed to assist with later recovery. However, in this case it was the French who'd benefit from knowing where to find the valuable anchor.

'No, Master. Just let it go. Is the starboard battery ready, Mister McCloud?'

'Ready sir and loaded with grape, although whether we can fetch the top of that cliff is another matter. Look, you can see them taking their positions among the rocks.'

Mouat could hear the steady clanking of the pawl as the bower anchor was hauled out of the ooze. He'd been warned that the stench from the mud that the anchor brought out would be almost unbearable, the result of a century and more of fish waste being thrown into the harbour. Well, that was the least of his worries. A quick look over the side showed the longboat still being manned. Now, what would the coxswain want at this moment? He should be down at the capstan or in the longboat.

The coxswain was even older than Mouat himself. He'd volunteered for the King's navy – or at least that's what it said on his first ship's muster-book – at the same time as Mouat had been sent to sea as a youngster in the same ship. It was a feudal arrangement, left over from an earlier way of doing things in the Shetlands. They'd served together almost continuously since then and in fact Mouat expected the coxswain to join him in retirement in this new part of the world, if that's what he decided to do. There was a level of trust and mutual understanding between the two men that just didn't exist between the captain and his officers. The coxswain's accent was more pronounced even than Mouat's and when they spoke together there was little chance of anyone else understanding them.

'Can I speak to ye, sir? Perhaps away from the capstan might be best.'

The sailing master glared suspiciously at the coxswain, but it was quite clear that his presence wasn't wanted. He'd learned over the past three months to accept this relationship even though it transcended the normal ship's hierarchy.

'What is it then?'

'It's no-go sir, the men won't have it. They can see those Frenchies up on the cliff and they know that's the only way out. They'll fight for you like Devils in a regular engagement, sir, but there's not one o' them will pull his oar long and dry with musket balls falling around his ears and no way of replying.'

Mouat started to point to the nine six pounders whose muzzles were elevated as far skywards as they could be, with their unwanted quoins lying on the deck beside them, but the coxswain interrupted before he could speak.

'No, sir,' he replied firmly, 'they know very well that no ball nor grape from those little guns will carry to the top o' that cliff, not even if ye knocked out the back trucks. They request – most humbly they asked me to say – that ye give the order to spike the guns and scuttle the sloop here in the harbour. They'd rather take their chances as prisoners than die in a useless cause.'

The coxswain stood square in front of Mouat, not giving an inch and showing no sign of nerves at addressing his captain in this way. He could sense his countryman's indecision and knew that if he left it alone, he'd lose the point.

'And for my part, sir, I agree with them. We've come a long way together, and I don't see much chance o' ye surviving the next hour if ye insist on forcing that passage. That French lieutenant up there will be pointing ye out to his best marksmen, ye and the sailing master. It would break my heart to see ye fall in a lost cause, not after all we've been through and with the war nearly over an' all.'

He laid his hand on Mouat's arm and looked him right in the eye.

'Think o' your missus, man. Think o' the bairns, if ye don't think o' yourself.'

***

Mouat watched from the longboat as *Gramont* settled into the stinking mud at the bottom of the harbour. It was only five fathoms where they'd anchored, and the three tall masts stood proudly clear of the water. He'd thought of chopping them down but had been deterred by the sight of French infantry marching onto the waterfront before the castle. Nobody could see what happened below decks where the carpenter had smashed his way through the oak planks, but he'd have exposed his men to a merciless fire if they were seen to be dismasting the sloop. The guns were a different matter, and the gunner had spiked them before the first French soldiers saw what he was up to. Not that it would do much good, for a decent armourer could fit new bushes to the whole lot of them in a day or two.

On the shore a squad of French soldiers was already taking charge of the British sailors as they landed. Each man had his bag with spare clothes and his most valued possessions, but they had little hope that they wouldn't be pillaged. Mouat could see a lieutenant waiting to secure the two commissioned officers, he looked pleased with himself, as well he might. This was an easy victory for the French expedition and Mouat firmly disagreed with the notion that apparently had swayed the council of war to vote as they did, that defeat was inevitable. The French guns had still not made an appearance and it would be difficult and time consuming to raise the protected batteries that were essential to survive under the guns of Fort William. The southern approach to the fort, where the attackers were preparing their siege lines, favoured the defender and they'd take days to establish themselves on the more advantageous Signal Hill or Gibbet Hill to the east. And when the French battering train was in place, what then? A week to make a practicable breach? In that time a British squadron could appear and change the situation in an instant. Mouat's thoughts were disturbed by his first lieutenant.

'Well, that was a short commission, sir. Just three months from joining at Portsmouth to scuttling at St. John's.'

He took another look at the sloop's masts and the discoloured water where she'd come to rest.

'There's one good thing come out of it though, sir.'

Mouat looked suspiciously at McCloud, he could see no good in this situation at all and was busy composing the words he'd use to Captain Ross when they met. Words that would express his outrage for the garrison's capitulating without giving him enough warning to get his sloop to sea. He'd be firm to the point of rudeness to get his point across, but it would do no good to provoke an argument that could lead to a challenge, there was no glory in a duel between prisoners-of-war.

McCloud's smile barely stretched his lips, but it was a smile, nonetheless.

'We never will smell that stink from the bottom of the harbour, sir.'

***

CHAPTER NINETEEN

Bacalao

Friday, Second of July 1762.
San Sebastian, at Sea. Cape Race northwest-by-west 25 leagues.

On a day such as this, one could even grow to appreciate these northern waters, where the air was cool and a clean shirt lasted longer than a forenoon. Don Mancebo breathed deep as he watched the sun rise over the wide, wide Atlantic. He'd regained his humour, at last, but it had been a long slow process. He should have known that a bearer of bad news was never honoured for his efforts. Oh, they'd taken him seriously, both the governor-general and the commander-in-chief, but they had no spare boats and even the trivial damage that *San Sebastian* had suffered from the British frigate was placed at the back of a long line of repairs that were urgently needed for the ships already in Havana. Why they hadn't foreseen their country's entry into the war was beyond Don Mancebo's understanding; the signs had been there this past year for all to read. But no, at his news it appeared that every captain in the Spanish Indies decided that his ship needed urgent attention before he could do battle with the British. *San Sebastian* had languished at anchor while its captain pleaded for the resources that would heal her wounds.

Then, without any warning, he'd received the secret orders that had brought him north, and he'd sailed with his battle scars still showing. Furthermore, he'd been stripped of his twenty-four pounders to make up deficiencies in the Morro Fort, and two hundred of his seamen and all of his marines had gone with the guns. All that Havana could spare him were two worn-out boats to replace those that the British frigate had destroyed. Well, he was here and there wasn't a boat in sight on this, the richest cod fishery in the whole world. Secret orders or not, it was time that his second-in-command was told of their mission.

***

'What are the people saying, Señor Guterres?'

The first lieutenant put down his coffee cup and considered his captain's question. For the first few days after they left Havana so abruptly, the ship had been abuzz with rumours about their destination. Most were disappointed to be leaving the grand squadron that was going to show the British navy, and the French, how real seamen fought their battles. Some, perhaps seeing the state of readiness of the ships, were pleased to be sent away, and the further the better. None however had come up with a plausible destination. When *San Sebastian* passed through the Florida Strait, the smart money had been on a return to Spain, perhaps to join in the enterprise to bring Portugal back to the Spanish Crown. When they cleared the Bahama Bank and set a course to the north-northeast, the wise heads spoke of the Atlantic Drift, and how it would carry them to the latitude of the Azores, before they broke away to the east, and steered for home. When even that theory proved false the bets were called off and even the wardroom was left wondering where in this world they were bound.

'Until this morning they'd run out of suppositions, sir. But a half dozen of the oldest hands claim to have fished these waters before the last war and now there's open speculation about our reclaiming the cod fishery. If you keep heading to the north then even that theory will be proved false. I expect to start hearing about the Northwest Passage and the East Indies any day now. I might even put a modest bet on that myself.'

Don Mancebo leaned back in his chair and smiled. It was the first genuine, unforced pleasure that Fernando had seen on his captain's face since the day that they'd met the British frigate, and that was more than four months ago. It brought an answering grin from the first lieutenant, the only acknowledgement of their long friendship on this tedious passage.

'You should save your money, Fernando, it is indeed the fishery. King Carlos has stated that one of his war aims is to reclaim the Spanish rights to fish the Newfoundland Banks, and perhaps even the Gulf of Saint Lawrence. Now, this is certainly not to be spoken of, not to the other lieutenants and not even to the sailing master. My orders,' he motioned towards the desk where a single sheet of thick paper with a broken seal lay as though it had been recently consulted, 'are to investigate the state of the fishery and by our presence here to establish our interest, and indeed our rights to a share of it. King Carlos sees this as an important demand at the peace negotiations, after we've shown the British that they're not the only naval power in Europe. Do you know anything about the fishery, Fernando? I remember that your grandfather sailed with the Basque fleet, long ago.'

'A little, sir. I know that the British have a few schooners but mostly fish the inshore waters in small boats during the summer, and they salt and dry the cod ashore before they send it away. They ship directly to the customers in the Caribbean islands, the West African coast and the Mediterranean, even to Portugal and Spain, I understand.'

Don Mancebo was listening carefully to his first lieutenant. He knew nothing about the cod fishery and his orders had prevented him inquiring at Havana, or even within his ship. He was taking a risk in bringing Guterres into his confidence, but it was already reaping its rewards.

Guterres wondered whether to continue, but one look at his captain's rapt attention told him that he should.

'Our own fishermen have always fished the Banks from schooners and brigs and big luggers, and they salt the cod and bring it home for drying. The French do the same, ever since they lost their harbours on the mainland. Of course, they gave up St. Pierre and Miquelon early in the century and I don't expect there's anything for them there. If the

French fish at all, it will be far out on the Banks and outside the season that the British do their business, I'm sure.'

Don Mancebo kept the delight from his face. He hadn't dared to hope that Guterres could know so much, but then, his first lieutenant had spent some time sailing in merchantmen when he hadn't been favoured with a commission to a man-of-war. Merchant sailors were a mixed lot, and their experience was generally far wider than could be found in the wardroom of a King's ship.

'I know the British have factories at St. John's and Placentia, but are there others? Here, let's use this chart.'

Guterres had never seen the chart before. His captain must have been given it in Havana; possibly it had been sent out from Spain with the orders for this mission.

'Here's St. John's, sir, and here's Placentia. I had heard that these places have regular defences, forts of a sort or at least batteries. This is where the supply ships come from England and it's where much of the cod is gathered before it's sent away.'

'What sort of building would they have here, for salting the cod?'

'Salting and drying, sir,' he corrected his captain. 'Sheds for salting and racks on the shoreline for drying. It's quite an industry, I understand. It's centred on these two places but almost every inlet, every bit of shelter on this whole coast, has its own sheds and racks. I think I said, sir, that the English fish the inshore waters, so access to the Banks isn't important to them. All the way around this north coast; Conception Bay, Trinity Bay and Bonavista Bay,' he traced with his finger the deep inlets that marched away towards the northern coast of Newfoundland, 'then south to Bay of Bulls and beyond, they all salt and dry and either ship the cod to St. John's and Placentia or directly to the customers.'

'Then that explains why the Banks are empty; we haven't seen a single fisherman since dawn.'

Guterres looked thoughtful. He'd heard a lot of tales in

his days in merchantmen and it wasn't always easy to disentangle fact from fiction and with the best of intentions, the truth mutated over time and with repeated telling. In his grandfather's day a significant part of the King's navy had been trained on the Grand Banks. The English only fished the summer season in the inshore waters but those who fished the Banks did so in any season. It was reckoned that a winter on the fishery turned a landsman into an able seaman when it would take a couple of years in a man-of-war. And it hadn't always been a peaceful enterprise. Yes, the English mostly fished the coast, but some of them joined the French, Portuguese, Dutch, Spanish and a half dozen other nations on the Banks. There was open warfare at times, and blood was spilled over the humble cod. He could understand the French and his own countrymen being absent, and the Portuguese would be needing every seaman they could muster to man their fleet, but where were those Englishmen? Where were the schooners and brigs and sloops that sailed from Bristol and the west country ports to harvest the white gold?

'I think, sir, that there must be more to it, if you'll pardon me. The English will have chased everyone else away now that the summer season has started. But there should be some English fishermen. On a day such as this the Banks should be full of vessels. Something's amiss, sir.'

Don Mancebo gazed thoughtfully out of the window. There wasn't a sail in sight on this whole, wide, blue sea. He'd heard tales of the fishery as well, not as much as Guterres, but enough to know that he was right. Something had cleared the waters of every nation's fishers.

'There's one other thing that my orders insist upon. In the event that I come across any French ships, I am not to tell them our business nor to combine with them in any operations.'

Guterres raised an eyebrow at that. The Bourbon family pact had been broadcast far and wide and was common knowledge in Havana by the time *San Sebastian* sailed away. It had grown in his mind into the new bedrock of Spanish foreign policy. Certainly it was unlikely that they'd find any French ships here, but if they did surely it was to their advantage to work together against the English.

Don Mancebo couldn't resist assuming the air of a man who understood these grave matters of policy.

'When this war ends, Spain will be negotiating as much with France and Austria as it will with England. King Carlos doesn't want his hands tied by implied favours that need to be repaid, not in the fisheries in any case.'

The first lieutenant nodded his understanding.

'So we must be seen by the English and French but must neither fight the former unless there's no risk to *San Sebastian*, nor co-operate with the latter.'

'I stand under correction, sir, but in any case, we're in no condition to fight with our twenty-four pounders left at the Morro Castle.'

Don Mancebo made the slightest inclination of his head, not wishing to be seen agreeing with an implied criticism of the governor-general of Havana.

'Well, Señor Guterres,' Don Mancebo reverted to a formal tone to end the meeting, 'it's our duty, I've no doubt, to discover what's happening here. The King wants to know, and I don't suppose his cousin of France is in a position to enlighten him, nor would he wish to ask. I think we'll start here, at Bay of Bulls. In this wind we can leave there and run down to St. John's in the same day. Be so kind as to tell the sailing master to set a course under easy sail and double the lookouts. I wish to arrive off the bay at dawn tomorrow.'

Guterres stood to leave then stopped dead and turned to his captain with a wide smile.

'One thing I hope we can achieve, sir. I haven't tasted good *bacalao* since we sailed from Ferrol. It used to be the

navy's Friday dish before we lost the Banks fishery and the very thought of it is tormenting me.'
***

CHAPTER TWENTY

Collision of Interests

Saturday, Third of July 1762.
Argonaut, at Sea. Off Bay of Bulls.

A fine south-westerly breeze had hurried *Argonaut* back towards the Avalon Peninsula and now, with the sun about to rise over her starboard quarter, the frigate was ghosting in towards Bay of Bulls.

'I've sent Mister Petersen to the masthead with my own telescope, sir.'

'That's very trusting of you, Mister Fairview.'

Holbrooke was feeling in high spirits. The weather had been fine, the victualling store at Halifax had favoured *Argonaut* with more fresh provisions than any frigate had a right to expect, and the men were all healthy. It felt good to be in command of a King's ship with the loosest of orders to find and report the enemy and to annoy him as much as possible, naturally without prejudice to the first part.

'I fastened the lanyard over his head myself, sir. Dick Turpin had no finer necktie.'

Even Fairview had caught the mood. It was said of the sailing master that his jests were a danger to good order and no laughing matter, but this one was almost amusing, if one allowed that the old ones are the best. Holbrooke did it the honour of a wry smile and a low chuckle.

It was a sparkling summer morning off the Newfoundland coast and the far hills showed in brilliant and exquisite detail, even before the sun had fairly hauled its bottom clear of the horizon. The sea was lightening before their very eyes and even the troughs between the swells showed blue with a hint of turquoise as they rose to their peaks. Holbrooke looked around the horizon. Nothing, not the slightest sign of a sail on the whole blue wilderness, no hint that Europeans had been fishing these waters for centuries and that whole trading systems depended upon the harvest from these waters. Petersen's hail interrupted his thoughts.

'Captain, sir, there's a deal of smoke over Bay of Bulls, I can't see what's causing it.'

It was just like Petersen to know the name of the bay, and that was one of the advantages of sending a master's mate to the masthead as well as the regular lookout. Smoke over Bay of Bulls? It wouldn't be surprising, for by all accounts it was home to fifty or so people and they'd be setting their fires for breakfast by now. But *a deal of smoke* seemed too much for fires from cottage hearths. Did the fish curing process involve smoke? What fuel was available; peat, or wood or sea coal? There was so much that he didn't know, and it made his suppositions fragile at best. Nevertheless, he'd heard of salting and drying cod – he carried some few hundredweight in *Argonaut's* fish room – but not smoking. Surely it was haddock that was smoked, and in the Scottish fishing ports at that.

'Take her right into the mouth of the bay, Mister Fairview. Mister Shorrock!'

He cast around the quarterdeck, with no success.

'Pass the word for the first lieutenant.'

'Here, sir.'

Shorrock had clearly been at his breakfast when he heard the call, and he looked as though he'd intended to square away his stock before coming on deck, but his captain passing the word brooked no delay.

'You see that there's something afoot in Bay of Bulls, Mister Shorrock. Have the men had their breakfast?'

Shorrock looked around in despair and saw Fairview's covert nod of his head.

'Yes, sir, they have.'

'Good. I don't plan to be surprised, so beat to quarters, if you please, and clear for action.'

Argonaut had cleared for action very, very many times

and each time had its own memorable character. Sometimes it was done urgently in the face of the enemy with a sleepy crew summoned untimely from their hammocks, sometimes in a howling gale, and sometimes as an exercise against the ticking of the captain's watch. Today it was almost a pleasure. Almost. This clear, dry weather and calm sea with nothing in sight to add unwonted urgency lent an air of gaiety to the affair.

'Cleared for action, sir and the men are at quarters.'

Holbrooke looked along the main deck. He could tell a lot from the attitude of the gun crews. Sometimes they looked resentful and occasionally apprehensive, but today there was a light mood in the air, as though they were on a picnic. And why not? Newfoundland was an ornament in King George's crown, a colony of the mother country and nothing in this war had yet disturbed its peace. Holbrooke guessed that it was no longer true, but it was good that the men were in high spirits.

Argonaut stood into the land under tops'ls and heads'ls, carving a clean, even furrow in the profoundly blue sea.

'No fishermen, Mister Fairview.'

'None, sir. You'd have thought the boats would be out by this time of day, and in such weather.'

Holbrooke made no reply but studied the approaching land through his telescope. That smoke was certainly more than fifty or so people could produce in their homes, at least in the normal course of events.

'Captain, sir. I can see topmasts in the bay. Two of the line and maybe a frigate or two, and I believe they're setting their tops'ls. Yes, there they go, fore and main tops'ls in regular order.'

'Heave to, Mister Fairview. This is close enough.'

'Could it be *Antelope* and her squadron, sir?'

'I think not, Mister Fairview. Petersen wouldn't be deceived, he wouldn't mistake a fourth rate and a frigate for two third rates, and we know that none of Lord Colville's ships are this far north. That's the French squadron for sure. They've despoiled Bay of Bulls and now they're moving on.'

'Sail ho! Sail to leeward, seven points on the starboard bow! A ship-o'-the-line, I reckon, sir. Not a fisherman nor a supply ship, in any case, and too big for a frigate.'

There was urgency in Petersen's voice now. A few ships setting sail from a deep inlet was no present danger, not with the whole ocean to leeward, but a strange sail in the offing, potentially trapping *Argonaut* against the land; that was another matter.

'T'gallants and courses, Mister Fairview. Wear ship, bring her onto the starboard tack, full and by.'

'Aye-aye sir.'

'Mister Shorrock, a moment of your time.'

Shorrock hurried aft, stepping cautiously over the train tackles and avoiding the tubs of slow match.

'What do you make of her?'

The topmasts of the ship to leeward had just become visible from the deck. They must have been in sight for a good few minutes from the masthead, but both Petersen and the lookout had been absorbed in what was going on in Bay of Bulls. Holbrooke made a mental note to speak to the master's mate. It was an easy mistake to make, but potentially deadly for all that.

'Ship-o'-the-line, sir, for sure, but there's something odd about her. Not French I fancy, nor King George's.'

Shorrock studied the topmasts in silence. Holbrooke had never had that ability to tell a ship's nationality and its rate from nothing more than a glimpse of her tops'ls. He knew, of course, the essential distinctive features, but he'd never managed to distinguish such fine details. It wasn't his eyesight, he knew, but it was a lack of time spent at mastheads studying such things. He'd been promoted to command too early to develop the skill, while Shorrock had spent years at sea before he gained a commission and many more years as a lieutenant, with hours and hours at the masthead.

'Spanish, sir,' he said with finality, 'a fourth rate much like the one we met back in February. It could be the same for all I know.'

Spanish! What was a Spaniard doing here off Newfoundland. Spain had been excluded from these waters for decades, why were they now taking an interest?

'Strange that we should see French and Spanish here on the same day, sir. It's almost like they're making a rendezvous.'

Shorrock expected no reply from his captain, but he'd said his piece, and he picked up the telescope again to continue his study of the approaching fourth rate. *Argonaut* tacked, Shorrock heard the orders, the rush of feet and the creaking of the yards against the mast as the frigate's stern came through the wind. He'd noted the possibility that this was the same fourth rate that they'd mauled four months ago, but it was only as a comparison, a point of reference. Now, however, he was starting to wonder. He couldn't have said what it was specifically that made him suspicious; the rake of the masts, the length of the tops'l yards, the distance between the fore and the main, and the main and the mizzen, but he was becoming increasingly certain.

Argonaut settled on her new course and was thrashing to windward to escape from the trap, whether it was deliberately set or mere bad luck. Shorrock closed his telescope.

'It's the same Spanish ship, sir, the *San Sebastian* that we met in February. She's somewhat more tender than she was then, as though she's light on ballast, but she's the very same, I'm certain.'

Holbrooke nodded. There was no need for him to look again at the Spaniard, his opinion wasn't worth a shaved groat compared with his first lieutenant's.

'Well, then we meet again. I wonder whether he's recognised us yet.'

***

'Captain, sir. I think I can just make out another sail, four points on the larboard quarter, a little way off the land. It doesn't look like a ship, sir, more like a schooner or a lugger…'

The report ended abruptly and looking up Holbrooke could see that the lookout was speaking urgently to Petersen, offering the telescope and pointing to the north.

'…maybe a cutter, sir, standing out to sea on the starboard tack, much like us, sir. Yes, a cutter for sure, just a single mast and a gaff mains'l.'

'Well, a day for reunions, sir, but I can't see her from the deck yet. I expect that's the cutter that fouled *Garonne's* broadside back in the Iroise. A reconnaissance of St. John's, perhaps?'

'Possibly, Mister Shorrock. But the French could have been here as much as ten days now and I expect in that time they've at least attempted something against St. John's. It doesn't seem like de Ternay's style to sit on his backside in the Bay of Bulls and do nothing more than burn a few boats and cottages. Perhaps more of a dispatch vessel than a reconnaissance. Now, what's that Spaniard about?'

Holbrooke took a swift scan around the blue horizon and the grey shore. He was safe enough, for now, with his windward position. But it was a puzzle to imagine just what was happening. Probably of all the three commanders, he was the only one to know the identities of all the ships that were converging off Bay of Bulls. The *San Sebastian's* captain must be wondering whose ships those were standing out to sea, and whose cutter that was coming down from the north. Probably he'd identified *Argonaut* as the frigate that had humiliated him in February, if not then at least he'd know it as a British sixth rate. If he were in that position, in command of that Spanish fourth rate, what would he do? It all depended upon what orders her captain had. Was he here to disrupt the fishery, to rendezvous with his French allies, or to gather intelligence. If only he knew…

'Sail ho! Sail to windward, sir, coming down fast.'

This was all too much and Holbrooke stopped himself just before he showed his exasperation by stamping his foot on the deck. What had been a perfectly manageable situation a few minutes before, was fast becoming a dangerous-looking trap. Heavy units of two enemy nations to leeward and now an unknown sail to windward with a rocky coastline cutting off all escape to the west. He had to know the identity of that new sail!

'Mister Shorrock, you'll oblige me by taking your glass to the masthead and telling me what you make of this newcomer.'

Holbrooke saw his first lieutenant swing himself into the weather main chains and run up the ratlines like a man half his age. Petersen saw him coming and he and the lookout dropped down to the main tops'l yard to make space. It only took two minutes, but in that time the fine breeze had brought *Argonaut* and the new sail half a mile closer together. Now the anonymous scrap of white that Petersen had seen was revealed as the fore and main t'gallants of a substantial ship.

'A frigate, or a ship-sloop sir, and one of ours I think, but I'll know in just a minute. If it's a frigate it's a small one, perhaps one of our twenty gun sixth rates.'

Holbrooke picked up the speaking trumpet and aimed it aloft.

'Thank you, Mister Shorrock. Come down as soon as you're certain.'

A British frigate or a sloop. That would be *Siren* or *Gramont* then. Patrick Mouat had *Gramont,* and he was just a commander, but *Siren* had a post-captain, Charles Douglas.

'Mister Lister, what's Charles Douglas' seniority? Run down to my cabin and check the list.'

Holbrooke knew the answer, of course, but it was as well to be certain. So much of the next few days rested on that date.

'He was posted in March last year. He's eighteen months junior to you, sir.'

Holbrooke nodded. Then unless Douglas had been superseded by someone more senior before the frigate had sailed from Sheerness, *Siren* would be subject to Holbrooke's command. A cautious man might wait until he could hail the smaller frigate but the whole thing was very unlikely. Holbrooke had heard that *Siren* was awaiting a convoy only three weeks before *Argonaut* had sailed for the Brest blockade, and even if a new captain had joined in that short interval, it was unlikely that any captain senior to Holbrooke would be commissioned into the smallest class of post-ship in the navy.

'Make the signal enemy in sight to leeward and keep it flying. Then make the signal for frigates to come under the admiral's stern.'

In the British navy there were only a few signals that were universally understood, and every squadron commander published his own as soon as he hoisted his flag or pennant. The moderately comprehensive list that Hawke had distributed to the Western Squadron would almost certainly be unknown to *Siren* and *Gramont*. It was lucky that Holbrooke could make himself understood with just these two flags, but it would only work if Douglas understood *admiral* in this case to mean the senior of the two frigates.

'It's *Siren,* sir, and the *San Sebastian* has hove to. I'll come down now.'

Shorrock ran back down the ratlines as fast as he'd ascended. It was just the slightest bit difficult for Holbrooke to wait the five minutes until *Siren* was close enough to read the signals. He could be entirely wrong and be sending out orders to a man of vastly greater seniority than him, or Douglas may choose not to understand the signals. It was the first time that Holbrooke had been in this situation of command over another post-captain, and he was unsure how it would go.

'*Siren's* acknowledging, sir, and she's bearing away. It looks like she's steering to join us.'

'Thank you, Mister Fairview. Where's the Spaniard? Ah, I see he can't interfere. Heave to if you please, on the larboard tack, and let *Siren* come under our lee.'

***

CHAPTER TWENTY-ONE

A Fine Cutter

Saturday, Third of July 1762.
Argonaut, at Sea. Off Bay of Bulls.

'The weather-gage is a fine thing, sir, if you can win it.'

Fairview had brought *Argonaut* to with the frigate's head to the northwest, and now *Siren* was moving slowly into position to run across her stern. He nodded in approval as the smaller frigate stripped her canvas until she was propelled by nothing more than a flying fore-tops'l and what windage was left in her other close-reefed square sails. It would be a hasty conference, for sure, but this was no time to be transferring captains by boat, not with ships-of-the-line of two enemy nations just a few miles under their lee.

'I intend to keep the weather-gage, Mister Fairview, in the face of all provocations, but I'd dearly love to know what's happening at St. John's. That cutter knows, I fancy.'

The cutter was beating steadily up towards Bay of Bulls and her captain was evidently aiming for a meeting with de Ternay's squadron. Holbrooke looked at it wistfully. As an admiral might long for a frigate to extend the reach of his squadron, so a captain with only two frigates under command longed for a sloop or a cutter. He climbed onto the gunwale and hooked his arm through the mizzen lanyards, taking the speaking trumpet from the quartermaster's hand.

'Captain Douglas, I presume,' he called across the gently lifting sea.

This was one of the advantages of heaving to. The wind in the rigging was reduced to a whisper and the sounds of the waves against the hull were stilled to nothing more than a regular drumming, the normal heartbeat of a ship on the ocean. *Siren* was likewise quiet, with only enough canvas to maintain her steerage way.

'Aye sir,' came the reply in a broad Scots accent, born on the east coast, Holbrooke guessed, somewhere to the north of Edinburgh, 'and ye'll be Captain Holbrooke. I'm at your service, sir.'

Well, it was as easy as that. With those few words Holbrooke and Douglas had established their relative seniorities and Douglas had declared that there was no hindrance to his taking Holbrooke's orders. That last point was important because it would be a brave man who countermanded any instructions that Douglas had from a more senior officer. No doubt Captain Graves, the governor of Newfoundland, had given him orders, but the changing situation here off the Avalon Peninsula had rendered them obsolete. In this case *I'm at your service* was a literal statement of *Siren's* availability for tasking and not a mere conventional pleasantry.

'What do you know of the situation, Captain Douglas? Where have you come from?'

'I saw these fellows ten days ago,' he said gesturing towards the French, 'and I sent *Gramont* to St. John's while I made for Placentia. The fishing fleet there won't move. There are perhaps two hundred of them, of all sizes. They won't go to sea, not to catch fish nor to run for Louisbourg or Halifax. They're more afraid of the French at sea than they are of having their boats burned on the beach. I've heard nothing from Captain Mouat, so I've come around the Cape to see for myself. D'ye think they've taken St. Johns? Is that a Spaniard over there? What the devil is he doing here?'

Holbrooke marshalled his words, he had only a few more moments before the ships drifted apart.

'I followed the French across the Atlantic and I've just come from alerting Lord Colville at Halifax. They've brought a small army with them, a brigade it looks like. St. John's must be under siege or perhaps taken by now, I expect that cutter will know and it's bringing the news to the French flagship. The Spaniard – *San Sebastian* – will be in as much want of information as we are. He's waiting to see what happens, but I've no idea what he's doing here.'

Holbrooke could see that despite Douglas' sailing master's efforts, *Siren* would soon draw too far away for easy conversation.

'Take station to windward and conform to my movements. We'll follow the French squadron.'

It lacked originality as a first attempt at disposing his new squadron, yet it was important. Douglas would probably have naturally taken the leeward station without any orders, but Holbrooke wanted to keep his own ship nearest the *San Sebastian*. He couldn't have said why, but he had that feeling that of the two enemies, the Spaniard's intentions were less easy to predict than de Ternay's.

'Mister Fairview, get underway and follow the French squadron. Stay at least three miles clear and keep the strictest watch on *San Sebastian*. If he looks like getting to windward, haul your wind immediately.'

'Aye-aye sir. Don't you worry about the Spanish gentleman though. Look, he's staying well clear, he's bearing away as we speak.'

***

The French squadron was backing and filling as it organised itself off the mouth of Bay of Bulls, the Spaniard was keeping his offing, apparently unwilling to either fight his enemy or speak to his new friends, and the cutter from St. John's was coming up tack-upon-tack in the failing south-westerly breeze.

'He'll fetch the French flagship on this next board, sir. We may see something then. That's if the wind holds.'

Shorrock was right, but there was something odd to Holbrooke's eye. The cutter didn't need to make so long a board to seaward, it should have tacked five minutes ago. Fairview thought so too; his raised eyebrow and frequent use of the binnacle compass told Holbrooke that he also suspected that all was not as it seemed. That cutter's captain would want to report to the squadron commander without delay, but here he was, squandering whole minutes of precious time.

The cutter's course took it further and further to seaward, and now it looked as though its captain was heading deliberately for *San Sebastian*. The Spanish captain was of the same mind, and his response was to bear away even further, as though he was determined to avoid any contact with the French.

'I expect the cutter's lieutenant has decided that his commodore would like to hear what the Spanish navy's doing in these waters. Well, he'll be disappointed unless he's ready for a long chase. Look, the Spaniard's come so far off the wind he'll have to wear ship soon. If ever there was a ship displaying a *not at home* card, it's that one.'

Shorrock was enjoying watching the movements of the enemy ships. It was evident that they weren't co-operating, and that the Spanish at least didn't even want to speak to the French.

Boom!

They all looked over towards the French where a puff of smoke showed that the flagship had fired a gun.

'A flag at the fore topmast, sir. I wonder what that means?'

Holbrooke could guess. The cutter was being recalled and the gun was to emphasise the flag.

'The cutter's coming about, sir. He'll have to bear away to reach *Robuste* now.'

There was a flurry of canvas as the cutter's stem hung in irons for a moment, then some enterprising soul backed the jib, and she paid off onto the larboard tack. It wasn't well done, almost as though the cutter's crew wasn't familiar with their vessel, and that was a strange state of affairs after a long Atlantic passage.

Shorrock was watching the cutter as Holbrooke looked over at the French squadron. A second gun, and the flag was dipped and run up again. Evidently de Ternay didn't understand the cutter's movements either.

'She's hard on the wind, sir, as though she's steering towards us.'

'Is the starboard battery ready, Mister Shorrock?'

'It is, sir. Loaded with ball, although it hardly seems right to fire nine pounders at a poor little cutter.'

'Hold your fire until you hear my whistle, Mister Shorrock.'

An unnatural hush had fallen over the ship, the disciplined silence that came with a worked-up crew ready to go into action. For now, until the great guns should speak, Holbrooke could still give his orders in conversational tones. He brought up his telescope to look more closely at the approaching cutter. It all looked normal. Perhaps there were more men on the deck than he'd have expected, and the guns weren't run out. But what could the cutter's lieutenant expect to achieve with those four tiny guns – four pounders at best – against the two frigates? Now he could see someone beside the wheel waving at him, an older man in a blue uniform coat, and he could see that it was cut in the style of a British captain or a commander.

'Mr Fairview, heave to on the starboard tack. There's no need to signal *Siren,* Douglas will follow our movements.'

***

Shorrock met the officer as he came over the gangway. He'd seen the commander's uniform but had reserved the pipes and the side boys that were due to such a person: they were for an officer with a commission to a ship in service, and there was no telling who or what this man was. A cutter was a lieutenant's command and in any case this one was quite obviously French. There were questions to be answered before the navy's jealously guarded ceremonial honours were rendered.

'Patrick Mouat, late master and commander of the ship-sloop *Gramont.*'

'Carter Shorrock, first lieutenant under Captain George Holbrooke of His Majesty's frigate *Argonaut.* Follow me, sir, if you please.'

Mouat looked about at the ordered decks as he walked behind Shorrock. He acknowledged Fairview's unspoken greeting; it seemed that the two men knew each other, but that was hardly unusual.

Holbrooke was awaiting events in his cabin. It wouldn't do to have the meeting under the full gaze of the ship's company. He'd already guessed that it was Commander Mouat, separated from his sloop, but the man may be an imposter, or he may have lost his ship in circumstances that warranted a court martial. In any case, these things were best done out of sight of inquisitive eyes.

Mouat told his story well enough, but it was clear that he was a weary man, as well he might be.

'So we spiked the guns and scuttled her, sir. Unfortunately, I had to let the masts stand, there was no getting at the standing rigging with a host of Frenchmen taking aim at us. They were furious, of course, and set us to work salvaging the sloop, or *corvette* as they called it. They pressed the officers and men, without any distinction. Well, she was afloat yesterday afternoon but the stink of her was unbelievable, what with the fish remains and whatnot on the bottom o' the harbour. The gunner flat refused to drill out the spikes that he'd put in the guns, and threw his tools overboard, spare bushes an' all, when they insisted. All hands followed him – it was like a mutiny, I suppose – so they put us all under guard in a couple o' big fishing boats that were run up on the beach. Well, I'd had enough and when I saw this cutter come in just before sunset, I determined then and there to cut it out and make our escape before the dawn. We tied up our guards and took a pair o' boats – there are any number of them abandoned in the harbour – and rowed over to the cutter while it was still quite dark. We dealt with the deck watch without any noise, all the rest o' the men and the officers being on shore. It wasn't yet dawn, barely enough light to aim a musket, and the wind turned foul as we swept out through the Narrows.

The French on the heights were ready to receive us, of course, but we were a poor target in the twilight. I lost one able seaman dead and two wounded. I'd have lost many more if we'd waited for the dawn. However, there wasn't a vessel left in St. John's that could face even our few guns and once we were a cable clear of the shore we had nothing to fear except the French squadron, which we'd heard was at Bay o' Bulls. Ye may have seen us hesitate when we rounded Cape Spear just south of St. John's. That was when we saw all those ships to the south of us. But one of my seamen swore that he recognised *Argonaut,* so we stood on. Then *Siren* came into sight and the rest was just a matter of keeping out o' range o' the French guns.'

Holbrooke listened in fascination. This was a truly stirring tale. Mouat may have lost his ship, but that was just the fortune of war and could be laid squarely at the garrison commander's door. To have taken a French cutter and escaped through a narrow, deep-cut passage under the very guns of the French infantry was a feat worthy of recognition.

'My last orders were from Captain Douglas, sir. I was to stay in St. John's to support the garrison commander, but it was he who surrendered without even giving me warning.'

'Yes, of course.'

Douglas should be involved now, if only to confirm Mouat's orders. Holbrooke looked out of the window. The wind had dropped and the sea with it; there was just a long, low swell from the southwest that rocked the ship as she lay under her backed fore topsail.

'Mister Lister, be so kind as to ask Mister Shorrock to step down into the cabin. A fresh glass of sherry, Captain Mouat?'

'If you please, sir,'

'Ah, Mister Shorrock, are the French and Spanish ships far enough away for us to call Captain Douglas over?'

'Oh yes, sir. The French have no wind at all and *San*

Sebastian has only enough for steerage way, sailing large. Mister Fairview says that the wind will turn easterly in the dog watches. I'll hang out a signal now, sir.'

'Very well, Mister Shorrock. It's well past dinner time, I know, but would you tell my servant that Captain Douglas and Captain Mouat will join me, and could you pass my compliments to Mister Chalmers also? Perhaps you could bear to eat a second dinner.

Holbrooke could see that Mouat appreciated being called *captain,* even when he had no ship and as a commander no natural right to the title. He remembered when he too had been a commander and had suffered the deliberate insults that were implied when he was named, with heavy insistence, as *Commander* Holbrooke.

***

Holbrooke was determined that dinner should be a brisk affair and that the business of the day should be held until the loyal toast had been drunk. In Shorrock and Chalmers he had faithful allies, and he found that Douglas was of the same mind, even though there was no particular need for haste. Fairview had declared that the calm would last into the dog watches and then turn easterly before the first watch. How he knew that was anyone's guess, but Holbrooke had long ago accepted that his sailing master had a personal relationship with the forces that determined the weather. An easterly wind would serve admirably, and that would be the time to execute any plans.

'Well then, gentlemen. It appears to me that we can do nothing for St. John's until Lord Colville or General Amherst should send an expedition to retake it.'

Mouat nodded his head in agreement.

'Fort William's a pathetic affair, sir, but the French are determined to strengthen it. They're using their prisoners as forced labour and any Irish fishermen that choose to are being brought into the army's ranks. It's the usual story; extravagant promises concealing the grave danger if they're captured under an enemy flag. It'll take a regular siege to dislodge them, in my opinion, unless they're bombarded from the heights to the east. I noted the names of their ships as I heard them in conversation, sir. *Robuste,* a damned great seventy-four with thirty-six pounders. Oh, excuse me please, Mister Chalmers.'

Chalmers nodded. He's been at sea for over six years and had heard far worse.

'*Eveillé* is a twenty-four pounder sixty-four. *Garonne* is a fifth rate of thirty guns, some of them are twelves but I didn't hear how many. Then there's *Licorne,* a frigate but fitted as a storeship.'

'*Licorne* did you say? I do believe we've met her before, Captain Holbrooke.'

'That we did, Mister Chalmers. Off Little Inagua Island in 'fifty-seven, then a few months later in the Chops of the Channel. She was fitted out as a storeship even then, and not exactly keen for a confrontation. However, they had a convoy to escort and *Kestrel* being only a little sloop, we did our best to avoid each other.'

Holbrooke paused in thought for a moment while his guests waited.

'I take your point about a siege, Mister Mouat, but it's not yet clear that they plan to stay. They must be aware that there's no hope of reinforcement now that we know they're there. They may last to the first cold of autumn, and if they do they may hold on through the winter, but they must surely know that next spring they'll be turned out. Now, it seems to me that Captain Mouat has brought us all the news from St. John's, and we can achieve nothing against the French garrison. However, less than half of the fishing fleet resides there and we should do our best to safeguard the rest. Here's what I propose to do.'

***

CHAPTER TWENTY-TWO

Fall From Grace

Saturday, Third of July 1762.
Robuste, at Anchor. St. John's Harbour, Newfoundland.

The interview was short and brutal, lasting no longer than the time between the lieutenant's boat coming alongside and the flagship reaching its anchor berth. De Ternay had appointed him to the cutter, he'd placed his trust in the young man and given him an acting commission, and that trust had been betrayed. There were no excuses for a vessel being taken from a defended harbour and de Ternay gave the lieutenant no opportunity to fabricate any. He'd been summarily reduced to his former rank of *aspirant* – a midshipman – and it was unlikely that he'd ever rise to a higher station with that very public failure hanging around his neck. De Ternay felt particularly bitter about the whole episode. He'd persuaded the admiral at Brest that he needed a cutter for the expedition and had personally selected the man to command it. This morning he'd watched it beat up towards his squadron from St. John's and expected a full account of the capture of the place before he arrived in person. Now he had to hear it all from d'Haussonville, and could expect a heavily edited account of the brigade's proceedings.

De Ternay wasted no more time on the useless officer, but had himself rowed ashore the moment that *Robuste's* anchor plunged into the dark and fetid waters of St. John's harbour.

***

'Then, in your opinion, is the fort capable of being made defensible, Monsieur?'

D'Haussonville shifted uneasily in his seat. He wasn't a nervous man, but this de Ternay, with his direct stare and uncompromising questioning, made him uncomfortable.

Also, he knew very well that this was a leading question. The expedition was expected to spend no more than a month in St. John's – if it should be so fortunate as to capture the place – and nearly a week of that time had already passed. Three weeks then; it was barely enough time to destroy Fort William and certainly not enough to make it defensible.

'It could be done,' he replied cautiously. 'I'm using the prisoners and the inhabitants as labourers, and my engineer tells me that it could be rendered proof against a *coup de main* before the winter. A siege is another matter, but I have enough guns to establish batteries on the high ground overlooking the fort, Signal Hill and Gibbet Hill as the English map names them. It will never be proof against a determined enemy siege, but it can stand until next year and then perhaps it can be reinforced from France.'

De Ternay's intense stare was reducing the unfortunate brigade commander to a mere shadow of his real self. In any other company d'Haussonville was accustomed to holding the centre stage. He'd been selected for this command partly because it was assumed by his military superiors that he'd be able to overawe this very junior naval captain. It hadn't turned out that way.

'Of course, if I garrison this fort there will be no army to carry out the rest of your orders.'

De Ternay showed no sign of having heard him. In his opinion the Comte's statement, delivered partly as a challenge, was too obvious to warrant a reply.

Yet this was the nub of the problem, and it was caused by the very success of the expedition, for de Ternay had not expected to capture St. John's. All his planning – and he'd kept it largely to himself – was predicated on d'Haussonville's brigade being turned back at the walls of Fort William. In that case he'd destroy what he could outside the fort, re-embark the soldiers and take his squadron to range along the coast of Newfoundland, Nova Scotia and Île Royale, ravaging the fisheries and raising a panic in all the British colonies in America. He knew that he'd have little opposition before the year's end, for the British had sent the vast majority of their ships and every able-bodied soldier to the campaign against Havana. However, the ease with which St. John's had fallen into his lap changed everything. If he could put the place into a sufficient state of defence, and if he could balance the number of people against the available supplies, then d'Haussonville or his deputy could perhaps hold it through the winter. In the spring anything was possible, and surely Choiseul would find it useful in the peace negotiations. *Uti possidetis* was the agreed starting point for the peace talks, Choiseul had said. The negotiations were being undertaken on the basis that territories belonged to the possessor at the time of the negotiation. Probably Choiseul wouldn't want to keep Newfoundland, but he would certainly be able to exchange it for something more important to France; Belle Isle, Martinique, Guadeloupe, the list of French failures and territorial losses was hard to bear. It was interesting, though, that nobody any longer mentioned Canada or the greater New France; it appeared that their loss was final and irrevocable.

'Have you secured the food supply, Monsieur?'

'Yes, all of the food stores are under guard. My men are foraging in the country surrounding the town to bring in whatever crops are ready. I fear it won't be enough to sustain five hundred soldiers through the winter though.'

'How many men do you need to secure the fort, assuming that it can be repaired before the winter?'

D'Haussonville had been expecting this question. Privately he'd prefer not to go wandering about the oceans looking for places to attack. Having taken St. John's, and being confident that the British couldn't scrape together an expedition to oust him – not before the winter, in any case – he was quite content to rest upon his laurels. There was another factor: in Fort William he was the master of events but as soon as he set foot aboard a ship of the squadron he was reliant upon de Ternay even for the means to get ashore. Yet, the orders, and they had come directly from Choiseul himself, had been explicit, and if they were to be disobeyed then he was determined that the expedition's commander should make the decision. That was one advantage of having a man such as de Ternay in command: he wouldn't willingly call a council of war and d'Haussonville certainly wouldn't demand one. Let de Ternay take the blame, for he would undoubtedly claim the credit if there should be any.

***

De Ternay had inspected the fort and walked through the shabby little town. D'Haussonville's men had caused little damage and it appeared that the British garrison had shown a distinct disinclination to fight to retain the place. He had to admit that the soldiers had done well in the week that they had been in possession. He could see the fresh earth where the walls were being repaired and the battery down on the waterfront had already been strengthened with dressed stone robbed from the larger houses in the town. And there were people everywhere! It wasn't surprising that so few had fled the invasion, there really was nowhere to go in this inhospitable land. One thing was for certain, if the place was to be held through the winter he'd have to send these civilians and prisoners-of-war away before they consumed all the provisions.

The walk ashore had done him good, and it had helped him make the decision that he knew should be made. Now, in his own great cabin, with the lanterns lit against the advancing darkness, he could settle down to write what he was sure would be one of the most important letters of his life.

'Perhaps I should start by describing the state of the town and the fort, Monsieur?'

He had a good secretary, a man after his own heart who thought through every move in the game before committing himself. Yes, he should prepare Choiseul by singing the praises of d'Haussonville's brigade that had taken St. John's and by portraying it as a place that, with a little effort, could be made secure until the following year. He remembered his discussion with the great man at the de Ternay chateau. Choiseul had been uncertain of the outcome of an attack on St. John's. He'd offered alternatives, including, bizarrely, an attack on Scotland or Ireland, on the assumption that Fort William would hold out. That wasn't how his written orders were phrased, but he felt he knew Choiseul's mind. In fact, he was gambling his professional future on understanding the unwritten part of his orders.

'Very well, a preamble then, and read it to me when you've finished the first draft.'

He found the scratching of his secretary's pen soothed his mind as he mentally rehearsed his reasoning. His orders, both verbal and written, had given him considerable discretion as to how he employed his force. It was quite clear that Choiseul expected him to exercise his own judgement as the situation developed. Would he be thanked for abandoning St. John's to carry out raids elsewhere? That British frigate had reappeared like some sort of evil spirit, and it had been gone just long enough to report to the British commander-in-chief at Halifax. Probably Lord Colville didn't have enough ships to oppose his own squadron, but he surely had sufficient to make a policy of raiding the British settlements difficult to achieve. Any day now the Newfoundland squadron would arrive from Britain, and that would give Colville something approaching a parity in force. De Ternay felt a particular bond to his two third rates, having brought them out of the Vilaine river in the teeth of the British blockade. He hadn't done that just to lose them in some mad adventure on the American coast, some raid that would make no difference at all to the course of the war. He knew the value of his two ships-of-the-line and his two frigates, and he was certain he wouldn't be thanked for losing them in a pinprick raid on an insignificant North American seaport.

'May I read the preamble, Monsieur?'

De Ternay nodded and his secretary read aloud the two pages that he hoped would set Choiseul into an optimistic frame of mind. It was well-written. His secretary had a way with words, and he understood what his master was trying to achieve. After that introduction it was easy to declare that – subject to Choiseul's approval – the town of St. John's and its fort would be put into a state of defence that would secure it through the winter. Expeditions would be dispatched to destroy the infrastructure of the cod fishery over the whole of the Avalon peninsula and as far as they could penetrate along the remainder of the Newfoundland coast before winter. That part would be easy; wooden drying racks and salting sheds and the little boats that the English used for the inshore fishery would burn readily during the warm summer, and there was little else of value. De Ternay would use the larger prizes – the schooners and brigs – to send the prisoners-of-war back to France and, in order to reduce the mouths to be fed, those of the French brigade that weren't required to garrison the fort through the winter. In the final paragraph he requested supplies of food before the deteriorating weather cut St. John's off from France, and consideration that a relief expedition be sent in the spring, if Choiseul should choose to retain the place through the next year.

It was done, and de Ternay listened as his secretary read the completed draft.

'A bold move, Monsieur, if I may say so,' the secretary said when he'd finished. 'You are aware, I'm sure, that the Duke may feel that you've disobeyed his orders in staying in St. John's. Nevertheless, his directions do imply a wide range of possibilities after you arrive here, and he might just as well ask why you chose to abandon such an important town when it was so swiftly taken.'

And that was just the point, de Ternay thought. He had a solid accomplishment and throwing it away in pursuit of chimeric gains in other places seemed ludicrous. Well, so be it. He'd send the best of the schooners to Brest tomorrow and hope for a fast passage and a rapid return from Choiseul. He could hope for a reply towards the end of August, and surely in that time the English couldn't gather together an army and a fighting squadron from what was left after so many ships and regiments had been sent away to the far Caribbean.

***

Daylight lingered long during these summer months, and it was strange to think that this town was on almost the same latitude as his home in the Loire valley. There was less than a degree of difference, and yet for six or seven months of the year St. John's was almost uninhabitable while his chateau generally enjoyed mild winters and warm summers; it was an altogether healthier and more enjoyable place. But at last the sun had dipped below the western hills and the lights of the town, the fort and his anchored squadron were starting to show as bright pinpricks against the gathering darkness. The wind had dropped and he now detected another disadvantage of this place as the stink from the harbour hung in the still air. Well, he wasn't going to be forced into his cabin by a disagreeable smell and he resolutely paced the length of his poop deck in the solitude that only he, of all the hundreds of people on board *Robuste,* could enjoy.

The letter had been sent and the dice were cast, and he knew that he really should think of the future and not the actions of the past. And yet, Choiseul's reaction to that letter would probably be a turning point in his career. Since the day he was sent to the Knights of St. John at Malta he had rigorously obeyed the instructions of his superiors. That policy had served him well but from today he could no longer console himself with that thought. Objectively, he had deviated from his written orders and even though he was convinced that his actions were for the best, he knew that it wasn't his opinion that counted. High command, he was finding, carried obligations beyond those of junior officers, and he had to make hard decisions that may not always be deemed to be correct. His star had been in the ascendent since he'd brought the first ships out of the Vilaine, but he knew very well that a wrong decision could bring it crashing to earth. A fall from grace was a hard fall indeed.

Then a thought occurred to him, an almost impious idea that verged on superstition. He had taken his vows in the Order of St. John, and here he was, the de facto governor of the port of St. John's. He took comfort from that even though he knew that it was nothing more than a fortunate conjunction of two instances of the same name.

***

CHAPTER TWENTY-THREE

The Intendant

Sunday, Fourth of July 1762.
Argonaut, at Sea. Placentia Road.

'A fine passage, sir!'

Fairview had the self-satisfied smile of a man for whom the past twenty-four hours had passed in just the way he'd predicted. They'd suffered a few hours of calm in the dog watches, with the ships of all three nations rolling to the south-westerly swell, like so many ducks bobbing in the run below a mill wheel. Then, without any preamble, the wind had come fresh and warm and a little north of east, bringing squalls and showers to send the assortment of ships from Bay of Bulls to their various destinations. The French had stood out to seaward, presumably to give themselves sea room on what had become a dangerous lee shore. On seeing that, the Spaniard had stood away to the southeast and was soon lost in the murky weather over towards the Banks. Holbrooke had decided to split his forces. He sent *Siren* to the north to round Cape St. Francis and warn the fishing settlements in Conception Bay and Trinity Bay while the cutter would follow *Argonaut* to Placentia.

Holbrooke had written out an acting commission for Mouat as Master and Commander of the cutter. There'd been a momentary hiatus when it became apparent that the little vessel, as a tender to a flagship, had not been given a name by its previous owners. It couldn't be called *Gramont's Prize,* because that unlucky sloop was no longer in commission, nor did *Argonaut's Prize* or *Siren's Prize* seem right as neither Holbrooke nor Douglas would benefit by its capture. Nevertheless, it was a commander's command and therefore by impeccable naval logic it was rated as a sloop-of-war, regardless of its number of masts. It must have a name, and one that, as far as everyone could remember, wasn't already in use.

Mouat thought for a moment.

'Well, sir, Saint Andrew has never been honoured by a ship's name in the British navy, although there were many in the old Scottish navy, I'm told.'

Shorrock snorted in derision.

'Only the Dons name their ships for saints, and the French sometimes.'

Holbrooke was very willing to let Mouat have his way, as a recognition of his zeal. However, he could see that it would be contentious, even if not in the way that Shorrock anticipated.

'Not quite so, Mister Shorrock, we already have *Saint George* and *Saint Albans*. I see no objection to another saint's name. However, I believe we're venturing into politics by naming a ship after Scotland's saint, it's too soon after the 'forty-five rebellion and I suspect it would raise eyebrows in Whitehall. Any other ideas, Mister Mouat?'

'Well, sir, my home is in Shetland and our saint is Ninian. I doubt whether he's known at all south of the Tyne, so if a saint's name is acceptable perhaps *Saint Ninian* would be suitable.'

'What do you think, Mister Chalmers? You're our expert on saints.'

'Oh, an excellent name, sir, and it has no association with the Stuart dynasty that I know of. The Venerable Bede thought highly of Saint Ninian. Do you have to ask their Lordships' advice on this matter?'

'No, I think not. On distant stations such as this I can just get on with it, at least where unrated ship are concerned. They'll soon tell me if they don't like it, and then I'll have to think again. However, I can't see any objection to the name, and you may make it so, Mister Mouat.'

And so His Britannic Majesty's Sloop of War *Saint Ninian,* boasting four French four pounders and looking suspiciously like a cutter, was commissioned as the latest vessel in King George's fleet. There was no ceremony other than the hasty reading of Mouat's commission and the only spectators were the ever-present gulls that whirled and swooped and squabbled and screeched, indignant that any ship could sail the Newfoundland waters without leaving a tasty trail of fishy waste in its wake.

Argonaut and *Saint Ninian* made a fast passage on the wings of the easterly wind and before the sun rose on the new day they had weathered Cape Race, Cape Pine and Cape St. Mary. By noon they were standing slowly in towards Placentia Road in a bay that was usually a hive of activity in the summer; today it was strangely deserted.

'By the mark, five, shoaling, sir, and nasty smelling mud it is.'

'Two miles from the castle, I fancy.'

'Very well Mister Fairview, this will do. Anchor here if you please, and signal *Saint Ninian* to come alongside. Where's Mister Chalmers?'

***

Mouat proved to be an accomplished pilot and Holbrooke had nothing to do but watch the unfolding scene as *Saint Ninian* reached sedately and confidently through the gut and into the broad lagoon beyond. The castle looked abandoned but a glance through his telescope told Holbrooke that some soldiers at least were working on the curtain wall that commanded the approach to the Gut. Clearly they knew about de Ternay's squadron and the French brigade, and yet there was a distinct lack of energy. The soldiers were there, certainly, and he could see picks and shovels rising and falling, but there was no sense of urgency.

'I wasn't aware that you'd been here before, Captain Mouat.'

'I was here between the wars, sir. I signed on as mate o' a supply ship for a season, then master for another. That's how I met Mister Fairview, we were masters o' supply ships sailing in company. I know Placentia like the back of my hand. It hasn't changed, and the Castle is the same, just a bit more of it's crumbled since I last saw it.'

Holbrooke exchanged a glance with Chalmers and they both studied Mouat as he directed the little cutter through the Gut. He was around fifty by the look of him, and Holbrooke knew that he'd been commissioned a lieutenant during the last war. There'd been little time to get to know the man, but nevertheless Holbrooke would have expected to have heard this vital information and it vindicated his decision to keep *Saint Ninian* with him. Perhaps it was that casual mention of shipping as a mate. For a lieutenant to sail as the master of a merchantman was unusual enough, but it was almost unknown to sail as a mate, except in an East Indiaman. Probably he hadn't been strictly accurate when he requested leave from the Admiralty to be absent abroad. That would be it, he must be embarrassed at whatever need – financial probably – that drove him to it. However it was, Holbrooke felt lucky to have the man with him.

'I expect it's still John Harris who acts as the governor of the place. *Intendant* is the title they use here, after the old French style. You wouldn't think it was sixty years since we kicked them out o' Newfoundland, the way the people here hold onto the old ways o' doing things. I don't know who commands the company o' foot, though, I never had cause to meet him as a merchantman's mate, nor as a master.'

'This man Harris, I heard from Captain Douglas that he can be difficult and he's not one to bend to a King's officer's will, is that your recollection?'

Mouat smiled at that as though he was remembering some amusing incident.

'Oh, that's John Harris all right, sir. A viceroy by his own anointing and for the last dozen years he's been making life hell for the commander of the garrison and whoever's sent over as governor o' the territory. I didn't get a chance to say this in your cabin, but if he's keeping the fishing fleet from sailing, it'll be for his own purposes, and nobody will dare to contradict him. I expect he fears he'll lose authority if they sail away. Then again there's the harbour dues; not one o' those masters or owners will feel that they should be paying for the privilege of berthing in the Gut if in fact they're at Louisbourg or Halifax.'

***

The cutter crept slowly towards a crowded wharf where a half dozen men were unhurriedly warping two luggers away to make space. The whole Gut was crowded with vessels; brigs, yawls, sloops, cutters, luggers of all shapes and sizes. Standing apart from the crowd, four or five anchored schooners looked capable of making the passage across the Atlantic or south to the American colonies, but on the whole it was a decidedly coastal affair. It was easy to see how the thought of a passage even as far as Île Royale would be unattractive to many of these fishermen.

'Do you see John Harris on the wharf, Captain Mouat?'

With only a hundred yards to run Mouat's whole attention was on handling the cutter. He looked up briefly and saw all he needed to see.

'No, sir, and I expect he'll want ye to call upon him, begging your pardon. That's the way he is, always careful to assert his authority, unless he's changed, and I doubt that.'

This was Holbrooke's first sight of a Newfoundland settlement, and he was seeing it at its worst. Wherever he looked he saw men in idle clusters or singly, all watching the approaching cutter with dull disinterest.

Chalmers was also struck by the air of lethargy that hung over Placentia like a grey, sodden cloud.

'There must be two hundred vessels here, as Captain Douglas told us, and a good five or six hundred men on shore. They don't look pleased to see us.'

The cutter nudged the wharf sending a ripple through its ancient, infirm timbers that made a few of the men stagger. However, there was no offer of help with the lines and it was lucky that the light breeze pressed the cutter against the piles until two men could jump ashore and drop the spliced eyes of the warps over the tops of two of the piles. Mouat looked at them appraisingly. The piles would hold in this breeze, but he'd need something more substantial if the wind changed.

'Well, what now?' Holbrooke asked Chalmers quietly. 'I've half a mind to wait here until someone comes to greet me.'

Chalmers had been looking over towards the Castle, rather than towards the town.

'There are three soldiers coming this way,' he said pointing to the road that led from the Castle.

Holbrooke followed his pointing finger and focussed the telescope. Three officers, and one looked as though he could be a captain. That must be the garrison commander.

***

Captain Trouville of the Fortieth of Foot was an old officer who had served his time entirely in Newfoundland. His company hadn't been called upon to face the enemy since it was formed forty-five years ago and sent to Newfoundland to secure this recently acquired territory and its valuable fishery. The company's welfare and indeed its very existence wasn't a high priority for the generals at Horse Guards, and Trouville had followed the example set by his predecessors in avoiding, as far as possible, anything to do with the army at large. He'd received recruits, uniforms, pay, muskets, ammunition and rations with reasonable regularity, and even the occasional orders and advice, but otherwise his was a world apart from regular soldiering. His men spent a good deal of their time about their own business. Most had families in Placentia, and their own plots of land and a few even owned or had shares in fishing boats. Trouville spent more time about his business interests than he did in maintaining the fabric of the Castle and the fighting efficiency of his hundred-or-so men. He'd long ago learned to co-exist with the Intendant and although it wouldn't be true to say that their interests were the same, they were at least usually not in conflict with each other.

An Upright Man

Not even the Louisbourg and Quebec campaigns had disturbed Trouville's peaceful routine. Then, out of the wide blue, a frigate had come calling talking of a French invasion and urging the fishing fleet to abandon the town and sail away to the ends of the earth. In that case he'd have no good reason to stay in Placentia. Without the boats there was nothing very much worth protecting and he could see that his duty would call him to take his men on the long overland march to St. John's, to a very uncertain meeting with a properly trained and motivated French force. It didn't bear thinking about, and he'd breathed a sigh of relief when *Siren* had sailed away. As he strode towards the wharf he rehearsed just how he'd persuade this next sea officer to leave them at peace, to take their chances with the French, if they ever came to Placentia, which he doubted.

'Good morning, sir. Captain Trouville commanding the detached company of the Fortieth of Foot. Whom do I have the honour of addressing?'

Holbrooke was surprised that the other two officers weren't introduced. The manners of a line regiment appeared to have been forgotten along with the duty to maintain the town's defences.

'Captain George Holbrooke of His Majesty's frigate *Argonaut,* and this is Captain Patrick Mouat of the sloop *Saint Ninian* and Mister Chalmers, my chaplain.'

Trouville looked twice at Mouat. He knew immediately that he'd seen him before but couldn't quite think where. He ignored Chalmers entirely. Neither of them mattered, it was the captain who had to be persuaded, not the commander and not the clergyman.

Holbrooke waited to be invited to walk over to the Castle, or wherever this soldier exercised his command, but there was no such suggestion. Instead, Trouville immediately started talking.

'I had the honour of meeting Captain Douglas of the frigate *Siren* a few days ago, you're acquainted with the gentleman, sir?'

'I met him yesterday.'

Chalmers was watching the two men as they jostled for position at the starting line. He almost smiled at the performance. He knew Holbrooke very well and could recognise the signs that he was less than impressed with Trouville's attitude. His friend was almost too easy-going, but he'd watched as Holbrooke had learned the hard way that he needed to maintain his position. He could see the danger signs already.

'Then no doubt you're not here on the same errand, sir.'

Holbrooke visibly bristled and drew himself up to his full height.

'You're aware, Captain Trouville, of the French expedition, I'm sure. Well, they've taken St. John's and I'm here to bring the fishing fleet to a place of safety. Now, if you can tell me where I can find the deputy governor, Mister Harris, I believe, then I'll make the arrangements with him and leave you to your own business and to await General Amherst's call to action or the French descent upon the town, whichever comes sooner.'

Holbrooke looked around as though he expected Harris to appear at any moment, and it was not an unreasonable assumption when a King's ship came a-calling. Trouville was visibly shocked. He'd thought the French expedition was a mere harassing attack; that they were intent on burning a few boats but hadn't enough power to take either St. John's or Placentia.

'St. John's has fallen? What's become of the company of foot?'

'Set to work at Fort William as prisoners o' war,' Mouat replied callously, 'their casualties were light, as you'd expect in such a brief affair.'

'And unless you have sufficient force to resist six hundred French infantrymen supported by a siege train,' Holbrooke held Trouville in his gaze as he spoke, 'I suggest you consider how you can best contribute to preserving this fishery, for as I understand the matter, it's the only thing of value in this place.'

Holbrooke continued to observe Trouville as the unfortunate soldier's head swivelled and his eyes were drawn inexorably to the walls of his castle. Its state of decay was obvious even viewed from this distance, and Holbrooke's words had struck home.

'Perhaps we can continue this discussion in my cabin, Captain Trouville.'

***

The Intendant lived in one of the few stone-and-brick houses in the town. It was set back from the hurly-burly of the dockside with its smells of fish and tar, and overlooked the scene with a lofty disdain from the crest of a low bluff. There were other houses beside the Intendant's, each hoping for the same disassociation from the business of the town, but they were all pale imitations compared with the true seat of power.

The two unnamed land officers had been sent to the Castle and now, with Trouville walking half a pace behind Holbrooke, there was no doubt who commanded the King's forces in Placentia.

John Harris awaited them in what looked like the business part of the house. It was a small room furnished in shades of brown and dark red that cast an immediate gloom over the party of four. No refreshments were offered and it was clearly with great reluctance that Harris offered seats. He looked suspiciously at Trouville and regarded Holbrooke, Mouat and Chalmers with a studied disdain that boded ill for the meeting.

'A second King's ship within a week. I trust you aren't here to tell me that I must abandon my town, Captain Holbrooke. I believe I've made my position clear on that matter. Ah, Mister Mouat, I hardly recognised you in that uniform. No longer a merchantman's master, I see.'

Mouat merely bowed. Holbrooke had made it plain that he alone would negotiate with Harris. The intendant looked pointedly away when he realised that his attempt to undermine Mouat had failed.

'You may do as you wish, Mister Harris. Stay or go, it's all the same to me, and likewise every master of a vessel in the harbour must make his own decision. But I'm here to tell you that I'll be addressing them all as soon as I leave this house, and I fully expect them to heed my advice. Now, Mister Harris, I'm giving you the opportunity to further the King's business and to save this fishery from complete ruin. If you choose not to take it, well, I'll proceed without you and record your opposition in my report…'

'You'll not address the town without my permission, Captain, by God you won't.'

'…as I was saying, I'll proceed without you, and you'd be well advised to reconsider.'

Holbrooke walked to the window. His gesture was unmistakable, and Harris would have needed a will of iron to avoid following him. What he saw brought an involuntary gasp. *Argonaut's* boats were alongside and already disgorging the ship's full complement of marines, some thirty-five in total. Lieutenant Murray was directing the landing, and the two unnamed officers of the Fortieth of Foot were bringing their own men at a fast march from the fort.

Harris glared at Trouville who merely bowed in response, without a hint of emotion. Mouat was less successful in hiding his feelings and when Harris turned towards him, he smiled and nodded knowingly.

Holbrooke turned towards the Intendant.

'You see, Mister Harris, this town will be visited by the French within the week, and having discussed the situation with Captain Trouville, we've agreed that for all practical purposes it's indefensible. As I said, you're welcome to stay here, but I'm confident that when they understand the situation as it really is, each and every owner of a fishing boat or supply schooner will join the convoy that will depart for Louisbourg tomorrow. I can offer you a passage in *Argonaut* but can't compel you to take it. Perhaps a

An Upright Man

French prison appeals to you more than the great cabin of a King's ship.'

***

CHAPTER TWENTY-FOUR

The Laurentian Channel

Tuesday, Sixth of July 1762.
Argonaut, at Sea. St. Peter's Island north four leagues.

Never since the Great Flood had such a ramshackle collection of vessels put to sea. There were over two hundred of every possible variety but with a unifying feature that all but twenty of them shared; they were built for the inshore fisheries and had spent their working lives harvesting cod from the deep bays of the southeast corner of Newfoundland. Never, not in their worst nightmares, had the owners of those boats – and they were almost all owned by their crews – considered sailing past St. Peter's Island out into the exposed Laurentian Channel. Yet here they were, each sporting some kind of sail and making a creditable four knots west-south-westerly before the providential northerly breeze.

'I wouldn't have thought to see its like, not in any place short of bedlam.'

Shorrock wiped the sweat from his forehead as he gazed in wonder at the convoy. He had the watch and was keeping *Argonaut* close to the south of the untidy gaggle. So far it had needed no more than the occasional hail to keep the worst of the sailors from wandering too far. They were more in danger of colliding with each other than they were of straggling. He looked over his shoulder to see *St. Ninian's* tops'l far away at the rear.

'How far to Louisbourg now, Mister Fairview?'

'Fifty-five leagues or thereabouts, little different from when you asked me at the last turn of the glass.'

Fairview was busy taking bearings of St. Peter's Island, hoping to lay down its longitude more accurately than it had been thus far. The island, along with Miquelon, had been British since 1713 but it had never been considered important enough for a proper survey to be attempted. Fairview knew that James Cook – the man of the hour since his role in the fall of Quebec – had come this way two years before, but even he hadn't stopped long enough to make a definitive survey.

'Thereabouts, Mister Fairview? I'd hoped for better from you.'

Fairview ignored the remark and bent to take another bearing while Shorrock, cheated of his fun, carefully quartered the horizon with his telescope. It was hard to see past the fishing boats to the north; he'd have to rely upon the lookout whose lofty perch commanded a view over the stubby masts of the convoy. To the west, the south and east he had as good a view as he could hope for and the horizon ran as straight as a rule, without the slightest impurity of line that would indicate a sail.

***

'Good morning, Mister Shorrock, Mister Fairview. I see the mist has burned off. Is *St. Ninian* in sight?'

'Dead astern, sir. You can see her tops'l from the taffrail, just to the right of those schooners.'

Holbrooke barely glanced at the cutter; it was enough to know that Mouat was keeping his allocated station. He'd anticipated a difficult time, bringing all these fishermen away from their homes in Placentia, but actually it had proved to be easy. When they understood that the threat from the French was immediate and real, and that the garrison would be embarking for the journey to Louisbourg, leaving the place defenceless, they'd quickly realised the wisdom of following *Argonaut*. As the inevitable problems had shown themselves, and boats began to develop problems with their rig, or started to take on water, the sense of community spirit had brought help from their friends. They'd scuttled two of the oldest boats within hours of leaving Placentia and even now a half dozen were under tow by the larger schooners, but that was to be expected with such a huge convoy of coastal fishermen setting out into the wide ocean.

There was little of value left behind in Placentia; just the houses, the sheds and the drying racks and a handful of souls who chose to stay to look after the place. The Intendant had refused a passage in *Argonaut* but at the last moment, as the vast armada was setting sail, Holbrooke had seen Harris and his wife hurrying aboard the only brig in the convoy. Mouat had confirmed what Holbrooke suspected, that it belonged to the Intendant.

Holbrooke noticed that Chalmers had come on deck and was also gazing out to the south and east.

'I had always thought that an escort should position itself to windward of a convoy, Captain Holbrooke, and yet, unless I'm mistaken we're firmly placed to leeward,' he paused to orientate his body to the breeze and nodded in satisfaction. 'There must be a good reason for your abandoning your principles in this manner.'

'Ah, good morning, Mister Chalmers. How very observant of you. Let me show you a chart to explain the situation.'

It took just a few seconds for the midshipman of the watch to fetch a chart from the master's sea cabin. He spread it out upon the top of the binnacle and pinned down the curling edges with a variety of small, heavy rigging implements that a passing bosun's mate conjured out of his pockets. There was barely a murmur from Fairview. It seemed that once the principle had been established, he had no real objection to hazarding his charts under the sun's baleful gaze; it was the salt spray that he objected to, and that most strongly.

'Here's the situation. You see that we have to cross this wide gulf before we can reach the safety of Louisbourg. It'll take us two more days if this wind holds, more if it shifts into the sou'west. Now, we know that de Ternay was last seen at St. John's but I don't expect he'll stay there very long. Placentia must be on his list of targets, and if he sailed yesterday, and if he's using his frigate intelligently, we could be sighted at any moment. Then there's the Spaniard. He was last seen making for the Banks, and once he knows that they're deserted, I expect he'll come this way as well. But you see, all of our enemies – or those that we know of – are to the south and east, and that's why I've positioned *Argonaut* as I have. If either of them should go into Placentia and find it empty, they won't take long to guess where we're heading and set off in pursuit, and then Mister Mouat will warn us.'

'A fine disposition, if I may say so. However, if I might make an observation.'

Holbrooke nodded cautiously.

'You've always told me that it's dangerous to assume that the enemy will do as you expect. What if they appear from the northwest, from the Gulf of St. Laurence? You have no protection in that direction.'

'True enough, but what would you have me do? Conjure up another frigate from thin air? *Siren* could join us today, it's at least possible, but short of that we're on our own until we sight Louisbourg. We must make the best of a bad job.'

'And if you should be overtaken by the French or the Spanish, or both?'

Holbrooke didn't immediately answer but stared at the far eastern horizon.

'In that case, my dear David, we must sell ourselves dearly to allow these fishermen to escape.'

'I'm sure you will, but are they worth it? Is the sum value of all of these worth a King's frigate and a prize cutter? Is this the same dubious arithmetic – more art than science – as was the case with the convoy to Savannah?'

'Oh, it's a similar calculation. The navy can't be seen to abandon half of the Newfoundland fishing fleet to its fate, and particularly not after I all but ordered them to abandon their homes and follow me to sea. It's the same dubious arithmetic, as you put it. Not hard coin, but the more subtle effects on the City, on votes and on this vast pool of seamen that the navy calls on for recruits. There's no question; I'll have to fight, whatever the odds, so long as there's a chance of half of these fellows escaping. Ah, here's the coffee. You'll join me, I hope.'

***

It was a peaceful forenoon, and they drank the first cup of coffee in silence. *Argonaut* raised barely a ripple as she rose and fell to the long, low swell while the quartering wind whispered softly and politely in the rigging. The early mist was but a memory and a fine blue sky with only a few clouds hurrying away to the south gave promise of a glorious summer day.

'Beg your pardon, sir…'

Shorrock had thrust himself in front of Holbrooke and his great bulk cast a shadow that encompassed both captain and chaplain.

'…*Saint Ninian* is signalling. It's hard to see, what with the sun, but it looks like he's sighted a sail to the east.'

Holbrooke looked over the frigate's quarter but there was nothing but a blank horizon.

'Very well. Wear ship, Mister Shorrock, make all sail and reach out to the east, perhaps east-nor'east, and let's see what Mister Mouat has reported. You may surrender the deck to Mister Fairview if you want to look over your guns.'

Now *Argonaut* was battling the wind, sailing a point free on the larboard tack in an effort to get to windward. If that was de Ternay, or *San Sebastian* then his station must be between the enemy and the convoy. And was that a smirk on the chaplain's face?

'Masthead!'

Holbrooke shouted through the speaking trumpet, his voice carrying easily to the lookout.

'You know what you're looking for?'

'Aye sir. A sail within three points of the bow. Nothing yet, sir.'

'And nothing more from *Saint Ninian,*' Fairview added, 'No, I lie, sir, Mister Mouat is signalling. Ah, it's *Siren* that he's sighted.'

The quarterdeck let out a collective sigh of relief. They all knew that *Argonaut* must fight any enemy, of whatever force, to give the fishermen a chance to escape. They were none of them shy of a battle, but unless the French had sent one of their frigates ahead, it was going to be a one-sided affair, with little honour in the outcome. Nobody would remember a brave frigate that fought a losing battle to save a band of fishermen.

'Very well, Mister Fairview. Then make a signal for *Siren's* captain to report to the commander. Mister Mouat will have the sense to repeat the hoist; you gave him the appropriate flags, I expect.'

'I did, sir. But *Siren* should be in range in ten minutes.'

'Well then, Mister Fairview. Bring the ship about and let's get back to our station. There's a deal too much activity in this stretch of water for my liking.'

'Yes, sir. Captain Douglas won't take long to catch us, not when we strip to our tops'ls to stay in station with these old tubs.'

Fairview indicated the convoy, and it was true that the motley selection of vessels didn't have a look of speed about them today, either singly or as a whole. They'd done well to keep up four knots overnight, but it wouldn't take much to slow them down again. What really worried Holbrooke was the prospect of the wind shifting to the southwest. In that case their three-day passage would easily stretch out to a week or more, and then provisions would start to become a problem. Under normal circumstances only the brigs and schooners expected to stay at sea for more than a day or two, and most just didn't have the capacity to stow food and water for a week.

'And Mister Fairview, I think we'll work our way to windward of the convoy. With *Siren* coming up from the east, it's unlikely that we'll be surprised from that direction. It will please Mister Chalmers, if nothing else.'

***

Fairview handled *Argonaut* superbly as the frigate threaded its way through the mass of small craft. Most of them had the sense to hold their course, but a few thought it best to attempt to clear out of the great ship's path. It was understandable but it added an unpredictable element to Fairview's calculations. No sooner had he settled on a course that would take him clear across the bows of a group of their charges, than one would break away and make a dive for what he thought was safety. Holbrooke would usually have watched this with interest, eager to learn from a master of the art, but today his mind was elsewhere.

There was something amiss. He couldn't quite say what, but it was like Macbeths witches – *by the pricking of my thumbs, something wicked this way comes* – and he couldn't settle his mind.

'Masthead, keep a good lookout all around.'

Shorrock stared at him. It was unlike the captain to give an unnecessary order when he knew very well that the lookout would scan the whole horizon, whatever else of interest there was. But perhaps he was right. With two hundred of a convoy and *Siren's* tops'ls likely to be visible at any moment, the lookout could well be distracted.

'Nothing, sir. I can't even see *Siren* yet.'

That was the lookout's way of telling Holbrooke that he didn't need to be reminded of his duty.

Holbrooke paced the quarterdeck. The feeling wouldn't leave him, and he was reluctant to go below to hide his agitation, even though he knew he was putting the whole quarterdeck on edge.

'Sail ho! Sail three points on the starboard quarter, sir. It looks like a frigate's t'gallant. Could be *Siren*, sir.'

Holbrooke instinctively looked out over the hammock netting in the direction that the lookout had indicated. It was a foolish gesture as *Siren* couldn't possibly be visible from the quarterdeck. It merely served to emphasise his unease. Well, Douglas would catch up eventually, and with his t'gallants set it would be only a few hours. Yet still something was worrying Holbrooke as he continued his pacing. Out of the corner of his eye he saw Shorrock and the gunner walking the main deck as the gun captains checked their breechings, their train tackles, their worms and sponges. The ship wasn't even at quarters and already everyone was preparing for battle. Was that his example, or did others feel that awful pricking of the thumbs as well?

'Keep *Siren's* signal flying Mister Fairview.'

Another useless order. Fairview wouldn't dream of striking the signal without a positive order to do so, and his querying glance at his captain confirmed that. Holbrooke felt he needed to explain.

'I want Captain Douglas with me as soon as possible. Mister Shorrock, you may fire a gun to leeward when you consider that *Siren* can see our signal.'

He may have ignored one of the basic principles by stationing *Argonaut* to leeward of the convoy, but he wasn't about to commit the cardinal sin of splitting his force when he knew – he absolutely *knew* – that there was an enemy about. The gun would emphasise the need for haste in a way that no additional flags would ever do.

***

Dinner, and the hands were all at their mess tables, noisily partaking of the principal social event of the day. Now Holbrooke was starting to feel foolish. *Siren* had come along hand over fist and Douglas would be expecting to be told why he'd hastened at breakneck speed through two hundred fishing vessels, every fourth one of which made a desperate attempt to disfigure the frigate's paintwork. Oh well, he'd have to make the best of it, but it would certainly sound less than convincing, and Douglas would have an embryonic contempt for his senior officer.

'Back your main tops'l, Mister Fairview, take the way off her.'

Holbrooke waited for *Argonaut* to settle down and for *Siren* to come up on his quarter, then he walked to the lee rail and drew a breath, still considering what he'd say.

'Sail ho! Sail five points on the starboard bow. It looks like a ship on the larboard tack running down to us, sir. It's no merchantman, more like a ship-o'-the-line.'

Holbrooke stopped dead. A ship-of-the-line coming down from the Saint Lawrence. It could hardly be British; Lord Colville had outlined the movements of what was left of his squadron after all the best were sent away to Havana. There were no others, not this side of the Atlantic and certainly none coming down from the Saint Lawrence. It couldn't be de Ternay either. The Spaniard then? *San Sebastian* could have investigated the Grand Banks, noted the general air of inactivity and decided to risk looking into the Gulf of Saint Lawrence. Certainly that ship's captain was eager enough to try anything, even poking around in what was now Britain's private lake. There was just time for him to have reached across to North Cape and doubled back. The wind would have served, too.

'Mister Shorrock. Beat to quarters and clear for action.'

That should at least give Douglas a hint, and sure enough he heard the answering drum roll from *Siren*.

'Captain Douglas, you come in the nick of time. I believe that may be the Spanish fourth rate to windward. In any case, take station astern of me. If it is, we'll have to fight.'

'We will at that, sir.'

Douglas was having to shout into the wind, but his enthusiasm was evident, even though two small frigates against a fifty-gun ship was hardly an appealing prospect. Holbrooke and Douglas had the advantage of a few more guns but they were much lighter and while the Spaniard's thick oak sides would keep out most nine pound shot, the frigates' sides would yield easily to twenty-four pound balls.

'If I get the chance we'll take her between our fires, Captain Douglas. You take larboard and I'll take starboard. Try to rake her if you can. We must harry her until she gives us up as a bad job. The convoy's the important thing, and we must avoid too much damage to ourselves while the

French are about.'

Douglas waved in acknowledgement. How much did he understand of Holbrooke's plan? It would be disastrous if he threw his frigate alongside *San Sebastian* and attempted to board. Holbrooke would be forced to support him and then the fishing fleet would be left without protection and in all likelihood would turn back to Placentia. But then, it may not be the Spaniard at all.

'God speed now, Captain Holbrooke.'

Siren fell away to take her station astern of *Argonaut*. Holbrooke was aware that Fairview was filling the main tops'l and that his frigate was starting to move ahead.

'Make all plain sail, Mister Fairview.'

Shorrock came aft. His face was suffused with pleasure and he was positively rubbing his hands in anticipation.

'The ship's cleared for action, sir and the hands are at their quarters. I've taken the liberty of running out the guns, it being such fine weather.'

He looked searchingly at his captain.

'We'll finish what we started with that Spanish gentleman, I've no doubt, sir.'

'We may well, Mister Shorrock, we may well, but it's not yet clear that it's an enemy, more less the Spaniard. Why, it could yet be one of our own fourth rates that Lord Colville forgot to mention.'

Shorrock smiled broadly. He didn't believe a word of it.

'Deck ho! It's the *San Sebastian,* sir, I'm certain of it now.'

***

CHAPTER TWENTY-FIVE

Attrition

Tuesday, Sixth of July 1762.
Argonaut, at Sea. St. Peter's Island northeast eight leagues.

'Bear up, Mister Fairview, bring her hard on the wind.'

'Aye-aye sir.'

Siren had already put down her helm and was evidently intending to tack across *San Sebastian's* head. Holbrooke spared the other frigate a glance to confirm that Douglas had understood his part in the action. A tiny ship like that shouldn't be engaging a fourth rate, but there was no alternative. *Siren* was the smallest vessel that could rightly be called a frigate. She was nominally a twenty-gun, nine pounder, but in fact she carried another two nine pounders on her *demi-batterie* on the lower deck, and two smaller guns on her quarterdeck, somewhat like the old *Fury*. Nevertheless, she was small and frail, not much more able to withstand fire than Holbrooke's first ship, the sloop *Kestrel*. Well, Douglas looked as though he knew what he was doing.

'Now, we'll see if this Spaniard has learned anything since we last met. What do you think, Mister Shorrock, is Douglas planning to rake his bow?'

Holbrooke watched closely; the Spaniard's moves over the next few minutes would give him a good idea of his intentions. For it wasn't yet clear what on earth a Spanish fourth rate was doing in these waters when Havana was in deadly peril, the East Indies was under threat, and the Spanish army was marching into Portugal.

'Ah, *Siren's* hard on the wind, trying to let the Don get closer. Look, you can see his scars from the last time we met. That's a ship's carpenter's job; no dockyard has worked on those timbers, I'll be bound.'

Shorrock was entirely taken up with the drama of the

moment. It mattered not one jot to him that a wrong move from Douglas would expose *Siren's* thin planking to a hail of twenty-four pound shot. All that mattered was *San Sebastian's* response.

'Will he turn? If he bears up *Siren* will be in a pretty pickle, but that will take him away from the convoy. He'll bear away, surely.'

Holbrooke kept his council. The Spanish captain must recognise *Argonaut*. That being the case, surely his first thought would be to engage his old adversary, the ship that had humbled him before. Why hadn't his battle damage been repaired? It was five months since they met to the northeast of San Juan and Holbrooke was certain that his adversary had been steering for Havana by the Old Bahama Strait until he'd seen the chance for what he thought were easy pickings in a British West Indies convoy. It was important to know, or at least to make an educated guess. *San Sebastian* must have been an unwelcome visitor to Havana, bringing news of war and a list of repairs. At that moment an extra, damaged, fourth rate must have been seen as a liability rather than an asset. Had *San Sebastian* been sent to Newfoundland to clear the space in the dockyard? Furthermore, the governor-general must have known that his city would soon come under siege – and Holbrooke was aware that he was stretching his few facts as far as they'd go – perhaps the fourth rate didn't have her full complement of men and guns.

'Ah, he's bearing away, sir.'

A glance told Holbrooke that his first lieutenant was correct. Those great, bluff bows were turning to starboard and a flurry of activity at the sheets and braces told him that *San Sebastian* was preparing to wear ship.

'Bear away, Mister Fairview, let's see if we can get a shot at his bows.'

The familiar sights crowded into Holbrooke's view. The long nine pounders were run out on the starboard side. The gun captains crouched at the breeches, peering along the barrels. With short sweeps of their left palms they directed the layers to swivel the ponderous weights with their handspikes, following the target that was almost steady in their sights. Their right hands were raised to say that their guns were ready to fire. The smoke of the slow match streamed away to leeward as a man at each gun held the linstock ready to thrust into the gun captains' hands.

'Fire when you're ready Mister Shorrock.'

The first lieutenant stood like a statue, watching for the correct moment. Holbrooke noticed that *San Sebastian* had only run out her upper deck guns, her twelve pounders. Perhaps there was something in his hypothesis…

'Fire!'

Shorrock bellowed out the command. There was a pause, no more than a second but it felt like half a minute, and then the guns spoke, and *Argonaut* staggered to the recoil.

'Two or three hits sir, but it's long range for nine pounders.'

Fairview was keeping up a commentary and behind him Holbrooke's secretary, watch in hand, was making notes for the report.

'Helm a-weather, Mister Fairview, follow his stern around.'

A ragged crash announced that the Spaniard had opened fire, but where the balls landed was anyone's guess. The battle was too fast paced, too many ships manoeuvering in a small area, and it was difficult to see whose shot landed where. For *Siren* was firing too and it looked like her broadside had done some minor damage to *San Sebastian's* stern.

'Nothing from her lower gun deck, sir, and her port lids are firmly closed. I reckon she's a flute.'

'Flute or not, those are twelve pound balls, Mister Fairview.'

Another broadside from the starboard battery. This one was better aimed, and Holbrooke saw splinters flying all along the Spanish ship's side.

'*Siren's* wearing all the way around, sir. I suppose Mister Douglas didn't have enough way to tack again.'

This was becoming the most curious battle that Holbrooke had ever engaged in. For some reason the Spanish ship was reluctant to close with either of the frigates. It was becoming clear that they were short of guns, but ten twelve pounders a side could still destroy a frigate in short order. The correct action should be to get alongside one of the frigates so that the extra weight of broadside could do its work. There must be something else; it was almost as though the Spaniard feared a boarding action. Could that be it? Could he really have lost half of his men at the same time as a whole deck of guns? It was the logical thing to have happened, to take the guns and the gunners to defend Havana. Shorrock hurried aft.

'I've been watching him, sir. I could swear he doesn't have enough men to work the guns that he has, and those are few enough.'

'Yes, I've seen that too, and he doesn't relish close action in case it should come to boarding.'

'Shall I tell off the boarding parties, sir?'

Shorrock's eyes were shining through the smears of black powder smoke on his face. There was no doubt what he'd do, but was it right? A boarding was always risky, and a defeat would mean the loss of the whole convoy. A victory would still leave him encumbered by a prize that must be manned and sent into port, when at any moment de Ternay could appear over the horizon. No, in this case his duty was clear, he had to frustrate the Spaniard and bring the fishing fleet safely to Louisbourg. That was the whole point of the King's Newfoundland possessions, the fisheries. Spanish prizes were a secondary consideration.

'I think not, Mister Shorrock. Our task today is to wear him down and force him to retire. He doesn't have a friendly dockyard in two thousand miles and he's all alone. My guess is that he won't risk serious damage. Look,

Captain Douglas knows what's needed, see how he dashes in to fire then withdraws again. Mister Fairview, you'll oblige me by doing likewise.'

Crash! Another broadside and the answering booms from *San Sebastian's* twelve pounders came hot on its heels. The problem was that neither side wanted to risk closing to a range where the battle could be decisively ended. This really wouldn't do. One of those heavy balls would hit something vital soon, a fore topmast or the rudder, and then *San Sebastian* would be able to brush aside the smaller *Siren* and get among the fishing boats. Only the larger of the three ships could benefit from this long-range sniping.

'Mister Shorrock, Mister Murray, Mister Fairview!'

The first lieutenant and the captain of marines hurried to their captain's side; Fairview was already there. Murray's men hadn't been engaged at all, the range being too great for muskets or swivels, and he looked fresh and eager in his still-clean clothes.

'Now, gentlemen. That Spanish ship has only half its complement of guns, and those that are left are twelves at best; I imagine the others were taken from him at Havana or possibly San Juan. It appears to me that he lost half of his men at the same time. He doesn't want to get close for fear that we'll both board him, and he's shy of taking damage so far from a Spanish yard. My concern is to keep *Argonaut* and *Siren* intact in case the French should come looking for us before we reach Louisbourg. I therefore don't want to linger too close to those twelve pounders.'

Shorrock and Murray exchanged glances. If that was the case, then they could see that the engagement would only be ended when one ship took an unlucky heavy blow.

'However, if he's so keen to avoid damage, we can play on that. Muster the boarding parties and I'll have Mister Fairview run up as though we intend to board. I won't do so, but let's see what he does about that. Don't tell the men that they're not to board, it must look convincing. I expect we'll get close enough for your marines to fire a few volleys,

Mister Murray.'

Argonaut shuddered as a pair of twelve pounders smashed into the hull below the gunports. If Holbrooke had been in two minds before, that settled the matter. His ship couldn't take much more of that and *Siren* even less.

***

Holbrooke watched in satisfaction as the marines and all the seamen who could be spared mustered on the starboard side of the fo'c'sle. A glance through a telescope would have made it clear to *San Sebastian* that a boarding was contemplated. Now Holbrooke watched carefully through his own telescope. In any normal engagement the Spaniard would be mustering his own marines and seamen to repel boarders and – if the opportunity occurred – to counter-attack onto the enemy's own deck. He saw a half dozen men manning swivel guns, but none of the blue uniforms of the Spanish marines. Of course, if Havana needed men for defence of the city, they'd take marines first. He was becoming more certain of his hypothesis.

San Sebastian was on a broad reach, paralleling the fishing fleet and some two miles to windward, apparently prepared to carry on this campaign of attrition to its logical conclusion. Then the slow fishing fleet would be at the Spaniard's mercy, and it would be surprising if a tenth part of them survived to make Louisbourg or the dubious safety of Placentia.

'Take her in, Mister Fairview. Make it look good, we have to persuade them that we're planning to run them aboard.'

'Aye-aye sir.'

Argonaut started moving up towards the two-decker with *Siren* on her windward quarter. Not for the first time Holbrooke regretted the paucity of the naval signal book. There was no hoist for *prepare to board the enemy,* and none of the existing hoists came anywhere near that meaning. Nevertheless, Douglas must have seen the preparations to board, and he was mustering his own men on the fo'c'sle.

This must be handled carefully, because it would be a disaster if Douglas boarded alone. He couldn't possibly prevail against twice the number of Spaniards defending their own deck.

'Mister Fairview, have the signal *take station astern* bent on but not hoisted, if you please. As soon as we sheer off you can hoist it and draw Captain Douglas' attention to it.'

Fairview nodded to the signal midshipman who, having heard what his captain had said, rushed off to the flag locker to prepare the hoist.

'Aye-aye sir. The Don's spreading his wings, I see.'

Holbrooke hadn't noticed it through the gathering bank of powder smoke, but now his attention was drawn to the Spanish ship, he could see t'gallants falling and courses being braced and sheeted. It could mean that *San Sebastian* hoped to draw ahead and cross *Argonaut's* bows, but it could also mean that the fourth rate was declining a close action with the two frigates.

'We're still faster, sir. Look, we're head-reaching on him.'

Holbrooke glanced up at the sails. If he furled anything above the lower yards, it would be immediately obvious that he had no intention of closing to board. He looked at the courses. The smoke was thicker now, probably hiding those big lower sails. It was hiding the boarding party too, but the Spaniard must have seen them before the smoke became too thick.

'Spill some wind from the main course, Mister Fairview, as discreetly as you can, and make that signal to *Siren*.'

Douglas had proved an intelligent ally so far, and Holbrooke hoped that he'd understand the meaning of the signal. The Spaniard was being ushered away but he was still dangerous. At that moment another shot, aimed higher this time, struck *Argonaut's* hammock railing, passed right through, and smashed a marine into pulp. The men either side of him barely flinched but pulled the still-twitching body into the centre of the deck and returned to the ranks of their fellows.

Shorrock's broadsides were still firing regularly, and his gun captains were making good practice. As he watched he saw *San Sebastian's* taffrail disintegrate as it was apparently hit by two nine pound shot. He saw the ship's captain walk aft and stare hard at the pursuing frigates. This was the moment; Holbrooke could feel it in his bones. That captain could put up his helm, throw caution to the wind, and force a close action with *Argonaut* and *Siren*. He could almost see the indecision on the man's face. Probably he had specific orders to avoid any action that could imperil his ship, and closing with two tough, active British frigates would certainly put his ship in danger. Holbrooke saw the momentary pause, then the slow turning away. Within Minutes *San Sebastian* had tacked and was steering away to the northeast.

'We'll follow, Mister Fairview, and keep that signal flying for *Siren* to take station astern. In fact, lower it and hoist it again, to emphasise my wishes. I don't want Mister Douglas to have to deal with a Spanish fourth rate, however keen the Don is to avoid close action.

***

'A satisfactory engagement then, George.'

Holbrooke and Chalmers had taken supper in the great cabin and were now enjoying a glass of Madeira as the sun dipped towards the horizon. Shorrock had the deck, and he'd have the setting sun right in his eyes as he looked forward, but here in the cabin they could enjoy the silvery glow that darkened to blue-black in the east. *San Sebastian* had disappeared towards Cape Race, the correct course for Spain, or to loop around the Atlantic Drift and cruise back towards Havana. Holbrooke didn't expect to see that ship again.

'Forgive me, David, is that a question or a statement.'

'A statement, I think, but one that you may challenge, if you feel so inclined.'

Holbrooke watched the wine in his glass against the

gleam of the cabin's lantern.

'For my part I won't challenge it. My objective – and I accept that others might not find this very honourable – was to protect the fishing convoy. Had *Argonaut* been dismasted, and the convoy taken, then Lord Colville would rightly criticise me. No doubt if I'd brought in a Spanish fourth rate prize, he'd have been delighted, particularly as I was sailing under his orders; he's quite impoverished you know, despite his title. Nevertheless, I feel he'd have thought less of me for it. We'll be in Louisbourg in two days, and I expect to see Colville there. If not then it's on to Halifax, but in any case, we'll deliver the fishing fleet.'

'Yes. I don't doubt that de Ternay has turned his eye to Placentia by now.'

'Oh, it could be a few days or a week, but I can't believe he'll rest easy in St. John's knowing that the greater part of the fishery lies to the west and the north. My only regret is that we lost Marine Spruell today. He was a good man. He'd served in this ship since it was first commissioned, and I shall miss his face and his Hampshire accent now that he can no longer take his turn as cabin sentry. His home is only a few miles up the Alton Road from Wickham, you know, almost the next cottage you pass after father's. He had no wife, but his mother still lives; I shall have to visit her.'

'Well, there's no need to put him over the side. There'll be a regular graveyard at Louisbourg and he'll last until then. His mates will like that.'

It was Chalmers' turn to look reflective, as though he was choosing his words carefully.

'You know, you should make your tactics today clear to Lord Colville. I don't know of another sea officer who would have resisted the urge to board a fourth rate when it was supposed – and I believe it's true – that you had equal numbers of men. Yet it was certainly the right decision.'

'Well, I thank you for your confidence, but it's a tricky situation. Nine parts of the navy will never understand why I didn't board and a good number of those will attribute it to ignoble instincts. No, I think it's better to state the bare facts, that we saw off a Spanish fourth rate and brought home an important convoy. Anything else risks my reputation.'

Chalmers bowed and raised his glass, and they drank in silence.

***

CHAPTER TWENTY-SIX

A Lonely Vigil

Wednesday, Twenty-Eighth of July 1762.
Argonaut, at Sea. off St. John's, Newfoundland.

'There you see it, Gentlemen, St. John's in all its glory. Perhaps you could show us the sights, Captain Mouat?'

Argonaut rose and fell to the southerly swell as she lay with her backed fore tops'l nicely balancing the rest of her rig. *Saint Ninian* was rather less comfortable under her lee, that long bowsprit didn't really lend itself to heaving to in a swell, and every time it dipped into an advancing wave the cutter's head swung wildly to leeward. Mouat gave his command a last anxious glance then turned to the matter in hand.

'That's Cape Spear that's sheltering us from this southerly wind, sir, but after that they didn't give much thought to naming the features. North Head to the north o' the entrance and beyond that Cuckold Head before ye come to Quidi-Vidi Gut. South Head on the other side o' the Narrows. There was supposed to be a battery to the west o' South Head but when I was there it was nothing more than a flat space with an earthen wall that was washed away a little more wi' each rain storm. The French may have made something of it, however; they were moving guns all over the place. That's where they fired their muskets at me as we made our escape. If we were closer you could see the iron rings let into the cliffs, to warp ships out when the wind's foul.'

Holbrooke studied the entrance through his telescope. South Head was easy to see once it was pointed out, but the angle was wrong to determine whether the French had armed the battery. It must have been very uncomfortable sweeping out of the harbour with the French infantry firing down upon the cutter, even in the near darkness; it was a wonder that Mouat only lost one dead and two wounded.

'There are strong points let into some rocks either side of the Narrows, to stretch a cable or chain across, great iron staples, much heavier than the warping rings. There was no cable in place when I was there, but the French were very active and they may have rigged something.'

'Not a place to be taken by boldly by sailing in then, Mister Mouat?'

'I think not, sir, at least not while there's an active commander defending the Narrows.'

Mouat shuddered as though remembering his contested passage, with French musket balls raising splinters where they struck the deck all around him.

'That's Signal Hill above North Head, you can see the mast and there's a house there for the signalman. I walked up there to see the lie of the land, before the French arrived; it's a grand view on a clear day.'

Holbrooke spared a moment for Signal Hill then trained his telescope through the Narrows again.

'You can see Fort William from this angle, sir, that grey mass at the far right before the cliffs obstruct the view. It's quite hard to see unless the sun is full upon it. That's the northern end of the wharves and jetties and you can just make out part of the town where it runs up towards the fort. There's a sort o' lower battery right down on the waterfront.'

'There's a lot of activity down below the fort, Mister Mouat, but I can't see any of the French squadron.'

'They'll be anchored further up the harbour, I expect, sir, if they're there at all.'

'Beg your pardon, sir, but I think I can see the stern of a frigate just swinging into view.'

Shorrock had good eyes and Holbrooke looked more closely at the point to the south of the fort where the cliffs of the Narrows cut off his view. There was little wind at sea, just a moderate breeze from the southwest, and it was anyone's guess what that would mean for ships anchored in St. John's harbour. It looked as though the frigate, for Holbrooke was sure of it, had been lying with its head to the northeast but a fluke in the wind had swung the ship around so that its stern could be seen. Then it disappeared as suddenly as it had come.

'The winds at St. John's can be quite unpredictable and fierce, even when it's calm outside.'

'It's a pity we can't see right into the harbour, I'd dearly like to know whether the other Frenchmen are in there.'

Shorrock swept the horizon with his hand shielding his eyes from the glare. It was a wise precaution with only one of the four French ships accounted for.

'We know de Ternay well enough now to at least guess at his decisions. In these waters he'll keep his squadron together. He may dispatch a frigate on a scouting mission, but if there's one frigate in St. John's, then *Robuste* and *Eveillé* will be there too. Still, it's worth being vigilant, Mister Shorrock. One thing's for certain, if they're in St. John's, they can't surprise us. They can't sail out in this uncertain wind and it'll take them half a day to warp out.'

Holbrooke took another look at the Narrows, imprinting the features upon his mind.

'Well, Gentlemen, Lord Colville's orders are that we're to watch the French and gather what intelligence we can. I think we've seen enough here. Captain Mouat, you'll take the inshore station but don't let yourself become embayed if the wind shifts into the east. Mister Fairview, as soon as Captain Mouat has left us, get underway and take station to the east of Cape Spear, at least a league distant, if you please. Captain Mouat, you have your signals board?'

'Yes, sir, all nicely packaged up.'

He held up an oilskin-wrapped package that contained

the list of private signals that Holbrooke had devised. Lister had glued it to a thin piece of deal to preserve it and had wrapped it against the elements.

***

'I gather this could be a long vigil,'

Chalmer nodded as Mallett offered a second cup of coffee. The wardroom had laid in enough for a normal spell of blockade duty off Brest but not for a transatlantic voyage. Those stocks had been exhausted soon after *Argonaut* arrived off Newfoundland, and there was none to be had in Louisbourg or Halifax, at least none that anyone would admit owning. The last cup of coffee had been drunk in the wardroom a week ago and invitations to the great cabin were now highly prized.

'Long and lonely. A month, I expect, but it depends upon a number of factors. Amherst is putting together a scratch army to eject the French, and that will take time. Lord Colville is frantically fitting out the few ships he has left and the army can't leave until Colville is ready. Graves could be here in *Antelope* at any moment, to take up his duties as governor. When he does arrive off St. John's he'll be surprised to hear that he's already lost *Gramont* and that *Siren* has been retained by Colville.'

'Did Lord Colville give you any orders for Captain Graves?'

'Yes, they're here in my desk, and I'm to tell him to leave *Argonaut* be. *Antelope* is to join Colville at Halifax, or at Louisbourg if he's advanced that far. I fear he won't like being told to abandon the territory that he's supposed to be governing. But there's another factor. Their Lordships must know by now that there's a French squadron laying waste to the Newfoundland fisheries. If the French are known to have two of the line, then I expect three to be sent to dislodge them, but I can't say when they'll arrive. I stand by my estimate of a month. In August I expect a convergence of expeditions from the west and from the east, and then de Ternay will have to shift to hold onto what he's won.'

'You believe, then, that he's intending to stay. Can he hold out until the winter? I assume that Amherst won't be in a position to attempt anything until after the end of September.'

'It depends upon de Ternay's orders. Is this an attempt to take and hold Newfoundland so that it can be exchanged for one of the islands that France has lost in this war? If so, then the French have committed the cardinal sin of sending too small a force. They may think that Britain has no ships and no men left on the American station, now that Louisbourg and Quebec and Montreal have fallen, but that's an illusion. It's in the very nature of Britain's mastery of the sea that we can re-deploy our forces at will. I find it hard to believe that de Ternay can hold out until winter, and even if he can, how will he be supplied? No, I suspect this is a raid, probably designed to demonstrate that France still has the power to hurt Britain. Newfoundland was chosen because it could be achieved with the number of ships available at Brest.'

'Yet I see no columns of smoke. If this is a raid then we could expect de Ternay to waste no time in destroying the fort, the town and the fishery before moving on.'

'And that's what's been worrying me, David. It makes no sense.'

***

CHAPTER TWENTY-SEVEN

Other People's Letters

Tuesday, Twenty-Fourth of August 1762.
Argonaut, at Sea. Off St. John's, Newfoundland.

A long vigil indeed. Holbrooke strode *Argonaut's* deck through that glorious August of 1762 as the frigate ploughed its lonely furrow off Cape Spear. There was no word from Colville, but then he'd expected none, and no vast British armada appeared on the southwestern horizon. *Antelope* arrived from England with a small convoy. Captain Graves read Colville's orders, questioned Holbrook, swore and stamped his foot then promptly departed for Halifax. De Ternay didn't stir from his anchorage and there had been no daylight attempts to send messages back to France. Nevertheless, as Holbrooke admitted to himself, anything could have happened during the frequent fogs or on dark and moonless nights, when a fast vessel could warp through the Narrows and be gone before it was betrayed by the rising sun.

Argonaut had settled into a routine. With no letters from outside to take up the officers' time and no spells of action to take the men from their maintenance tasks, the ship could be cleaned and repaired to a standard that drew the praise of even the bosun and the carpenter. The forenoons were the time when all hands turned to, even those who had just had the morning watch on deck. Sails were hauled up and dried, the damage from the fight with *San Sebastian* was repaired so that anyone would have thought it was the work of a King's yard, and every part of the ship had that freshly overhauled look about it.

It was on one of those forenoons, as Holbrooke was inspecting the new garboard strakes on the longboat, that he was interrupted by a shout from the lookout at the main t'gallant head.

'Deck there. It's a bit murky out to the east, but I thought I saw a topmast just above a low bank of fog. Can't be certain, sir, I only saw it for a moment. There it is again, I think.'

It was an uncertain sighting, to say the least, and the lookout's tone betrayed his indecision. Holbrooke had been plagued by such reports for the past month. Still, it was good policy to treat each one seriously, for the day would certainly come when one of them revealed a Frenchman trying to sneak into St. John's. Holbrooke was as sure as he could be that although de Ternay may have sent messages to Paris, he had received none since *Argonaut* had been on watch. It was one thing to escape from the harbour on a dark night or in fog, but it was quite another to make a precise landfall in the same conditions and carry a ship safely through the Narrows with no lights for guidance.

Fairview glanced at his captain who nodded slightly in agreement, then he summoned the mate of the watch.

'Mister Peterson, take the telescope and call down what you see.'

Holbrooke watched as the lookout dropped down to the main masthead to make way for Petersen. He saw the master's mate make his way up to the t'gallant masthead as a cloud moved away and the fogbank on the starboard bow was bathed in the full light of day. A moment or two of stillness as Petersen adjusted the focus, then a positive and lusty hail.

'Sail ho! Sail four points on the starboard bow, maybe four miles away. It looks like a brig, sir, standing in for St. John's on the larboard tack under tops'ls, a Frenchman by the cut of her tops'ls.'

Fairview watched his captain expectantly, but Holbrooke wasn't to be rushed. A brig had no chance of escape in this south-westerly breeze, not with a keen frigate to windward.

'Anything else, Mister Petersen? Take a good look.'

An Upright Man

Another pause as Petersen scanned the whole horizon. There were patches of fog at every point of the compass, just like the one that had hidden the brig, but none showed the telltale topmast that would give away a ship's position.

'Nothing, sir. Plenty of fog patches but I don't believe any are big enough to hide another sail.'

'Thank you, Mister Petersen and you may tell the lookout to visit my servant who'll give him a glass of brandy. Now, Mister Fairview, I'll leave it to you, but I want that brig under my guns before dinner.'

***

Sometimes, just occasionally, things turn out so well that the world seems a better place. The brig was the grandly named *l'Orient*, three weeks out of Brest with supplies for Monsieur de Ternay at St. John's, including a small canvas bag of coffee beans that Holbrooke couldn't officially know was at that moment being transferred to the wardroom. The rest was the usual miscellaneous stores, powder and ball, and dry provisions. When questioned about dispatches the master shrugged and declared that he knew nothing of such matters, had been given no letters for Monsieur de Ternay or anyone else, and hoped that his brig would be ransomed rather than taken as a prize, it being so far from a British port, and he could offer a surety from his own purse.

Holbrooke ignored the man's obvious lies and nodded to Shorrock, who knew what was needed and took a rummage party to the brig. Nothing escaped Shorrock. He'd searched more ships than half of the frigate's officers had seen sailing the oceans, and in only half an hour Holbrooke heard the discreet tapping at his door and excused himself from questioning the master.

'Two bags, sir,' Shorrock said grinning. 'One official mail and one personal, all neatly labelled so that we don't open the wrong one.'

'Well done, well done indeed, and you did well to keep it from our prisoner. I imagine he hopes that his offer of ransom will be taken and he'll be in St. John's tomorrow with his dispatches. Where did you find them?'

'Behind the cabin stove, it's a common place to hide papers. False bulkheads in the hold to hide seamen from the press, and a cavity behind the cabin stove for papers. I've rarely known it any other way, sir. The good Lord alone knows why they take us for such simpletons. Perhaps they think we won't dirty our hands searching in such places.'

'Well, I expect we'll learn something of interest. Lister's a good hand with a heated knife and he may fool them that they haven't been opened.'

'You're going to accept the ransom, sir?'

Shorrock knew very well that the Admiralty frowned upon the time-honoured custom of accepting ransoms in lieu of taking prizes. Captains liked it because it avoided the prize having to be condemned by a vice-admiralty court and allowed an almost immediate distribution of shares to the men. Their Lordships saw it as a lost opportunity; the French retained both the ship and its crew and all that they lost was a sum of money. Often the prize in question was insured by underwriters based in London through a complex set of middlemen and brokers, so even the monetary loss didn't hurt the French. It was a custom from an earlier age but it was still occasionally done where the situation warranted it.

'It depends upon what I read in the dispatches. If it's to our advantage to let him go into St. John's then so be it, but if I'd rather de Ternay didn't read his own letters then I'll send him with a prize crew to Halifax. Now, if you'd ask the bosun to entertain the French master, we can get on with this affair.'

***

It was a strangely tense moment as Lister opened the bag with the unmistakable seals of the French ministry of marine. He'd done this before and while it wasn't a perfect job, it might fool de Ternay's secretary. With one of the surgeon's long, slim, very sharp knives, heated just so, he carefully separated the seals from the thick paper of the wrappings. There were two seals to each of the three packages within the bag and they were chipped and scarred, having suffered in the Atlantic passage. It was quite conceivable that whatever Lister did to them would be taken by his French counterpart as the normal marks of wear.

Chalmers made the first pass through the letters. There were the usual greetings and remonstrances from the various yards that supplied ordnance and cordage and beef and all the other necessities of life at sea in a man-of-war. There was a notice of promotions in the French navy; painfully few in these closing days of the war, and then, finally the all-important letter from the Duc de Choiseul.

'This is rather like reading other people's letters, don't you think, Captain Holbrooke.'

Chalmer's had a wry smile. He knew as well as Holbrooke that official mail was fair game, while personal letters were not.

'That may be so, but they're letters that can help our country and perhaps more immediately prevent us wasting lives in misguided adventures. Please be so kind as the read the main points of the letter.'

Lister suppressed a grin. It wasn't often that anyone cared to question the captain's ethical stance.

Chalmers cleared his throat and began.

'Monsieur de Ternay is congratulated by the Duke himself on his efficient and timely – yes, that's the phrase used, efficient and timely – capture of St. John's. He's reminded that the purpose is the destruction of the fishery, not the occupation of British territory. It's not too late – Choiseul says – to make an attempt at Louisbourg or even to work back across the Atlantic to Ireland or Scotland. How was he greeted by the Irishmen in St. John's? Has he recruited a significant number? The Duke expresses his confidence that de Ternay will take advantage of whatever opportunities present themselves for the annoyance of

France's enemies. That's the tone of it, and it does seem to suggest de Ternay will be bound to leave St. John's when he reads this; if he reads it.'

Holbrooke sat still, thinking. It had been a bold move to open the letters in the first place and Colville could take the view that they should have been brought to him unopened. But that would have taken time; days for the prize to be sent to Halifax, perhaps a chase to Louisbourg if Colville had left Halifax, and more days to return to St. John's. No, he was confident that he'd be judged to have done the right thing.

'Ah, I've found something else, something perhaps in Choiseul's own handwriting. Very elegant indeed, I'm surprised he allows a ham-fisted clerk to write his letters.'

Chalmers straightened himself as though in awe of reading the great man's words written by his own hand.

'If in your judgement you can hold St. John's through the autumn and into the winter, I leave it up to you whether to remain there. You should know, however, that there is little chance of sending supplies to you once the enemy establishes a blockade, which they surely will. You must consider the numbers of people – of mouths to feed – and reduce them accordingly by sending prisoners and surplus soldiers back to France. As always, I must rely upon your judgement.'

'That's the sense of it but I'll need more time to make a faithful translation. I would comment though, that the whole letter has a sense of frustration, perhaps that de Ternay hasn't strictly obeyed the orders he'd been given.'

Holbrooke was deep in thought, trying to make sense of his adversary's situation.

'Hubris, perhaps, Captain Holbrooke. We must admit that de Ternay did very well in bringing those ships out of the Vilaine river, and if that's our opinion, then you can imagine how Choiseul views him. Last year he was a lieutenant with no hope of being posted in this war; now he's the commodore of the only French squadron that's actually doing anything positive. This letter hints at a certain vagueness in his orders, a licence to act as the situation

An Upright Man

seems to demand. Is he taking this too far? Does he really believe that he can hold St. John's? Yes, hubris I think, and we all know where that leads.'

'I'm sure you're right, Mister Chalmers. Hubris indeed and on balance I feel that Monsieur de Ternay is quite capable of making his own mistakes without any help from us, or from the Duc de Choiseul. There'll be no ransom and these letters must be seen by Lord Colville as soon as possible. Mister Lister, pass the word for the first lieutenant and I believe Mister Petersen deserves a run ashore in Halifax or wherever he finds the commander-in-chief, so pass the word for him also.'

***

He'd given his orders and Shorrock and Petersen had left to make the arrangements for a prize crew and victuals and all the myriad items that had to be considered before the brig could be sent away. He could think in this solitude, he could make rational decisions having pondered all the consequences. He'd been wrestling with a particular question ever since he'd decided to send the brig back to Halifax rather than ransom it. He'd sent the official mail away, of course, but he'd retained the personal letters. He knew that once they were in Halifax they wouldn't reach their intended recipients until long after the war was over, if they did at all. Perhaps he could do better than that and it may give him the opportunity to gather some useful information. The French on Signal Hill above North Head must have seen the brig being taken. Supplies, ammunition, dispatches, they must know that all of those were gone, never to be seen by de Ternay's squadron or the French brigade at St. John's. They would still, however, hold out hope for the personal letters. It was quite normal to send mail sacks under a flag of truce, particularly if there was no animosity between the two sides, although it was more normally a decision for a commander-in-chief or a flag officer. Sometimes the letters were opened in case vital orders had been sent under a personal cover, but it wasn't usual to do so.

It was a humane act, and that consideration alone would have swayed Holbrooke. But there was something else. Mouat had spoken of the cable or chain across the Narrows, of the work to arm the batteries and the repairs to the fort, and it would be useful to know how far the French occupiers had gone in improving the defences. Also, although he'd assumed that de Ternay's squadron was at anchor in the harbour, he hadn't seen anything more than the stern of a single frigate. For all he knew de Ternay could be elsewhere. He ran the risk of Lord Colville's displeasure, but he thought he knew him well enough to take the gamble.

'Pass the word for Mister Chalmers.'

The chaplain had evidently finished his supper and he looked content and well-fed as he took a seat and accepted a cup of coffee. He took a sip and pursed his lips.

'You know, yesterday your coffee was as welcome as the purest water to a wanderer in the desert. Abraham's tribe couldn't have been happier. Yet today, I find that it doesn't compare well with the beans that we took from the brig. Oh, perhaps I shouldn't say any more, I remember now that it's frowned upon to pillage from a prize.'

Holbrooke laughed out loud.

'It is indeed. It's called *breaking bulk,* and it's almost a capital offence. However, the wardroom running out of coffee is a serious matter, and I've been living in fear of Mister Shorrock requesting to buy some of mine. Now, if yours is so superior, the tables may be turned. But that's not what I called you for. I intend to send the mail in to Monsieur de Ternay tomorrow under a flag of truce. I have Lieutenant Murray in mind, but his French is poor and I'm hoping that you'll consent to go with him.'

'Not Mister Mouat in the cutter, then, George?'

'I think not. He was a prisoner of the French not so long ago and the cutter belonged to them; I wouldn't want there to be any confusion about his status or for that matter the cutter's. It must be a commissioned officer and it would be helpful to have someone who speaks French. I can't spare Mister Shorrock, not with Petersen away with the prize. Lieutenant Murray with your able assistance seems to be the best embassy.'

Chalmers took another sip of his coffee; a small, polite sip accompanied by a sour expression.

'Of course, it will be my pleasure, particularly if I have the chance to meet Monsieur de Ternay. It will be like greeting an old friend.

'Ha! I'm afraid that's quite unlikely. It would be more normal for you to be met by an aide on the wharf, relieved of the sack of letters and sent on your way, but if you do meet him, please send my warmest regards. And do you know, I really mean that. I've never met the man and probably never will, but I feel that I could like him.'

When Chalmers left, Holbrooke couldn't help noticing that he'd only drunk half of his coffee. Perhaps there was something in occasionally breaking bulk after all. He'd have to ask Mallett to negotiate with the wardroom steward for a share of this fabled French coffee.

***

It was late in the forenoon before the longboat returned, and Chalmers had what looked like a case of wine at his feet and he carried a bag almost the same size as the sack of letters that he'd delivered.

'I did meet Monsieur de Ternay. A most gentlemanly person, although rather anxious, I think, behind his severe exterior. He sent you this case of wine and when I told him about your desperate need for drinkable coffee, he sent this bag of what his purser described as the finest beans from the East. His purser was distressed at the thought of anyone having to drink English coffee, and I have to say that I now understand his concern. Mister Murray also received a case of wine. He's writing up his notes now, so that he gets it all down before you rack him.'

Holbrooke smiled at that. He hoped he wasn't

becoming the sort of captain that his officers feared to approach, but he'd spent so much of his time in command worrying about not being stern enough that he could allow himself a little severity.

'For my part and for what it's worth, Monsieur de Ternay's squadron is all at anchor, all four of them, and a great gaggle of schooners and sloops as well. They've burned most of the smaller vessels, and the stages and racks for the cod, and the drying sheds. It's quite a scene of devastation. They've set up batteries in the Narrows – Lieutenant Murray will have the details – and what looks like a good-sized cable from a man-o'-war's anchor is coiled beside the fixing points on the north side. The fort's been repaired too. I'd say that the ships are ready for a rapid departure, but the French army is settling in for a long stay.'

'That's all very well, David, and as you say Lieutenant Murray will have a report for me. But what of de Ternay?'

'Well,' Chalmers gathered his thoughts, 'he sends his best wishes and thanks for the letters of course. He suspected you might be the same captain that he met twice in Quiberon Bay, and I took the liberty to confirm that.'

Chalmers paused as Holbrooke digested that information. So de Ternay knew he was up against a man that he'd beaten twice already. How would that affect his thinking?

'As I remarked, he's a gentleman, but one with a formidable air of command. I really found it difficult to imagine him as a mere lieutenant only last year, he looks as though he was born as a fully formed flag officer. For all that, I liked him and the good opinion that I formed from Garnier's friend Marignac is doubly reinforced. It's plain to see that his duty comes before all else, with perhaps the exception of his religion, but I expect they're very nearly one and the same thing to him.'

'And his staff officers, how did they behave?'

'Oh, they're all in awe of him. The commander of the soldiers, the Count d'Haussonville, came briefly to offer his thanks for the letters and he seemed wary of speaking at all in de Ternay's presence. I wouldn't say that they're at odds, but I don't expect there's a free flow of information between the two. And now I think of it, there wasn't a single item in the official mail addressed to d'Haussonville, although he had a good number in the personal bag. I wonder whether that's significant.'

'Well, the French still have the sort of divided command on expeditions that we suffered in the early years of the war. It does sound as though this is an attempt to have a clear chain of command. I can only imagine what this Count d'Haussonville thinks about it all.'

'De Ternay is a man at the peak of his accomplishments, George. Hubris,' Chalmer's held up a finger to emphasis the point, like an Old Testament prophet, 'it will be de Ternay's nemesis, you mark my words.'

***

The south-westerly breeze had stiffened and as the daylight faded the brig was sailing full and by on the starboard tack to make its offing and round Cape Spear. It would be a long, hard beat to Halifax, unless the wind changed, but Petersen had a good prize crew and the brig's French crew were outnumbered and firmly overawed by the file of marines that guarded them. There'd be no trouble. The French on Signal Hill would have watched as it disappeared to the south, bound for Halifax. Holbrooke gave his night orders to Fairview then turned for his cabin.

***

CHAPTER TWENTY-EIGHT

Unlimited Liability

Saturday, Eleventh of September 1762.
Argonaut, at Sea. Off St. John's, Newfoundland.

Northumberland's great cabin seemed strangely empty. Holbrooke had attended a number of briefings over the past week and at each of them sea and land officers had crowded in to hear the plans for the removal of the French from St. John's; a very junior frigate captain's voice had been lost in the tumult. However, it had been quiet for the last day, presumably while Lord Colville and Colonel William Amherst – the younger brother to the commander-in-chief of all of North America – laid their final plans for a landing. Now it was only those two commanders and Holbrooke, and he felt as though he was under examination.

'Well, Captain Holbrooke...' Colville looked embarrassed for a moment, 'oh, you start, Colonel, you know what you need.'

Amherst bowed slightly and studied Holbrooke for a moment. They'd met a few times before, but it had always been in a great crowd. He and Holbrooke were of nominally equal rank, but Amherst came from a social circle that orbited many strata above Holbrooke's, and in this case he commanded a modest army while Holbrooke had only a frigate. Nevertheless, it was Holbrooke who had been in contact with the enemy for the past three months, not Amherst, and he felt like an old campaigner by comparison with the fresh soldier.

'My army will be landing the day after tomorrow, Captain Holbrooke, on Monday, here at Torbay. It's not generally known but it soon will be. Now, it's a somewhat ad-hoc affair, we have no flatboats and none of the preparations that went into the landings on the French coast, but of course the enemy can only mount a very limited defence, not knowing – I trust – where the blow will land. I'm told that you have experience of this kind of operation. Saint-Malo and Cherbourg have been mentioned, and Saint-Cast. Fort Niagara too, I understand.'

Amherst left it hanging, not quite as a question but more of a statement that begged verification. Holbrooke's heart sank when Amherst mentioned landings. He'd had his fill of perilous descents upon enemy beaches and even more dangerous withdrawals. He reached involuntarily for the scar that he carried on his ribs – a souvenir of the disaster at Saint-Cast – and he was aware that his eyes narrowed in memory of the pain and terror of the moment when the French bayonets thrust down upon him as he struggled in the surf. A moment only, and then he was himself again, and he desperately wanted to lighten the mood and get to the point. He had no interest in presenting his credentials as though he were striving for a clerk's position in a government office.

'Yes, I had the honour to be engaged at all of those places. I sometimes wonder whether I've taken more knocks on land than at sea. How may I be of service?'

Amherst glanced sideways at Colville who nodded vigorously. He too thought it better to go straight to the heart of things. Some men relished parading their honourable wounds, but Holbrooke was evidently not one of them.

'If all goes well, if the French aren't inclined to oppose the landing, then it will just be a matter of rowing ashore and marching on St. John's. It's only seven miles away and even though the roads are poor – nothing much better than cart tracks – we should be there in a day or two. Now, I can't afford to assume that the French will leave us in peace, so I need the advice of someone who's been involved in this kind of operation. Advice, and – I hope – active participation. Someone needs to command the landing until I'm established ashore, someone of sufficient rank to keep my battalion commanders in order…'

'He means you, Holbrooke,' Colville was becoming impatient with this dancing around the matter. 'You're the best man I have for the job, if not the only man; what do you say?'

Holbrooke opened his mouth to speak but this time Amherst was too quick for him and he didn't want the second part of his needs to be overlooked by a too-hasty agreement.

'Not just the landing, Captain, but the march on St. John's too. I have campaign carriages for any number of guns and Lord Colville has offered me as many cannons as I need, and sailors to serve them too. However, the artillerymen that I've scraped together are only those that were left behind in Louisbourg when the main body was sent to Havana – well, you can imagine – and there's not a man with any real experience among them. I fear that they'll let me down, so I need an artillery commander also, and a man of experience to move everything along. It's an unlimited liability…'

'So here's the question, Holbrooke, and it's something my friends in the army tend to overlook. Is your first lieutenant fit to take command while you run riot on the shore? Shorrock isn't it? I can't have a frigate drifting aimlessly across the oceans for want of command.'

Holbrooke almost laughed. In one breath he was being asked whether he'd accept the job, and in the next whether Shorrock could deputise for him. If the answer to the latter was yes, then the first question was unnecessary. He inhaled and smiled encouragingly.

'Mister Shorrock is more than capable of command, my Lord, and I, of course, would be honoured to serve in the capacity of commander of the landing and commander of Colonel Amherst's artillery, and anything else that might further the King's business.'

'Thank you, Captain Holbrooke. One more thing. If I have to send a frigate away it will be best if it's *Argonaut*.

Siren strictly belongs to Captain Graves, and he'll have his own plans, no doubt. Admiral Hawke on the other hand is thousands of miles away and has presumably already become reconciled to losing your services. How are your stores, your wood and water?'

'I can stand an Atlantic passage, sir, but not much more.'

'Well, let's hope your next port of call is Halifax before I send you home. Nevertheless, be prepared, Captain Holbrooke, be prepared for anything.'

***

Dawn on the thirteenth, and a sullen sun rose reluctantly over the red rocks of the point that enclosed the eastern side of Torbay. It held no heat and it cast but a pale illumination as its rays fought their way through the low-lying mist. Holbrooke looked to the left and to the right. A dozen longboats were advancing steadily along the mile-deep bight that sat at the far western part of the bay. He'd personally briefed the lieutenants, master's mates and midshipmen that commanded them and he could see that his orders were – for the most part – being obeyed. Every boat carried a signalling staff at its stern, and each had a distinguishing number painted on either side of its bows. By reference to the tabulation in his pocket he could instantly say which ship had provided a particular boat, the name of the boat's commander, the unit of soldiers that it carried, and lastly its station in this modest invasion force. The pattern should have been easy to discern – four columns a hundred yards between columns, each column comprising three boats spaced fifty yards from stem to stern – but of course it wasn't that easy. One boat commander's idea of a hundred yards might be wildly different to his neighbour's in the next column, and fifty yards could in fact be anything between twenty and eighty. However, Holbrooke wasn't concerned and in its essentials it was a well-ordered squadron that rowed into the bay. Barring accidents, the first four boats should run ashore at the head of the bight more-or-less simultaneously.

Each of the longboats carried about twenty soldiers, so this first assault wave comprised two-hundred-and-forty men. They weren't the battle-hardened grenadiers that he'd seen at Fort Niagara or at Cherbourg or Saint-Malo, in fact there were hardly any coherent infantry units in the whole army. Amherst had swept up every able soldier between Boston and Louisbourg and in many cases they hadn't seen a shot fired in anger. God help them if the French had guessed the location of the landing and were waiting with a couple of batteries of six pounders loaded with grape and cannister. It was possible but hardly likely. Colville had ordered a very visible reconnaissance of every likely cove within five leagues of St. John's, and it was only in the dim light of the middle watch that he had moved his squadron into Torbay. Holbrooke had been part of that planning and he agreed with the assumption that d'Haussonville couldn't possibly protect every little cove and bay. All the roads were bad and any artillery that he did send to the likely landing sites was in grave danger of being overrun as it attempted to withdraw to Fort William. By all military logic he must surely concentrate his precious field artillery on the heights around the town and fort and harbour, and only defend the beaches with an infantry screen.

'Make ready the signal for the assault, Mister Carew.'

The midshipman had been ready since the boat had left *Argonaut's* side. He was sitting upon the flag so that there was no chance of it advertently showing, and the flag was bent on to the halyard. It would take barely a second or two to hoist it up the short mast.

Pop! Pop!

They were firing now, and Holbrooke noted that the puffs of smoke were concentrated on the beach they were heading for. That was to be expected. The bight was rimmed with rocks along its whole mile-length, and it was only at its head that a strip of grey sand and gravel offered the opportunity to put soldiers ashore in good order.

An Upright Man

Pop! Pop! Pop!

Too soon, Monsieur, Holbrooke thought. At that range only a lucky shot could score a hit on the boats. And the commander of the French force that guarded this cove was squandering that first carefully loaded volley that could have had a profound effect on men pouring ashore from the boats. This random shooting also gave some idea of the numbers that they'd face. Twenty, perhaps as many as thirty, unless some of them weren't firing yet. A soldier in Holbrooke's boat gasped and grabbed at the air as a ball plucked his hat from his head, sending it spinning into the sea. The soldier next to him laughed nervously and the sergeant growled an order for silence.

Holbrooke looked over his shoulder at the second long boat in the second column. Amherst was in that boat, leading from near the front, but sensibly not risking himself in the very first ranks to reach the beach. He wasn't looking in Holbrooke's direction at all but was standing up in the stern sheets, peering ahead.

Two hundred yards to the beach. They should make it in less than two minutes, and they'd only have to suffer one or two volleys before the soldiers would be ashore. Of course Holbrooke had gone over all those calculations time and time again.

'Hoist the signal, Mister Carew. Coxswain, stretch out! Come on you men, let's see whose boat can win the honours!'

Holbrooke's longboat leaped forward as the oarsmen increased the tempo and length of the pull. They knew as well as Holbrooke that they had to cross this dangerous last stretch as quickly as possible, and it was the sailors who were in the greatest danger, while the soldiers had at least some shelter inside the two lines of oarsmen.

'Pull! Pull! Put your backs into it!'

The coxswain was on his feet urging the oarsmen to expend every last ounce of energy. The seamen were in shades of blue and white, with checks and stripes and plain colours fighting for dominance, but without exception they each sported a red neckerchief. The soldiers made a colourful contrast, although it was strange to see so many different facings on the men's coats as at least half a dozen regiments were represented in this one boat. The soldiers were looking nervous, but the captain and the sergeant appeared confident enough.

'Pull! Pull!'

The firing had stopped. That French commander must be making sure that every musket was loaded ready for the crucial volley. It was futile, of course. Two-hundred and forty men were about to land on the beach and the French defence could not make a significant difference to their numbers. There was no hope, none at all, of turning back the British landing, for Holbrooke had already recognised that William Amherst wasn't the sort of man to withdraw once he had set his feet on dry land.

They were in the surf now, ploughing their way through the little waves that ran slantwise across the beach. Holbrooke heard the well-remembered sound of the boat's forefoot running up the sand and felt the jerk as the boat came to a stop and the stern started to drift sideways under the influence of the waves.

'Off you go, bow oars.'

The forward oarsmen were already discarding their oars by the simple expedient of pushing them overboard into the water and within a second or two they'd vaulted over the bows and were holding the boat steady. The soldiers looked uncertain for a moment, then at a shout from the sergeant they too started jumping over the bows, using the sailor's shoulder and heads to steady themselves. They were each trying to jump clear of the water and onto hard sand. It was a small but important point that if at all possible they should be put ashore dry-shod. It was a crippling problem if soldiers had to start a campaign with wet feet and no prospect of getting them dry again. Fortunately the tide was flooding, so the sand beyond the reach of the waves was quite dry.

As the last soldier left the boat Holbrooke leaped ashore with Carew close at his heels. He immediately noticed something strange, there was no sound of firing, but a good deal of cheering from the men he'd put ashore. He looked inland and saw a sight to gladden the heart of any old campaigner: a column of French soldiers were hurrying over the sand dunes and slanting away towards the south. They hadn't even waited to deliver the volley that surely must have accounted for half a dozen of the British soldiers. Holbrooke couldn't fault their commander's decision. If they'd delayed to deliver the volley, they could easily have found that their retreat had been cut off. It was one thing to withdraw in good order before an enemy that hadn't yet put itself into an attack formation, but quite another to extricate themselves from a general engagement. D'Haussonville couldn't afford to lose twenty of his men in defence of a lost cause. They'd achieved their purpose in identifying the enemy's main line of advance and now, like all reconnaissance screens, they must carry the information back to their commander without risking being overwhelmed. So far, Holbrooke was impressed with the commander of the French land forces.

***

They toiled all through that day to move the whole of Amherst's force ashore. Then they started on the field artillery, and then the ammunition, the rations, and the siege equipment. It was mostly the sailors who did the work while the soldiers established the perimeter and started sending out patrols to find the enemy and to give warning of any counterattack. They found nothing. The small village of Torbay was empty, with not a Frenchman to be seen and not a single inhabitant of the country left to greet them.

Amherst paused in his inspection of the lines.

'This man knows his business, wouldn't you say, Captain Holbrooke?'

Holbrooke paused in giving his orders for siting the guns. The field guns must be positioned to defend the tightly packed area that Amherst's army was quickly filling, and the face of the dunes where they gave way to cultivated land and low scrub offered an obvious defensive line. The long days of summer were over; the light was fading fast and there was much to do.

'I would say so. He'll need all his men to hold the land between Quidi-Vidi harbour and St. John's. If he loses the high ground, he loses the fort and we'll be able to fire at his ships at our leisure.'

'If you were commanding the French, where would you attempt to hold us, Captain? Would you defend a line from Signal Hill inland, or would you meet us further north?'

Holbrooke looked briefly at the very sketchy map that Amherst held. It was better than nothing, but it asked more questions than it answered.

'If he holds that line from Signal Hill then he's hazarding his whole campaign on a single roll of the dice. There's nowhere to withdraw his men except to Fort William, and that will leave de Ternay's squadron exposed. No, I'd try to block our advance here, where Quidi-Vidi Pond is fed from all these streams. They don't look like real obstacles but they'll slow us down and your army will be vulnerable trying to cross them. From there to the sea, that's where I'd stand.'

Amherst looked thoughtful.

'I agree, Captain, but I wonder whether d'Haussonville has the numbers for a campaign like that. He must still be wary of our landing a second force to the south of the town, and he knows very well how vulnerable the fort is from that side, it's the way he came himself to take the place. A strong defence of Signal Hill and Gibbet Hill, and a garrison for the fort and some kind of reserve will soak up every man that he has. A defence at Quidi-Vidi would be a bold tactic, and if it fails, he'll have all the fewer men for the last line of defence. I'm sure you're right though. Signal Hill is the vital ground, but we have to get there before we concern ourselves with its taking.'

'Will your men stand a long campaign, Colonel?'

'Ah, now that's the most important question of all. I'm sure they have one general engagement in them. A battle for the heights then a siege; they'll pour out their life's blood for that. However, a vigorously opposed advance lasting days, with experienced French infantry contesting every natural obstacle is quite another matter.'

He sighed and smiled at Holbrooke.

'On balance, I think you may be right, and we may have to fight for the crossing of Quidi-Vidi. Well, tomorrow we'll see what we'll see for I don't intend to tarry here. We'll march at first light. Will the artillery be ready to follow?'

'Aye Colonel, the guns will be ready.'

***

CHAPTER TWENTY-NINE

A Master Stroke

Wednesday, Fifteenth of September 1762.
Signal Hill. St. John's, Newfoundland.

Holbrooke lay flat on the ground with his telescope resting on a rock. How he'd found himself here, as far forward as any man in Amherst's army, he couldn't tell, but the words *unlimited liability* had certainly come home to haunt him. As the French had retreated before the advancing British, so he'd found himself drawn ever closer to the most advanced units of the force. He'd been back with the staff officers as the army had rushed at the hastily prepared positions on the Quidi-Vidi stream but as it became clear that there would soon be an opportunity to mount batteries to fire down upon the French in Fort William, he'd come forward. Amherst had a captain of artillery, but he'd spent his whole service in fortresses. He'd been plucked from Louisbourg for this expedition, and didn't yet have Amherst's trust.

'What do you see, sir?'

The infantry major who shared the dubious cover of this rock had a small field telescope, the sort that could be conveniently carried in a coat pocket, and it was useless at night. Holbrooke had his own quarterdeck telescope, a Dolland instrument, one of the first to be sold with lenses constructed on the achromatic principle. There was almost no distortion when viewing dim lights or shapes at night and he could see details of the French positions that MacDonell couldn't hope to see.

Holbrooke could sense MacDonell's impatience and eventually he took pity and handed over the telescope. The major was no fool. He rested the unwieldy telescope on the shoulder of a lower rock, not on top of the one that they were sheltering behind. The sky was overcast, hiding the moon and the stars and the night was as black as pitch, but

An Upright Man

Holbrooke could feel the easterly wind and could see that the covering of cloud was thinning. Any moment now the sky would start to lighten as the moon peeped through the scurrying clouds, and an incautious head raised above a rock could easily reveal their position.

'Thank you, sir, this is a wonderful instrument. Perhaps too large for normal campaign use, but today it answers the purpose admirably. Ah, I can see their defensive line, just a hundred yards away. A reduced battalion position perhaps, more than a company at least. They must have placed a third or a half of their whole force on this hill.'

Holbrooke said nothing feeling it better to remain silent with the enemy only a hundred yards to their front. He wasn't surprised that d'Haussonville was so strongly defending Signal Hill for he was certain that it was the key to Fort William and the town of St. John's.

MacDonell studied the enemy positions for a full two minutes as the sky to the east became perceptibly lighter. Holbrooke could sense the restlessness of the sergeant and two light infantrymen who'd been allocated as their guards. They had no doubt about the danger that they were exposed to by remaining here and were anxiously watching the sky.

'Can you bring your guns up here, sir? It's very steep and broken.'

'Certainly, Major, but for now I think our rightful place is further removed from the enemy's lines.'

MacDonell nodded. Perhaps he hadn't noticed how the darkness was becoming differentiated, how the deeper dells and spaces between the boulders had an altered quality of blackness. Not shadows, not yet, but it was clear that a revealing moon would soon change the aspect of the hill. The major started to wriggle backwards in preparation for a stooped withdrawal.

'Psst.'

That was the sergeant. MacDonell froze and Holbrooke pressed himself more firmly into the damp bracken.

Nobody spoke and Holbrooke could hear nothing untoward, just the noises of the French lines and the sigh of the wind through the scrubby trees that dotted the hill. He cautiously craned his neck around, carefully keeping his face tilted forward to avoid its pale disc being seen. There were dark shapes moving stealthily below them, between their dubious cover and the advance British positions.

The sergeant moved his hand downward, an unmistakable gesture. Holbrooke could just see the patrol now. Six men at least and they were moving slowly and stealthily across the slope of the hill only some twenty paces below his position. It was an obvious precaution, intended to give warning of a surprise night attack, but it could just as easily prevent the sort of reconnaissance that Holbrooke and MacDonell were engaged in. They were looking from side to side as they cautiously picked their way through the boulders and scrub, but MacDonell had chosen a good position to observe the defences, and their dark clothes gave no point for the patrol's eyes to fix upon. Holbrooke found he was holding his breath. He exhaled quietly and tried to breathe normally. The sergeant, Perry was his name, a Boston man, had rested his hand on the arm of one of his soldiers, to reassure him and to keep him still.

Seconds passed like hours and now the French patrol was directly on Holbrooke's line of retreat. He saw them stop as one of them examined the ground. Then a break in the clouds let in a shaft of moonlight and they moved away to the west, hurrying so as not to be caught in this dangerous no-man's land between the two opposing forces.

They waited until the French patrol disappeared over the curve of the hill. MacDonell looked cautiously at Holbrooke who nodded in reply, and they started to slide back down the hill, across the trail that the French patrol had made. They were below the point where they had seen the enemy and MacDonell raised himself off the ground and started a crouched walk back towards the British lines and safety. They heard a shout, a musket fired and as one accord they threw caution to the wind and ran pell-mell down the hill. Holbrooke noticed that Sergeant Perry brought up the rear although he looked as though he could easily have outrun the two officers.

***

'What do you think, Captain Holbrooke? If I can take that French position on Signal Hill tomorrow, how soon can you have a siege battery established?'

Holbrooke felt at a disadvantage in his wet and mud-stained clothes. With the exception of MacDonell, all of Amherst's staff officers were reasonably clean and dry as well they might be in this campaign tent sheltered in a deep dell out of sight of the French. Still, it was he that had crept so close to the French lines that he had come close to being captured while these soldiers had been waiting on his word before finalising their plans. He drew the colonel's map towards him and studied it briefly.

'I can have half a dozen twenty-four pounders in place the day after the hill is secured, and I can bring up the mortar battery two days later, perhaps one day later if the weather holds. There's a path here that runs south with the sea on its left and this stretch of water, St. George's Pond on its right. I didn't walk the length of it…'

Amherst smiled and his staff officers nodded knowingly. That would have been an open invitation for his reconnaissance party to be observed by the French.

'.. but it looks like it's been cleared of the larger boulders, and the ground is firm.'

Amherst looked again at his map. It was badly soiled and had suffered from overuse since Holbrooke had first seen it.

'This second mound, Gibbet Hill, it's between Signal Hill and Fort William.'

'It is, but Mister Mouat saw it while he was in St. John's, and he's certain that it's low enough to fire right over it into the fort. I wouldn't want to set up my batteries there, it's too close to the fort. Signal Hill is just a mile from Fort

William and that's close enough to make the French consider their position. If they're obstinate and we have to make a breach, then we might have to move forward to Gibbet Hill.'

Holbrooke still had those moments where he wondered why his word should hold any weight. He wasn't a soldier after all, and two of Amherst's staff officers were professional artillerymen and should by rights take the lead in this discussion. But then he'd brought an artillery train across the American wilderness to Fort Niagara, and he'd played an active part in the siege, and that was more than anyone else in Amherst's army could boast. And, of course, he was a post-captain and certainly not to be ignored.

Amherst tapped his finger thoughtfully on the chart. His army was hardly much larger than d'Haussonville's and it was certainly less effective, man-for-man. There wasn't a complete company among them, and every platoon had its share of the sick, lame and just plain lazy. Like much in warfare, he was engaged upon a massive game of bluff. He had to persuade the French that the outcome was inevitable and to do that he must be bold and strike without hesitation. Holbrooke was right. Fort William couldn't hold out long when the battery had been established on Signal Hill. It was a greater range than one would have wanted, and much of the battery's fire would be wasted, but it would only take a tenth of the shots to land within the fort's walls to make his point. The mortars would be more effective, but they hadn't yet been landed. The question now was whether he could take Signal Hill in one swift action. He opened his watch. Three hours until there would be enough light to launch an attack over the rough ground. With a decisive snap he closed it and replaced it in his pocket.

'Gentlemen, we attack an hour before sunrise; let us hope for the usual pre-dawn fog. Major MacDonell, I hope you'll do me the favour of leading the assault. There will be no guns, this is a purely infantry affair, but I want those fellows cleared off the hill before midday. If you can do as much, then perhaps you can chase them off Gallows Hill also, but that's a secondary objective. Captain Holbrooke, will you have the guns ready to move as soon as you get the word? You might feel that you should follow close behind Major MacDonell in order to determine the moment that success is assured.'

***

Holbrooke shivered. He hadn't been cold four hours before when he'd been lying in the wet bracken near the summit of the hill, but here at its foot the hoped-for fog was at its thickest and its clinging tendrils infiltrated every part of his clothing. There was no need to hide; there wasn't the slightest chance of being seen from the top of the hill and even the sounds of Amherst's force preparing for the assault were muffled. An auspicious morning for a surprise attack, although the French couldn't possibly be expecting to be left alone in command of Signal Hill, not as it was so obviously the vital ground for a siege of Fort William.

He could barely distinguish the shapes of the soldiers preparing for the attack. The nearest group – a half platoon – was commanded by the same Sergeant Perry that had accompanied Holbrooke up the hill just a few hours ago. He recognised the two soldiers that had made up the same party, looking like battle-hardened veterans beside their nervous companions. Perry nodded at Holbrooke in a friendly manner, just like the tough, self-sufficient New Englanders that had rowed and poled his fleet of bateaux and whaleboats up the Mohawk River back in 'fifty-nine.

A barely recognisable form in a red uniform coat slipped into the space beside Holbrooke and a slighter figure in a plain blue coat.

'I'd like to formally thank you, Captain Holbrooke, for offering me this opportunity to serve at the front.'

Lieutenant Murray had been cajoling the guns forward ever since the force landed at Torbay and his rightful place was two miles in the rear, ensuring that all was ready to move as soon as he had the word. However, it was clear to the simplest mind that he didn't want to miss this battle and an hour ago Holbrooke had sent Midshipman Carew to call him forward. He'd considered phrasing it as an offer, in terms that Murray could reject, but that was just a cowardly way of going about the matter. There wasn't the slightest chance that Murray would choose to remain with the siege train when he was being offered a place in what was intended to be the only general engagement of the campaign. In any case it was so important that the guns should be moved at the first opportunity, or told to stay or retreat if the battle didn't go well, that Holbrooke really needed a deputy with some authority. Carew was there as a messenger, but his rank carried no weight in the army.

Holbrooke spent a few moments explaining to Murray what was to be done. It didn't take long because the marine officer had been in Holbrooke' confidence for the past few days.

Another mist-shrouded figure appeared from the left.

'Twenty minutes, sir,' Captain MacDonell said, 'and I'm pleased to see Mister Murray will be with you. You'll be well advised to stay behind my party, sir, and if you keep an eye on the Sergeant there,' he nodded to Perry on Holbrooke's right, who grinned in response, 'you'll be on the right track.'

'Then the very best of fortune, Captain MacDonell. Win me Signal Hill for my guns and I'll deliver the fort to Colonel Amherst in half a week.'

The two men shook hands and Macdonell moved away to the left, like an actor in the guise of a ghost, exiting the stage.

Holbrooke busied himself checking his pistols' priming and flints. He carried two and his sword while Murray had a short carbine. Carew contrived to look self-conscious as he fussed with his two pistols and a cutlass. Holbrooke knew how he felt, as though he were a child playing at pirates in the yard at his family home.

A brief look at his watch, five minutes to go. There was

a sound like a lazy wind sweeping through rushes as all around him the infantrymen hauled themselves to their feet. Then the soft calls of sergeants and corporals giving last minute instructions. A low order and then the unmistakable sound of five hundred bayonets being slid out of their scabbards and fixed to muskets. The withdrawal was like the scraping of a carving knife being honed before addressing a joint of beef, but there was no sound on this earth like the metallic click of an army's bayonets being fixed to its muskets.

Holbrooke looked at Murray. To his knowledge the marine had only fought at sea, and never on land, but he was behaving as though this was his natural habitat. Carew looked uncertain but Holbrooke knew that he'd steady up when they started advancing. Amherst's men seemed confident and on the face of it they should prevail today. But as much as a sea battle, an engagement on land was an uncertain affair, and it would only take a trivial setback to send this motley army running back the way it had come.

Then, suddenly, the whole line was moving forward. Holbrooke hadn't heard the order to advance, it must have been given in confidential whispers to each company and platoon, but it had certainly been given. He saw soldiers stumbling over the rough ground, but every one of them advanced at the same pace. A cold breath of wind came stealing in from the east, then another, and suddenly the fog cleared above them. It was like walking through a dream, nothing could be seen twenty yards ahead or on either side but overhead and to their left a crescent moon, halfway to its zenith, cast its pale light on the scene and the first rays of the rising sun were lending a rime of silver to the ragged edges of the fog.

***

Boom!

The first cannon fired from the French lines. A six pounder, but where it was aimed was anybody's guess. Perhaps on either side of the British line the fog had lifted entirely, but here it still lay at their feet and obscured their view forward. A rattle of musketry, but it was a hundred yards or more to the left. He heard cries of pain and cries of anger and defiance. Somewhere in this turgid miasma men were falling and dying, but nothing as yet had penetrated Holbrooke's enchanted circle. Only Murray and Carew and Sergeant Perry and his platoon were in sight.

They stumbled on over the rough ground, expecting white-clad Frenchmen to appear in front at any moment. The firing was general now and a cheer to the right told where a part of the British force was charging forward. And the fog was thinning. Suddenly Holbrooke realised that he could see ten yards in front, then twenty, and then without any warning the whole battlefield, still cloaked in a pre-dawn gloom, opened before his eyes. A British officer to his right waved his sword and shouted and the whole line surged forward. He stretched out his arms to keep his little group under control; it was no part of their duty to enter into bayonet duels with the enemy. He could see it was a struggle for Murray, but Carew was quite content to stay by his captain's side.

In any case, they weren't in the front rank anymore. Sergeant Perry and his Bostonians had angled across their front and were busily chasing a group of Frenchmen who had broken and were running for the top of the hill. It was a brutal little battle and as each of the enemy was overhauled he was summarily bayoneted. Holbrooke had seen it all before of course, and he'd been on the other side of the bayonet charge too, but it was still a horrifying sight.

Ah, there were the French guns. Six pounders as he suspected, and they were firing cannister. As he looked, Perry's men charged at them from their left and the alarmed artillerymen had only time to fire their last shots before they joined the general retreat. And it was a fateful last salvo. The battery of four six pounders was pointing straight at MacDonell and the company behind him. One minute they were all cheering lustily and moving forward in a mass, and the next there was a clear passage carpeted and walled about with kicking and writhing limbs where the packets of musket balls had cut through their ranks. There was no sign of MacDonell.

Holbrooke looked around. The French were beaten, that was a certainty, and in a few minutes he could send for the guns to start moving forward. He'd have the batteries established before sunset and then tomorrow he could deliver the final notice to d'Haussonville, in the form of roundshot. The next day, or the day after, it would be mortar bombs that they'd have no means of answering except with a capitulation. But meanwhile there was time to look for MacDonell.

They found him lying on the ground surrounded by the dead and dying from that French battery's terrible last salvo. He'd been hit in both legs, above the knees, and the dark red blood was surging out with the same rhythm as a bilge pump in the morning watch. Holbrooke had seen enough wounds to know there was little hope but he did what he could with the big handkerchiefs that he and Murray both carried as field dressings. They staunched the flow of blood and tightened down on the arteries using two bayonets from discarded muskets, just as they'd use Spanish windlasses in marrying a pair of shrouds. In what seemed like moments a bearer party arrived and carried him away. He was unconscious by then and perhaps that was for the best.

***

By the time that Holbrooke reached the bare top of the hill, the only Frenchmen to be seen were dead, wounded or prisoners, except for the last few fleeing into the fog towards Gibbet Hill, dragging the remains of a battery of guns in their wake.

'Well, Mister Murray, I think our work here is done; this is an excellent place to establish a battery, so make all haste and let's get the guns moving.'

***

CHAPTER THIRTY

De Ternay's Fog

Wednesday, Fifteenth of September 1762.
St. John's, Newfoundland.

'This weather will be the death of us all. Is there any news from Monsieur d'Haussonville?'

De Ternay's normal composure was being tested by a lack of information. He'd heard the musketry and the sound of the artillery's small cannons, but it had faded away now and only the occasional discharge broke the silence. The firing had appeared to be coming from Signal Hill on the north side of the Narrows, but this fog not only obscured the view but it distorted the sounds making it difficult to judge the direction. It was infuriating; Signal Hill was only just over a mile from where *Robuste* lay at anchor and in all probability a battle had started and ended but he didn't know what had been fought over and – worst of all – who had won the engagement.

'Nothing, sir. Shall I send a lieutenant to inquire?'

There was only one man in the squadron who could match de Ternay's Olympian detachment, and that was his secretary whose icy stare had, at one time or another, brought every officer in the ship into subjugation.

'No. Call away my boat, I'll go myself.'

***

Fort William was in an uproar, and it required no questioning to determine that whatever the engagement, the French forces had come off worst. Exhausted and wounded men streamed down from the slopes of Gibbet hill, appearing as spectres through the enveloping fog. Many of them looked anxiously over their shoulders in fear of pursuit. A company, evidently d'Haussonville's reserve, was marching in the opposite direction to the retreating, beaten soldiers, apparently to form a new defensive line.

An Upright Man

The captain at their head saluted elaborately as he passed and gave de Ternay a rueful smile.

An aide conducted de Ternay to the brigade headquarters deep within Fort William. The evidence of a battle lost was visible in the faces of the men who slumped, exhausted, against the walls.

'The enemy has taken Signal Hill, Monsieur.'

D'Haussonville made an attempt to pull himself together in the presence of the commander of the expedition, but he looked tired and discouraged, the very picture of a defeated man.

'They attacked at dawn through the mist and as far as I can tell I've lost some fifty men, killed wounded and captured.'

'You're certain, Monsieur? The British have taken Signal Hill? Have you considered a counterattack?'

'A counterattack? I don't have the force for it, not if I have to man the batteries at the Narrows and defend the fort. That company that you saw is my entire reserve and I've sent them out to hold Gibbet Hill. No, there will be no counterattack today. Tomorrow perhaps…'

'Tomorrow? Do you talk of tomorrow, Monsieur? We know that the British have landed a siege train; the moment this fog disperses you'll have twenty-four pound shot hammering at your walls. And I wouldn't be surprised to hear that they'll be landing mortars soon. There is no tomorrow, Monsieur d'Haussonville, it's today or not at all. Now, I've given you all my marines and it appears that only a fraction of your force was engaged today; is there nothing you can do?'

D'Haussonville shook his head wearily. He wished with all his heart that this forthright sailor would go to the Devil and leave him in peace to organise the fort for the coming siege. In a few weeks the weather would turn and then the British would surely have to withdraw.

'Then you must re-embark your brigade. We've fulfilled our mission; the fishery is in ruins and now we must go.

How quickly can you get your men aboard?'

D'Haussonville looked shocked. Only a few days before they had been talking about sustaining a garrison through the winter. He had no thoughts of withdrawal, only of the hard arithmetic of the number of mouths that he could feed through a cold Newfoundland winter. De Ternay could see that the man needed a push.

'Monsieur d'Haussonville,' de Ternay said in a determined voice, 'I didn't bring these ships out of the Vilaine river in the teeth of a British blockade to lose them in a squabble over codfish. My squadron will depart at the first opportunity and if you haven't embarked you'll have the choice of starving in your fort or surrendering to the British. It's now eleven o'clock. My boats will be at the wharfs below the fort at two o'clock.'

'That is impossible! I need to hold the British at Gibbet Hill and I need to fire the fort's magazine. My guns must be embarked, and I have patrols out who know nothing of a withdrawal…'

'Monsieur d'Haussonville. This is my positive order; you are to commence embarking your men this afternoon. I can't say when I'll depart, it depends on the weather and the British squadron, but it will probably be at very short notice. Those of your force that are not embarked at that time will be left behind. I hope that is entirely clear.'

The Comte d'Haussonville had not been spoken to in that manner since he'd commanded a company in the far distant days of the last war. He simply didn't know how to respond, and after a few breathless seconds de Ternay solved his problem for him.

'Then I'll expect your men at two o'clock. Good day Monsieur.'

***

First came the massive baulks of timber to form the bed for the gun carriages, then the shot came swinging up the hill suspended two-at-a-time in a net slung below a pole borne on the shoulders of a pair of sailors. The barrels of

An Upright Man

powder and the tools of the gunner's trade – worms and sponges and rammers – all followed and very faintly and far-off Holbrooke could hear the sounds of a hundred soldiers and sailors hauling the twenty-four pounders up the hill by brute force. The artillery officers were busy pegging out the battery lines while the infantry established their positions on the forward slope, protecting the guns. Holbrooke had the feeling that his usefulness had ended, that the professional artillerymen could take over and, when the fog lifted, start the wearying process of battering Fort William into submission.

'A good morning's work, Colonel Amherst. Your men seem to have done all that was asked of them. Now we just need the fog to clear.'

'Yes indeed, Captain Holbrooke, and no small thanks to you that the batteries are being established so quickly. Do you have any thoughts on the weather?'

Holbrooke laughed and looked over to the west.

'If this was any civilised country then the fog would have burned away with the sun. The wind's picking up from the west, and usually I'd say it would blow the fog away, but really, I can't be sure. I just have the feeling that the visibility won't improve until this westerly has blown through, perhaps tomorrow.'

'Well, we can wait. I can maintain a siege for perhaps a month but if the French hold out after that I'll need to withdraw my army to Halifax and leave them in possession until the spring. Will their ships try to flee, do you think?'

Now, that was the question. He couldn't imagine that de Ternay would willingly allow himself to be bottled up in St. John's through the winter. Surely he'd want to escape, whether his land commander decided to stay or not. The harbour at St. John's didn't freeze, thanks to the warm water of the Atlantic Drift, and in principle de Ternay could delay his departure indefinitely. But he must be aware that his time was running out, that their Lordships in the Admiralty would have cobbled together an overwhelming battle squadron and that at this moment it must be on its way.

'He'll try to escape. He needs a westerly wind to get through the Narrows and he needs Lord Colville to be blown off station. He could fight, of course, and he has a greater force than Lord Colville, but he has no yards hereabouts and he must fear a superior British force arriving at any day.'

Holbrooke looked thoughtful and tested the wind again. The fog was as thick as ever, but the wind was definitely stronger in the gusts.

'I need to report to Lord Colville and he'll probably want me to rejoin my ship. It looks like your men have it all under control now.'

'Well I hope so, Captain, although I'll miss your wise council. However, you go with my thanks. You know that MacDonell died of his wounds?'

'I did not, and I regret it deeply. He was a fine soldier.'

***

'I'm pleased to hear that Amherst is well on the way to Fort William, and my thanks for looking after his guns. I'll be looking to you and Captain Douglas to watch St. John's, Holbrooke. My sailing master is certain that we're in for a westerly gale and God knows *Northumberland* won't be able to stay on station if he's right. We'll lose a point of heading on every tack, and we'll be over the Banks and rolling our guts out before nightfall. The rest of them will be even worse. You'll have to make do with verbal orders, Holbrooke, I can't hold you a moment longer. Now, if de Ternay comes out you're to follow him wherever he goes and break off to report as you see fit. If he steers for the Gulf of Saint Lawrence or for Halifax or Boston, then you're to find me immediately. However, my guess is that he'll have had enough of these waters and he'll make for Brest. In any case, his squadron's too big to be allowed to wander around the oceans without our leave. Douglas is to keep *Siren* on station, whatever the French do; he'll be my only remaining frigate. Although how he'll know that he's to stay here is a mystery because I can't get a message to him now. Oh well, he'll do as he sees fit, I'm sure.'

'Very well, sir, and the best of fortune to you.'

'You know, Holbrooke, your friend Carlisle always spoke well of you, and I can see now what he meant. God go with you, and I hope we meet again.'

***

Two o'clock came and went. The ship's boats should have been appearing out of the fog by now carrying the advance parties of d'Haussonville's brigade, but not a single one was to be seen. All the information that de Ternay had received since he met d'Haussonville was from his flagship's first lieutenant who was in charge of the embarkation. He'd sent a short note saying that only a very few soldiers had arrived and that he'd seen more formations marching out of the fort towards Gibbet Hill than were coming down to the wharfs. The lack of information would have infuriated a lesser man, but de Ternay refused to engage in idle speculation. He couldn't see the shore from his flagship, and he had to rely entirely on messages being passed. He'd told d'Haussonville that he must embark his brigade; if the man chose not to then that was his misfortune.

He looked at the dog-vane on the quarterdeck, it was nearly horizontal even here in the shelter of the harbour, so out beyond the Narrows it must already be blowing a gale. He could guess that the British ships-of-the-line would soon find it impossible to maintain their stations, if they hadn't already fled to the east. In any case, this was almost certainly his last chance of escape and regardless of what d'Haussonville did, he'd take it.

'A lieutenant, if you please, Captain. I have a message to send to the squadron.'

The flag captain knew better than to point out that he had only one lieutenant remaining after he'd fulfilled de Ternay's wishes for supervision of the wharfs, and that this last lieutenant had spent the night on deck and the forenoon preparing the ship for sea. He was on his knees with fatigue but then, it was a hard service, and nobody should expect anything different.

'Take the *bachot*, I believe it's the only boat remaining, and give my respects to the captains of *Eveillé, Garonne, Licorne* and the prize corvette. They're to be at single anchor by four o'clock, cleared for action and at quarters. It's my present intention to withdraw all the boats from the shore at five o'clock, whether the brigade is embarked or not. They're to slip their anchors – not weigh them – at exactly six o'clock. Each ship will be towed by its own boats until it can make its own way, and we depart the harbour in the order *Robuste, Licorne, Garonne, Eveillé* and the corvette. They're to avoid action with the British. If they lose sight of the flagship, the course is nor'east by east to take a northerly track for Brest. Now, repeat that to me, if you please.'

De Ternay refused to give an impression of uncertainty by nervously pacing the quarterdeck through the afternoon; instead, he calmly attended to his paperwork in his cabin. At three o'clock he heard the best bower anchor being weighed. That just left the second anchor which wouldn't be so significant a loss when it was slipped. At half-past four o'clock the same last remaining lieutenant came to his cabin to report that he was ready to take the *bachot* to the wharves.

'There's to be no indecision, Lieutenant. All the boats must leave the wharves at exactly five o'clock and every last seaman is to be on board. That is my command, and you may repeat that to anyone who cares to disagree.'

***

The fog was thinner than before, and the visibility was just good enough for *Northumberland's* sailing master to find *Argonaut* and heave to in the frigate's lee. Holbrooke was wet and shivering when he reached his own deck, and frankly grateful to have survived a boat journey at the very edge of prudence. Colville really had left it until the last moment and not another boat would leave any of the ships until the gale had passed through.

'Mister Fairview, Mister Shorrock. We're to hold our station off the Narrows when the squadron's blown to leeward.'

Shorrock nodded but it was Fairview's responsibility to execute the orders.

'Aye-aye sir. Look, they're going already; they don't choose to risk their sails and spars fighting this gale, and I can't say that I blame them. We're perhaps two miles off North Head by my reckoning and there's just a point of southerly in the wind to keep us clear of Cape Spear.'

'Very well, Mister Fairview. Bring her closer in to about a mile and start soundings, if you please. If the French don't want to spend the winter in St. John's and risk being taken when the fort capitulates, they must seize their opportunities when they can. This de Ternay loves a fog, and if he's the man I think he is, he'll be through those Narrows before dawn. Now, beat to quarters, if you please, and clear for action. Double the lookouts and relieve them every half-glass. There's to be silence on deck to give us a chance of hearing them if we can't see them.'

Ten minutes to bring the ship to quarters and then a deathly quiet came over the frigate's deck. Holbrooke's mind was starting to turn over de Ternay's possible actions when the leadsman's voice pierced the muffled silence.

'No bottom No bottom on this line.'

'Mister Fairview. The leadsman is to pass his sounding back by a reliable runner, unless he finds fifteen fathoms, then he's to sing out loud and clear.'

***

'Anchor's slipped, sir. The boats are holding her.'

De Ternay could feel his ship come alive as its bows were no longer held into the wind by the anchor. He looked over the side to where he could just make out the scummy water that was drifting lazily down the side under the impetus of the wind. He made no answer to the flag captain's report; he knew very well what to do.

The great three-decker's head was pulled slowly around to starboard. Larboard would have been quicker, but with no clear sight of the shore it was too dangerous to make a leeward turn. It was all a matter of guesswork, but the sides of St. John's harbour were steep-to, and they'd certainly see the shore before they ran aground. In any case, it was now or never.

They passed *Licorne* on their starboard side. That was a good marker, and they could make the turn into the Narrows as soon as the frigate had passed astern.

'Helm's a-weather…'

The sailing master was addressing the flag captain as was only right and proper.

'…we can set the main tops'l now, sir. Two reefs, I think.'

There was a rush as the topmen ran out onto the yard. The falling sail was visible from the quarterdeck and when it was sheeted in, the ship lurched forward adding a knot of speed.

'*Licorne's* following, sir.'

The fog was a little thinner here and the sides of the Narrows could be seen, crowding in upon *Robuste*. He could hear the soldiers at the batteries jeering as the ships made their escape. They were in no doubt as to what was happening; they were being abandoned to their fate. De Ternay didn't care what they thought. He'd given d'Haussonville every opportunity to evacuate his brigade and yet he'd done nothing.

De Ternay could feel the open ocean and he could no longer see the cliffs of the Narrows. They must be through. Now they had to wait for the other four ships of the squadron. A quick look astern showed *Licorne* sheering off to starboard to avoid running into *Robuste's* stern. There was no question of a lee shore, not with this westerly gale that was tugging at the reefed main tops'l.

An Upright Man

'Bring her to on the larboard tack, if you please. Get the boats alongside and then we can get underway.'

The flag captain gave his orders and *Robuste's* head turned to the north. There was still no sign of the British but then they'd hardly be this close in to the shore.

'Fifteen fathoms sounding, sir, and deepening.'

Good, they were making an offing. All of his ships should be clear of the Narrows by now. He could see a number of shadowy shapes drawing nearer but he couldn't tell exactly how many. He'd have heard something if one of them had struck a rock in the harbour or in the Narrows. He was comforted that *Eveillé* was bringing up the rear. Her captain was a steady man and he'd find a way to alert his commodore if there was a problem.

'Boat's crews are aboard, sir, and all the boats are towing astern.'

'Very well, bear away and set reefed tops'ls, jib and fore stays'l. Your course is east for Brest.'

Robuste was moving clear of the land and now the wind was howling through the rigging and even under reefed tops'ls the log was showing six knots. There were occasional gaps in the fog, and through those gaps *Licorne* could be seen as a constant presence close astern.

'A sail, sir, on the larboard bow.'

The sailing master was pointing at a patch of fog that was more substantial than anything around it. A ship, certainly, not a two decker, a frigate perhaps. British for sure.

'Stand by the larboard battery. Fire when your guns bear.'

Robuste had a fearful broadside comprising two decks of thirty-six, eighteen and eight pound guns and all thirty-seven fired within a few seconds of each other. At that range it should have been a crippling broadside that reduced the enemy frigate to a shattered wreck, but at the last moment as the gun layers were making their final adjustments the fog closed in and obscured their prey.

There were no points of reference in that howling grey wasteland and no means of knowing whether their broadside had reached its target. Well, at least it would alert the rest of the squadron to the enemy's presence. A frigate, he was sure, and he'd stake everything – he was indeed staking everything – on the British battle squadron being far offshore by now. They may have heard the broadside but in this westerly wind they couldn't possibly beat back to where the sound had come from. Now was the time to deceive the enemy, to strike off in an unexpected direction.

'Three points to larboard, Captain, make your course nor'east by east.'

***

The lookout saw the tops'ls too late and Fairview's frantic effort to wear ship away from the threat was doomed to failure before it started. That great menacing shape could only be a French seventy-four, and therefore de Ternay's flagship. It was there and then it was gone, and its disappearance was followed by the sound of its broadside and the weird illumination of the fog, like the ghostly light on a misty mere at dawn, but greater and more menacing. There were two distinct crashes, as roundshot smashed into the frigate's frail hull; they felt like thirty-six pounders. Two lesser crashes could have been eighteen pounders. The fog felt like a friend as *Argonaut* slipped away to the north.

'Two men dead at number three gun, sir. Wilkins and Jefferson, and two wounded.'

Shorrock knew better than to run straight into a damage report after he'd told his captain about the casualties. Holbrooke needed a moment of reflection, a moment to consider how he might have avoided those deaths and injuries.

'I saw it, Mister Shorrock. It didn't look so bad from here. I'm sorry, they were good men.'

Shorrock nodded and continued.

'The gun's trunnion has been shot away. Four shot

holes all above the waterline and Chips is getting at them now. One of the lanyards on the starboard fore shrouds has parted and the bosun has that in hand.'

'Thank you, Mister Shorrock. That was unexpected. You were right to hold our fire though, we may see a better target yet. Now, they have four in their squadron, and Mister Mouat's sloop. Mister Fairview, can you tack?'

'Aye sir. I have enough way on.'

'Then bring her about and let's see if we can follow at the rear of his line.'

'Sail on the larboard bow, sir. Nearly a mile off, I'd say.'

'Thank you, Mister Fairview. I fancy the fog's still lifting. Keep us at least a mile away in case they're tempted. Ah, there they all are now.'

Fog is a strange thing. One minute a man can't see the back of his hand and then, as though a curtain is lifted on a stage, the outside world comes sharply into view, only for the curtain to fall again. That was how Holbrooke saw the whole French squadron and Fairview was able to determine its course, before it was lost again.

'Nor'east by east, sir, or thereabouts.'

'Then join the line, Mister Fairview, and keep the rear ship in sight. This will be a long passage, I expect.'

***

CHAPTER THIRTY-ONE

No Refuge

Saturday, Twenty-Fifth of September 1762.
Argonaut, at Sea. Ushant, north-northeast 5 leagues.

Quarter to five o'clock in the morning, no moon and the brisk north-westerly wind brought dangerous squalls with hard rain to chill the bones of the watch on deck. Holbrooke tripped over the hatch coaming as he came on deck and it was only the messenger, a lad of about fourteen, that saved him from an undignified arrival.

'Good day, sir, Two bells in fifteen minutes.'

Shorrock looked disgustingly cheerful for a man who'd been on watch until midnight and had been roused only four hours later to take the morning watch. It was Holbrooke's fault, of course. Following de Ternay's squadron across the Atlantic in a sixth rate frigate carried the constant danger that one of the French ships would double back – during the night or in bad weather – and trap *Argonaut* between two fires. He'd thought about it, discussed it with Shorrock and Fairview, and had come to the conclusion that only the sailing master and the first lieutenant – the only lieutenant in a small frigate – could be trusted with the night watches. During the day, when the visibility was good, the gunner had augmented the watch bill, but otherwise it was just his two most senior officers.

'The wind's as you see it. These squalls come and go and the two reefs in the tops'ls seem to be holding us at eight knots. Ushant's to the nor'east at five leagues,' he added dipping his head towards the larboard bow. 'Our course is east, and Mister Fairview assures me that we'll find the Iroise if we hold that heading. It's all quiet and most of the watch on deck has had some sleep. Nautical twilight at nine minutes past five, sir. Will you want to beat to quarters?'

Holbrooke was still warm from his cot but already the

cold, damp air was searching through his cloak, seeking for gaps in his defences.

'Good morning, Mister Shorrock. Has there been any sign of the French?'

'Not since I reported them before the moon set, and they were all in their normal stations then, but that was seven hours ago. They were four miles ahead and making straight as a rule for Brest. Nothing since.'

Shorrock swept his hands wide as if to show that nothing could possibly be seen on a night like this after the moon had set, not without it showing a light, and the French squadron had been most particular about darkening their ships as sunset.

Holbrooke knew all about the last sighting of the enemy. He'd been on deck as the moon dipped below the horizon and again at eight bells, just an hour later, and he'd haunted Fairview every hour through the graveyard watch. While Shorrock and Fairview had been watch-and-watch about through the night, he'd never had more than an hour's sleep and often not that much. For the danger was very real and very present. At any moment the French seventy-four could appear out of the darkness or through a squall and then one broadside would see the end of *Argonaut* and most of her people. Well, all he could do was remain vigilant, even though it was visibly wearing down his senior officers, and vigilance required that he send the men to their quarters before the first light of the new day.

'Yes, Mister Shorrock, beat to quarters if you please.'

The drummer had been ready since Holbrooke's marine sentry sent the word that the captain was astir, and he plied his sticks with gusto. The ship was already cleared for action of course, so it took no longer than the time required for the men to roll out of their hammocks and make their way to their stations. This being a frigate where the men berthed on the lower of the two decks, they could man the guns without having to stow their hammocks. Usually Holbrooke would have insisted upon it in any case, but he recognised that his people also had a limit to their endurance. The ship would be at quarters for perhaps one turn of the half-hour glass – until the horizon could be seen – and then the watch below could turn in again and resume their interrupted sleep. It took at least ten minutes for a man to retrieve his hammock from the nets and rig it, and that was ten minutes of wasted opportunity for rest.

'The hands are at quarters, sir, and the ship's cleared for action with the exception of the hammocks.'

'Very well, Mister Shorrock, a very creditable time, I believe. Now let's see what we can see.'

It wasn't sunrise, far from it, but below the eastern horizon, below the hills of Brittany if Fairview was to be believed, the sun was sprinting upwards. This day being so close to the equinox, the interval between bible-black night and a clearly visible horizon was at its shortest. Slowly, almost imperceptibly, the blackness ahead gave way to grey with a hint of an orange dawn.

Every telescope on the quarterdeck was busy quartering the horizon and every man with nothing better to do was also watching. High above the deck the lookouts stared through hand-shaded eyes, hoping to be the first to sight the enemy. The man at the masthead won the point.

'Sail ho! Sail fine on the starboard bow. It looks like the French, sir. Three, no four of them. I see the fifth now.'

Now that they were pointed out, and as the light improved second-by-second, they could be seen from the quarterdeck. Fairview took a bearing for form's sake, and straightened up.

'Two leagues, sir, I reckon. They'll be tucked up at Brest before they pipe to dinner.'

Holbrooke let out the breath that he'd been holding. The long days of tension were over and as soon as he'd seen de Ternay's squadron past Point St. Matthew, he could tack and stand out to the west to make his offing before tacking again to weather Ushant and reach up the channel for Portsmouth. He could be home in two days if the wind held. And yet there was a feeling of anticlimax, of a job not yet completed. He'd hoped with all his heart that he'd find a portion of Hawke's Western Squadron off Brest, cutting de Ternay off from his refuge. With this north-westerly there would be no escape to seaward and he'd make sure that *Argonaut* so disrupted them that they'd be easily overhauled. In any case, he was certain that they all needed to be careened, particularly Mouat's *Gramont*. The sloop, or corvette as the French were no doubt calling it, was noticeably slower than the others. It had been an extraordinarily fast passage from St. John's but with these constant westerlies it should have been even faster. Of course, Hawke was keeping a distant blockade of Brest, and his ships would be at anchor in Plymouth or Torbay. The best he could hope for was a pair of frigates and that wouldn't be enough to stop de Ternay's headlong dash for home. Still, he'd done his duty and seen them into Brest, or soon would do.

'Sail ho!'

The lookout at the man t'gallant head's voice was urgent, quite a different tone to when he reported the French. He'd been expecting to see them as the day lightened, but this new sighting was something unexpected.

'Sail four points on the larboard bow. Men-o'-war, sir, three or four of them but I can't quite make them out.'

'Mister Petersen…'

Holbrooke didn't need to finish the sentence. These new ships weren't yet in sight from the quarterdeck, and it was evident that they must be identified as soon as possible. Petersen grabbed the deck telescope and ran for the main shrouds.

'Whoever they are they've run the passage and they're just approaching Point St. Matthew, sir. I trust they've embarked a good channel pilot.'

Fairview shook his head at the thought of men-of-war making that dangerous passage without a pilot. Holbrooke was more concerned about their identity and his heart beat faster as he considered the possibilities.

'Deck there. I can see four third rates, sir, and I'm almost certain they're British. My God, they've set their stuns'ls aloft and alow; they're cracking on at a furious rate. It looks like they're trying to cut off the French squadron from Brest.'

'Well, never say die, sir. Here's the inshore squadron right on time. Monsieur de Ternay needs to make a fast decision. He can just make the Passage of the Raz if he wears now. It'll be too late soon.'

Fairview kept a mental map in his head, and he could visualise the whole of the Iroise and the outer approaches to Brest. No doubt he was right, but de Ternay had a better appreciation of the situation, being at the focus of the three parts in this drama.

'Ah, he's bearing away. He's wearing.'

'Up helm, Mister Fairview, let's see if we can cut him off. Shake out those reefs. Will she bear stuns'ls?'

'Tops'l stuns'ls, sir. Anything else is risking our yards.'

'Very well Mister Fairview. Mister Stitch, make the Western Squadron signal for enemy in sight to leeward.'

***

Argonaut yawed wildly as the long Atlantic rollers hit her stern. It was the frigate's most uncomfortable point of sailing; in fact it was almost every ship's least desirable point. Nevertheless, she leaped forward in pursuit of the fleeing French.

Holbrooke tried to put himself in the enemy's position. What must be going through de Ternay's mind? He was so close to completing his mission. Holbrooke knew nothing of d'Haussonville's brigade that had been left behind at St. John's. From his perspective it looked like a successful expedition that was in peril at the last moment before its final triumph. Clearly de Ternay had decided that the four British third rates would pass by Point St. Matthew, braving perhaps a single salvo from the shore battery's heavy guns, and place themselves squarely across the Goulet, blocking the way to Brest. He'd seen it and taken the kind of decisive action that Holbrooke had come to expect of him. Now he was running for the Passage du Raz and then presumably for one of the other Atlantic ports, La Rochelle or Rochefort. Yet he had a world of dangers before him. There was a British blockade along the whole of the coast, sustained from the captured Belle Isle. He wasn't clear of danger by any means.

'The sloop's lagging behind, sir, just as we expected. He must be making a full knot less than the others.'

'Just so, Mister Shorrock, and I suspect that de Ternay won't wait for him, not if it risks that squadron catching them.'

He looked over on the larboard quarter where the four third rates were now visible in the bright light of day.

'Mister Fairview, are we head reaching on the French?'

'Only on the sloop, sir. If anything, the others are faster than us; they have the wind two points on the quarter, of course.'

That was an important point. Until they were through the Raz, de Ternay's squadron would sail as fast or faster than *Argonaut* because the wind was further off their quarters. Once through the Raz it would be a stern chase and he could hope at least to match their speed.

'They're five miles ahead, I reckon, sir.'

'Then I rely on you, Mister Fairview, to get every knot of speed out of *Argonaut* that you can, every tenth of a knot.'

'Deck there!' Petersen shouted from the masthead, 'I can just make out a signal from the lead third rate; general chase, I believe, sir.'

Then whoever commanded the inshore squadron was intent upon catching the French, Well, it would be a long chase and night would fall before there was any resolution. But there was always the sloop…

***

A breakneck chase with too many independent components, yet it was resolving itself, minute by minute into a simple contest. It was clear from the start that the British squadron was being left behind. Perhaps it was a strange wind shadow created by Ushant and the low-lying Molene Islands, or it was the confused sea caused by those same islands as the strong northwester piled up the waves to crash upon their rocky shores. Whatever it was, the four seventy-fours were being left further behind as each minute passed. The signal for general chase still flew bravely in the lead ship, but it was clear that unless *Argonaut* could slow the French retreat, they'd be long gone by the time the British squadron passed through the Raz.

The four leading French ships were also leaving *Argonaut* behind. They looked supremely elegant with the wind on their quarter compared with the British frigate's wild yawing and rolling. At this rate they'd still be in sight when *Argonaut* came through the Raz, but they'd be so far ahead that it was unlikely that Holbrooke could come up with them before sunset. And then what? If he couldn't engage them with any hope of success in the ten days that they had sped across the Atlantic, there was no hope of doing so with France under their lee. Then there was the sloop. Mouat had said that the rigging would need setting up anew after it was brought up from the filthy ooze at the bottom of St. John's harbour. Perhaps that was such an odious job that it wasn't done with any conviction. Perhaps the stink had stayed with the ship and debilitated its crew. Whatever the cause, *Argonaut* was catching the sloop at the rate of a nautical mile or even two every hour.

'What do you make the range now, Mister Fairview?'

'The sloop's three miles ahead, sir, and it's five to the narrowest part of the Raz. We won't be up with her until she's through. Wind's picking up though, I'd like to take in the stuns'ls. And take a reef in the tops'ls.'

Holbrooke looked aloft. The stuns'l yards were bending extravagantly. Perhaps Fairview was right, but it would severely reduce their speed.

'There goes her main t'gallant, sir, and her fore t'gallant.'

Holbrooke turned in time to see the drama. The drag of the t'gallant masts over the side caused the sloop to yaw and she was almost upon her beam ends before the situation was recovered. In a few minutes she was back on her old course, running fast for the Passage du Raz. But her speed was drastically reduced.

'What do you think now, Mister Fairview?'

'Oh, we'll catch her before she's through the passage, that is if we don't pull out our own sticks. The wind's come up in the past few minutes and I don't believe it's a passing squall. We should furl the stuns'ls and put two reefs in the t'gallants and a reef in the tops'ls, sir. I won't answer for our spars otherwise.'

'Very well, Mister Fairview, make it so.'

Argonaut's crew was well worked up and the furling and reefing took only ten minutes. Holbrooke could feel it, *Argonaut* was slower by about a knot, but still they were gaining on the sloop. The leading four ships had clearly abandoned their smallest member, perhaps they felt no kinship with this British prize. With a wide spread of canvas they'd passed through the Raz and hauled their wind by two points. They were heading southwest-by-south into the Bay of Biscay. Perhaps de Ternay didn't relish losing his squadron to the British blockades of the Biscay ports and he was steering for Cape Finisterre. Would he make for a Spanish port, or continue right through the Gut into the Mediterranean? It hardly mattered. Unless something changed radically Holbrooke's battle was confined to the eighteen-gun sloop now.

***

'Lay me alongside to windward, Mister Fairview.'

'Aye-aye sir. He'll pass the outlying rocks of Pointe du Raz by half a cable. Look, the sea's bursting over them. One wrong move and he'll be ashore.'

'Mister Shorrock. Stand by the larboard battery.'

Holbrooke was gripping the quarterdeck rail. Why didn't the sloop strike its colours? It would only take the loss of a mast or the bowsprit to put her aground on the rocks off the point, and then she'd break up in a moment. Even if the sloop made it through, *Argonaut* would be hard on its heels and there would be no more chance of escape on the other side of the point than there was on this side. A thought occurred to him.

'What's the coast like around the point?'

Fairview knew what Holbrooke meant. Was there a sheltered sandy cove where the sloop could be run ashore is safety?

'Rocks and more rocks, sir. He'll be sheltered, somewhat, but he'll bilge as soon as he strikes and be dashed to pieces in a few minutes. He can't be hoping for that.'

'Larboard battery ready, sir. Loaded with ball.'

'Put a shot across his bows, if you please, Mister Shorrock. Number two gun. If that doesn't bring him to his senses then you can give him a full broadside.'

Bang!

Number two gun fired. Where the ball landed was anyone's guess, it was lost in the broken sea of the Pointe du Raz.

'Her ensign's still flying, sir.'

Holbrooke held up his hand, he wanted to give the opposing captain every opportunity to strike. Nothing. The French officers looked a dogged lot as they went about their task of getting every knot of speed out of their ship. He realised that there'd been no answering shots from the sloop. Probably its guns had been taken for Fort William. He remembered those six pounders on Signal Hill; in all likelihood he'd already met them.

'Another, Mister Shorrock, number four gun.'

Bang!

He saw that one, a spout of water leapt up a quarter cable ahead of the sloop. Holbrooke waved his arms and received a slow shake of the head in return.

'Broadside fire, Mister Shorrock.'

The larboard battery fired almost as one, except the number four gun that had not yet reloaded. The result was both spectacular and tragic. Within an instant the sloop's fore topmast and jib boom were over the side and it looked as though her rudder had been shot away. The unfortunate ship veered uncontrollably to larboard and, with the full force of the northwester at her stern drove hard towards the cruel rocks of La Vielle, the furthest outcrop of the Pointe du Raz. They watched in silence as the sloop struck and her remaining masts went by the board. A big sea swept over the hapless ship, then another even bigger that slewed her stern around and broke her back. Holbrooke looked through his telescope but there was no sign of life on the deck, it had been swept clean of everything; masts, windlass, wheel, binnacle, lockers and hammock nets.

'There's nothing we can do, sir. No boat of ours will swim in this sea.'

Holbrooke stared through a blank-face. Never in all his career, in all his battles, had a victory seemed so hollow. He pulled himself together with an effort and spoke stiffly.

'Very well, Mister Fairview. Take us around the Isle de Sein and when you can, tack back towards the Iroise. I'll be in my cabin.'

***

HISTORICAL EPILOGUE

At Sea

In early 1762 British forces commanded by Admiral Rodney and Brigadier General Monckton captured Martinique, leaving the French Caribbean possessions reduced to only those in the southern part of the island chain, and Saint-Domingue. With their navy yet to recover from its defeats at Lagos Bay and Quiberon Bay and its futile attempts to reinforce Quebec, there was every prospect that St. Lucia, St. Vincent and Grenada would soon also fall into British hands. To make matters worse, the loss of Belle Isle in 1761 had provided an excellent base of operations for the British blockading squadron; France's Atlantic seaboard was locked down tight. The French shipyards were busy building replacements for the fleet and French agents were scouring the shipyards of Europe for spare capacity to build men-of-war. Meanwhile, and until the new ships should be available, all that the French navy could do was to try to keep a fleet in being, protected in its main bases at Brest, Rochefort and Toulon. The French hope of the Spanish fleet turning the tide of the war at sea was dashed when a large part of it was committed to defending Spain's colonial possessions.

Lord Anson's death in June 1762 brought in a new administration for the navy, initially under the leadership of Lord Halifax, but by then the important decisions had all been taken and the British fleet was well on the way to complete mastery of the seas.

Western Europe

Prince Ferdinand continued to frustrate the French armies that poured into Westphalia and the other German states with each new campaigning season. It was this failure to capture Hanover that was King Louis' greatest concern because he and his ministers were convinced that Britain would exchange anything to retrieve the King's personal German fiefdom. However, if they noticed that George III didn't have the same attachment to Hanover as his grandfather had, they failed to take it properly into consideration, and it's questionable whether it would have been the bargaining chip that they had hoped to place on the table.

Central Europe

Frederick of Prussia continued to raise new armies to hold his territorial gains against the combined armies of Austria and Russia. Nevertheless, a tactical mistake in the autumn of 1761 left the Prussian state on the verge of collapse and it was only saved by the death of Empress Elizabeth of Russia in January 1762. Her successor Peter initiated peace negotiations with Frederick, taking the pressure off his army and saving Prussia from defeat and destruction.

Portugal

One of Spain's principal war aims was to invade Portugal and bring its territory and people into union with Spain, and during 1762 King Charles launched three separate attacks across the border. It looked easy, Portugal at that time was a poor and sparsely populated country with little strategic depth and the distance from Spain to the Atlantic coast was only around a hundred miles along most of its length. However, the Spanish reckoned without the military support that Britain sent and perhaps more importantly they underestimated the determination of the Portuguese people. By September 1762 the first invasion had failed, the second was faltering, and the third was yet to start.

North America

French territory in North America was reduced to a few settlements in Louisiana and in the centre of the continent to the west of the Ohio. The English-speaking people of the thirteen colonies were starting to come to terms with the idea that they were no longer threatened with enclosure by French soldiers and settlers moving down from Canada. Louisiana was so far away that it was of little concern except to the people of Georgia, who also worried about Spanish Florida on their southern border. The mood in America was one of expansion to the west, and they were impatient with the continuing war which they largely saw as none of their business. They felt increasingly constrained by the demands of their colonial masters in Whitehall and although it's difficult to find evidence of anyone openly considering independence, many were thinking of ways to loosen the leash.

The Long War

France had lost territory in North America, the Caribbean, West Africa, the East Indies and, most humiliatingly of all, their own home island of Belle Isle. There was no consolation in Germany where they were no more than holding ground. Their only conquest that had any bargaining power in peace negotiations was Minorca, and they had already promised that island to Spain as part of the secret treaty. King Louis saw Spain's entry into the war as critical, and if they could take back some of the sugar islands and if Spain could successfully invade Britain's ally Portugal, all may not yet be lost. Thus, Britain's declaration of war with Spain in January 1762 was greeted with joy in Versailles. However, the Spanish navy had not been given enough time to mobilise and the army wasn't ready for the stern test of invading its neighbour Portugal across a difficult border. For France and its allies, the prospects of a favourable outcome from the war still looked bleak.

***

FACT MEETS FICTION

The Third *Pacte de Famille*, 1761

There were three Bourbon family pacts during the eighteenth century. The first was in 1733 during the War of Spanish Succession and was agreed between Philip V of Spain and his nephew Louis XV of France. The second was made in 1743 during the War of Austrian Succession and was also between King Philip V and King Louis XV. The third Bourbon family pact and the one that we're concerned with was agreed between King Carlos (Charles) III and King Louis XV. Charles and Louis shared a common grandfather in another Louis, known as The Grand Dauphin, and were therefore first cousins. Charles had only been on the throne two years when he was persuaded into this disastrous treaty and it seems likely that he was heavily influenced by his older cousin who had, by that time, ruled France for forty-six years. The treaty committed Spain to join the war in May 1762 if France had not achieved a peace settlement by then. Britain, being aware of this secret treaty, decided that it was better to fight Spain before her ponderous bureaucracy had managed to bring its fleet and army to full readiness. King George duly declared war in January 1762.

The Chevalier de Ternay

In my research for this series of books, I continually find the same historical characters taking leading roles time and time again. I've become quite attached to some and the Chevalier de Ternay is one of them.

The Battle of Quiberon Bay was fought in November 1759, as told in the seventh book in the Carlisle & Holbrooke series, Rocks and Shoals. It was a resounding victory for Admiral Hawke's squadron, and it established British naval superiority for the remainder of the war. In an attempt to escape capture or destruction, a number of French ships sought refuge in the muddy and shallow Vilaine estuary, that empties into the eastern side of Quiberon Bay. They were still there in January 1761, but by the extraordinary efforts of the Chevalier de Ternay, then a junior French sea officer, most of them escaped over the following six months. De Ternay's actions in bringing out the ships from the Vilaine are some of the most inspiring events of the war and are told in the twelfth book in the series *Treacherous Moon*.

When France needed a bold and undaunted leader for an expedition to Newfoundland, de Ternay was promoted over the heads of all of the rest of the French *Capitaines de Vaisseau*, and it appears that the King and his ministers were satisfied with de Ternay's actions because thereafter he enjoyed rapid promotion. In the following war as a *chef d'escadre* – a rear admiral – he escorted the first French troops to America to assist the rebel colonists. He died on active duty and is buried in the grounds of Trinity Church, Newport, Rhode Island, close to where Lucia and I were married in 1982.

John Jervis, Earl St. Vincent

In late 1762 John Jervis commanded the fourth rate forty-four-gun ship-of-the-line *Gosport* on the North American station. His ship wasn't engaged against de Ternay's squadron but Jervis went on to become a successful captain and admiral and commanded the squadron that beat the Spanish at the battle of Cape St. Vincent in 1797, flying his flag in the first rate *Victory*. He was created the first Earl St. Vincent and became one of the country's most successful First Lords of the Admiralty during the Napoleonic Wars.

Sergeant Perry

It's wonderful when I can find a firsthand account of a battle, and Sergeant (later Captain) David Perry, of Boston,

Massachusetts, has provided a magnificent record of his involvement in the battle on Signal Hill and the subsequent recapture of the town and fort. His service started in 1758 at Fort Ticonderoga and continued into the Revolutionary War. You can find his account by searching for <*Captain David Perry's Website*>.

The French Squadron

What ships did de Ternay bring out of the Vilaine and which of them formed his squadron for the raid on Newfoundland? The historical record isn't clear on the subject, particularly with respect to the sixty-four gun third rate ship-of-the-line *Eveillé*. Perhaps there is more information available in French archives but for now I can't be certain of the answer. Consequently *Eveillé* appears in *An Upright Man,* for she was certainly present at Newfoundland, but not in *Treacherous Moon.*

The Newfoundland Raid

De Ternay's raid happened in much the way that I have written. D'Haussonville easily overcame the lacklustre defence of St. John's and then he and de Ternay settled in for a long occupation, ignoring Choiseul's orders to stay no longer than a month. In hindsight the result was inevitable, and when Colonel Amherst's force landed in Torbay, only a few miles north of St. John's, it was all over for the French expedition. The battle for Signal Hill sealed the fort's fate. When the fog arrived and de Ternay saw the opportunity to save his squadron, he abandoned d'Haussonville and almost his entire brigade and fled towards France. D'Haussonville held on for three more days until a British mortar battery started sending shells into the fort, when he was forced to surrender. De Ternay was blocked from sailing into Brest and made for Coruña where he spent the rest of the war, writing letter after letter to justify his actions.

De Ternay was in essence a very junior officer propelled to high command by his own exertions. Did he make the right decisions in Newfoundland? It's difficult to say, but having alerted the British to his presence, any further raiding in the North American station would have put his squadron in mortal danger. France had any number of brigades but few naval squadrons, and two ships-of-the-line and two frigates were worth far more than d'Haussonville's army.

It's difficult to determine what effect the raid had on the eventual outcome of the war, but it was certainly the only French naval success in the closing stages, and it must have demonstrated to Newcastle and Bute that France still had the power to hurt Britain's pocket.

Signal Hill

At the time of de Ternay's raid *Signal Hill* near St. John's was known as *The Lookout*. I've used the modern name to avoid confusion with the many time that *Lookout* appears in the story referring to a stalwart seaman scanning the horizon from the top of the mast.

San Sebastian

The Spanish fourth rate *San Sebastian* is entirely fictitious, as is Don Ezequiel Mancebo and his crew. Nevertheless, King Charles of Spain and his redoubtable chief minister, General Wall, certainly considered that regaining access to the Newfoundland fisheries was an important reason for going to war. I've used Don Mancebo and his ship to imagine how they'd stake a claim – not just with Britain but with France – in advance of the peace negotiations.

***

Chris Durbin

THE CARLISLE & HOLBROOKE SERIES

There are now fourteen Carlisle and Holbrooke Naval Adventures. The series starts in the Mediterranean at the end of 1755 when Captain Edward Carlisle's small frigate *Fury* was part of the peacetime squadron based at Port Mahon to watch the French fleet at Toulon. Carlisle was a native of Virginia but in the years before American independence it was quite normal for well-connected men from the colonies to take a King's commission. In fact, there is an information board at Mount Vernon that records George Washington's wish to join the navy and his mother's refusal to allow it. Imagine how different things might have been if he'd found himself on the quarterdeck of a man-of-war instead of leading the allied armies to ultimate victory against the British during the war of independence.

Carlisle had a master's mate, George Holbrooke, the son of an old friend who had retired in England. Holbrooke's heart wasn't in the navy; he wanted to become a lawyer but the family finances wouldn't stretch that far. His performance at sea was disappointing, to the extent that Carlisle was considering dismissing him. However, when war broke out the following year Holbrooke rose to the challenge and as the navy struggled to mobilise against the French he achieved rapid promotion and was soon in command of his own ship.

Each book in the series is centred on one of the two principal characters, either Carlisle or Holbrooke, and they take centre stage in alternate episodes. There are broadly two books for each year of the war and I hope to carry the series through the period of strained relations between Britain and its American colonies, into the war for American independence.

The series is available in Kindle, Kindle Unlimited and in paperback formats, and I plan to publish two new books each year. The easiest way to obtain a copy is through Amazon.

I'm also releasing audio editions of the books and I hope they'll be published at the rate of four a year until they catch up with the print and Kindle versions. The audio books are available through Amazon, Audible and iTunes.

***

BIBLIOGRAPHY

The following is a selection of the many books that I consulted in researching the Carlisle & Holbrooke series:

Definitive Text

Sir Julian Corbett wrote the original, definitive text on the Seven Years War. Most later writers use his work as a steppingstone to launch their own.

Corbett, LLM., Sir Julian Stafford. *England in the Seven Years War – Vol. I: A Study in Combined Strategy*. Normandy Press. Kindle Edition.

Strategy and Naval Operations

Three very accessible modern books cover the strategic context and naval operations of the Seven Years War. Daniel Baugh addresses the whole war on land and sea, while Martin Robson concentrates on maritime activities. Jonathan Dull has produced a very readable account from the French perspective.

Baugh, Daniel. *The Global Seven Years War 1754-1763*. Pearson Education, 2011. Print.
Robson, Martin. *A History of the Royal Navy, The Seven Years War*. I.B. Taurus, 2016. Print.
Dull, Jonathan, R. *The French Navy and the Seven Years' War*. University of Nebraska Press, 2005. Print.

Sea Officers

For an interesting perspective on the life of sea officers of the mid-eighteenth century, I'd read Augustus Hervey's Journal, with the cautionary note that while Hervey was by no means typical of the breed, he's very entertaining and devastatingly honest. For a more balanced view, I'd read British Naval Captains of the Seven Years War.

Erskine, David (editor). *Augustus Hervey's Journal, The Adventures Afloat and Ashore of a Naval Casanova*. Chatham Publishing, 2002. Print.
McLeod, A.B. *British Naval Captains of the Seven Years War, The View from the Quarterdeck*. The Boydell Press, 2012. Print.

Life at Sea

There are two excellent overviews of shipboard life and administration during the Seven Years War.

Rodger, N.A.M. *The Wooden World, An Anatomy of the Georgian Navy*. Fontana Press, 1986. Print.
Lavery, Brian. *Anson's Navy, Building a Fleet for Empire, 1744 to 1793*. Seaforth Publishing, 2021. Print.

***

Chris Durbin

THE AUTHOR

Chris Durbin grew up in the seaside town of Porthcawl in South Wales. His first experience of sailing was as a sea cadet in the treacherous tideway of the Bristol Channel, and at the age of sixteen, he spent a week in a tops'l schooner in the Southwest Approaches. He was a crew member on the Porthcawl lifeboat before joining the navy.

Chris spent twenty-four years as a warfare officer in the Royal Navy, serving in all classes of ships from aircraft carriers through destroyers and frigates to the smallest minesweepers. He took part in operational campaigns in the Falkland Islands, the Middle East and the Adriatic and he spent two years teaching tactics at a US Navy training centre in San Diego.

On his retirement from the Royal Navy, Chris joined a large American company and spent eighteen years in the aerospace, defence and security industry, including two years on the design team for the Queen Elizabeth class aircraft carriers.

Chris is a graduate of the Britannia Royal Naval College at Dartmouth, the British Army Command and Staff College, the United States Navy War College where he gained a postgraduate diploma in national security decision-making, and Cambridge University, where he was awarded an MPhil in International Relations.

With a lifelong interest in naval history and a long-standing ambition to write historical fiction, Chris has completed the first fourteen novels in the Carlisle & Holbrooke series. They follow the fortunes of a colonial Virginian and a Hampshire man who both command ships of the Georgian navy during the middle years of the eighteenth century.

The series will follow its principal characters through the Seven Years War and into the period of turbulent relations between Britain and her American colonies in the 1760s and 1770s. They'll negotiate some thought-provoking loyalty issues when British policy and colonial restlessness lead inexorably to the American Revolution.

Chris lives on the south coast of England, surrounded by hundreds of years of naval history. His three children are all busy growing their own families and careers while Chris and his wife (US Navy, retired) of forty-one years enjoy sailing their Cornish Crabber on the south coast.

Oyster Boat *Terror*

Chris is a volunteer skipper on the restored Victorian oyster boat *Terror* that takes passengers on day trips around Chichester Harbour. *Terror* is the last survivor of Emsworth's oyster trade that flourished until the early twentieth century and is a genuine link with the past. You can find more information by entering <*Oyster Boat Terror*> in your web search engine.

Fun Fact

Chris shares his garden with a tortoise named Aubrey. If you've read Patrick O'Brian's *HMS Surprise* or have seen the 2003 film *Master and Commander: The Far Side of the World*, you'll recognise the modest act of homage that Chris has paid to that great writer. Rest assured that Aubrey has not yet grown to the gigantic proportions of *Testudo Aubreii*, though at his last weigh in, he topped one kilogram!

***

FEEDBACK

If you've enjoyed *An Upright Man* please consider leaving a review on Amazon.

Look out for the fifteenth in the Carlisle & Holbrooke series, coming soon.

You can follow my blog at:

www.chris-durbin.com.

***

Printed in Great Britain
by Amazon